The CG Assignment

The CG Assignment

YVONNE GRIESE

BALBOA.
PRESS

A DIVISION OF HAY HOUSE

Balboa Press books may be ordered through booksellers or by contacting:

Balboa Press
A Division of Hay House
1663 Liberty Drive
Bloomington, IN 47403
www.balboapress.com
1 (877) 407-4847

Because of the dynamic nature of the Internet, any web addresses or links contained in this book may have changed since publication and may no longer be valid. The views expressed in this work are solely those of the author and do not necessarily reflect the views of the publisher, and the publisher hereby disclaims any responsibility for them.

The author of this book does not dispense medical advice or prescribe the use of any technique as a form of treatment for physical, emotional, or medical problems without the advice of a physician, either directly or indirectly. The intent of the author is only to offer information of a general nature to help you in your quest for emotional and spiritual well-being. In the event you use any of the information in this book for yourself, which is your constitutional right, the author and the publisher assume no responsibility for your actions.

Any people depicted in stock imagery provided by Thinkstock are models,
and such images are being used for illustrative purposes only.
Certain stock imagery © Thinkstock.

Print information available on the last page.

ISBN: 978-1-4525-2860-1 (sc)
ISBN: 978-1-4525-2861-8 (e)

Balboa Press rev. date: 05/01/2015

There are many people who helped me along the complex journey of writing a novel.

My husband Mark has been unswerving in his encouragement. Thank you darling, it is wonderful to be sharing my life with my best friend.

Merry Watson was the catalyst who got me started and ran our C3 Church writers' group with great wisdom and authority. Many thanks to Merry and the members of the group who were always inspiring.

To my son Klute, thank you so much for taking the time to plough through my first draft and give such helpful feedback without crushing my spirit.

I could never have come to this point without the professionalism and optimism of Balboa press.

Many thanks to the whole team who nurtured me through the daunting process of editing and publishing.

This book is dedicated to my grandfather Bill and father Darcy, who both survived the hell of war. They each demonstrated to me the unconditional love of a father's heart.

Part One

1

But be not afraid of greatness; some are born great, some achieve
greatness and some have greatness thrust upon them.
—William Shakespeare, from *Twelfth Night*

The Kingdom of Heaven – Angelic Control Epicentre (ACE)

It occurred to Nathaniel that if he were a human, he'd be breaking out in a cold sweat about now. Yes, undoubtedly this state of affairs would create stress levels of the highest order—if he were a human, that is. He'd be tossing up the pros and cons of obedience (maintaining a tranquil demeanour and staying put) versus rebellion (letting out a soul-shrinking scream and hightailing it through the nearest exit like someone on a bad acid trip). Then, horror of horrors, he'd probably choose rebellion, a downright appealing option—for a human, that is. And then he'd probably—if he weren't an angel—lose it big time and …

What bizarre train of thought was this? Was he losing his mind? Having another of his escapist fantasies? Both of these were at best scary possibilities, and his heart sank at the mere notion. A guardian just couldn't afford to dabble in vain imaginings, and that was all there was to it.

He began to tremble, starting at the toes and gradually working up to the teeth. When the chattering started to attract some attention, he knew it was time to get a grip. Exercising maximum control, he closed his eyes, counted to ten, and then covertly panned the room by lifting both eyelids and looking from right to left without moving his head.

Oh, hallelujah! Call off the ambulance! This was not a dream sequence that had run amok. He was in fact in the vestibule of the ACE Head Office and really was standing in the blue-ribbon-elite waiting area!

A ball of nervous excitement exploded in his spirit, and he lit up like a meteor in full fall. Multiple dream scenarios flashed through his mind, not least of which involved Nathaniel the Faithful receiving an award for outstanding guardian achievements.

He decided that such an auspicious occasion warranted a wing check, so he looked over his right shoulder towards a gold-framed mirror on the far wall. Wouldn't you know it? After two centuries of nonstop guardian duty, those feathers were still well preened and thick, all the gold tips as good as new.

Turning now to face the mirror, he thought—not for the first time—how good it was to be thirteen feet tall, clearly above the angelic average. In a moment of unbridled vanity, he beamed with pleasure and allowed his eyes to linger on the reflection smiling back.

Oh yes, the old Nathaniel was certainly a step above the guardian norm. Those eyes were the colour of fresh snow, and the diaphanous robes floated like a sea of light.

He swayed from side to side and sashayed into a half-turn and then remembered where he was and glanced around to see if anyone was watching. Fortunately the two ushers were looking towards the entrance. Turning to see what had caught their attention, he was just in time to spot what had to be a grade AA warrior accessing the vestibule.

Everything went as quiet as death. A herald announced Zimron the Valiant as the guy strode through the entrance, screening all and sundry with eyes that flashed gold and white like a Morse code signal box. Energy crackled and bounced off walls as he approached the blue-ribbon waiting area.

The guy stood at twenty feet minimum; he boasted muscles that would turn a panther white, and bedazzled everyone with his gold-and-orange robes, which were reminiscent of a sunrise—or sunset, depending on your perspective.

Nathaniel's flirtation with pride came to a swift and humiliating end. But then again, in terms of one's eternal destiny that was a good thing—disturbing and deflating, but ultimately good. Choosing the path of maturity, he decided to start up a conversation with the only opener that came to mind: "Do you come here often?" A pathetically lame attempt, sadly reflective of how lame he felt at the moment.

Zimron turned towards him, eyes flashing at twice the pace as before, brows furrowed. He said nothing.

Nathaniel cleared his throat and plunged on. "This is my first proper appointment time, actually. I've heard reports, of course, from friends who—"

"Three times!" boomed a voice.

Nathaniel jumped a foot and yelped. He was absolutely mortified but managed a weak "Three times?" in return.

"Yes, I've been here three times. The first was when Moses was approaching the Red Sea and needed a miracle. The second was when the walls of Jericho were about to come down, and the third was during the Crusades."

Well, if Nathaniel had felt a bit threatened before, he was downright panicky now. "Oh, really?" he squeaked in a voice that was a full octave higher than usual. "I did pop in for just a quick roll call two centuries ago at the start of my guardian apprenticeship. Scared wingless I was. Those archangels were so awesome that I fainted and the ushers had to carry me out. It was a categorically tragic humiliation!" He pronounced the last sentence with a flourish of hands, but it turned out to be anticlimactic, because Zimron had wandered off to address one of the ushers.

At this point, Nathaniel tottered dangerously close to the Highway of Offence. Honestly, warriors could be so rude! Happily, that mental collision course was disrupted when multitudes of bells rang out, signalling that it was time for someone to go in. Over the loudspeaker came the cry, "Zimron the Valiant to the inner chamber, Zimron the Valiant to the inner chamber," and as if that weren't enough, the words echoed off every wall and along every hallway.

Zimron galvanised into action and flew off without as much as a goodbye.

"Nice knowing you," Nathaniel muttered. He was wondering what to do next when one of the ushers signalled him to come forward. This guy was friendly but at the same time very businesslike, a combination that luckily had a soothing effect. He flashed a smile of encouragement.

"Nathaniel, our records tell us that you were quite overwhelmed when last presented to an archangel. How are you expecting to respond this time?"

"Well, if I haven't improved in two hundred years, I might as well give the game away!"

The usher threw back his head and laughed. He must have mistaken that last heartfelt comment for a joke. "That's very melodramatic, but don't fret. This time we're going to do some serious prep work on you beforehand. We shouldn't keep you waiting much longer."

"Excellent! Thank you very much!" Nathaniel bellowed. *What in heaven's name does prep work entail? It sounds ominous!* "I can handle this, I can handle this, I can handle this," he whispered, panic levels shooting up off the graph. Oh, brother, now would be a good time to do some relaxation exercises if he could just find a good focal point.

It didn't take long. The north-facing wall of the vestibule was made from finest crystal and overlooked a snow-dappled mountain range, which soared to mingle with suspended clouds and then plunged into fruitful valleys. *Perfect!* He spent several minutes contemplating alpine glory while doing non-demonic meditations and Holy Ghost–anointed deep breathing.

Needless to say, all of that did zilch to calm his nerves. Well, what was an angel to make of this situation? An hour ago he'd been in a guardian training session trying to improve his take-off times and struggling to maintain a loving attitude towards Jamsen, who was beating him hands down. "And all of that's important, because how can you hope to better yourself if you have slow times or a flawed character?"

Nathaniel realised immediately that he'd accidentally said that last thought out loud, but a quick peek revealed that no one was taking any notice because a new lot had just arrived for processing. He began to breathe again.

You could have knocked him over with a daisy when that messenger had turned up and interrupted the session to announce that Nathaniel the Faithful was wanted at Head Office. All the guardians had just stared open-mouthed as he took off and winged after the messenger who'd already taken flight.

Just then someone called out his name and caused Nathaniel's thoughts to flip back to the present. He turned around to look straight into the eyes of a seriously stern-faced administrator who stood sceptre-straight with hands on hips.

"Can you hear me, guardian?" demanded the AA in tones that snapped Nathaniel into both fight and flight modes.

"Yes, administrator!"

"It's time, guardian!"

"Right!"

Nathaniel felt as though he'd just been summoned to the death chamber. This new guy spoke like a prophet of doom, not nearly as comforting as the last. He followed the administrator, who opened some purple satin curtains and then flew along a hallway and into a media area.

What a brain-muddling zone this was. AAs were charging in every direction, a blur of various shades of blue. Many were wingless, and all were built for skill. Myriad screens ran reports from every universe as the cameras of Heaven panned over Creation. Fluorescent letters ran across the walls giving updates of trouble spots, and the atmosphere pulsed with the glory of worship, which was being transmitted live from the Throne Room.

"This way, guardian!"

Talk about charisma challenged! Plate-face took off flying again at the speed of light so that Nathaniel was hard pressed to keep up. Countless workstations and information storage cells whizzed by until in the distance could be seen a flashing red sign which projected the words "Preparation Area" out into the cosmos.

"I can do this, I can do this, I can do this," said Nathaniel. This was no time for timidity. As they came closer to the sign, he was relieved to see two smiling ushers who came flying out to meet them.

The AA took a deep breath and began to call out to all and sundry, "Nathaniel the Faithful to see—"

"Yes, yes; we know who it is," said the one with sea-green eyes which sparkled with humour. "Thank you, job well done," he added.

The AA disappeared, and the ushers came to stand at each side of Nathaniel, all of which went a long way towards lowering his stress levels. "Greetings, friends," he said with some relief. "Pleased to meet you!"

"Greetings Nathaniel," they replied in perfect harmony as they nudged him under the sign. "We're honoured to be sharing this sacred experience with you."

He opened his mouth to ask what in Heaven they'd meant by that last statement but heard, then saw, a wall of water so massive it rendered him mute. A mountainous wave came crashing over them and created an undertow which sucked him into the vortex of what seemed to be an ocean.

He was dragged endlessly through water which swished and churned as if it were in a giant washing machine, and just when he was feeling as if his time might be up angel-wise, he landed like a beached whale in a giant chamber. He felt as though he'd landed on top of a live electric socket.

Oh … boy! Energy-wise this place made the Media Room look like a twopenny firecracker. Dazzling lightning slashed through the atmosphere, and ear-splitting thunder booms reverberated off every surface.

Nathaniel agonized briefly over the likelihood of him coming out of this blind and deaf. Or—worst case scenario—blind, deaf, and a basket case. Then he started to vibrate, which led to bone-snapping shakes until his only conscious thought was *Thank God for the ushers!*

They held on until he was an inch away from disintegrating and then dragged his lifeless form for miles across to a spot labelled "Anointing Oil." Once they were positioned there, one held him firm while the other reached across to a wall which had a huge lever attached to it. He pulled the lever down and immediately a vat of oil was upturned over Nathaniel, filling him to saturation point.

It left him feeling quite euphoric. To be totally honest, it was downright intoxicating! Mere minutes spent soaking in the mind-melting nectar was enough to make him slump like a wino in one usher's arms and smile inanely at the other one, who had now flipped the lever back up and was hurrying over to assist.

As they lifted and then carried him across the room, he turned first to one and then the other of his new brilliantly wonderful friends and continued to grin through an ever-thickening stupor.

They placed him gently on a huge down-filled cushion where he just slouched, in no hurry to move. His fuzzy brain could make out neither hide nor hair of what was happening, but he wanted to enjoy every last second of whatever was going on. Finally, after what could have been minutes or hours, he heard an usher speaking through the haze.

"Archangel Michael is ready to see you now."

"Diju say 'Archanshel Michael'?"

"Yes, that's what I said."

Nathaniel took several moments to come up with his next response.

"Sherioushly guys, I mean sherioushly now … am I on *Candid Camera* or *Thish ish Your Life?*"

He beamed from ear to ear as they exploded into fits of hilarity, holding on to their sides and leaning on one another for support. So much for all those who'd said he couldn't crack a joke!

"Seriously, guardian, Archangel Michael wants to see you" said Ol' Green Eyes. "It's an important occasion when someone gets promoted! Up you get, and let's get to the Inner Chamber!"

And with that they rocketed off, pulling Nathaniel with them. Light years flashed by as they soared through the heavens. Workers everywhere looked up as if something had grabbed their attention. Faces lit up, and thousands waved happily. This was not the sort of reaction he was used to getting.

Gradually he began to think a little more clearly, and in fact by the time the ruby-encrusted entrance of the Inner Chamber came into view, he was maintaining a modicum of decorum. Minutes later they executed a perfect landing, with Nathaniel positioned between the two ushers.

"Excuse me, friends," he said, finally staring straight ahead at an imposing three-storey solid gold door. "I hate to appear slow on the uptake, but did you say 'promoted'?"

"Indeed I did," replied the one on the right.

"Yes indeed he did," reiterated Green Eyes, who then stood to his full height of seven feet and called out in commanding tones, "Nathaniel the Faithful to see Archangel Michael!"

The door opened, and Nathaniel was carried in on a tide of worship. The glory of the Lord lifted him to great heights until everything and everyone was forgotten, transfigured as he was with adoration.

"Oh how wondrous and glorious you are Lord!" he cried again and again like a cracked record. "You are beyond beautiful, and words will never be enough!" A song of adulation rose up in his heart and found fulfilment as he joined in harmony with the millions of others who worship around the throne unceasingly and endlessly, forever and ever.

After what seemed like a moment but could have been hours, he came to in a sumptuous room. Despite the thick presence of the Spirit, he found the strength to stand. This was mercifully unlike the fiasco two centuries ago when he'd had to be carried out comatose. That prep work seemed to have done the trick.

He straightened his robes, then looked up just in time to see Zimron passing by. The warrior stopped and looked directly at Nathaniel for two full seconds with eyes flashing like there was no tomorrow. He then nodded and waved on the way out. Nathaniel was still misty from his time of worship and had to go cross-eyed to focus and wave vaguely in the right direction.

He began to look around and get some bearings. This place was the full six-star article! Every surface was encrusted with precious stones: sapphires, rubies, emeralds, amethysts, topaz—you name it. And there, ensconced in a sea of emerald velvet, was the archangel himself.

"Well, well, it's young Nathaniel! How are you feeling after two centuries of guardian duty?"

His voice was a harmony of three octaves. Nathaniel blinked twice and shook his head to make sure this wasn't a dream. Nope; he was wide awake, and the Archangel Michael was sitting right there before him.

"It's been a privilege and an honour, sir!" he shouted. Seriously, what does your average guardian say to the warrior who'd led the Great War of Heaven; the one who'd battled head-to-head with Satan?

"Did you find the Rogerson family interesting?"

Michael glowed amber from head to toe. He had a ruby aura, for crying out loud. And there'd been nothing even remotely interesting about the Rogerson family.

"You look like a fire!" he blurted; cool under pressure and supremely irrelevant.

"And you look ethereal, Nathaniel, which is why the enemy always underestimates you."

"Excellent!"

"See that as a positive, my friend. The Lord designed you for special under-the -radar missions."

Michael pressed a ruby which turned out to be a button, and down came a screen which he began to scan.

"It says here that for two centuries you have been faithful and obedient even when you were terrified beyond words."

"Right!" This was embarrassing beyond words. All of his panic attacks had been observed and recorded!

Michael smiled and went on. "You have demonstrated a heart of compassion and sacrifice, and we are convinced you would enter the very portals of Hell to protect your charges."

"Thank you, archangel!"

Nathaniel bellowed his response to cover a growing unease. Were they going to ask him to go hurtling head first into Hell, yelling out "Praise the Lord!" as he went up in flames?

"For these reasons, Nathaniel, you have proven yourself worthy of promotion to a managerial position."

Nathaniel's spirit screeched to a halt, reversed back from Freaking out Freeway and began to motor happily along Hope Highway. He knew that his body language changed from slumping to standing erect, but Michael continued to speak as if nothing had happened.

"As you know, Satan is always searching out and targeting humans who demonstrate a willingness to be trained up as prophets of darkness. He uses such prophets to deceive multitudes in his quest to draw as many as possible into the consuming fire. The Lord, of course, foresees everything and uses even the very strategies of the adversary to bring forth his own deliverers.

"You will play an integral role in one such campaign. The scene has been set for a remarkable individual to rise up in the twentieth century with a mandate to operate powerfully in the dispensing of miracles. The divinely appointed human, whose identity is known only to the Lord, will be able to communicate directly with God and lead untold thousands into truth.

"The campaign will centre on two family lines in which there are unique characters aplenty and all the ingredients for the making of such a person. He believes that you will fit in perfectly with that scenario and that you have what it takes to oversee a cross-generational work."

Curiouser and curiouser, thought Nathaniel. "You were saying that the Lord desires to stay under the radar."

"Yes, it's imperative that Satan takes a while to catch on to this so that work can get well underway. You have proven yourself to be discreet, and as I said, Satan has foolishly underestimated you. To provide a cover, at least at first, we are assigning you as guardian to one of the participating humans, a person called Florence Forsythe. By the time the enemy realises that something bigger is afoot, we will be off and running. Are there any questions?"

Are there any questions? Does a Zebra have stripes? He thought long and hard and then said the thing that was uppermost in his mind.

"How can this come to pass? I am merely a faithful and ethereal guardian."

"Don't be afraid, dear friend; you have already been prepared for the task at hand. Believe that to be so, and then act upon it. You will be positioned in the Forsythe family at the Earth time of 1890, eight years before Florence is to be placed into her mother's womb.

During those eight years, you will undergo intensive training and gradually get into your role. You will also be able to assist Tristan, who has the job of guarding Florence's father, Alec. If you want to know the truth, he's finding it all a bit of a struggle. Zimron was called in today because he and his warrior team will be working with you at various points throughout the decades. Are there any more questions?"

"When will all this begin?" Nathaniel asked, speaking in little more than a whisper now.

"It will begin as soon as you receive your new mantle! Step forward, angel!"

He obeyed in spite of almost crippling fear. A thrill zigzagged through him from head to toe when Michael placed both hands on his head and began to call out with the roar of battle.

"Give him the heart of a lion, Lord!" The walls shook. "Let the new mantle rest upon him, and let the new name settle within his heart!"

"I have a new name?" Nathaniel called out in what turned out to be strong and resonant tones.

"Yes, angel, you have a new name!" laughed Michael. "From this point on, you will no longer answer to the title of 'Nathaniel the Faithful' but will be known to all as 'Nathaniel the Bold: Cross-Generational Case Manager!'"

2

Man will err while yet he strives.

—Johann Wolfgang von Goethe, from "Prologue im Himmel," *Faust* pt. 1, 1808

Aberdeen, Scotland, 1908

Alec Forsythe slowed down the rhythm of the pedals and strove to harness his thoughts. With effort he shut out mind and heart to all but the present surrounds, allowing his eyes to scan from east to west. What a bonny sight it was! Springtime in Aberdeen, which now boasted its own hospital, university, and even electricity generating station. It made glad the soul of a Scot.

True to the nickname Silver City, its granite buildings were beaming diamond-like in response to sunny caresses. As he rode along, it seemed as if the dying rays of dusk were mingling with the cool breezes of approaching night in a gesture of farewell. He began to experience some measure of buoyancy, and in a moment of sheer abandon he surrendered to the various sensations.

Times like this afforded a man scant moments of peace, and he must grab each one or he would not stay strong. Dear Lord, there were burdens aplenty to being a stationmaster and a family man. But 'twas his cross to bear, and bear it he must.

He turned into the service lane and did a smooth dismount at the back of the old terrace. Unlatching the timber gate, he pushed the bicycle over to lean on the backyard fence and stopped to admire his personal Eden. A grin broke open his usually dour face.

What a feat it was for a man to supply such a haeme for his family! Starting to feel pretty cock o' the hoop, he strode along the stone path, stopping for a moment, hands on hips, to examine the vegetable patch and rose garden before stepping through the door into the back porch.

Off came the beret and coat. Then, with a grunt or two, he removed his heavy boots. It was heaven indeed to slip into cosy slippers! Making his entrance into the kitchen, he warmed all over at the sight of Helen holding the fort afore the wood stove. As she handed him a cup of broth, he rewarded her with a smile and a nod before moving on to the serious task of inspecting his bairns.

The atmosphere in the living room was fine indeed, with nary a thing out of place. The air was thick with cooking smells, and every nook and cranny was spotless. A glance over to the study revealed lads that were washed up, ready for tea. Indeed they had their books out and were immersed in schoolwork. What a scene to fire the furnace of a man's spirit! A bubble of joy floated up from somewhere within and settled in the area of the heart.

But all this changed when Alec drew closer to the study. Arrows of anxiety ruptured the joy, and within moments his thoughts and emotions were all out of kilter. He tallied up not six children, but four! He galloped along the hall, checking bedrooms. Muscles at the base of his neck started to tighten, and his stomach sent up a wave of heartburn.

"Helen!" he roared. "Helen! Would ye come here, woman!"

Helen peeped around the kitchen doorway. "Alec, now dinna be getting yerself upset …"

"Dinna be getting myself upset? Dinna be getting myself upset? Lord Almighty, woman; where in all damnation are Florence and Hamish!"

*   *   *

Flo hated Hamish. She poked out her tongue and stabbed his back with sinful thoughts. There he was, striding along in breeches while she tripped over in skirts and stockings. And all he ever did was laugh without helping at all.

She plopped down onto a low stone wall. Muttering away to the fields and birds, she wiped her damp face with a petticoat and struggled to get a mess of curls back into ribbons. But at the sight of her brother disappearing over a hill, she groaned and gave up the fight with her hair. It wasn't fair!

Up she jumped. She gathered the biggest stones that her tiny hands could hold and gave way to a fully-fledged tantrum. Stones flew everywhere, and screams of fury echoed out over the silent heather. Then, in mid-throw, she spied some wildflowers the colour of snow. She meandered away from the path to touch the fragile petals, lost for a moment in their beauty.

The trouble was she just couldn't stay angry with Hamish for long at all; how could she? With him she felt alive all over. Aye, he made her laugh till her stomach ached when she didn't hate him; like this morning when they'd stolen apples from Mr. MacKenzie's orchard at the end of Miller's Lane.

That old man had huffed and puffed so as he tried to catch them. A funnier sight she'd never seen! They'd scrambled over the fence just afore he spied them, and while he muttered and cursed they hid out of sight. Flo's heart had hit her chest so hard she feared it would pound its way out and fall to the ground!

For just a few wee seconds, guilt about the stolen apples blacked out the memory and brought on a frown and much lip nibbling. Aye, it was a great sin to steal and to laugh at old people. But in no time at all, the frown turned into a pout. How else was she to get any fun? At home there was nary a laugh or even a smile to be found! Aye, and not a hug anywhere! There was only a lot of getting into trouble, and Flo was very good at that! Hamish was calling to her from over the hill now, and she stamped her foot at the sound.

"Ye old slow-coach; a tortoise could beat ye!" he yelled. "Flo canna beat a tortoise; Flo canna beat a tortoise!"

She would not be likened to a tortoise! Hoisting up layers of material, she threw herself into struggling up to the top of the rise. She was in the midst of planning different ways to kill Hamish when a field of daffodils came into view. Taking a big breath, she ran and plummeted into the middle of so much beauty and rolled over to lie spreadeagle looking up at the sky.

A smile began in her eyes and made the edges of her mouth twitch before breaking her face open in a big grin. Aye, it didn't matter what Hamish thought. She was better than him in spelling and maths; better than everyone in spelling and maths!

Her mind drifted. Yesterday she and her best friend Nellie were lying just like this, side by side in a patch of heather looking up at the clouds and making up tales. Then Nellie surprised her.

"Y'er so special being the baby and the only girl, Flo," she'd said. "Do ye always feel like a princess?"

Flo's eyes had filled with tears and she'd turned her face away. "Oh aye! Mother laughs and dances wi' me all the day, and at night Father gi'es me a hug and kisses me good night."

It was sinful to tell such lies, but Flo couldn't stop them pouring out. Then Nellie said something right strange.

"Y'er so lucky, Flo," she sighed. "I'm lost in the midst of five sisters. And I dinna have Godly parents like yers."

She wasn't upset with Nellie for saying that. Nellie was her best friend, but didn't understand how she suffered under religion. She'd never even been to the cinema!

An icy breeze suddenly breathed o'er Flo and set her to shivering so that she sat up startled and looked around. That was strange; there was nary a puff of wind around. Oh horrors, was that a sunset she could see? She was late, late, late! Scrambling to her feet and looking down, she groaned at the sight of torn skirts and holy stockings.

There would be a caning tonight for being "unladylike and disrespectful." Her head and shoulders dropped in unison; her world was a black place indeed. She decided to run away. Her head and shoulders snapped back into place. Aye, that was a fine answer indeed!

But where would she go, and what would she eat? It wouldn't do to freeze and starve to death. A lass needed a fire and food on the table. She took one last lingering look at the bonny field of sunshine, whimpered at the thought of what was ahead, and then pursed her lips and headed for home.

*   *   *

Far out! He'd only just managed to grab the girl's attention before she was caught in the dark! Nathaniel shook his head as the auburn-haired vision in shredded petticoats and stockings trudged along muttering away to herself. Those killer sepia eyes didn't miss much, but she'd never seen him. Keeping right on the ball, he spread his awesome new super-gloss maxi-wings and lifted up into the air.

He'd never gotten over being chuffed at the way his managerial robes flashed like lightning bolts with every move (go the uniform!). Not that he'd ever let that be a distraction. He was a picture of on-the-edge vigilance, fully pumped and ready for trouble!

No one could accuse Flo of being boring; he'd give her that. In fact, he'd lost count of the number of times he'd snatched her from the very jaws of disaster. And this assignment had been going for only ten years. It didn't pay to think too far into the future; that would shoot the heart out of a guardian's confidence.

Her parents were proving to be a strategic challenge. Human love was, to say the least, complex and bewildering, but he'd dealt with that issue on countless other missions, and centuries ago one of his superiors had advised him to deal with it one step at a time.

For a moment he hung suspended, trying to recall which archangel had given out that piece of eternal wisdom. Then, needless to say, when the subject of "archangel" popped up, his mind spiralled from the present back to that metamorphic, never-to-be forgotten day.

Oh, hallelujah; that soul-rattling moment when the archangel Michael had raised him up to Cross-Generational Case Managerial status! Nathaniel lit up with ecstasy at the recollection; yellow and blue waves pulsed out for miles around. It had taken him days to get over the shock and put together even a couple of logical thoughts.

But news always travelled like a meteor through the old angelic grapevine. Man was everyone impressed when they heard about the promotion! And surprised. In fact, they were beyond surprised. More along the lines of shocked.

The yellow and blue waves blended into a muddy green and started to wilt. Might as well face it; the degree of shock expressed by everyone and sundry at the time was downright offensive.

Whoops! Where was he and what was he doing? In Scotland; check. Guarding Florence Forsythe; big check. Nathaniel brought his thoughts back into the harness and flash-scanned the scene. He charged at a couple of random demons who had snuck closer, scaring them witless with his favourite high-level screech. Satisfied that the airwaves were stamped with CGCM authority, he proceeded to escort his charge as she set her jaw and steeled herself to approach the front door.

* * *

11.30 p.m. that night

Alec wouldn't be sleeping a wink tonight. He finally surrendered to this truth, gave up pretending to read about Daniel in the lions' den, and headed instead for the pantry where he knew there were some leftover pikelets. Aye, there they were, just as he'd pictured, neatly placed under the linen doily. Close to drooling, he lifted the doily, snatched several of the wee round delicacies, and pulled the honey pot close. Then his hand stopped in mid-air on its way to the cutlery drawer.

Heaven have mercy; he hadn't let the children commit the sin of improvidence by having seconds tonight, and now here was he, caught in that very web. Guilt stroked him with icy fingers. Well what was a man to do? It was no wee thing to handle the stomach-gripping terror of raising a family in the fear of the Lord!

With new resolve and rising sweat levels, he thrust around in the drawer to secure a knife and began spreading honey as if his life depended on it, all the while salivating at the prospect of indulging in the sweet, wicked treat. Scrambled thoughts went hither and thither and came to rest on a memory of Flo. The knife stopped in mid swipe.

Oh Lord his heart had near melted at the sight of the lassie tonight coming in late as usual with yellow petals caught in her chestnut hair! He'd kept himself strong by mentally reciting over and over the Bible verse about spoiling the child by sparing the rod.

The knife clanked onto the bench, and a pikelet went mouth ward. How he agonised over her fullness of spirit. Aye, and he'd caned her soundly so his family didn't detect any weakness. But she was a light in his life, blessed with beauty and a sharp mind. She brought colour into the grey monotony of his days.

As for young Hamish, he was all that Alec himself had wished to be. Through the years he'd sent nary a glance the lad's way, for just to look at his countenance could bring a glow and smile to his face. It wouldn't do for him to get big-headed.

Hamish won the favour of all—even Helen, whose face softened at the sight of him. But it was Alec's role as a father to drive vanity from his children, so he couldn't soften. With a cringe of shame, he remembered giving an extra caning to Hamish tonight not so much to discipline the boy but rather to toughen himself.

He all but inhaled the pikelets and was caught up for mere seconds in a sugar reverie. But as the last mouthful disappeared, so did the fleeting respite from sombre reality. His shoulders dropped and eyes closed at the thought of his dreary job at the railway.

Somehow he had to find the will to crawl out of bed on the morrow when it was pitch black, as always. Then he would push down yet another bowl of porridge before venturing out into the freezing cold at the crack of dawn.

Nay, not in a year of Sundays would he jeopardise his hard-earned reputation as a man of integrity and constancy. He'd lived with shame as a lad trapped in a household of drunkards, and the Lord knew every one of their filthy acts committed against him in secret. He'd vowed one night in his little wardrobe of a room—vowed as a mere ten-year-old lad—to leave when he could and build a life that was clean.

The post at the railway had been the answer to a lad's prayer. Aye, it was merely a cleaning job, but it included a room at the back of the stationmaster's house and enough money to buy food. He owed them his life and wouldn't let them down. The Lord knew how hard he'd laboured to restrain his carnal tendencies and gain respect in the Church of Scotland. But gain it he had.

Helen was a wife who knew her rightful place. She ran their home as if it were an army barracks and would do nought that was unseemly. Heath, Charles, Robbie, and Angus had obeyed him since they were bairns, thank the Lord. He licked the last of the honey from his fingers with eyes closed in reverence and set about eliminating all telltale signs of the midnight debauchery.

So where had he erred in the case of the other two? The only way that wee imp of a lassie had got petals all through her hair was by fair rolling around in a field of daffodils! For mere seconds a smile curved across his face, and before heading to bed for another futile attempt at sleep, he knelt down in front of the fireplace.

"Heavenly Father," he whispered, "Thou kenst that I am a hypocrite who is unworthy tae ask ought for myself. I beg only for Thy forgiveness and that Thou wouldst have mercy on my wife and family; especially Flo and Hamish. Keep them safe from Satan, and guide them in Thy paths. Father, I ask for this in the name of Jesus Christ, Thy precious Son. Amen."

Presently he felt fair enveloped by a peace-heavy embrace. Burdens seemed lighter somehow, and where there had been anguish of soul, there was comfort. He rose upright, resolved to fight another day, felt his way around furniture in the last flicker of lamplight, and then began to navigate the dark hallway leading to the bedroom stairs.

*   *   *

There it was again; the Lord's response to a human prayer. Down came a waterfall of light, peace, love, hope, you name it—all the good, fully awesome stuff. Condemnation fell over webbed feet, scurrying into the shadows while hissing at Tristan and him. Righteous anger galvanised Nathaniel into action so that he lunged at the retreating back and chased the demon from the property. Pride's face was contorted with terror. He stood in the light for thirty seconds before letting out a maniacal scream and bolting off.

Alec was immersed in the mammoth challenge of climbing the stairs. He didn't have a clue that heavenly light surrounded him, and he knew jack about the damage he'd just inflicted. *What would it be like,* Nathaniel wondered, *to have just a pinprick of revelation at your disposal to build your life on planet Earth with?*

"Humans battle against many foibles, don't they?" whispered Tristan. He was staring open-mouthed.

At first Nathaniel didn't know how to respond to that understatement. Tristan wasn't the sharpest knife in the drawer, but he meant well. Finally he found the words.

"And the Lord loves them … and loves them … and loves them," he said with a grin. "And even when they're drowning in a tsunami of wretched foibles … He loves them still."

3

Forsythe Cottage, 1915

Damnation! The place was as quiet as a morgue. Flo stuck her head out the window. "Och, better tae live in a convent as a nun for all the fun there is tae be had here!" she shouted.

She spat out the couple of swear words she knew while opening and slamming kitchen cupboards, searching for some form of treat.

Eureka! She struck gold in the shape of fresh-baked apple tarts. They would serve mightily as a diversion. With an apron full of treats, she scurried outside and plopped down on the soft grass against the western wall of the kitchen with legs splayed wide.

Briefly at ease, she munched away while gazing at the dusk sky in wait for sunset. Hamish had brought her to this very spot years ago, and she'd never forgotten.

"Ye dinna ken how grand a sunset is until ye see it, Flo" he'd said, his bonny face all aglow. "Come and I'll show ye the best spot for the watching."

The very thought of Hamish caused her eyes to well up, and that was the end of the apple tart escape. What was she to do now with Heath and Charles long gone to wives and Robbie and Hamish off to the fighting?

"Dammit! I just canna bend tae the quiet now, Hamish!" she screamed. "How could ye go and leave me alone here wi' Angus? Dinna ye ken that he and I ne'er had a bond?"

Just then there was a movement at the back gate as someone came in from the lane. Flo snorted in disgust at the sight of her sister-in-law, who waddled along the path singing hymns to herself. The woman fair spent half her life at the church.

Surely there was not any God, or at the least not one that she'd be worshipping. Flo hadn't seen any sign of mercy and goodness in her life. It was torment enough to live for the past six months in this hell called home without her soulmate Hamish. But she'd also been forced to endure bloody prim and proper Victoria!

*   *   *

Victoria was close to the limit of endurance with fatigue; she hadn't felt energised for months. Her friends insisted that there was something called "the nesting stage" which came upon a lass when heavy with child.

At the onset of this condition, the expecting lady apparently became highly invigorated and wanted to indulge in peculiar behaviour, such as scrubbing ceilings or wallpapering the house to prepare for the bairn. Meanwhile she did nought but sleep.

Nevertheless, her great success at the church luncheon today had been very uplifting. Reverend Miller's comments had been quite gratifying, and he'd said nary a word to any other. It was all due to the date scones, a specialty of hers. Aye, they never failed to impress!

"Mrs. Forsythe, I must make mention of your scones," he'd said with an approving smile. "You have surely impressed us again this year, lass. Your husband is a fortunate man indeed!"

Oh Lord, the complement had caused great embarrassment, and the mention of her husband had brought on tears. Fair threw her into confusion! She'd come out hot all over, juggling the hot coals of modesty and pride, which she was experiencing in equal measure.

But aye, it was good to reach the comfort of home. She was so slow of late that every task seemed to take an eternity, and now 'twas only hours before Hamish would come. Six long months had passed since they'd last kissed, and oh she longed to look bonny for his arrival.

But even more pressing was the desire to lift her swollen feet and bathe her stretched stomach with oil. As she did her penguin walk towards the bedroom and privacy she spied her sister-in-law entering the kitchen. That lass was a constant source of misery to Victoria, so she attempted to increase speed in a bid to escape notice. But it was not to be.

From the kitchen came a jolly, welcoming voice. "Evening greetings, Victoria! I kent I'd heard someone enter through the back door. Oh dear, ye look fair pale. Ye must rest and put yer feet up for a time. It'll be no time at all ere Hamish knocks on the door."

"Aye, that is what I intend tae do Florence," said Victoria, feeling more than a wee bit uneasy. This was indeed mystifying. The young vixen had never shown herself sympathetic in the past. "I shall have a time of privacy in the bedroom, and ye can be sure that I will be fully prepared for Hamish's arrival."

"Vera well," replied Flo in light melodic tones, "I will see ye when ye're ready."

Victoria didn't have the energy for further thought about the lass. She gained the haven of her bedroom, located a bottle of fragrant lavender oil, and subsided into a favourite armchair, feet up on the bed. Off came all constricting clothing, layer by layer, until there was just her corset to unlace. With that done, she sighed and began to rub her stomach with the soothing oil and let her thoughts flow free.

How well she recalled the fuss and ado that had broken out when she, simple Victoria Allen, had snared Hamish Forsythe, the most eligible bachelor in town. Every lass envied and hated her, and their mothers had been shocked beyond belief to think that he would choose her above their bonny daughters.

And oh, the vicious rumours they'd spread about her integrity and the way they'd laughed at her simple upbringing! But she'd not held it against them; it was of no concern to her what folk believed about her. He was sinfully handsome for sure, with the charm of six men. And oh, but he had a way with words. But she loved Hamish with her very soul, and that was a fact.

"Ye give a man reason tae get up each morn, bonny Vic," he'd said one time. "Not only are ye more bonny than a hill of heather; ye have a heart of pure gold. Gie me yer whole heart, for I will take nought less."

"Ye have my whole heart as ye ken full well," she'd laughed. "Tis yers forever, an' if ye break it I'll ne'er forgive ye!"

But because of Germany's lust for power, they now had this godforsaken war, and Hamish was fully bent on joining his fellow countrymen. He couldn't be talked out of enlisting, so sure was he that nought bad would happen to him. If only her private womanly business were regular, she'd have known that she was already with child ere he left.

In her heart she'd suspected, but she could say nought when he was leaving to fight for the cause of freedom. Aye, silent she remained until his departure, and now here she was as fat as a cow and able to see him only on leave. With a sigh of resignation, she spread her feet out wide and fully surrendered to the comfort of self-pity.

What happened then was the stuff of nightmares. Someone knocked on the door and began to slowly open it, revealing the tip of a soldier's hat! Panic overcame exhaustion. She galvanised into action, scrambling to her feet and then lumbering around in search for something that would give cover. Heart pounding, she yanked the quilt from the bed and wrapped it around her swollen belly. But that proved to be a less-than-perfect solution. Now she looked as immense as an elephant instead of a cow and was sweating like a pig. As the rest of the hat and then a uniformed shoulder came into view, she prepared for the worst and began to scream.

"F'God's sake, dinna come in! Dinna come in!" she screeched in banshee-like tones. Was she hallucinating or, God forbid, was this truly happening? Her stomach twisted into a sailor's knot as the figure entered the room.

And then there was Flo wearing a soldier's hat and coat and a huge grin. Victoria was rendered mute and paralysed as the lass collapsed onto the bed in laughter.

"Oh, Victoria, that was so bloody amusing," Flo spurted between huge gulps of air. "Ye looked fair ready tae face a firing squad!" She uttered more gasps and guffaws. "Dinna fret yerself, lass; when Hamish arrives I will keep him wi' me until ye're fully prepared. Ye must trust me, sister-in-law; we are family now after all!"

And with that she skipped out, still overcome with mirth. Victoria remained speechless and just stood staring at the door. Minutes later she began to shake from head to toe and couldn't stop. With great effort she crossed to the bed and collapsed in a heap with the bedcover still wrapped around her elephantine body. Tears began to flow and pour down each side of her face and into her ears. Was that lass a mere simpleton or actually the devil incarnate?

*   *   *

Flo hummed as she clattered around in the kitchen preparing beef stew, Hamish's favourite. It was most agreeable to confound Her Highness like that! She didn't have to be such a drudge! Flo alone made Hamish happy. There was not a doubt in her mind that he hadn't rocked with laughter since his wedding day.

As for marriage and children, she wanted nary a thing to do with them. You wouldn't find her all aflutter with the first young suitor who approached. And there were many who had. Nay, she sought someone singular; someone like her Hamish. A very prince who would lift her onto his white horse and carry her away—as far away as possible from here!

She dipped the stewing chops into salted flour and placed them in a large pot which had a few inches of beef stock in it. Over the top came layers of chopped onions, carrots, potatoes, and peas, and then the closed pot was placed on the wood stove to simmer for two hours until all the flavours were mixed into the stock and the flour had thickened the juice.

As she was taking off the apron, there was a bustling sound to her side, and her mother appeared at the door, pushing it open with her elbow while carrying a pile of wood for the fire.

"Mother, what're ye trying tae do tae yerself?" said Flo as she leapt across to the door so as to catch Helen afore she fell. "Ye mustna try tae carry such immense loads any more. Ye've only tae ask me and I'll do it!"

"For heaven's sake, Flo, ye dinna need tae treat me like an invalid!" snapped Helen. "Stop yer fussing and mind that ye clean up yer mess here in the kitchen when ye're finished!" With that she struggled into the lounge room and resolutely made for the fireplace wi'out a backward glance.

For several moments Flo gripped the sink and wrestled privately against familiar icicles of rejection, which slithered like swords through her heart. There and then, in the kitchen of the house where she'd been since a bairn, she made a decision. She wouldn't let herself care ever again—that is, for ought other than Hamish.

When her breathing returned to normal, she lifted the large pot of hot water off the stove and emptied the contents into a basin. With a cake of soap and a cloth, she began to clean the kitchen utensils with purpose.

It would be marvellous indeed to see Hamish again. How she'd missed his bonny face and cheeky smile! Last week they'd received the news that he was to come home on leave and would arrive today on the 6.00 p.m. train. Father would meet him at the station, while they must be satisfied with waiting at the house.

So here she was, imprisoned with Princess bloody Victoria and her precious pregnancy. How tiresome it was to endure her endless complaints! The lass merely carried one wee bairn, not the problems of all Scotland!

She attacked a very grubby basin with the scrubbing brush as countless memories of Hamish surfaced. There was nary a dull moment with him around, and many an adventure to enjoy. She recalled that he stopped his teasing when she showed signs of emerging womanhood. From that time he became protective and treated her with kindness and affection. Aye, the kinship between them was a soothing balm throughout the years.

*   *   *

As Flo scrubbed a pot to within an inch of its life, Nathaniel left her side to answer a call from Heaven. He tuned into the message pulsing through space, and his alertometer revved up a hundred notches. This was a Code Orange from the Lord! The last time he'd received one of these was a century before, and he'd blacked out under the pressure. Who knew what he'd do with a Code Red? There hadn't been anything above a Yellow for him since that passing-out debacle. Through a mindless mist, he heard the Lord calling.

"Answer if you hear me, Nathaniel!" the much-loved voice was saying. "Nathaniel? Nathaniel!"

Nathaniel was once again stuck slap bang in the middle of fight and flight. He struggled to send out a reply, but the result was just a mass of static which made no sense at all. The guardians were beginning to look his way, curious about the strange electrical currents swirling around. He had to focus.

"I hear You, Lord," he squeaked. It wasn't much; but it was all that was to be had.

"You must be ready to act quickly, Nathaniel. Alert all the guardians to prepare for a double catastrophe which is imminent and will greatly affect everyone in the family."

Everything was starting to go into slow motion for Nathaniel, and his body was separating from his mind. "There will be a double catastrophe," he repeated in robotic tones. "It will affect everyone in the family."

"Yes, that is correct" said the Lord. "First Alec is about to receive a telegraph from London at the station telling him that Hamish Forsythe did not board the train with the other soldiers heading for Scotland. It suited my purposes to take him, Nathaniel; he was injured and did not survive."

Immediately a question shot like lightning from Nathaniel's spirit. *Why is the Lord telling me now and not last week—or last month, for that matter?* He went all out to retrieve it, but bullseye—it hit the throne.

The reply was immediate. "I am telling you at exactly the correct time. Not too early, not too late."

With a growing sense of doom, Nathaniel asked the question now sitting heavily on his heart. "And what was the second thing, Lord?"

"The second thing is that Victoria will go into early labour and the doctor will have to be fetched urgently. It will be a difficult birth, and the premature baby will be fragile—a touch-and-go situation. When that time comes, I have every confidence that you will follow my instructions to the letter and communicate clearly to the other angels." And with that, the communication lines were closed.

"I can do this, I can do this, I can do this," chanted Nathaniel while he worked to reconnect body and mind. It didn't take an archangel to figure out that Flo, so poisoned with jealous hatred, had played a key role in facilitating an emergency situation for Victoria. He hoped she would feel guilty long enough to cooperate for a while. Timing would be paramount here, so he needed to have a special talk with Tristan—a slow, super clear talk. That angel was definitely not too quick on the uptake. No wonder religion had been able to slither into Alec's life and steal his joy.

It was time to call the other guardians. "Do it afraid, Nathaniel," he said to the air. "Do it afraid!" he repeated with upraised fist. Then he sent out the signal. Within seconds they all congregated above the roof. They were aware that something big was afoot and were looking to him for wise and courageous leadership.

Wouldn't you know it; his left eye had developed a tic. Pushing through a potential panic attack, he kept both eyes wide open to compensate and began to update them with all the authority he could muster.

"I'm afraid it is bad news and bad news, team," he blurted. Not the best start, but better than nothing. "The Lord has taken Hamish, and now Alec is about to receive the dreaded telegraph about this. Also, Victoria will deliver early, and it will be dicey for both mother and baby. No time for questions, only action!"

"Are you okay, Nathaniel?" asked Helen's guardian Micko.

"Perfectly okay, thank you, Micko! And yourself?" His eyes were beginning to water from staring like a drugged owl.

"I'm fine. I just thought—"

"There is no time for thought; only action! Tristan, you and I must see to Alec. The rest of you, protect the house and wait for my next signal!"

Tristan remained nailed to the spot, stammering. "B-b-b-but w-w-why?"

"I believe I said there was no time for questions, Tristan!" declared Nathaniel. "Let's go!"

He took off with what he hoped was a leader-type manner, blinking furiously and wiping his eyes. Now to concentrate on the humans who would be caught up in this upheaval?

At the moment, Alec was a huge concern. He already flagellated himself daily for all manner of trivia and would be fully masochistic now, blaming himself for everything including the weather. But Nathaniel hoped there was still enough to work with. His good intentions augured well for prayer power, and even though he was tragically overzealous, that was still better than laissez-faire.

Glancing back, he was relieved to see Tristan close behind. He nodded, and then the two of them descended to land on either side of Alec at the railway station. They each placed a hand on his back and channelled strength into his spirit in preparation for the telegraph, which was just now coming into the railway master's office.

*   *   *

Alec's mouth went dry when he read the telegraph. All through the years he'd lived with a private dread that the Lord would punish him for secretly favouring Hamish. And now the dread had become a reality. Hamish, with his boundless energy and hunger for life, who had answered the call to fight for the cause of freedom, was dead ere his life had really begun.

He couldn't bear this; it was not possible! He had never revealed to Hamish his deep love and affection, and now the chance was forever gone. Never again would he see that cheeky grin or laugh secretly at his son's impish humour. From this day on he was damned to live in a grey world.

Nay, it was too hard. It was too hard! The dam walls of emotion broke, and he dropped weeping to the floor, curled up like a bairn. He prayed from the very depths of his soul, forgetting to use his best Holy Book English and instead calling out to the Lord in a thick Scottish accent.

"Oh God, God, God, oh God," he called, "ye ken how frail we are; aye, and how much we're needin' yer mercy. Strength, Lord—gie us strength! And gie us angels all 'round tae protect us!

Keep yer hand of grace on the family! Have mercy, God, and watch o'er the bairn that's tae be born! Have mercy, Father, mercy!"

*   *   *

A cloud popped over the horizon, and Nathaniel adjusted his eyes for long distance. There it was—a horde of demons sent to cash in on the crisis. Discouragement, Panic, Infirmity, and Death, to name a few, were hurtling along, and it was pretty flipping clear from the angle of a thousand bug-eyed stares that he was the first target.

A missile of despair whistled forward, aiming straight for his heart. Nathaniel hit the deck at Alec's feet, but the wretched barb still hit him in the leg. He dislodged it, but the poison was already entering his spirit, and his courage was waning. He was halfway through reciting "Do it afraid, Nathaniel" in slow motion when out of the blue Alec's prayers went up a notch.

"Almighty Lord, I ken that ye are God and there is nought other!" he cried. "And it says in the Holy Book that ye are a God of love who doesna betray yer followers. Ye are faithful and true above all others! It says that if Ye are for us, none can be against us! In the name of Jesus, take this burden by the scruff o' the neck and gie us strength. Gie us strength! Show yer fist tae Satan and carry us through this grief!"

The cloud stopped in mid-flight and begin to retreat. Alec continued to weep and call out in the kind of despair that only comes from humans who are at the end of their rope. Man alive, the guy would get a two out of ten for rhetoric, but he had the heart of a warrior.

Nathaniel felt power surge through his spirit. The dread which had threatened to surface began to fade, and a cry of battle erupted from his mouth. He grinned at Tristan, and the two of them held hands to let the prayer currents refresh and empower them. Soon Nathaniel's cry turned into a roar.

Within milliseconds a division of soldier angels flew in and surrounded them, brandishing swords and grenades and looking to Nathaniel for instructions. Heady with the smell of victory, he declared that Tristan should minister to Alec and the soldiers should follow him.

"They're ours for the taking, guys!" he yelled. "They dare to come against the army of the Most High God!" With wings outspread, he flew towards the cloud, and with another shout he hurtled head first into the centre of the enemy ranks.

4

Can I see another's woe, and not be in sorrow too?
Can I see another's grief, and not seek for kind relief?
—William Blake, from "On Another's Sorrow," 1789

Two days later

The screams, the weeping, and the groaning of anguish continued without relief, and Nathaniel's valiant workers were heartsick having done all they could. It was up to the comforters now to tend to the grief-stricken as they waited on the Lord's grace to bring healing.

Nathaniel checked once more through misty eyes to see that there were guardians at every watchtower, dog-tired though they may be. He flinched with empathy as Victoria once more screamed out her despair. On she went for hours, bearing down in childbirth, bringing a life into the world while she wept over a death.

In the name of everything holy, how was an angel supposed to figure out the whys and wherefores of a human's plight? They were awesome, these created beings who fought against so much darkness with so little light.

Flo was still alone in her room, curled up tight and repeating over and over that she'd lost the love of her life. He started to pace back and forth at the foot of her bed while one of the comforters administered peace oil. This whole super-sensitive thing was not his scene at all, and he felt as out of place as a trout thrashing about in a lily pond.

Poor old Alec was a basket case now, crippled by a deadly cocktail of guilt and grief. Tristan's chances of getting the guy to receive any help at the moment were less than nil in a thousand, but he was still giving it a red-hot go. When Nathaniel saw that he was literally trying to wrestle Alec into the sitting position, he decided that it was time to intervene.

"He's not responding, Tristan," was all he could think of to say.

"But he has to, Nathaniel. He has to!"

"Maybe so, but he's not; and that will have to be the end of it."

"But I don't understand how he will get over this."

"And I don't understand a lot of things, the reason being that I'm merely an angel and not God."

Tristan let Alec slump back down onto his bed. "Counselling isn't really our forte is it?" he whispered.

"You can say that again, angel," said Nathaniel with a sad smile. "You can say that again."

5

For man does not know his time. Like fish taken in a cruel net, like birds caught in a snare, so the sons of men are snared in an evil time when it falls upon them suddenly.
—Ecclesiastes 9:12

The battlefields of France, 1918

Exploding shells ripped open the few minutes of peace, and Tom's stomach churned as he ploughed his way through the shin-deep mud of no man's land. Front line duty was hell enough, but doing a turn on fatigue could send a man bonkers.

What with being covered in mud and wet to the skin with no hope of drying out for days, a bloke hardly felt human. A sergeant wouldn't normally do this shift, but Tom couldn't bring himself to send men out night after night without at least sometimes having a go.

Suddenly a star shell went up, and there they were, lit up and nowhere to hide. He clutched the life-giving soup in his shaky hands and stood stock-still. His mouth was too dry to pray out loud, and his mind was numb anyway, so he just stayed put, as they'd all been taught, until darkness enveloped everyone again.

Not far to go now before he could hand over the soup to his men on front line duty, and then there was nothing for it but to once again cover the hundred yards back to the shelter. It might as well be a thousand miles; an hour it had taken him to get this far. Finally he reached the trench and got a hero's welcome.

"You're a godsend, Serge!" said the first soldier, smiling straight into his eyes. "Fair dinkum I don't know which is worst; front line or fatigue."

Tom's face heated up, and he mumbled a reply and moved on to the next soldier until all the soup had been handed out. He couldn't do small talk with other blokes. It wasn't that he didn't want to; he'd just never learnt how.

One thing he liked about this lunacy called war was the mateship, where a bloke like him could feel close to other blokes for the first time in his life. Back on the farm in Aussie land, he'd spent most of his time alone with his animals and crops.

He turned and steeled himself for the torture of the return trip. At least this would be the last for tonight, as dawn was just around the corner. And how many of the men he'd just visited would be still alive come daybreak? It didn't pay to care so much, but how did a bloke stop himself?

He and the other soldiers on fatigue duty began to inch their way back. Ten yards along there was a cry of "hit the deck!" from the front, and Fritz's machine guns began to rattle. Tom didn't relish being face down in mud, but survival took over. He chucked the utensils aside and landed with a squelch as the bullets sprayed over and around them. What felt like an eternity later, all was quiet and they were on their feet again, soaked and frozen to the bone.

Gradually his feet covered ground, and as the minutes ticked and crept along, the hope of safety buoyed his spirits a little. Only some yards to go now, and it looked as if he would live to face another day. A hundred feet to go; fifty; twenty. No banter between the men, who had the look of horses headed for home.

The only comfort ahead was a corner in a makeshift camp, but compared to where he'd been tonight, that seemed a big improvement to Tom. The days dawned warmer lately, and with some fancy footwork, he could get somewhere in the sun. That is unless there were wounded who needed it more than he did.

As the first dawn light split the sky, a blessed sight came into view. The banner of the Salvation Army flew in the face of Hell. By jingo they were amazing, those Salvos! In the midst of all this torment, they were there night and day, bringing love and comfort.

His heart welled up with gratitude that he didn't have a hope of putting into words. Already they were up, busy preparing food and coffee, and ready to minister to any wounded or dying. The sounds of life in the camp welcomed him as he approached, and he got a sense of coming home—the closest he'd ever got to that feeling anyway.

He handed in the food containers, received a smile and his own ration of the wonderful hot liquid, and closed his eyes as the first mouthful made its way down his food hole. A friendly voice called out from a dugout, and there was Bill. He had a spot next to him that would be in the sun soon and where Tom would be able to settle in and get some shut-eye.

He said his thank yous and then settled into the spot and leant against the dirt wall to finish off the soup. That's when he felt the let-down after being on tenterhooks all night. Exhaustion set in, and he fought against self-pity. There was no one at home who wept or prayed for him. Was there a God in heaven who gave a rip whether he lived or died?

Machine guns sprayed only yards away as he huddled in the flimsy safety of the camp. Soon it would be daylight and Fritz would give it up for a few hours. He tried to lift his own mood by thinking about his leave coming up next month. Fancy a farmer like him going to a place like London! Maybe he'd get to see the King and Buckingham Palace. He'd be warm and dry. There'd be girls around, and all kinds of food at the eating places

It'd feel good to be in a big group when the Aussies hit the streets. Even though he always felt he was on the fringe of things, the other blokes didn't mind having him around. He didn't cause any waves; just tried to do right by the men. He reckoned that was how he'd earned the rank of sergeant.

Gradually, in spite of the discomfort and sounds of men coughing, praying, or crying, he grew more and more drowsy. He sighed and rested his head back. Finally, with some relief, he felt himself drifting off into sleep.

6

But men must know that in this theatre of man's life it is reserved only for God and angels to be lookers on.
—Francis Bacon, from *The Advancement of Learning*, 1605

England, 1918

Flo was fair caught between ecstasy and terror. London turned her giddy, and her nerves were threatening to break out in public. The Welcome Inn Eating House did not seem so respectable now that they were seated and had a chance to look around. Soldiers and lasses were drinking and cavorting every which way, and she was close to losing Nellie, who hadn't spoken for an age but just sat with her mouth open wide, looking for all the world like a stunned mullet. *For the love of God, that girl is such a simpleton at times!* Flo fumbled around in her bag for a cigarette and lighter, all the while attempting to look elegant. Nellie wasn't going to ruin her fun! It was a dream come true to be here, and she didn't want anything upsetting her chances for adventure.

They'd been allowed to travel alone only because Uncle Robert had offered to meet them at the station on arrival and escort them to safety. The man truly was fair generous even though he and his wife, Gael, were as dull as doorknobs. But they were churchgoers and had a bomb shelter in their backyard, so father was happy.

Och, her father's priorities were full shallow and meaningless! He'd given her a list of rules as long as the Thames. "The List" had the purpose of keeping her from falling into sin whilst in the den of iniquity which was London. And what was there for her at home? Her mother was caught up day and night helping Victoria with the baby, and she couldn't remember the last time she'd seen a smiling face.

Anyway, his dour ways hadn't left her holiday in ruins. Nay, to her great relief London had met all expectations for excitement, and she felt a stirring of joy and hope in her heart for the first time in three years. She'd broken nigh on all the rules on the List, an accomplishment of the highest order. She and Nellie were adults, not mere bairns!

She finally located a cigarette and matches and lit up with a flourish, looking around as she inhaled the smoke. But the exhale came out as a sort of long, slow "O" because she spied a group of somewhat raucous lads in uniform who were studying them from a bus across the street.

Not for the first time, she secretly faced the truth that she often didn't feel very mature at all. Her heart thumped against the wall of her chest like a bass drum, and she could hear the sound of her own blood swishing and pumping around.

* * *

Nathaniel fidgeted around getting a better position on the sign above the Welcome Inn Eating House. The English were getting on with life as usual, which was par for the course. Zimron was sitting nearby and putting in zero effort towards conversation; also par for the course. Call him simple, but how was he supposed to communicate with a centuries-toughened warrior who had the personality of a swamp rat and made him feel like a midget? Seeking a distraction, he glanced down to check on Flo.

"Well, that's number twelve," he said with a chuckle.

"Number twelve of what?" replied Zimron.

What Nathaniel thought was, *Hallelujah, the warrior speaks!* What he said was, "That's the twelfth rule that Flo's broken since she arrived in London." He broke into a monstrous grin and crossed his arms, warming to the subject. "Lighting a cigarette is the ultimate call to war. She'd be feeling pretty chuffed after that."

* * *

Zimron was totally lost for words; the usual thing. He was in charge of a hundred warriors who each had a thousand soldiers under them. Domestic life was not his scene. This was kindergarten stuff for him—human soldiers on leave in a peace zone. But the Lord had told him to pop over here for two hours.

His and Nathaniel's roles hadn't dovetailed before, and they didn't have much in common. But he had to say something or the guardian would write him off as rude. How did you compare the situation of Florence smoking with that of soldiers trying to find a moment's peace in the midst of war? After at least a minute, he felt ready to reply.

"So the smoking is a big deal then?" he said.

*   *   *

Nathaniel visibly flinched and threw his hands in the air before he'd had a chance to collect his wits. Wouldn't you know it; Zimron had thrown him for a loop again by coming up with an off-the-wall question hours after Nathaniel had made a perfectly reasonable comment.

"Um, yes it is, actually" he replied through gritted teeth. "She knows that her parents would be outraged if they saw her. She's acting out her own anger and sense of injustice."

He glanced across through slitted eyes to measure Zimron's reaction to that comment and decided that he was showing a modicum of interest. In a moment of abandon, he threw caution to the wind.

"How do your charges deal with the anger they must feel at the injustice of their situation, Zimron?" he asked.

The warrior was now looking at him with a decidedly stunned expression, but Nathaniel was ready this time and maintained eye contact. After all, it was a sensible question and deserved a decent answer. "How do they deal with the anger?" he finally said. "How do they deal with the anger? Hmm. To tell you the truth, Nathaniel, the injustice of their situation is so enormous that it's beyond thinking about or dealing with on any level. They are way past anger. Anger is a luxury they can't afford."

"Right!" Nathaniel felt like a baboon conversing with an astronaut. Seriously, there was just nowhere to go after that comment. Nothing for it but to get back to checking on Flo. There she was, with her friend Nellie, petrified and beside herself with excitement.

*   *   *

Zimron directed his attention to the bus which had recently pulled up to the kerb. Four soldiers laughing and clowning around had alighted from the vehicle and been quick to notice the two beautiful girls sitting alone. And they just happened to be all under the care of soldiers who answered to him. His spirit was quickened.

In the time that he'd been here amongst all this froth and bubble, the Lord had already pinpointed numbers of young men who were to be taken when they returned to France. He would assign extra counsellors to each one to make sure they had every chance to be ready for eternity.

Equally important were the ones who were to be preserved for reasons he was not to know at this time. The pressure had not lifted off his spirit yet, so he knew there must be more to come. He was really into the zone now. The Lord was still speaking, and nothing less than 100 per cent accuracy would do.

He also had to be exact to the last letter when it came to informing the relevant authorities so that all would be in the right place at the right time. One mistake on his part could have unthinkable consequences.

*   *   *

Flo was so lost in her own panic that it took several shaky inhalations afore she registered Nellie's voice, which seemed to come in a whisper from the foggy distance.

"I'm scared, Flo" she breathed. "In truth, those soldiers are lookin' our way, and the expressions on their faces says they're wantin' for excitement."

"And we're wantin' for excitement too, Nellie, in case you've forgotten," hissed Flo between her teeth as she gave the lads a welcoming smile which was a borderline grimace. She heard Nellie's intake of breath beside her.

"Well, cobbers, look at this; some fair dinkum London beauties!" said the cockiest one, who had the strangest accent Flo had ever heard.

"Scottish actually," she replied, her smile starting to fade a little.

The other young men exploded with laughter and began to tease their friend.

"Always the ladies' man is our Bill," said one, "only ever opens his mouth to change feet."
More laughter broke out on all sides.

"We'll never be short of sheilas with you around, mate," added another.

Flo sneaked a quick look at Nellie and saw that she was smiling and seemed more relaxed. Maybe these men with the strange accents just wanted to be friends.

"And what on earth is a sheila?" she asked in mock innocence. "We're just two young lassies who've nary a clue where y're from."

"That's right! We've nary a clue!" echoed Nellie, her face flushed and eyes bright. Flo grappled with her first frissons of guilt since leaving home. Nellie was as naive as a newborn bairn, and Flo had vowed to care for her.

"Well, lassies, allow us to clarify," replied Bill who did not seem to care that the laughter was at his expense. Afore she and Nellie could respond, he sat himself at a nearby table and the others did the same.

"The truth is, lassies, we're from the end of the world; from a place called Australia, where the sun shines and the kookaburras laugh."

"And what might a kookaburra be?" asked Nellie. "Is it like a hyena? I've read that they make a sound nigh to a laugh."

"She wants to know if it's like a hyena, mates," said Bill.

"Yes," said another, "just like a hyena—except it flies!"

Yet again the soldiers laughed—louder this time. People at nearby tables turned to look, and Flo squirmed with shame. Nellie had her eyes to the ground and didn't look happy at all. These lads were too coarse and unruly by far.

But then the quiet and bonny one who'd been keeping to himself up till now stood and walked across to their table and began to speak.

"You had no way of knowin' what a kookaburra was girl," he said. "It's a bird that's only found in Australia, and when it does its call, it sounds as if it's laughin' fit to burst."

"Oh I see" replied Nellie. She smiled her gratitude, and the other three men lifted their eyebrows at each other.

"And what would your name be?" asked Flo.

"My name's Tom," said the soldier. "Blimey, I could listen to you girls talk all day." Their eyes met and smiled to one another.

For the first time in her life, Flo felt a flicker of interest in a man. This Tom had a face that was carved and creased in a way that was fair stirring, and his skin had been out in the sun for a lifetime. He was a sergeant and looked bonny in his uniform. Of course he didn't compare with her brother; no man could. But he seemed kind, and his accent was pleasing.

*   *   *

Yes, Tom was lost; guardians just knew these things. It wasn't rocket science to figure out that he was totally mesmerised by Flo's beauty. Nathaniel looked from one to the other, and the light dawned when he saw an interchange of souls.

"The Lord told me that something momentous was on the horizon for Florence, Zimron," he said. "Looks like that something could be a husband."

Zimron surprised him by replying in a flash. "I've been thinking the same thing, Nathaniel. There'll be another six months before this war is finally spent. It's going to be a living hell over in France, guardian; enough to break the spirit of many. The Lord has been pinpointing for me which of the young men down there are to be taken, as well as the ones he wants kept. I would appreciate it if you would make contact with Caleb, Tom's guardian."

He stood up and stretched. "Well, the sense of urgency has lifted here, so I think that's a wrap" he said in mid-yawn. "Now I can stop treading water and get back into action. There are some strategies needing to be put into place."

"Yes, thank goodness for that." Nathaniel felt thoroughly miffed. Was he so boring that time spent with him was a total vacuum? Zimron didn't bat an eye. Nathaniel silently repented for the sarcasm, which had gone totally over the warrior's head anyway.

"It's been an experience spending time with you, Nathaniel" he said without making eye contact. "All the best with Florence's anger problem."

Nathaniel summoned up a reply. "Thank you, Zimron. All the best with the war."

He sent up a quick ripple of forgiveness as the warrior took flight. His mind then began to race ahead to all that had to be done. The Forsythes had already suffered the loss of Hamish and the premature birth of his baby. Now it looked as though Flo would be leaving to go to the other end of the world.

He checked back to the eating house to see how things were progressing and saw that there was an arm waving in a flurry back and forth. When he realised the arm belonged to Caleb, he jumped to his feet and waved back. Caleb gave him a wink and a thumbs up in return.

Nathaniel glowed with pleasure. The two of them had had a blast every time they'd worked together over the centuries. There were lots of different types of angels in creation, but there was no doubt about it—guardians were his absolute favourites!

7

I married beneath me, all women do.
—Nancy Astor, 1961

Aberdeen, Scotland, spring 1919

Call him bizarre, but Nathaniel reckoned the stone kirk had put its best foot forward today and risen to the occasion. There it was, ramrod straight and sporting a mix of winter white and kaleidoscope spring. Forget Westminster Abbey; this pile of stones was strutting its stuff in accommodating a wedding.

There wasn't what you'd call overkill when it came to colour in the place. Sunlight was showering onto the stained-glass windows so that old Bible stories were lit up like rainbows. Then there were the two brass urns standing watch at the front and spilling over with early spring flowers. Throw in the empty wooden cross and a few gold bits and pieces, and that was about as frivolous as it got, really.

The wedding party had just stepped across to the side alcove to sign the register, so the congregation would now endure the agony of a musical presentation. This was comic relief for the guardians, who all settled back to enjoy the experience.

Charlie McPherson charged life into the old organ, belting out the twenty-third psalm as though he were fighting for his and his family's lives, including grandchildren and second and third cousins. Then Jess Simpson began to sing her heart out along with the organ, her face a picture of ecstasy. She was caught up in the divine and looked and sounded ready to explode any second.

Nathaniel winced and then, along with Tristan and Caleb, fell about in hysterics on the back pew.

* * *

Flo finished with the signing, smiled at the minister, and then turned to Tom, who gazed at her with a look that spoke of desire. She watched her brother Angus and Nellie glance fair lovesick at one another before signing as groomsman and bridesmaid, and she knew that it wouldn't be long afore they declared openly their love. She knew she must hide her foreboding and not spoil their joy.

Tom was her ticket out of here, and she wouldn't let the chance pass her by. There was no getting away from it; she must marry or else curl up and die in Aberdeen. True, she wasn't bursting with love and passion, but she did feel something for Tom, and that was a miracle in itself.

He would protect her; of that she was certain. And he was taking her to a new world where they would build a life together away from rejection and pain. Aye, he was the knight she had hoped for.

She let that thought grasp her mind for a moment in hope of solace, but she couldn't deny the truth. She was marrying a man she didn't know, and she had agreed to follow him to the far end of the earth. Aye, there was terror enough there to stifle any hope and override any thrill. But relief at the prospect of leaving kept her resolute.

Thanks to the gods of music, Jess Simpson screeched out a final note. Flo was sore tempted to check for broken windows. The bridal party returned to the main kirk area, and Reverend Miller's voice rang out, fair bouncing off the rafters.

"Would the congregation please rise!" he boomed in his special "holier than thou" church voice. "May I present to you Mr. and Mrs. Tom Millet!"

Flo had hoped for some wee stirrings of joy at this point of the service. But she was so shocked to hear herself referred to as "Mrs. Tom Millet" that she didn't feel a thing. Surely the man had a brain the size of a peach seed. If he'd said "Tom and Florence Millet," she would still exist somewhere in the midst of this charade.

Well, at least she wouldn't have to attend this torture chamber called a kirk ever again, and she didn't have to smile, because these dim-witted folk didn't believe in smiles. Faith they thought that a grave face showed depth of feeling. Aye, and depth of feeling she had in abundance; enough to sink a battleship!

Her kinfolk looked as if they were sucking lemons at a funeral. They didn't think she would ever come to any good. Let them think what they would. They'd been rude and patronizing to Tom, who wasn't used to such treatment. But he didn't let it upset him. Just courteous to everyone was Tom.

*   *   *

Tom couldn't take his eyes off Flo in her white satin dress with spring flowers in her gorgeous red hair. She looked just like an angel. He was in seventh heaven. To be still standing when the war ended was amazing enough, but to be marrying the most glorious creature in the world was a miracle. He felt that any minute now he was going to wake up and find himself in a mouldy trench somewhere in France.

To think that her old man had given his blessing and the whole family was being so polite to Tom Millet, a farm boy orphaned since childhood. He'd always been a nuisance and an outsider passed around from one sister to the next, and now he was part of a family. It was too much to take in.

When the man of God called out those words—"May I present to you Mr. and Mrs. Tom Millet!"—Tom was so blown up with pride he was half expecting to come apart at the seams. He knew pride was a sin, but he already felt so unworthy being in a holy church and mixing with all the clean-living folk that he didn't have anything to lose. His only previous experience with Christians had been on the battlefield with the Salvos, who always seemed to be there—at the front, in the trenches—when needed. He'd seen plenty of them shot down while praying for dying soldiers. He wished he could be a Christian too, but he felt he could never be good enough.

*   *   *

Alec had never wept in his life, but he feared lest he would break down afore everyone and scream like a hungry bairn. Flo was leaving him. When she'd first come with the news, he'd wanted to lash out and wound her with his words. 'Twas only pride kept him as quiet as the grave.

He wondered how a man learned to feel ought but fear and grief. Folks spoke of joy, but he'd known nary a drop in his whole life. When Tom had come seeking to wed Flo, he'd wanted to punch the man between the eyes. But instead he'd stood erect, given his blessing, and remained civil throughout the preparations and now the ceremony.

As the minister called out the dreaded words "May I present to you Mr. and Mrs. Tom Millet!" it was as if Flo now didn't exist, and new grief was added to the gaping wound which had festered in his soul since Hamish's death. The two lights of his life were extinguished, and he was left in the dark alone. In the secret heart place that no one ever saw, he cried out to God.

"Gie me strength, Father, tae carry on," he pleaded. "Protect her, dear God; protect my wee lass and keep her safe."

*　　*　　*

Helen sat stiff and erect, arms crossed. She would ne'er forgive Florence for this desertion. What would become of her in her old age? Her heart curled with contempt just to look at that heathen who'd seduced an innocent girl away from her kinfolk. All her life she'd been a godly woman who did right, and she'd always put herself last. She obeyed her husband, kept herself from superficial pleasures, and didn't succumb to the lusts of the flesh. And what was her reward? A son slain in battle and a daughter left for the end of the earth!

The minister asked for the congregation to rise, and his serious countenance showed his disapproval. As he called out the words "May I present to you Mr. and Mrs. Tom Millet," Helen made an inner vow. *My daughter is now dead. I wipe my hands of her as of this moment.*

*　　*　　*

Unforgiveness and bitterness exchanged a smile across the top of Helen's head. They had lodged there for the duration of her life and could continue to hinder and poison the family. As for Alec, Condemnation still held enough ground at the moment to keep him emotionally impotent and keep his heart hidden from the world. For a time, at least, their future was secure.

*　　*　　*

Victoria felt the wood of the kirk pew knocking against her spine. Seriously, she'd never found a way to get comfortable on these lumps of wood. Hamish Jr. was causing her much anguish with his mischief today, and she didn't want to deal with his antics.

Outwardly she remained as still as the night, but behind the mask she felt exceeding overwrought. 'Twas true she was a woman of faith, but she was still hard put to hold back a rising of despair. It was well nigh impossible to ignore the jealousy that assailed her at the thought that Flo would be happy while she must continue on alone.

That attitude was sinful, but there it was. Somehow she must be rid of the anger that festered in her heart against the lass. Victoria was not clever and didn't pretend to be, but she knew the things that were important. Hatred was a poison that brought nought but torment, and that she knew full well. There was nought for it but to find a way to move past her grief if she were to live and not die.

As the minister announced, "May I present to you Mr. and Mrs. Tom Millet!" she came to a resolve.

"Heavenly Father," she prayed, "I forgive Florence for the pain she caused me. She didna ken what she was doing. And Father, please help me tae come tae the end o' my tears o'er Hamish. I choose to live, Father. Aye, I choose to live."

*   *   *

Nathaniel was on full alert. Man alive, there was everything under the sun going on here as the minister's words bounced off every wall. Then, in the middle of the pandemonium, both Alec and Victoria managed to push through their own pain and pray down a blessing. This kind of gutsy behaviour was, to be fist-clenchingly honest, the stuff of a guardian's fantasy. He felt his eyes mist up.

Guardians came from all over, robes billowing and light flashing. Angels never got tired of watching the Lord's dealings with humans. Quicker than you could say "Praise the Lord," a hug of peace enveloped Alec and healing rain poured over Victoria. Then the Lord's finger touched her forehead and stamped on it a promise of blessing beyond her wildest dreams.

*   *   *

Reverend Miller was finding this ceremony burdensome. He was fond of young Florence; aye, had always found her energy and spirit inspiring. O'er the years, her talent in song and keyboard had been a blessing to the congregation and indeed to him. The young lad seemed a nice fellow, unassuming and kind, and fair lost in love with his bride. He hoped they would be happy.

But her kinfolk hadn't been easy to deal with over the years. He couldn't turn around without bumping into Alec, who helped with everything under the sun. The man's gravity was fair suffocating. He was at every meeting and on every committee and did nought to warrant rebuke, so there'd been no choice but to make him an elder.

As for Helen, the woman didn't have an ounce of human kindness flowing through her veins. She could massacre joy with one look from that sour face.

Aye, but Victoria was a different kettle of fish. Against all effort, he couldn't ignore her beauty. She was a mother and homemaker next to none and had a heart of gold. He allowed his eyes to linger on her for a wee moment and inwardly sighed. Perhaps in time she would recover from her grief and the Lord would give him favour in her eyes.

It was time to make the final announcement, which always occasioned a thrill for the bride and groom. Reverend Miller placed importance on this part of the service, so he took a deep breath and called out, "May I present to you Mr. and Mrs. Tom Millet!" in crystal tones. He sent up a silent prayer for their happiness and asked God to give them a fresh start in Australia.

* * *

It was nothing short of mayhem city here now; a shemozzle of humans, demons, and angels. Nathaniel reckoned that family and friends had been hanging onto their last shred of hope for an eventual end to the service, judging by the way they were falling over one another trying to get to the exit. The kirk bells were close to rupturing their insides in a bid for festivity. They had a job ahead of them if the expressions on people's faces were anything to go by.

Flo stepped out into a burst of sunshine looking paradoxically like a person heading for the guillotine and was followed by Tom, who beamed from a mix of pride, shock, and rampant testosterone. The party one by one offered congratulations to the couple before spreading out onto the lawn. Finally the bells gave up the fight and folk began to get into the tea and sandwiches and chat amongst themselves.

The guardians scuttled the remaining demons, then all fell in a heap to get their breath back. A quick debrief with the team was in order, preferably before they fell asleep.

Nathaniel decided to ramp up the ante. Ignoring their groans, he instructed them to gather together around the kirk steeple for a meeting. Several minutes later, after much straightening of robes and preening of feathers, they assembled in obedience and waited to hear whatever he had to say.

"I'm exceptionally pleased with each one of you." He beamed with what he hoped was a smile of affirmation. "You've pulled together and shown the enemy that you are a polished, lethal team not to be taken lightly. I have every confidence that you will continue here successfully in Aberdeen." At this point he paused for dramatic effect. "That is the good news. On a more serious note, Caleb and I must prepare for change because our mission calls for us to continue on assignment in Australia. Although I know what a disappointment this must be for you, I have every faith that you will adjust and regroup in time."

The response to this announcement was disappointing in Nathaniel's opinion—blank faces and deadly silence all round. But a leader must remain positive, so he retained the smile and stayed upbeat.

"Unfortunately I cannot give any indication as to how long I will be gone. In my role as a cross-generational case manager, I must stay on the job until the Lord's will has been worked out through the decades. But I promise that I will find ways to keep in touch!"

His assurances were met with more silence and more blank faces. Had Satan hypnotised them while he wasn't looking? He chose to go on as if everything were normal. "Are there any questions?" he asked.

After many torturous seconds, Tristan stepped into the breach. "I think they're all a bit exhausted, Nathaniel," he offered. "That wedding was about as joyful as a locust plague, and what with the war and all, there's a lot to deal with. But I'm sure they're all excited that you're a CGCM, and they will miss you enormously once you're gone."

"Right! Excellent! Thank you, Tristan!" *Could someone just come along and bury me in the kirk graveyard, for crying out loud?* "Well, looks like we've done what we had to around here; let's all get a bit of rest while we can."

By the time he'd finished the last sentence, there wasn't an angel in sight.

*   *   *

Tristan was beside himself with weariness. He couldn't imagine what it would take for Alec to drop his multiple shields and just be himself. Then again, most humans didn't have a clue who they were and spent their precious few years on Earth doing a bad job of trying to be somebody else. Angels were lucky that way. They knew where they'd come from and who'd made them, and they knew who they were at any given point in time.

Nathaniel had been a much-needed support and a kind friend. Tristan's confidence had grown with him around, and things would be much easier from now on. But to be honest it would be good for them to be separated for a time. In fact, to be absolutely honest, he would call it a blessing in disguise. He had a heart of gold, did Nathaniel, but he found it hard to know when to let go.

He'd tried not to look too elated at the prospect out of respect for Nathaniel's feelings. However, he couldn't help breaking out into a bit of a skip while heading over to join the others who'd settled around the steeple. The guardians began to worship the Lord as one, singing "Holy, holy, holy, Lord God Almighty!"

He joined voice with the whole heavenly host. Then, rapturous bliss, the Lord poured out peace and joy and an ocean of love. Cries of "Hallelujah!" reverberated across the city of Aberdeen until the powers of darkness shook with fear and shrank back into the black corners of the earth.

8

But those who wait upon the Lord shall renew their strength; they shall mount up
with wings like eagles, they shall run and not be weary, they shall walk and not faint.
—Isaiah 40:31

Ascension Expressway to Heaven

"Oooooh … I'm gonna go up, up, up to the highest places, aaaaand … I'm gonna be look,
look, lookin' at heavenly faces!"

Over and over Nathaniel bellowed out the two lines he'd made up. Did he know how to
party or what? He was on his way to heaven and was totally—yes, totally—chuffed. The earth
would have to get on without him, even though there was something unique about him. Yes!
Those were the words he'd been looking for to round off a totally awesome song.

"Yeeees … The earth will have to get on without me, eeeeven … though there's something
unique about me!"

Perfect! He must pass that on to the songsters at the Throne Room. He sang it through from
start to finish a couple of times for good measure. Glory did he feel good, what with a holiday
coming up and after the great send-off his team had given him back on Earth.

They'd fallen over themselves promising to keep the show on the road, difficult though
that would be, and saying they'd miss him like crazy but would push on regardless. Needless
to say, their words were shamelessly over the top and lacked the full ring of truth. But he was
so brimming over with joie de vivre that he'd let it pass.

With every second of ascension, the darkness of Earth dissipated some more and made way
for increasing radiance. Already he could hear songs of worship coming from the throne and
bouncing off the mountains and oceans of Paradise. Then, rapture of raptures, a familiar vista

opened up. There they were—thousands of rainbows quivering in the reflection from the River of Life as it swirled and bubbled along.

Hallelujah! Nathaniel celebrated with a get-down-and-boogie mid-air dance. Letting out a shout of "Who's your Daddy!" he swooped downwards and laughed as the water rose to meet him. Then he plunged into the life-giving depths.

The heaviness of Earth's suffering and agony ebbed away as he duck-dived and floated, allowing the river to carry him towards the Throne Room. When he reached his destination, he swam across the current and stepped onto shore purified and good as new. If it weren't for the river, he'd have had Buckley's chance of making the vital transition to be ready for the King. But man did he feel good now.

He met up with a passing group and entered into harmony with their singing. Dancers clothed in silver and white leapt and swirled in the Worship Garden, where perfumes drenched the senses and golden pathways led to jewel-encrusted doors of the Throne Room. The weight of glory pouring out caused him to collapse for timeless moments, then he scrambled to his feet and scurried to get in and find a spot.

Bypassing the guardian section, he headed for the area marked "Case Managers." *Ooeee!* He lit up at the sight of jaws dropping everywhere as he floated by. Unfortunately, the resulting glow remained and in fact worked its way right down to the hem of his robe.

As destiny would have it, this moral lapse was soundly disciplined within minutes. Nathaniel had just started to step up into the case manager area when he was pulverised by the next wave of glory, ending up flat on his face, unable to move and with arms wrapped around the sign. The Lord's voice sounded like a hundred trumpets but was aimed at him alone.

"Now is a season for renewal, Nathaniel. It is preparation for a time to come when you will have to be on your mettle. At some point word will get out that you are in fact on a special mission, and Satan will be working overtime to sabotage it. But I alone know the time and place, while Satan is guessing in the dark. We will keep him guessing."

Then, before you could say "Mephibosheth," all communication ceased without so much as a "bless you, angel." Nathaniel flashed scarlet as he struggled unsuccessfully to get up from his humiliating position on the floor.

Looks like we're going to keep the old Nathaniel in the dark too, he thought.

Big mistake. Five songs later he was still expressing to the Lord deep and undying repentance for his sojourn into not only pride but resentment to boot. Every angel and his dog knew that resentment leads to bitterness (which is fatal) and that pride had got Satan into a never-ending mess of the worst order.

Finally there came a release and he was able to stand and mix in with the other CGCMs. He was wandering around amongst them, just revelling in every second when he happened to catch the Lord watching him. He stared back feeling like the proverbial rabbit caught in headlights until something wonderful happened. The Lord's face opened up into a wide grin, and he winked!

Nathaniel broke up laughing, overcome with joy, and went on laughing for hours. Laughter led to worship, which drew him into the glorious intimacy with his God that he cherished. For weeks this continued, until he finally ventured from the Throne Room and set off to catch up with old friends and visit favourite holiday spots.

He marvelled at the contrast he saw between humans on Earth and those who lived here in harmony with one another and with all created beings. And he was inspired afresh to do all in his power to see that the ways of heaven were revealed to the world.

When the passion for his calling began to pull at his heart, Nathaniel knew that the time to leave was not far off. One perfect golden day, he was surfing happily in a seaside wonderland and was poised to catch the biggest breaker ever when the Lord intervened.

The Spirit of God tapped him on the shoulder ever so gently. There was mercy, yes, but also absolute authority. Nathaniel felt himself being lifted up and then nudged towards one of the exit ramps. He struggled against regret and grief as the Lord breathed comfort and drew him away from the realm of endless glory and out towards the stratosphere.

But it was not in him to seriously rebel. Gathering courage, he abandoned all resistance and opened up mind, heart, and spirit to hear the beloved voice of his Lord. Life-giving words filled him, accompanied by anointing oil.

"Don't be afraid, Nathaniel; you are greatly loved. During this stay, your heart has been impregnated with love and compassion for all those who are in your care, angels and humans alike."

"Yes, Lord!" Was the Lord saying that he'd been lacking in love and compassion before?

"You were already a loving and compassionate angel. But with an increase in responsibility and pressure comes the need for increased anointing. Rest assured that you have been made ready for the next stage."

"Thank you for that assurance, Lord," he replied, reminding himself that it wasn't really possible to have too much love and compassion.

Nathaniel declared eternal allegiance to the kingdom and waved a fond goodbye to the friends who'd gathered to bid him farewell. Then he resolutely turned away, dived off the exit ramp, and headed downwards, streaking through space for countless light years until he began to enter the stifling atmosphere of Earth.

The darkness increased, and his spirit pulsed with mercy as sounds of suffering and pain reached his ears. Demons cringed backwards in passing as a reaction to the fresh glory that he carried. With the courage of a true angel of light, he flew straight through the midst of the enemy's ranks, not flinching or deviating from the path that led to his new battlefield of Australia.

Part Two

9

Incensed with indignation Satan stood unterrified, and like a comet burned … and
from his horrid hair shakes pestilence and war.
—John Milton, from *Paradise Lost*, book two, 1667

Head Office of Demonic Events Nemesis (DEN), Hell

This was typical of Satan—leaving him and these losers to hang around at DEN clueless and in a panic. A wave of sulphur mated with the stench of evil and drifted up Tetrak's nostrils. One whiff started him tripping, and he turned to say something to the others but was hit with everything from "up yours with a flag pole" gestures to "what're you lookin' at?" outbursts.

This was enough to set the spleen of hatred pouring into his spirit, and soon it was hard to hold on to any semblance of intelligent thought. He made no attempt to hide his scorn. They were a pack of halfwits who'd swindle a fellow demon just for a two-second buzz.

One thing was certain. If their great white leader didn't turn up soon, there was no telling what could go down out here. Where in hell was he?

* * *

Satan cringed before an old adversary—burnout. His spirit tightened in defiance. It was always the same nightmare picture. Energy levels plummeted and the old get-up-and-go gave up the fight, leaving his ego to crash-land in the gutter. Then, before you could say "What the …?" Madam Reality, the mother of all wet blankets, rose up and hit him in the face with three major downers.

The number-one punch in the guts was the reminder that despite popular opinion, he was not, in fact, omniscient. The number-two wallop was the glaring fact that in spite of all his brainstorming, he hadn't yet cracked the code to escape the judgement. And number three was a sure-fire soul crusher: maybe he never would.

Like he always said, there was a lot going for denial. He curled up in a corner, head in hands, as his mind slid like a giant jelly blubber into familiar, ice-cold chambers of desolation. A last-ditch effort to squeak out "I'm the Prince of Darkness, destined to rule" did nothing. Pride couldn't stand against the suction of truth.

As sure as night followed night in this rat hole, panic began to rise up like a tsunami which was gathering impetus by the second. When the tidal wave finally took form and came thundering down, he lost any semblance of rational thought, thrashing around and screeching like a wild animal caught in a trap.

On and on went the screaming, profanities, and threats, which echoed off soundproof walls and fell impotent to the floor of the tailor-made sanctuary. He headbutted the wall repeatedly, preferring a migraine to nauseating dread. Finally he let out an extended bellow that sounded like a rampantly randy bull and then collapsed spreadeagle on the floor.

Now pulverised into a state of numbness, he attempted to summon whatever cohesive thoughts were left banging around in his head. He had to think and somehow stir up the energy to face the clowns waiting outside, who were probably killing one another by now.

If anyone saw or heard even an inkling of these attacks, he'd be mince meat. He was on his Pat Malone without a doubt. Needless to say, there was no point praying for help. So here he was again, hanging over the edge of wretchedness with never a moment's peace. Perfect.

Not that he'd ever admit any of this to all the losers who'd followed him in mutiny centuries ago. What a moment of madness that was! His defence was that he'd been drunk with pride at the time. But what was their excuse? Given half a brain, they'd have seen the dead end that was waiting for them down the track.

Incredibly, they were still tagging along like two-year-olds in the belief that he had all the answers. Even though this was a testament to his leadership charisma, it was nevertheless pathetic. He could imagine them whistling and singing "Hi ho, hi ho, with Lucifer we all go" as they walked off the edge of time.

What really got in his craw was the lack of choice. He had to keep on forever plotting and scheming like some crazed character in a galactic computer game, trying to find an escape clause in cyber space.

Of course the mammoth downside was that the person he was trying to outwit just happened to be God, who also happened to be omniscient and omnipotent. His spirit seethed and bubbled with loathing just at the thought of his arch enemy.

The biggest high he had ever got came from hurting God. And there was a sure-fire way to pull that one off. He could always get a bullseye by destroying humans, because every time one of them went down the tube, the Allfrickingmighty ached reeeealy badly.

At the same time, it made the old Lucifer feel really good. He got a rush just thinking about the relief that came from inflicting misery! It put a Band-Aid over despair, if only for a moment. And one thing was certain—his ingenuity in that area knew no bounds.

The pièce de résistance was definitely war. As proof observe the myriad lives destroyed, twisted, or traumatised beyond help, plus the wreckage left for subsequent generations. He visualised countless scenes of carnage orchestrated through the centuries and imagined God's agony over every wound.

It wasn't long before his eyes glazed over from the intoxication of bloodlust. There were so many success stories and glorious victories to summon up. In fact, he was beginning to feel empowered. And that felt incredible. And hey, this was definitely starting to work for him!

Without missing a beat, he decided to go with this, rising to his feet and strutting around the perimeter of the room, muttering away as he recalled past atrocities. His confidence was growing by the second. In fact, there was enough energy for some positive self-talk.

A self-portrait grinned at him from the sideboard. "Lucifer, you old genius" he said to the portrait, "you're incomparable! Without equal! More dreadful than a thousand volcanos! Faster than the speed of light! Superman looks like a gnat next to you!" He broke out in manic laughter that escalated into hysterics. This was fantastic. How bloody brilliant was he? He kept up the monologue until the furnace began to charge and finally blasted away at full throttle.

"You've outdone yourself this time, you genius!" he cackled. He was ready to fire, and the timing was perfect. By now his middle management gurus had been hanging around long enough to be good and nervous. Granted, he was working with some lousy material there, but his projects were all so brilliant that even the minor leaders could do some real damage with them. He started to pace, getting psyched up to pull off the double whammy of whipping them into a frenzy while keeping them still grovelling in his shadow.

With most of them, that would be a cinch. They were all catatonic with fear around him and would do whatever they were told. But there was one slippery character he'd have to watch.

*   *   *

The situation in waiting room central was looking about to explode big time when Satan finally hit the scene looking pumped and … well … menacing. A wave of terror hit Tetrak, sending his system into body-wracking seizures which left him convulsing on the floor. So now he had hatred and terror mixed together with a dollop of disgust. What a cocktail! All up, this was the closest he'd felt to being alive in decades. It was totally orgasmic.

Satan began to move amongst them, spilling out vitriol as only he could; when it came to words of death, no one in Hell could match him. It was mind-altering stuff! Demons started to vomit, ooze slime everywhere, and curl up in the foetal position. Tetrak felt as though he were being fuelled up for another decade of murder and destruction. Then the One Who Must Be Obeyed came towards him.

"I'm over the pathetic convulsions, Tetrak!" he stated. The others all laughed hysterically. They wouldn't be laughing when he was finished with them.

"Y-y-y-yes M-m-m-aster," he replied. Somehow he just couldn't stop shaking enough to get his words out properly.

"Answer me clearly, for Hell's sake!"

Tetrak felt he was going to throw up, but he hadn't got to the position of project manager by being a weakling! He summoned the effort to collect his wits and shouted in top volume.

"S-sorry, Master! M-my mistake!"

"You're a wretched worm, Tetrak."

"Yes, Master! I'm a wretched worm!" He could see from the corner of his eye the smirks and sneers of his rivals.

"All right, we're agreed on that; so slither over here. I want to talk to you."

Tetrak had the fleeting insane thought that he should get down on his stomach and wriggle across the floor. Luckily the will to survive won out, and he stepped forward dutifully. Satan looked at him for several body-numbing moments and then sighed deeply and cursed before going on.

"It seems you have friends in high places, Tetrak. Personally I think you're a wanker, but my chief advisors tell me that you're a ruthless, slippery seducer."

Tetrak thought he'd explode with pride. "I do my best always, Master!"

"Well, you suck up better than anyone here, which brings us back to the 'wanker' tag. Anyway, the decision's been made, and you've been assigned to a high-priority mission." Another big sigh followed. "And yes, Mr. Ladder-Climber, it entails promotion. Call me a risk junkie, but I'm raising you to the position of cross-generational manager."

Now it was Tetrak's turn to sneer, which he did with all the venom he could muster towards those smart-arses who were now open-mouthed and literally turning green with envy.

Satan's voice dropped to little more than a whisper. "When you've finished your pitiable sniggering, Tetrak, there is something you need to know. Failure on this mission will not be tolerated. In fact, it will result in torment of the worst kind."

Tetrak felt the familiar agony of stomach-cramping dread. The Master had always motivated him with the fear of failure so that his reward at the end of a successful mission was just sheer relief at having not stuffed up. He forced himself to focus on every word Satan was saying. The lowlife was chatting away now in a light conversational tone.

"For starters, let me stress that you must exercise absolute confidentiality with this work. You are to be assigned to the Cutler family in Sydney, Australia. They come from a line that's been under my control for centuries, and our hold over the lot of them has been dominant, so we should be able to keep them working for us. However, we never take anything for granted. It has come to my notice that a new situation has evolved which poses a small threat. Needless to say, not even a chink can be left open for enemy infiltration into our established territory. And of course one lapse of focus from you and you're mincemeat."

Without warning he suddenly turned to the others and yelled, "Are you all listening?" which scared them brainless. It triggered in Tetrak another round of cataclysmic shaking that knocked him to the floor.

"It is vital, absolutely vital, that word does not get out about this!"

He eyeballed every demon in the room and hissed with menace into their horror-stricken faces. Much whimpering and shuffling of feet could be heard. Then he turned to Tetrak and went back to chat mode.

"Do you understand so far, demon?"

"Absolutely, M-m-master!" shouted Tetrak as he clambered back up to his feet and stood to attention. With sheer force of will, he kept from dropping his bundle. He was determined the others were not going to get their slimy paws on this dream opportunity.

"I want you to keep a low profile at the beginning stages, Tetrak. Your first task is to merely infiltrate the life of a human called Eleanor Cutler in the Earth time of 1907. She was raised in a loveless upper-crust home where she was never touched and often punished. Her face and body were good enough to snare Harold Cutler, who was wealthy and handsome. But it turned out he was also a womaniser and general prick."

"Brilliant, Master!" shouted all the demons simultaneously.

"Shut up, you morons!" was the screeched reply. "I'm trying to explain something crucial to a demon with a brain the size of a pea!"

"You're right as always, Master! I have a brain the size of a pea!" barked Tetrak. "Please continue your explanation!"

Satan clicked straight back to chatting. "This is where the tricky bit comes in. Eleanor was created with the gift of spiritual insight and has the potential to be a prophet of light. Luckily she retreated instead into darkness and solitude, which is right up our alley. The bottom line is that she's isolated and open to seduction. You've shown yourself to be talented in that department apparently."

"I like to think so, Master." Tetrak was already salivating at the thought.

"Once you have possessed her and established your beachhead within the household, your job will be to keep an eye on the rest of the family. Eleanor is too addled to be any threat, but the gift will pop up somewhere else." He again dropped his voice to a whisper. "When that happens, I want the relevant human for my purposes and my purposes alone. Do you understand?"

"Yes, I understand perfectly, Master!" Tetrak tried to hide his excitement in case Satan decided to knock it out of him. This was a plum assignment that included a full-on human seduction plus a promotion. Where was the downside? "Are there any further instructions, Master?" he asked in the most submissive tones he could muster.

"Yes there are. If you understand everything, then get the hell out of here and start work. You need to do your research and be fully prepared before you move in on Eleanor. Now as for you other sad excuses for management material …"

Tetrak didn't hear the rest of that sentence, because he'd already spread his bat-like wings and taken off flying. Once he'd covered enough distance, he finally let loose with maniacal screams of excitement which echoed through the caverns of Hell and made a mockery of the wailing and groaning of the damned.

10

The awful shadow of some unseen power floats though unseen among us.
—Percy Shelley, from "Hymn to Intellectual Beauty," 1816

Sydney, Australia, spring 1907

What a pack of clowns these Sydneysiders were, glued like a foetus to Mother England. They lived in a land with a burnt heart and lush green coast, oceans and worlds away from trouble in the southern tropics. Sydney was spread around a network of waterways and a vast harbour with miles of space. Yet most of them lived in crappy pocket-sized terraces joined together and closed in on themselves. You'd think they were dealing with overcrowding and an arctic climate. Tetrak couldn't believe it.

A whole generation was sweating like demented horses in multilayered outfits, cooking up heavy English recipes and eating all their meals huddled together indoors like the loony British instead of getting out in the sun and fresh air. "God save the King unto death, men!" he shouted, giving a salute and then falling around laughing.

In another sixty years they'd discover garlic and al fresco and strip down until some were walking around wearing nothing but flowers and "make love not war" tattoos. But in 1907 it was "life at the Pole."

Glebe came into view—a mishmash of the very rich and the really struggling. He zeroed in on the Cutler mansion. By all accounts you wouldn't call it a home, just "the place where the Cutler family lived." Sounded like his kind of joint. Eleanor Cutler was wealthy enough to have servants, cooks, maids, gardeners, and nannies—the lot. She was still as miserable as a flea on a toy dog of course. Now that she'd got going with her latest self-help project in the search for enlightenment, his job was looking a lot easier—especially now that she'd called in a medium.

Speaking of which, crazy Lottie was going for it in the living room, working her butt off calling up departed spirits left, right, and centre. Bless her emphysema-riddled lungs. The old tart was seventy-five years old if she was a day; sported a blonde wig, cherry-red lipstick, and a candy-pink rouge; and wore a purple dress and several strings of multicoloured beads. She looked like a rainbow with a hangover.

Now she began to go into a trance, and things got going big time. Furniture was moving every which way, lights blinked, and weird noises broke out. *Bring it on, baby!* Tetrak thought. This was a scenario custom made for his unique gifts. It was his time to shine!.

*   *   *

There were some seriously strange activities going on here. Lottie was still comatose, and so far several pictures had moved on the wall, lights were flashing on and off, and the table they were sitting around had floated up into the air three times.

Eleanor was feeling more agitated by the minute. She found it onerous to concentrate for very long in the best of circumstances, and Lottie really was taking an age to come around. The other members of the Enlightenment Society were showing no indication of unrest in spite of the extraordinary goings-on. Perhaps she just didn't have the fortitude for spiritual revelation.

What a disheartening thought! She'd harboured great hopes of meeting one of her parents today, or perhaps even an aunt or distant cousin—anyone who could give her some idea of where she'd come from. It was unbearable having this large black emptiness inside, almost as if she didn't actually exist. She felt like a body without a soul watching the world and going through the motions of living.

Now she was feeling not only agitated and disheartened but also overwhelmingly sad. If something didn't happen soon, she'd need to take a lavatory break to avoid exhibiting some kind of inappropriate behaviour, like screaming.

The answer to her dilemma came seconds later when a shaft of sunlight cut across the room. Eleanor glanced up just as a familiar face peeped around the door. All she could see was a pair of black eyes framed by matching black curls, but that was enough to make her stomach churn. Without a backward look, she hurried across the room and outside closing the door behind her as quietly as possible.

"Beatrice, you were told to keep away from this part of the house!" she hissed to her daughter. "What is that nanny of yours doing? Is she asleep?"

"I was wondering what you were doing, Mother," Beatrice replied.

"And what are you doing wondering about anything? You're supposed to do what you are told and nothing more. It would be a very pleasant surprise if you were to learn to be obedient."

The girl's eyes filled with tears. "But these meetings are so strange. They frighten me."

Eleanor looked into those eyes and felt nothing but loathing for herself as well as this girl, who stood out amongst the other children like a brown cow in a field of golden wheat. Because of Beatrice she must endure ongoing reproach and a constant reminder of love lost.

Ten years had passed since he'd been sent away, but she still ached just to think of the slender keyboard instructor with the exotic eyes and olive skin and a smile that said "I understand." He alone had seen the desolation that she tried to disguise and had been bold enough to make an advance.

He could bring a piano to life with those long fingers, and she had discovered that music was a soothing balm to comfort a broken heart. For just a passing moment in time, her life had mattered to someone and she had experienced respite from the agony of Harold's rejection and the humiliation of his countless affairs.

"Mother? Are you all right?"

Eleanor realised that she'd been staring blankly into the girl's face. She covered her discomfort with hostility.

"I want you to keep out of my sight for the rest of the day, child; do you understand?"

"Yes, Mother."

"Then go!"

Beatrice clambered away half blinded by tears, and Eleanor felt nothing. What sort of a mother would feel nothing? Was she just a walking corpse or an accident of nature? If there were a God anywhere, he'd either forgotten about her existence or had so regretted creating her that he'd cast her destiny into some sort of odious divine wastepaper basket.

"I hate you!" she choked out, shaking her fist in the air. "You're a sadistic, uncaring monster who abandons mistakes and leaves them to fend for themselves. I will find my own way and will not grovel to you!"

The tears ran free now as Eleanor bewailed her absolute isolation. Harold rarely went near her now, and the staff mocked her with their eyes. This mansion, which was the envy of so many, was a prison from which she would never escape.

As she continued to weep, her emotional state graduated from self-pity to absolute despair. This was dangerous territory, where thoughts of jumping off the roof seemed like a valid solution. Her only hope was with that group inside. Other members of the society had received visitations in past meetings; surely her time would also come.

She blotted her face with a handkerchief and stood contemplating the sitting room door. For just a fraction of time she wondered whether Lottie represented salvation or a hangman's noose. That was when the sound of pandemonium broke out behind the door. Without further thought, she grabbed for the knob and bolted inside.

Pandemonium it certainly was, with ornaments moving from one end of the dresser to the other and furniture shifting around the room. Several members were calling out and seemed to be looking around, but on closer inspection their eyes were glassy and sightless. Old Sarah Warnlock had swooned and fallen face down on the table.

Eleanor briefly considered opening the curtains and throwing water into various faces but then leant more towards running deer-like for the hills. But thoughts and emotions about anything disappeared in a moment, because Lottie began to speak. It wasn't what she said that rendered Eleanor catatonic; it was the fact that she was booming away in a deep male voice.

"Be still!" said the voice, and silence reigned supreme. "I have come with a mission today," it continued. "There is someone in this room with the gift of a third eye. My assignment is to operate as a spiritual guide to that person."

Eleanor's heart was sitting in the vicinity of her throat, and it was quite impossible for her to comprehend what she was witnessing. Then Lottie slumped forward like a piece of laundry and a light appeared behind her chair, hovering for a few moments in mid-air. It began to float around the table towards Eleanor, who was frozen to the spot. Like a fly caught in a web, she watched as the light came ever closer until it enveloped her completely. That same voice spoke, this time in softer and more seductive tones.

"It is you and you alone who can hear and see me, Eleanor."

How does he (it?) know my name?

"Eleanor, I know all the names at this table and I have pinpointed you as the gifted one."

The gifted one?

"Yes, you are special; a cut above the others."

A streak of exhilaration flashed through her body, and then the light lifted away and disappeared. In an instant all the society members snapped back to the present, looking around them in bemusement. Lottie adjusted her blonde wig, which had become decidedly skewed during the proceedings. She blinked a couple of times and seemed to be trying to gather her thoughts before slowly rising to her feet, hands on the table.

"There has been a most grand visitation today, friends," she announced in perfectly enunciated tones, which was a little off-putting, as she usually spoke with a cockney twang.

"You don't mean to say," replied Primrose, who was trying to pin her hair back into some kind of shape.

"Absolutely, my dear Primrose," replied Lottie, who was oblivious to all subtleties of humour. "A special spiritual guide has manifested here in this very room and has told me that Eleanor Cutler is the chosen one he was sent to help."

All eyes turned to Eleanor, and what she saw was not contempt or indifference. It was awe, pure and simple. She was the chosen one, the envy of everyone in the room. This was the most exciting moment of her life. How strange it was that only minutes prior she had contemplated jumping off the roof.

* * *

What a piece of cake that was. And they'd tried to tell him he was losing his touch! Tetrak was so puffed up with pride that he'd doubled in size and was feeling as though he could conquer the world. Nothing got his juices flowing like doing a visitation. All it took was a few quick magic tricks and some theatrical crap, and he could blow them clean away.

That interruption from the daughter was just the thing to send Eleanor over the edge. All those vows and curses aimed at the Almighty! All he'd had to do was turn up and it was a done deal.

Tomorrow's leadership meeting was going to be a high point for him. *Subject seduced, Master. Beachhead established, Master. What have you got to say to that, Master? Oh yeah, bring it on.* He couldn't wait.

* * *

Beatrice thought that her crying was finished, so she started towards the house. But then the tears began all over again, so she turned and ran back into the garden. She just wouldn't let anyone see her with swollen red eyes, and that was that!

Peeping out from behind a camellia bush, she spotted her nanny sitting in the lounge room reading. It had been wrong to lie to Nanny Miller, but her mother's meetings were so strange that she'd wanted to see them for herself. The challenge now was to get back up to the bedroom without being seen, splash some water on her face, and then walk down the stairs to the lounge room as if she'd finished resting and felt better.

Darting from bush to bush, she came around to the side of the house and risked one glance around the corner. There was no one in sight. She shot over to the old oak tree, tucked skirt and petticoats into stockings, and scampered up the strong branches until she was level with her open bedroom window.

Just as she'd done countless times Beatrice now walked out along one of the main limbs, holding on to branches and twigs. With her heart pounding, she jumped through the window and landed in a heap on the floor.

Without even stopping to recover from that effort, she jumped to her feet and spent a moment straightening petticoats and hair. A quick splash of water on her face and she decided it was all right to be seen. This was just in time, as it happened, because seconds later Priscilla knocked on the door and called out.

"Are you all right, Bea? It's time for lunch," she said.

Beatrice steeled herself to tell another lie. "Yes, Cilla, I'm coming. I just felt a bit sick in my tummy, and nanny said I could rest for a while." She opened the door, trying to be brave, but one look into the hall made her spirits drop.

Priscilla looked like a gorgeous platinum china doll dressed up ready to be sold. They were both wearing candy pink today, but the colour did nothing for Beatrice. As usual, she felt like a kitchen hand standing in front of a princess. And that princess resembled her mother, whereas she resembled nobody.

Her sister's face displayed nothing but honest concern. Why did she have to be nice as well as beautiful? If she'd been horrid, Beatrice could at least have hated her without feeling guilty.

"Oh, honestly!" She charged past Priscilla, trying to ignore her stunned expression. "You are such a worryguts! I'm absolutely fine. I'm always fine and don't need anyone to fuss over me!" Ten steps later she stopped and turned back, overwhelmed by remorse. "I'm sorry," she whispered, eyes to the ground. "It's not your fault that I don't belong here."

"But you do belong, Bea; you do!" was the heartfelt reply. "You're the only sister I have. Who would I play with if you weren't here? Boys are no fun at all!"

Cilla was a kind, protective older sister, but she wasn't very clever. Beatrice forced a smile to look as if she felt better. "I'm famished, Cilla; are you?" she said.

"Oh, I'm ravenous; absolutely ravenous!" "Ravenous" was Cilla's new big word.

Beatrice held out her hand. "Let's go and have lunch," she said in her bounciest voice, "and then perhaps we can play for a while this afternoon."

11

Sydney, Australia, September 1913

Those Cutlers were a piece of work. They didn't give a rat's about each other or about any of their children. Tetrak couldn't remember the last time he'd had it this easy. The next chapter would be a walk in the park. Mum and Dad both had reasons to get out of the house, and as for the girls, stampeding buffalos wouldn't be able to keep them from the Cavendish ball next door.

The plot was thickening nicely like pea soup. Eleanor was chuffed out of her brain after being asked (thanks to intervention by Tetrak) to address the annual spring meeting of the Enlightenment Society tonight. A pack of wild rabid dogs camped at the front door wouldn't have scared her into turning it down. Of course that meant she had to rack her brain to organise for someone to act as chaperone for the girls.

Meanwhile, Harold was blowing steam from both nostrils, desperate to spend time with his mistress. It'd been an abstinence of two weeks now (once again thanks to some clever meddling by Tetrak) and the mercury was nearly going through the roof from frustration. Any longer and he'd have considered approaching his wife!

What did old Harry care how it all came together, as long as Eleanor went to her cursed meeting and the girls took off with at least the appearance of being chaperoned. He couldn't wait for them to be married off and out of his hair.

Even Tetrak was taken aback by his own genius. Eleanor had already taken off early for the meeting, and Harold would soon bolt out to fetch Libby Parker, that scatty broad who'd waited in the wings for ten years believing that one day he was going to leave his wife and marry her. Yes, and one day the sun would turn green!

By a strangely convenient coincidence, all of the usual possibilities for a chaperone were busy tonight, which meant that the girls would be left in the charge of their old nanny, Emily Miller,

71

who was eighty if she was a day. In other words, those fresh plums were virtually unsupervised. And hadn't that got Bea's juices going!

*　　*　　*

There it was, just across the hall on the sideboard where she'd left it. How ironic if her meticulous plans were to be foiled by a hairbrush! Beatrice scanned the area in a second and then tiptoed over, grabbed the brush, and turned to run back to the bedroom. As she did so, Richard saw her from the library! For a split moment his eyes bulged while his mouth opened and shut twice, which made him look like a trout in the last death throes. He adjusted instantly, of course, but she glimpsed the spontaneous reaction, which was satisfying and terrifying all at the same time.

Needless to say, the terror aspect put a dent in her confidence, so she spent a few moments sitting on the bed, summoning up courage. When her nerves had settled down again, she stood to groom her hair in front of the full-length mirror. After several minutes of solid brushing, she stopped to pose and study the final effect while striving to remain confident.

But sadly, in spite of her best efforts to see the sunny side, there was no escaping the fact that she was tragically skinny and ridiculously short. A well of discouragement began to build up behind her eyes. She'd dreamt of an opportunity like this for months, and her plan had seemed like a splendid idea several days ago, but tonight it looked absurd.

Now the tears began to flow, which was going to make her face blotchy. Ignoring that dire possibility, she allowed herself to cry for several minutes. When the last of the wave had passed, she spent more precious time nose-blowing and eye-dabbing. That was followed by another sojourn in front of the mirror.

Well, she was convinced of one thing at least. This colour did complement her. No more powder blues and strawberry pinks. From now on she would dress according to the dictates of her own heart. Mother and father would be horrified if they saw her bare shoulders, because of what the neighbours would think. But then she already had the permanent disapproval of both no matter what she did, so there was nothing to lose and much to gain by defying them.

Surely her hair was thick and wavy and looked attractive when left loose. It could be considered an asset even though it was not blonde. She turned sideways to study herself in profile for a moment and finally came to the conclusion that her eyes were an attribute; but when it came to breasts, the most you could say was that there was very little to speak of.

Oh bother, there is so little here to boost a girl's confidence! Her stomach felt as though it were in a triple nautical knot, but tonight was an opportunity, and she didn't want to miss it through lack of courage. She knew she must avoid thinking about consequences or risk being trapped forever with parents who wanted only to cramp her in a mould which didn't fit and never would.

Nobody had ever taken the time to notice the fire which burned in her heart. For months now youthful fantasies had been filling her mind while she went through the soulless routine of homework and piano practise. When was her life ever going to start? With emotions somewhere between anger and despair, she grabbed the velvet cloak from the wardrobe, encased herself with it, and headed for Cilla's bedroom.

*   *   *

Richard stood alone in the library, leaning against the wall with his eyes closed. He must try to calm down so that his heart would stop pounding. What had possessed Harold and Eleanor to leave their two youngest daughters in the care of old Emily Miller?

He'd not been a head butler for thirty years without learning when a storm was brewing. And there was certainly a mother of a tempest on the horizon at this very moment. He was still reeling from the glimpse he'd just had of Beatrice sporting a red satin gown and wearing her black mane of hair flowing to the waist. She must have managed to persuade one of the maids to take her shopping. God knew she had their sympathy.

The strongest emotion he was experiencing other than blind fear was compassion for the quiet, intense girl. He'd watched her through the years hungrily grasp the crumbs of approval which came her way only when she performed so brilliantly on the piano. One had only to look at her chocolate eyes and caramel skin to know that she was an unwitting thorn in the side for both parents.

Getting back to the blind fear, he searched his brain to discover the best way to protect his own position here. Beatrice knew that she'd been spotted, so he felt perhaps he should make an attempt (however feeble) to block their path. Then, if anything inappropriate were to transpire, Emily and young Priscilla would attest to the fact that he had tried to intervene.

Yes, that was a reasonable plan. Several minutes later it was still the only one he'd come up with. He straightened his jacket and strode into the hallway, narrowly missing a collision with both girls as they bolted ahead of Emily towards the front door.

Bea searched his face with those enormous eyes as she sidestepped him. "You're not looking your usual self, Richard. Should we call the doctor?"

"Not yet Beatrice, not yet … um … I … you see … I …"

Priscilla's pretty face showed an honest concern. "Are you all right, Richard?"

Richard was rendered mute and immobile by a sense of inevitability. Beatrice was now covered from head to ankle in her hooded cloak, and obviously her sister had no idea what was going on. He just stood and stared at Beatrice with a silent plea.

A range of emotions bounced off one another across Beatrice's face. "You worry too much, Richard," she finally said in little more than a whisper. "We're in good hands with Nanny Emily, and we'll be fine."

All incentive to act drained out through the soles of his feet. "Take care, young mistresses!" he called to their backs as they charged through the door to make the short trip down the road to the ball.

*   *   *

They strolled along at a comfortable pace, and Bea breathed in the beautiful spring air, her senses quickening at the sounds of music and life which floated in the air. Priscilla was dabbing lavender water behind her ears.

"What do you think was troubling Richard?" she asked. Bea grimaced inwardly with guilt.

"I know exactly what was wrong with Richard," she replied. And with that she unclasped the neck of her cloak and let it drop from her shoulders.

Seconds went by with no sound coming out of Cilla's open mouth. Bea couldn't remember ever seeing her sister speechless before. Emily looked as if she were frozen with shock, probably already predicting an end to her career as a nanny and seeing her life flash before her. Finally Cilla just said, "Oh Bea!" in a croaky voice.

Bea endeavoured to calm them down. "Don't worry. If mother or father find out what I was wearing, I'll tell them that I snuck out before you and you had no idea how I was dressed." They both looked decidedly unconvinced and uncomfortable.

"Oh, Bea!" repeated Cilla.

"If you say "Oh Bea" again, Cilla, I'll start screaming! The fact is, you're pleased to conform to expectations in all things, even if it means being covered from neck to ankle in pastels and lace for the rest of your life! You're blonde and pretty anyway, so that style becomes you. But I don't fit into the same mould. I've finished school now and completed my piano grades, and now it's time to fly a little and see if there's any place in the world where I belong!"

Bea was mortified by her own outburst and tried to hide the embarrassment by making a big thing out of reclasping her cloak. The three of them then walked the rest of the way in silence, her sister staring straight ahead with her lips all pursed and their nanny looking hopelessly depressed.

They reached the entrance to the Cavendish mansion, and a pompous old butler greeted them. Bea's heart was pumping with nervous excitement. She lowered the hood of her cape and undid the clasp so that her curls were let loose to tumble around her bare shoulders. Then she allowed the cape to be taken by a servant, thus revealing her crimson gown.

Never before had she received the sort of attention that followed—or any attention, for that matter. Women were shooting disapproving looks while several men were eyeing her up and down as if they were hungry and she was dinner. In her fantasies this kind of scenario would stir wordless excitement, but in reality it was disconcerting, to say the least.

Without stopping to think, she took off walking and headed for the punchbowl which was visible at the far end of the next room. Her heart was thumping as she spooned some punch into a glass and started gulping it down as quickly as possible.

Then someone tapped her on the shoulder and she flinched, nearly choking on the last mouthful. But happily it was William Stephens, a childhood friend. Relieved beyond belief, she chatted to him for a short time before she accepted his invitation to dance and allowed him to lead her towards the dance floor.

The party enfolded her as she approached the main ballroom, which had giant glittering chandeliers and was crisscrossed with blue streamers. Champagne flowed freely in celebration of Charles Cavendish coming of age. It was undoubtedly a very adult affair. She knew she must be careful, as she was already feeling the effects of that punch.

She and Cilla were by far the youngest girls there, and they should have been closely and effectively chaperoned under such circumstances. More to the point, Beatrice should have been closely and effectively chaperoned under such circumstances. Cilla would no doubt be positively angelic all night.

"You look ravishing tonight, Beatrice," whispered William. "I hardly recognised you when you walked in."

"Thank you, William," she replied, smiling at him through an ever-thickening fog. "I hardly recognise myself, actually. And coincidently, I also feel positively ravishing!"

12

9.00 p.m. That Night
The Cutler Mansion

Eleanor stood as still as a statue in the dining room, glass in hand and ears pricked. There was definitely someone walking around. She sighed with relief when the footsteps grew softer and disappeared out into the servants' quarters. Thankfully it was the kitchen hand finishing up for the night.

At the first sound, she'd thought it could be her husband and feared that the tiresome old goat might want her in his bed. She raised her sherry and toasted the mistress, who was apparently performing well. "You're welcome to him, girl; wherever you are," she whispered with a roll of her eyes.

The place was as quiet as a tomb. She took a long, slow slurp of the sherry and let it roll around her mouth and then slide down her throat. What a bonus to find that her wretched daughters were not yet home to make demands and destroy any chance of peace.

She tiptoed up the stairs, offering thanks to the gods for the servants, nannies, and mistresses who freed her from the tedious things of life. Eleanor Cutler had been a roaring success tonight. Some people were just meant for higher things, and if no one understood her unique calling, then so be it.

She let herself into her bedroom and the wonder of privacy, finished the sherry, and placed the glass on the bedside table. Oh, the sheer bliss and comfort of the dark! Now that the gift was operating so smoothly, many opportunities were opening up to her and she didn't need anyone.

Praises rose up in her heart for the gods of darkness. With arms spread wide, she swayed from side to side, beginning to lose the sense of time and space and slipping into a trance-like state.

Soon she sensed a familiar presence close by and someone touched her lightly on the shoulder. Her body tingled from top to toe. He had come to her again, her own faithful and intimate guide.

"Is that you, Tetrak?"

"Yes, Eleanor, it's me. You know that I will always come for you."

She felt him slide across her back. "Yes. I'm sorry for doubting you even for a second. I trust you, Tetrak." No one had ever cared about her but him. Her eyes filled with tears.

His words caressed her like a lover. "I am your friend and helper, special one, sent to guide you into all truth. Everything else is a lie."

Now she was weeping, shedding tears that seemed to come from wells of grief deep in her soul. "All my life I've been lied to; nothing but lies."

"But now I'm here for you, beloved. Just follow my light."

A glow began to appear beside Eleanor, and then a rush of pleasure washed through her body as the circle of light encompassed her for a moment. She closed her eyes and surrendered to the sensation, but after mere seconds it moved away. She whimpered with frustration as it crossed to a corner where there were chairs and a small table.

She followed instantly and sat in one of the chairs, staring into the midst of the light, mesmerised. "I would like to contact my father tonight, my dear friend."

"Call him forth, my child; call him forth and he will come. You have the gift."

Eleanor felt so empowered that she needed no one! How electrifying to be able to unlock death and call forth loved ones! She began to speak with authority.

"Father, I call you forth!" she commanded. "Come, Father; come and speak with me! There is much I wish to ask you."

* * *

Tetrak battled to disguise the loathing he felt towards this desperate human who'd grasped his morsels of affection like a starving dog and was now opening her heart to the underworld. His excitement mounted as the portals of Hell opened and demon powers began to enter the room.

Death, Rebellion, and Lust flowed freely through the gateway, and to his great satisfaction, heavenly guardians watched helplessly, waiting for the first sign of light. Everything was going according to plan, and the young daughters were surrounded by the shadows of Death.

13

Cavendish Mansion, 9.30pm

What a wonderfully marvellous party this was! Priscilla had her usual bevvy of beaus, but tonight Bea was also positively surrounded by admirers. To her delight, women young and old were obvious in their jealousy, try as they might to appear outraged.

After she had finished two glasses of champagne, all the young men were looking exceptionally attractive. She was laughing hysterically at one incredibly witty gentleman when her attention was caught by the sound of clapping. Lady Cavendish's voice was calling out above the din.

"I'm wondering if you could all look this way for just a moment please! We have organised entertainment tonight as a surprise, so please clear the dance floor by moving back into a circle around the perimeter of the room!" There was much shuffling and murmuring as the guests moved back far enough to provide a space. "Thank you; you're all very clever! And now, without further ado, may I introduce … the Flamenco Flames!"

Onto the floor strolled a middle-aged man with a world-battered face and dark olive skin. He was carrying with him a lone drum and a short stool, and without so much as a smile he sat down and began to execute a primal beat which thrilled Bea to the core.

A mature man and woman strode into the circle, unsmiling and smouldering. They started to move slowly as one, with their feet clicking and hands tapping in time to the beat. The woman wore a black fitted dress, and she moved like a panther, circling her partner and defying him with her eyes.

The drumbeat became faster and louder, and then there was a gasp from the guests when the woman lifted the hem of her dress as she twirled to reveal an expanse of brown leg. Bea was open-mouthed at this sight and gaped in wonderment as a second drummer seated himself next to the first. Together the pair lifted the beat to another level of volume and speed.

Then onto the dance floor glided three glorious young olive-skinned creatures, two of them women and one a beautiful man. Bea was immediately captivated by the young man's eyes, which were the bluest of blue. He looked like a suntanned angel.

The three younger dancers exploded into a spine-chilling routine, pounded the floor with their feet, and swayed and twirled until all five of the dancers and the two drummers had transported themselves and those watching into another dimension.

Bea was literally breathless, and she stared unashamedly at the male dancer. Her eyes were pools of tears, and her emotions were a mess. She had been to ballet concerts from an early age and the theatre many times, but never had anything impacted her to the core like his passion and energy. As she watched in a semi-trance, he glanced her way and held the look for a heart-stopping moment.

The music went to a final crescendo, and then the routine finished with a stamp of feet. The response from the guests was mixed as the dancers bowed and filed out. Those who'd partaken generously of the champagne called out "Bravo!" and applauded, while the sober ones gave a weak polite clap, disapproval written all over their faces. Bea smiled to herself. Lady Cavendish always liked to shock!

Conversation started up again all around the room, the band began to play background music, and waiters began to bring out all kinds of delicious desserts. But this was happening around Bea like a dream. All she knew was that she had to see the dancer again. Needless to say, that was a ridiculous notion, and she began immediately to debate with her own common sense, which of course told her to forget the idea immediately.

Then, against all rationale, anger rose up, surprising her with its intensity. She'd been sensible all her life. And to what end? Was she any happier now than she'd been as a little girl?

Time came to a standstill for Bea as she stood in her shocking red gown and cast her eyes around the room. A voice whispered in her ear, "Surely there has to be something better than this!" Her spirit jumped in agreement, and she made a decision to ignore her mind and follow her emotions.

At that point the band started up and a gentleman approached her for a dance. With her thoughts swirling, she explained her need to visit the powder room for a privacy stop and then turned and headed off in the general direction of the lavatories. Once she had covered a fair distance, she checked to see if anyone was watching, and then she changed course.

With her pulse galloping, she began to thread through the crowd, trying to keep a steady pace and not draw undue attention. One more glance around and she slipped out a side door and into the garden.

*   *   *

Sean O'Brien downed his second whisky as he sat brooding in the corner of the room which had been allocated to the entertainers. Papa Carlos was chatting contentedly with his grandson as they packed away their drums, and Jose and Paula were joking along with their two daughters. They were in the highest of spirits, as was usual after a performance.

He'd been dancing with them for a year now and normally would have joined in with their chitchat, but his thoughts were centred on the delicious little brunette he'd seen amongst the guests.

She'd blazed like fire against the dull backdrop of bored upper-crust matrons and their soulless daughters. And she'd noticed him; he was sure of that. But how could someone from his world hope to move in hers?

He silently chastised himself and began to change out of the dance costume, knowing that it would benefit him nothing to dwell on such things. A few minutes later, the main butler turned up looking as if there were a bad smell in the room and passed an envelope to Jose.

"Lady Cavendish wants you to know," he said in perfect King's English, "that she would have preferred that your wife was more modest in her execution of the dance. However, as she is a very generous employer, she has paid you your full amount."

Sean felt the muscles in the back of his neck tighten as once again the Miguels submitted silently to such treatment. Back in their homeland that family would be lauded as stars, but here the most they could expect was condescending tolerance.

According to them, their market garden on the city outskirts was barely covering costs and they couldn't afford pride, but that reasoning seemed senseless to Sean. He would never sacrifice pride, no matter the cost.

He turned away so that the butler wouldn't see his expression and listened as Jose politely thanked the pathetic little man who had such an inflated idea of his own importance. The Miguels were determined to shrug off the incident like brushing away an annoying insect and were in the mood to party. The best thing he could do with this black mood was take it away somewhere.

Maria could always see right through him. "We're going to a party at Papa Carlos's house, Sean." She questioned him with her eyes. "There's room in the buggy, and we don't mind dropping you home later. Are you coming, or would you rather find a good funeral to go to?"

"Very funny, Maria" he replied, forcing himself to smile. "It just so happens that I feel pensive today, and unlike you crazy people, I would like a little peace and quiet occasionally. I'm walking home."

"Well, that will take you at least two hours!" chipped Carolina. "But what else could we expect from a mad Irishman? You won't have to fight to be alone, Sean. The last thing we want is peace and quiet!"

"Dammit, Carolina," said Sean with a grin. "I'm half Spanish, and you know it! Am I responsible for my mother's choice in a husband? The only thing my father ever gave me was blue eyes. I wouldn't know him if we shared the same gaol cell."

He continued along a light-hearted vein, bantering with them as they gathered their things and took off into the night. Their simple happiness had always stirred in him a mixture of amazement and irritation.

They just mindlessly accepted the things in life which they couldn't change and were sickeningly grateful for the things which they saw as blessings. Well he wasn't going to settle for that. No one was going to talk down to Sean O'Brien!

He grabbed for his cigarettes, lit up with gusto, and inhaled deeply as he strode out into the peace and comfort of the rear garden. For several minutes he smoked and tried to calm down.

Then all his senses pricked when he became aware of a movement to the right. Turning instinctively, he was amazed to see the girl from the ballroom. At first he put it down to a flight of fancy, but then the fantasy began to speak.

"Hello," said the vision.

Sean just stared, waiting for her to disappear. "Hello." He exhaled slowly and nearly suffocated in smoke.

"My name is Beatrice, but my friends call me Bea." Her voice was soft, and she spoke with a posh accent. Her eyes were the colour of midnight, and she looked directly at him with the poise of the privileged. "I wanted to tell you that your dancing is wonderful; I've never seen anything like it."

Sean had learnt in life that it was better to say nothing at all than speak out and prove yourself an idiot. He remained silent, drinking in the sight of this stranger from another world. She did not say anything more, so he eventually plunged in.

"Well, my name's Sean, and my friends call me all manner of things which I'd rather not divulge." She smiled and waited for him to continue. He took her cue and swam in further.

"There is something that I would like to say to you." Now he was in very deep water and in danger of drowning. "When I was dancing out there, my eyes were drawn to you like a moth to a flame. You've a fire inside you, girl, and that is a fact."

*　　*　　*

Beatrice had been terrified that the gorgeous stranger would spurn her advances and leave her humiliated, so she was relieved and thrilled by his response. She walked towards him, her eyes never leaving his face, and stopped just out of reach. A new daring rose within her.

"If I have a fire inside me, it's you that lit it," she whispered, wanting to show him that she was not playing any games but was deadly serious.

He stood riveted to the spot, eyes flashing. Her boldness seemed to have taken him completely by surprise. Then he appeared to make some sort of decision. He slowly ground out the cigarette with his foot. His eyes never left her face as he stepped forward. Keeping his movements slow, he placed a hand on the back of her head and gently drew her towards him.

Bea didn't flinch. Wherever he wanted to go, she was happy to follow. She was heady with the thrill of stepping into such dangerous territory and of eliciting an instant reaction from a man such as this. All five senses were vibrating in response.

Then he kissed her and whispered wonderful words of desire in her ear. Her love-starved soul awakened to intimacy and touch like a desert flower blossoming after long-awaited rain. Desire overcame fear or ethics, and she began to kiss him back.

"Is this your first time with a man?" breathed the stranger.

His words had the effect of breaking the spell. She burned with embarrassment upon realising that he could tell she didn't know how to kiss. Then she sobered enough to remember that it was very late in the evening. Emily was sure to be looking for her, and people would notice that her red dress was missing.

"I have to return to the house. I'll be missed."

"When can I see you again?" He grabbed her by the arm. She hesitated for just a moment but was pleased by his fervency. *So I'm not that bad a kisser!*

"I can meet you in the lane which runs behind these houses after ten tomorrow night. All the house lights will be out by then."

"I will be counting the minutes!" he called as she hurried back to the house.

She slipped through the side door and ran behind a large group of extremely loud and inebriated revellers. From there she made her way through to the main body of people just in time to see Nanny Emily searching amongst the guests and displaying an expression that could only be described as one of panic. Bea waved cheerfully as if she were just strolling back from the lavatories, and Emily closed her eyes as if giving a prayer of thanks.

"Come, Beatrice," she called, "it's time to go home!"

Bea joined Emily and allowed herself to be half dragged to the exit, where a servant presented her with her cape. Emily expressed relief at seeing Bea once more enveloped in the cape, and Cilla pinned her with a look of pinched disapproval.

But Bea wasn't concerned about that. She'd spent her life attempting to please everyone, to no avail. Nothing could dampen her spirits tonight! They said their thank-yous, and as they began their walk back home, Emily started in with the inevitable lecture while breathing heavily.

"Now, girls, thank the Lord we have got through this night without any major crises—no thanks to you, Beatrice! I am not going to tell anyone about your behaviour, assuming that it was a one-off stroke of rebellion.

I would thank you, Priscilla, to say nothing also if you don't want your own freedom limited in future. Let us see if we can finish the evening out in peace and with some semblance of sensibility."

The girls said nothing in reply, and they spent the rest of the walk in silence. Bea was grateful for that, as it allowed her to relish the secret she harboured. She was beautiful and desirable, like a fire! And she had had her first kiss.

14

Three months later

At last everyone had gone to bed. The cat had been let out, and just the junior kitchen hand was awake and setting up for tomorrow's breakfast. Bea lifted her hair off her neck and sat back in the chair. It was too hot to think. The light from the candle should be too faint to attract attention, but she kept one ear open for even the slightest movement. She was struggling to put words to paper.

What does one say when the only good emotions one is feeling are those connected with leaving? She was not in the mood to entertain any regrets. Her pen remained poised over the inkwell, and she scanned the spotless, antiseptic showpiece that had been her childhood bedroom.

And now here she was with her life turned upside down. The first evening after the party, her courage had been tested to the limit. She'd nearly vomited with fear waiting for the last sounds of life to die off in the house. But that was nothing compared to the terror of clambering out of her lace-trimmed bay window and struggling down the old oak tree.

As a child she could slip down soundlessly to land like a kitten. But that night she'd broken a couple of branches, torn both stockings, and gotten her hair caught up in twigs and leaves. Then she'd fallen the last few feet and landed with a thump loud enough to wake the dead. But she'd leapt to her feet and catapulted off to gain the cover of the back lane.

What a starry-eyed virgin she was back then, feeling her way along to the rendezvous, body caught in the grip of awakened longing and mind flowing with girlish romantic notions. She was terrified that he might not show, which would prove that she was just a foolish child tripped up by vain imaginings.

When she saw him silhouetted in the moonlight, she feared for a moment that it was an illusion. But as she drew closer, there was no doubt that it was indeed him. And he was waiting just for her. The look in his eyes caused her last feeble fence of resistance to crumble into a useless heap.

He closed the gap between them as she stood glued to the spot. There were more kisses and whispers of desire. She melted into him and responded by copying whatever he was doing. He began to caress her, and she allowed the caresses to continue, caring not for any rules or regulations. Somebody wanted her; just her.

The next night and the next she'd met him, and Bea refused to feel guilty. The words "I love you" were intoxicating, and she would stop thinking clearly whenever they were said. She was no different to an alcoholic, because she returned to that lane again and again like a drunk rushing to catch the hotel the moment it opened.

Never in her short life had she ever experienced the pleasure of intimate touch and words of love. It was as if a volcano erupted in her heart and there was no holding it back. A thrill flashed through her body now at the mere thought of all the forbidden activities that she had abandoned herself to in the dark corners of the back lane. If the servants knew anything, they had remained blessedly quiet about it.

Once again Bea dipped her pen in the inkwell and went to write, but again her hand stayed suspended in mid-air. *What would Mother and Father have done if they'd known? Would they have agonized over it and fretted because of my lost innocence? Would they have cared about anything other than the prospect of social disgrace?* The only answer that came to her mind was *Not at all.*

Suddenly and unexpectedly, tears welled up and she was beset by a deep sadness. How tragic to feel completely alone at a time such as this. Priscilla would have some sort of reaction, probably confusion and horror. But there was nothing she could do about that. The two of them might be sisters, but they were as different as chalk and cheese.

Now the tears came with a vengeance and she cried buckets for all the things that had never been and as of tonight never would be. That fantasy in which Mother embraced her with affection and Father smiled with approval was just a mirage that had always disappeared whenever she reached for it.

Ten minutes and many nose blows later, she tried to compose herself. Those childhood needs were just sand slipping through her fingers. She knew she must maintain her resolve and grasp her chance for a future with substance. With her mouth set in a straight line, she made a last wipe of her nose with her sleeve. Into the ink went the nib of the pen yet again. Beatrice finally put pen to paper.

Dear Mother and Father,

When you read this note, I will be long gone. I apologise if I am a disappointment to you, but I have fallen madly in love and find that I am expecting a baby.

We are to be married tomorrow. You would not approve of my choice, so there is no point in my including you in the ceremony.

Please do not attempt to hinder me, as my mind is totally made up.

Kindest regards,

Your daughter Beatrice

She placed the note on her bed, swung a knapsack over her shoulder, and slipped out of her window as she had done a hundred times before.

Part Three

15

You saw me before I was born. Every day of my life was recorded in your book; every moment was laid out before a single day had passed.
—Psalm 139:16

Northern Extremity of Heaven—Birthing Province

This place was going off the map. The adrenalin haze was so thick you'd get lost trying to cross the room. It had taken only one solitary skinny herald to announce that the Lord was approaching, and the guardian recruits were beside themselves, falling over one another in mindless chaos.

Imogen stood riveted to the spot within the swishing robes and fluttering feathers. After a century of Throne Room duty, he was going to need time to adjust here. To be fair (to himself), it wasn't every day a meditative worshipper was thrust into an atmospheric transformation of such proportions.

His eyes darted everywhere as he tried to process the surroundings. There was one whole wall of crystal, the top and sides of which stretched beyond his field of sight. As he strained to look past all the heads and took in the view, he noticed that the vista changed before his very eyes from snake-infested jungle to open green meadows complete with fluffy white rabbits—probably the Lord's way of keeping His creative juices flowing. As for the rest of the place, the perimeter seemed to be shimmering from endless folds of gossamer curtains that reflected light and shuddered at each breath of air so that there were little rainbows bouncing in every direction.

He was just starting to get into the bouncing rainbows when the five-piece jazz band that had been grooving along peacefully in the background suddenly morphed into a fifty-piece orchestra belting out light opera. Fortunately his shout of terror wasn't heard over the din.

In the middle of all the action were the pure new souls which were due to start their Earth journey, each one protected by a nurturer. He was standing on tiptoe to peek into one of the bassinettes when the place suddenly went as quiet as one of those monasteries where the humans had decided for reasons known only to themselves that it was holy to say nothing for a lifetime.

The Lord filled the room. Angels ceased their strivings and fell to their faces, seemingly rendered senseless. Imogen was taken by surprise by this turn of events and found that he was the only one standing, albeit in an attitude of worship.

He briefly thought about finding the nearest corner and curling up in the foetal position. But then, without exception, everyone leapt up and exploded into worship with shouts of praise and adoration, and he was conscious of nothing but the beauty of the Lord and the struggle to find the right words to describe it. After what seemed minutes but might have been hours, the waves of worship eased and reason returned.

Apparently this was crunch time, when guardians would be selected, so thousands of pairs of eyes looked to the front, waiting for a command. The Lord signalled to one of the nurturers, a medium-sized all-white angel who stepped forward with his charge and began to address the assembly in a voice as soft as down.

"The first soul on the agenda is Michael," he breathed. "He is to be given to Beatrice O'Brien of Sydney, Australia, and will be born in 1914 at the start of the Great War of the twentieth century. His Earth-walk will be a troubled one, but he has the spirit of an overcomer."

Imogen heard the words "troubled" and "war" and went onto high alert. Michael showed all the signs of being a very high-maintenance candidate. To be honest, even a low-maintenance contender would be unappealing right now, because he was actually in two minds about the whole guardian thing. He would prefer worship duty any day.

The problem was that he knew any hope of remaining inconspicuous was small because he was not only measurably taller than the other nominees but also sprinkled lavishly with gold and silver feathers. Add to this the fact that he was flashing on and off like a traffic light because of the high-alert dynamic, and you had your basic no-win situation.

Avoiding any sudden moves, he bent his knees and slipped behind the nearest angel while he tossed up the pros and cons. On one hand, it would be exciting to work with a human who had the heart of an overcomer. But on the other hand, the guardian would have to be a super overcomer to hang in there. Then again, who wanted to be hanging around doing nothing? Then the Lord spoke.

"Nimrad; come forward."

Imogen craned his neck to see who'd been chosen for such a tricky assignment. Out of the crowd stepped an unassuming angel who had a short, stocky build and was coloured beige. It was his eyes that stood out. They were the colour of steel and set like flint, glinting in the light of the Lord's presence. He wasted no energy on emotion, maintaining a grave countenance and disciplined body posture.

The Lord spoke again. "You have proven yourself immoveable in the heat of battle, Nimrad, and have shown yourself to be one who never looks back. I have chosen you for this role because of your courage and compassion."

"Thank you, Master; I will give my best!"

"Yes, you will, as always. Be blessed beyond your wildest dreams, faithful one." And with that, the Lord touched Nimrad, who crumpled and landed in a heap on the floor.

More and more uncomfortable, thought Imogen. He wondered when he would be able to get back to the Throne Room. He was deciding which direction would lead to the nearest exit when the nurturer began to speak again.

"The next baby for allocation today is Katherine, who will be placed into the womb of Florence Millet in Australia during the Earth year of 1921. She will play a pivotal role and make a difference."

"Well, I wonder who the choice will be this time," mumbled Imogen under his breath. On the one hand it would be a great honour to be commissioned to a human soul who was to make a difference; no doubt about that. But on the other hand, he'd watched the guardians come in from service almost comatose with exhaustion and drained of light. He'd seen the fleeting regret in their eyes when it was time to return to the battle. Then again, it would be incredibly challenging and rewarding to be out on the coalface of battle, tasting huge victories.

"Imogen!" boomed the voice of ultimate authority. Everything went into slow motion, as it does when one is faced with a life-threatening situation. To his horror, many faces angled in his direction, eyes wide and mouths open.

"Yes, Lord," he said in the feeblest of manners.

"Come forward, angel! I believe you will be a perfect guardian for Katherine."

"You do?" Imogen felt like a ventriloquist's dummy opening his mouth and waiting for the words to fill it.

"Absolutely! I made you, and I know what's in you. Come!"

He willed his body to take one tentative step forward and then another until he stood in full view of everyone in the room. This was, of course, his worst nightmare coming to pass, but after all, it was the Lord he was dealing with. Mind you, little comfort was to be had there right now.

"I am most honoured by your confidence, Lord," he said, feeling now like a cornered mouse trying to debate with a lion. "On the other hand, I am a mere worshipper with absolutely no experience."

That was when the Lord touched him and divine glory began to pour out like a waterfall. He quickly lost any sense of his surroundings and got caught up with visions of planet Earth that began to flash on and off like a travel documentary. His last conscious thought was "I guess there is no other hand."

16

In the years of trial, when life was inconceivable, from the bottom of the sea the tide
of destiny washed her up to him.
—Boris Pasternak, from *Doctor Zhivago*, 1922

Singleton, Australia, 1919

Flo stopped under the one gum tree in the backyard, holding on to the kindling she'd collected as if it were a newborn babe. *Damnation, this heat must be coming straight from hell itself into Singleton!* she thought. *I'd sell my hair to see the ocean!* But the closest thing was the old dam in the northern paddock, and that was half empty because of the drought.

She scanned the naked horizon. This country had next to nothing in the way of people. And as for her wretched patch, there was nary a human as far as the eye could see. North, south, east, and west it was the same—just acres and acres of grass, wheat, animals, and flies.

She felt like a beached whale gasping for breath and hoping against hope for the tide to rise. Surely a tidal wave of anger had landed her here. And surely Satan had let Australia masquerade as her answer. But no point her trying to figure it out, and no future in standing under this tree all day.

Stirring up some crumbs of courage, she strode forward to cover the distance between the gum and the house and struggled up onto the veranda of what she referred to as "the house that Tom built." She was not ready yet to call it home, or even their house; "Flo's prison" was closer to the mark, or maybe "God's checkmate." "We are not impressed, God!" she announced to the endless paddocks.

Romantic Flo had dreamt of starting life afresh in a faraway land full of brave pioneers. But she'd landed in a nightmare desert sprinkled with pea-minded people. Clever Flo had found a brave soldier who would carry her away from life's problems. But he hadn't mentioned spiders, snakes, and flies!

Educated Flo had worked in an Aberdeen bookshop, immersed in the world of literature and surrounded by learned folk. Now she was a farmer's wife, socialising with cows in the back of nowhere on the bottom of the world.

She pushed through the kitchen door and placed the kindling next to the wood stove. Tom would be back from the milking soon and would be wanting his scrambled eggs, so there was nought for it but to get the fire going. That man had been grinning ever since they'd arrived here. He had the look in his eyes of a bull let loose in a herd of cows. As she carried out her duties, Flo thought that he'd best not ask any questions, lest she give him some answers!

With the efficiency of years of practise, she placed paper then kindling then sticks inside the stove and set the paper alight. Once the twigs and then sticks were ablaze, she added heavier wood and closed the opening. Before long the water in the old black kettle was boiling, and she added it to the tea leaves sitting in the equally old but bright silver teapot. Thanks to the gods of morning, there was enough time for a blessed cup of tea before she would hear the sounds of heavy boots coming from the back.

Just the simple act of pouring dark tea into a china cup offered a modicum of comfort, reminding her as it did of home. In went the creamy milk and a spoonful of sugar; then she carried the cup outside and settled in a favourite chair on the veranda. She closed her eyes as the first mouthful slid down her throat.

Aye, 'twas a barrage of shocks that had hit like an oncoming train over the last weeks. Especially the ones to do with her body! All the books she'd devoured as a girl spoke of a wife with her prince charming in a precious meeting of minds and hearts which bordered on the sacred. Poppycock; it was disgusting, all of it! Disgusting!

And to her shame, she'd experienced all manner of sensations in spite of Tom's social failings, which had seemed immaterial back in Scotland. He'd looked so handsome in his uniform, and because he'd said so little, she'd filled in the gaps herself. For sure, a blind man could see that there was actually little if anything going on in the man's head!

Now her traitorous body was responding to grapplings with a mere farmer. This was the stuff of horror stories! Down went the rest of the tea in big gulps, as if to wash away the memory of the previous night's episode. But still her mind swam with shadowy recollections of being fondled and licked and adored.

She folded her arms and scrunched forward. There was no choice for her here; she couldn't go back when so many bridges were burnt to a cinder behind her. Hamish was dead. Witty, smooth, charming Hamish would never cause her to collapse in laughter again.

The one person on Earth who cared for her was a slow, uneducated bear of a man who had animals for friends. It was clear that no one liked her here. She had never fitted in anywhere and never would. The pain was beyond bearing. With head in hands, she groaned and wept like a bairn.

*　　*　　*

Nathaniel eyed off the intruders and focused on looking bored, the plan being to make them feel as if they were about as threatening as a mosquito. The fact that he was pushing back a full-blown panic would, with any luck, remain his secret. The demons were almost within touching range now and ready to pounce at the first sign of weakness, so sending out a mayday alert was not an option.

Discouragement, Condemnation, and Rejection had followed them from Aberdeen and then hung around watching from a distance. Sadly Nathaniel had been tripped up again by the old "overconfidence and need to succeed" thing and hadn't called in reinforcements. He also hadn't allowed for Flo unravelling this fast. So here they were, caught up in a situation that was at best unstable.

Then to his horror, Flo began to lose it big time right there on the veranda. She started wailing like a dingo and cursing God, shaking her fist in the air like someone demented. In a tribute to all things uncool, he called out "Yipes!" before galvanising into action at the same time as the demons. They'd seen their chance and were grunting and oozing at the prospect of bringing destruction.

"Okay, move it!" yelled Discouragement to the others, who didn't need to be told a second time. They began to whisper into her ears words of death.

"Everyone hates you here," said Rejection. "They think you're the strangest thing they've ever met; and they're right!"

Condemnation slithered around her neck. "You're no good, Florence, and you never were any good," he hissed. "You're too clumsy and reckless and have never behaved like a lady should. You broke your parent's hearts because of your selfishness."

"Why don't you just give up?" said Discouragement. "There's nothing for you here or back home." Saliva dripped from his mouth as he became increasingly euphoric. "You wouldn't be missed, so why not just give up? Just give up, give up, give up …"

Their words joined together in a mantra that coiled around Flo's spirit. Nathaniel tried to hold open the coil, which was tightening and squeezing the life out of her. He nearly burst something crucial in the attempt, but she was in agreement with her enemies, so they were gaining in strength while he was losing ground.

She didn't know how cherished she was. The thought of losing Flo was intolerable because he had loved her for all these years, but power was draining from him like water down a plughole. For a moment it seemed that he could be on his last stand.

And that was when he heard it—faint at first, and barely to be felt, but there nonetheless. It was the voice of Alec Forsythe swirling through the heavens—prayers from his heart for his daughter.

"Mercy, Father God!" he was crying. "Keep her from harm, Jesus! Gie her strength; encourage her Father an' fill her wi' your love! Forgive me for not lovin' her better, Lord!"

On and on he went, crying out through his tears to the Lord. The demons began to cringe and curse and lose power, while Nathaniel felt his strength returning. "Bless you, Alec Forsythe," he whispered as his confidence ground out of reverse and kicked into first gear. With a massive grunt that worked its way into a shout, he ripped the coil of death apart and then set upon his enemies with sword flashing and fists flying.

The moment they began to retreat, he burst into songs of praise and cries of "Hallelujah!" and sent them packing like the mongrel dogs that they were. His laughter had an edge of hysteria to it as it echoed across the wheat paddocks and milking sheds. He'd just had a close encounter of the worst kind. A CGM didn't forget that sort of thing in a hurry.

*   *   *

When Flo finally came to the end of her tears, she sat up straight and looked around her. She whipped a hanky from her apron pocket, blew her nose, and wiped both eyes with her apron. What in God's name had come over her? These tears would get her nowhere.

With a face set like concrete, she stood to her feet. Then she began to pace back and forth on the veranda. She had Scottish blood running through her veins, for God's sake! And there was none more stubborn than a Scot. The bed she'd made for herself was fair lumpy, but self-pity would change nothing.

There wasn't the option of returning home. The amount of pride she'd have to swallow would be enough to fair choke an elephant, and anyway she didn't think her kinfolk would give her a hero's welcome. It was hard for a woman to survive in this world alone, so for the time being, she needed Tom. The truth was, men in general were a pretty sorry lot, and there was no changing that.

It would be hell to go back, and it was purgatory to stay. There was no doubt about it; she'd landed in a sorry pickle. But there was nought for it. She would have to give her heart wholly to building some sort of a life for herself in this wilderness.

*   *   *

Mary Eastman wiped the sweat from her brow with her apron and with her other hand balanced the bucket of warm fresh milk. By the looks of it, they were in for a scorcher come summer if it was this hot already. The caramel-coloured poddy calf slurped away, half drowning itself in the process. It drained off the last dregs and looked up, dripping white from nostrils to ears.

She smiled and stroked its head, taking her time to drink in the sight of the massive eyes and velvety skin. A few moments later, she took a hold of the bucket handle, straightened, and began to stroll contentedly back to the milking shed. The sound of buckets clanking and the heady smell of warm milk fresh from the cow were things that brought her comfort. This was one chore that she actually enjoyed, and her thoughts meandered as she walked.

Fancy that shy neighbour of hers bringing home a Scottish wife last month; a beauty to boot, judging from what she'd seen at a distance. It was pretty exciting to have a woman her age move in; maybe there was a chance of company for her out here at last. Of course she was not one to push herself on anyone. She'd given them plenty of time to settle in.

But she wanted to show herself friendly. She thought maybe tomorrow she'd take over some cookies and fresh eggs and introduce herself. Happy with her plan, she opened the gates of the holding paddock which surrounded the milking shed and strolled up the path to milk herself another cow.

* * *

Irene Drummond checked her reflection in the gold-framed mirror as she entered her sitting room. Robert loved her hair to be left long, and fortunately it was still thick and golden even after two babies. She deftly plaited the waist-length mane and coiled it in a coronet around her head, pinning it in place with the skill of years of practise. A quick twist of her body to the left and right gave her reassurance that all clothes were matching and sitting correctly, and a glance around revealed that everything was in its place.

She relished the early hours of the day and loved her morning practise when the children were still asleep, but she always checked that everything was in order before she lost herself in the music. After all, when you live close to the heart of town, you never know when someone might drop in.

After settling herself on the piano stool and opening the first sheet of music, she found herself thinking about the new arrival in Singleton. *Oh my; hadn't the locals been all aflutter a month ago when that fresh breeze swirled through the gossip grapevine!* Tom Millet was bringing home a Scottish bride.

Rumours had grown out of the little snatches of information which his sisters had released here and there, and Irene had listened to many conversations in which her friends had stretched their imaginations, trying to picture what the newcomer would be like.

But no amount of rumours could have prepared them for the sunburst which was Florence! She had exploded into their town all colour and action, with the look of someone seeking adventure and wanting to make friends.

Irene sighed deeply. Sadly the mood amongst her friends had quickly changed from curiosity to disapproval. The morning tea-party chats had taken on a sour taste: "What an odd creature she is in her weird outfits and hoity-toity manner. High-button boots, for goodness' sake!"

"Who does she think she is, strutting around as if she owns the place?" "How can anyone understand a word she says with that accent?"

Oh yes, at first they'd been like stunned rabbits, just staring at Florence in awe. But before long they began to clump together and give the foreigner a wide berth, punishing her for their own discomfort.

Irene began to run her fingers along the piano keys, and her heart danced with the notes as she brought to life "The Blue Danube." If she were lucky, she would have half an hour to drink in the ecstasy of beautiful music before the house awakened, and she wanted to drain every last drop allotted to her this morning.

The notes built on one another and lifted her above the pettiness of small-town thinking, and she could picture herself back in the concert halls of Sydney, watching her beloved father create magic with his violin.

As for Florence Millet, Irene had kept all her thoughts to herself. She observed the woman whenever she could and had come to her own conclusions. One thing was for sure; she would do all she could to make a friend of that fascinating creature.

17

Two years later

Tom let his horse travel at her own pace, knowing that Violet was just as exhausted as he was. It seemed to be getting harder and harder to round the cattle up and get through the milking. He knew he'd taken on more of them than he could handle easily, but he had to make ends meet.

He was pretty excited about the new dam he'd built twelve months ago. Over the last year they'd had some good, solid rain, and it had held that water like a beauty. He reckoned that there was nothing more satisfying than the sight of a full dam. He looked over to the west just in time to see the sun give a last grand show. It coloured up like a ripe orange, then plopped behind the horizon. It always amazed Tom how quickly it did that last dip as it disappeared.

He looked down at his faithful little foxy and grinned. "You're a good fella, Spot, aren't you?" he said, and the dog wagged its tail and looked up adoringly. No one loved a bloke like his dog! He knew that Flo didn't think he was wonderful like old Spot did, but he didn't mind. A simple bloke like him was lucky if a woman like her stayed around as a helpmate. He saw the way other men looked at his Flo, and he was always as proud as punch.

Tom dismounted at the stables, and Violet plodded tiredly up to the trough to have a well-deserved drink. He emptied some feed into her tray and gave Spot a quick game, wrestling him onto his back and tickling his tummy.

Turning towards the main house, he could see Flo through the window by the light of the kerosene lamp. Even though he was bushed, he felt desire stir up his insides just at the sight of her. But it wouldn't do him any good, because she hadn't been feeling well for a while now and would bite his head off if he touched her.

There she was, busily working in the kitchen that he'd made with his own hands. What a bonzer woman she was! When they'd first arrived here, he'd been worried sick. It seemed to him that it'd be only a matter of time before she'd pack her bags and leave. He'd tried his best to pray to the God that the Salvos believed in, but he reckoned that they were pretty hopeless prayers.

But by jingo, she'd stayed and stuck it out—why, he'd never know. She was a great cook. Her mother had taught her how to churn butter, make jam, bake bread, and keep a clean house. He'd always had a veggie garden, but now she'd added some patches of flowers to brighten things up. The only thing missing was a baby.

Again he felt the panic that had plagued his mind since marrying Flo. *Jeez, I must be a failure in the bedroom!* Even though she was desperate for a baby, she still only let him near her every blue moon. No wonder they were still childless. Well, there weren't any lessons for a bloke, so there wasn't much he could do about it. He reckoned that once every blue moon was better than never.

* * *

Flo stood dry-retching at the sink. It took every last ounce of willpower for her to stay in the kitchen getting something ready for dinner. How was she ever to stand the heat and loneliness here? Her neighbour Mary had been born in Singleton and was set to die here. That was not a life; it was merely a mindless existence. The girl was kind enough but was about as inspiring as mould growing on bread. But at least she was nearby if ever there was a crisis. Irene Drummond was more engaging; a townie who actually knew that there was a world outside of Singleton.

There was a sudden movement outside and the flash of a figure. After a brief shiver of fear, she realised it was Tom coming up the path. Once again, her reaction was twofold. First there was relief because she felt safe with him. But then there was frustration because he annoyed the living daylights out of her.

She hoped—not for the first time—that he wouldn't be wanting to come close. Her emotions went every which way when he was around, and her body couldn't be trusted at all. It was too difficult to deal with by far.

But more than that, there was another circumstance to deal with this morning, and that circumstance involved extreme nausea. Aye, there was no doubt about it. She'd been two months without a show and was as sick as a dog. She steeled herself as he turned the knob on the kitchen door and swung it open.

"G'day Flo," he said to her as he dropped his boots outside and stepped into the kitchen in his socks. "How're you feelin' today?"

"I'm feelin' quite strange, Tom," she replied. "Nay not my usual self at all." Turning to look at him with what she hoped was a meaningful expression, she continued. "In fact, I canna remember ever feeling like this before."

"Jeez, must be some new bug goin' around," said Mr. Genius as he lifted various lids to check out what was going for dinner.

"Nay. Wrong conclusion, my slow-witted husband," said Flo, rolling her eyes heavenward. "Now go wash yer hands before ye start poking around at the stove!"

As she watched him walk obediently over to the sink, she spoke to his retreating back. "I'm pregnant, Tom." she said. "Ye're going tae be a father."

He turned around in slow motion, held his arms out, and began to walk towards her. "Oh, Flo!" he gasped.

"Dinna touch me!" she shouted as she ran outside to vomit in the garden.

* * *

Resting against the chimneys on the roof, Nathaniel was getting acquainted with Imogen. He really was an amazing specimen—taller than most and with an impressive wingspan. His eyes were soft gold, and two-thirds of his feathers were gold and silver. Nevertheless, it was obvious that the newcomer was exceptionally green and hugely apprehensive.

"The Lord never makes mistakes with his choices, Imogen," he said in an effort to be part of the answer. "You must have what it takes to succeed in your mission, or He wouldn't have sent you here."

Imogen looked deep into Nathaniel's eyes, his own moist with emotion. "I don't know how to accommodate for the heaviness and darkness of Earth, Nathaniel," he whispered. "I fear the shock is more than I can bear."

"But bear it you will, my friend, because it is not in you to rebel against the Lord. That is why you are still in the Kingdom of Light and were not thrust down to Earth with the angels of darkness. And forever you will be with the Lord when all this is over."

"Do you really think so?"

"I believe it with my whole heart."

Nathaniel sat with him in empathetic silence, not daring to share his own deepest struggles. An angel had to do what an angel had to do.

18

Singleton Hospital Maternity Ward, November 1921

Sister Gladys Cooper cursed her bad luck at landing night duty tonight. A secret enemy must have been sticking pins into a doll or something. Since 10.00 p.m. the poor unfortunates who were rostered on with her had sneaked off regularly for cigarette breaks to cope with the pressure. And all this because of one woman's labour!

It wasn't a stalwart farm girl or a pragmatic town lady they had on their hands. This one was used to letting everyone know what she thought about everything when she thought it.

So far the torture had lasted for fifteen hours. She was having a time of it; no buts about that. But Lord have mercy, they'd be just as relieved as her when it was all over.

*   *   *

As Flo gritted her teeth through another monster contraction, that demon of a midwife spoke out another platitude. "You're doing well, Mrs. Millet; it won't be long now," she said in a chirpy voice. But she looked more like she was dealing with a person in the last stages of the black plague.

"Like hell it won't!" yelled Flo. "Ye said the same thing days ago! Is there a soul around here that tells the truth?"

She wasn't doing well, and she knew it. She'd been in torment for hours and was thinking of killing either that sugary midwife or herself. After mere seconds of relief, the next contraction began and quickly carried her to the realms of agony.

"This is madness!" screeched Flo as she rode the wave of pain until it came crashing back down. "Why dinna someone warn me? Is it that there's a secret pact between women tae keep it hidden?"

"Oh, for heaven's sake, woman, stop talking and push!" shouted Sweetness. "I'm telling you you're close, so gear yourself up for the final run!"

What had happened to all the sugar? Flo had to admit that she liked the shouting better. She readied herself for the next contraction, and when it came, she pushed with everything that she had.

"The head's appeared!" announced Sugar-Vinegar. "One more good push, Mrs. Millet, and you're there, so show us what you're made of!"

Flo didn't have to be told twice. She threw her heart into obeying the command even though she fair felt she was splitting in two.

"Yes! The head's out!" cried the infuriating woman. "The rest is easy, dear," she added with a benign smile.

Oh, so now she was the Virgin Mother. There wasn't time to think about that, because the next pain came, and before she knew it, the bairn was born.

"It's a girl, sweetie," said Sugar-Vinegar-Mother, "and she's bursting with vitality."

A girl; how wonderful! Finally there would be a wee companion to fill the big gaping hole in her heart. They would share everything together, and she'd never be lonely again. The name that had stayed in her mind for months now was Katherine. Yes, she would call the girl Katherine after "Katherine the Great."

19

Five years later

Kate curled up in as tight a ball as she could and tried to cry quietly. She'd been such a bad girl and deserved to be caned again. The last time she'd hidden in the wheat paddock, Mummy hadn't found her; but Daddy was better at finding things, and his voice was getting closer all the time. He called out her name over and over, and she wanted to run to him but was too scared.

Mummy said that it was "very unfashionable" for girls to run around getting brown from the sun. She felt they should stay at home and help their mothers. But Kate loved being free like the wind; she didn't know why.

She hated going visiting and having to sit still for hours. The last time they went to Mrs. Drummond's house, Kate sneaked outside to run and dance in the garden. But Mummy came and dragged her inside to be spanked and "fixed up." She was all red in the face, taking big breaths and telling her what a hoyden she was. Kate didn't know how to stop being a hoyden.

It was good spending time with Daddy. He didn't notice how bad she was. He'd told her that he went to school only until he was twelve years old and worked on a farm till he left for the Great War.

Her arm started hurting again, and there was blood everywhere. Daddy called out her name, and she wanted him to cuddle her. Finally the dam walls burst and she began to cry her eyes out.

* * *

Tom stopped still and listened. Yes, there it was, by jingo—a sound coming from the northern wheat paddock! He sneaked up to approach the scene of the crime very slowly until he could see movement amidst the wheat stalks. Closer still and there were sounds of crying plus flashes of red hair showing through. A few more steps and he was looking down on a little bundle of mischief covered in dirt and … and blood!

"What's happened, Katie?" he said, keeping his voice very quiet as he bent down to pick her up. "What have you done to yourself?"

"I'm sorry, Daddy!" she cried "I don't want to die! Don't let me die!"

By this time Tom had figured out that the blood was coming from a nasty cut on her arm. His heart slowed down its thumping just a smidgin. "It's only a cut, Katie; nothin' a visit to the doctor won't fix," he said. "Of course I won't let you die, nipper. What made you say that?"

"I went to the shed, Daddy." Katie was looking into his eyes with her green ones, which were drowning in tears. She was watching to see what he'd do.

At first Tom was confused. Then he remembered a few months back when Katie had been getting up to all sorts of mischief in the shed where he kept his machinery. He hadn't been able to bring himself to scold her, but he told Flo about it later.

He'd felt pretty bad then because Flo had gone off the deep end, yelling about all the ways Katie could hurt herself with one of his gadgets. "She will end up killing herself in that shed!" she'd said. Then she'd given the poor little thing a heck of a hiding. Once that wife of his lost her temper, there was nothing anyone could do to stop it.

He held Katie close, stroking her back and arms. "You won't die, nipper," he whispered, "Daddy's here now." He closed his eyes and drank in the ecstasy of his little darling snuggling up to him, sniffing against his neck all filthy and messy. "Now let's do something about this blood," he added, pulling a handkerchief from his pocket and tying it tightly around her arm.

"You didn't have anyone to look after you, did you, Daddy? Mummy said that your Daddy ran away to the gold mines when you were a boy."

The question shook Tom up a bit, but he answered the best way he could. "You're spot on there, Katie. And my Mum died in childbirth when I was only a little one. She just kept havin' babies until her body wore out, and she'd had more than you could count." He felt that knot again in his stomach.

"So who looked after you?" asked Katie, looking up into his face, hers creased with concern.

"My older sisters raised me along with their own kids, little one," he said. "They did their best, but it's not the same as your own mother. I got on good with my cousins, though. Mary's m' favourite; she's the same age as me."

"Don't worry, Daddy," said his little angel, "I will look after you."

"Will you now?" said Tom, giving her another squeeze. He didn't want to dampen her fresh young heart. She'd turned out to be a real companion, had Katie, coming out each day to help with some of the chores. She was a slight little thing, but she was full of life and hated being cooped up indoors. Word was his mother had been tiny too and danced like a dream—until she'd started having all those babies.

"Mummy will be so angry," said Katie. "I'm supposed to stay and help her."

"Yes, well there's not much we can do about Mummy bein' angry, nipper. The important thing is gettin' you fixed up."

He held back a sigh. It'd been hard on Flo losin' all them babies. He knew it had affected her badly, and nowadays she hardly ever let him go near her. He hated it when she took it out on Katie.

He'd gotten attached to his little girl. It was the closest he'd ever felt to anyone. He wondered what he was going to do with himself when Flo and Katie took off for Scotland in a couple of months. It did him no good to think about it. But Flo wanted to visit her family, so that was that.

"Let's get you to the doctor, nipper," he said in as light-hearted a tone as he could muster. "He'll have to sew you up by the looks of things. Bet you won't go back in that shed in a hurry, eh?"

*   *   *

Flo thrust open the kitchen window and slapped a damp washer across the back of her neck. Only November and already this hot!

"Och, I hated this country" she grumbled. "They should give it back tae the blacks!"

She shifted the cloth to the top of her head and stepped out onto the southerly veranda to try to catch a breeze. Thank goodness Tom hadn't made a fuss about her wanting to go back home for a while. He'd even agreed she could take Kate to meet all the Scottish cousins. He believed that homesickness was the only problem, and who was she to enlighten him?

The letters from home had slowly changed in their tone over the years, which made her believe that her kinfolk had softened. They were missing her and wanted to see Kate. This was her window of opportunity to go under the guise of a visit, reconcile with her parents, and then weave back into the heart and soul of Aberdeen.

Her brain was buzzing with what she'd need for the voyage in two months' time: glamorous attire for the weeks spent at sea, and plenty of warm things for Scotland. After this wretched heat, what a relief it would be to feel cold again and rug up before the old stone fire.

Tom believed she was staying in Aberdeen for eight months, so including the voyage there and back, he wouldn't be expecting her home for twelve months. Twelve months to decide her future. As she pondered these things, her thoughts were interrupted by someone shouting her name.

"Mrs. Millet! Oh, Mrs. Millet!" came the voice from the front of the house. It sounded like the postie but he didn't usually come all the way in. She deposited the damp cloth back in the kitchen and headed for the front door.

"Hello, Mr. Everidge!" she called in greeting. "What brings ye here?"

"Telegram, Mrs. Millet!" he replied with a wave and a grin. "Just arrived this morning. I always make sure folks get a telegram right away!"

Flo's heart sank. Her thoughts flew back to the telegraph which had come during the war announcing the death of Hamish. Even after all these years the memory stirred up dread. She pushed through those feelings to reach out and take the telegram. The postie stayed where he was and looked fair eaten up with curiosity.

"Thank you, Mr. Everidge," she said, holding on to the unopened envelope and pinning him with what she hoped was a formidable look.

The happy-go-lucky grin of the postie regrouped into an O of dread. It was some seconds before he found his voice again. "No trouble at all, Mrs. Millet," he managed to squeeze out. "Have a good day."

She stood as she was until he'd taken off on his bike, and then, with her stomach in a knot, she opened it. If there had been the whisper of a hope that her fears were ungrounded, it evaporated as she read:

DEAREST DAUGHTER STOP SADLY YOUR MOTHER DIED OF A HEART ATTACK YESTERDAY STOP BE COMFORTED IN THE KNOWLEDGE THAT SHE DIED HAPPY TO KEN THAT YOU WERE COMING HOME STOP

PLEASE DO NOT CANCEL PLANS STOP MY HEART IS BROKEN AND I LONG TO SEE YOU STOP YOUR LOVING FATHER STOP

Flo stayed absolutely motionless. She gazed out over the brown paddocks, trying to grasp this latest tragedy in the farce that was her life. With one finger of destiny, her hopes of reconciliation with her mother were snuffed out. The hugs and words of forgiveness she'd hoped for would never happen. The doors which she had thought were open before her now slammed shut in her face.

There'd been no goodbyes at the leaving, with so much pride and bitterness blinding her. All she'd wanted was to lash out and be rid of the anger which boiled inside. And now she would have to live with that being her last and final memory. Regret flooded her heart, and she feared she would drown in grief and loneliness.

She let out a mirror-cracking scream and big sobbing gasps which came from somewhere near her feet. Galvanising into action, she tore down to the driveway. Just as she'd done as a lassie on the moors, she grabbed stones and shoved them into the pockets of her apron.

Then came the mother of all tantrums. Stones went flying in every direction as she screamed out a tirade of rage towards God for being so unjust and towards Tom for bringing her to this godforsaken country. Shouts, curses, and screams took flight across the vegetable gardens, wheat fields, and quietly grazing cattle until at last she was all emptied out and gradually lapsed into exhausted silence. In the midst of the grief haze, she began to think of her father. She considered that maybe he would need her now that Mother was gone.

Way out in the distance somewhere, a nervous cough interrupted her musings. Closing her eyes to control the flash of anger, she looked wearily around.

"You okay, Flo?" Tom stood stock-still, his eyes like saucers. Plastered to his side was Kate, who gripped Tom's shirt and implored her with eyes the colour of the sea on a stormy day.

Flo hardly had the strength to reply. "She's bleeding," was all she could say.

"Yeah," replied Tom without changing his expression. "Reckon the doc'll have t'sew her up."

"I went to the shed, Mummy," added Kate. "But Daddy says I won't die."

20

Sydney Wharf, January 1927

A smorgasbord of emotions battled away in Flo's heart as she watched her husband struggle to keep up a brave front. He was frantically waving from the wharf, his face taking on the look of a grimacing mask. Ye couldn't call Tom bright; that was for sure. But he knew that something was up.

It had taken every last grain of her willpower to keep from screaming these last days. He'd hung around her like a winter fog, searching for an assurance which she couldn't give. How broken he would be when they didn't return. Guilt knocked at her heart, causing her to wave once more and then look away.

Tom hadn't come up to her expectations, and that was the end of it! Country life was not to be borne, and the city of Aberdeen took on more of a rosy hue in her mind with each passing year. When the sun shone at a certain angle over there, the place lit up like stars. Memories flooded in once again.

The Scots were good at making everything cosy in winter. She and Nellie used to sip hot broth before the fire, gossiping while the snow fell outside. How she missed the acres of yellow and white daffodils in spring and the hills covered in purple heather. She was already heady with anticipation of the sea voyage after the tedium of life on the land. How she missed the sea, which was ever changing, always alive and gloriously terrifying.

As she juggled feelings of guilt, excitement, and apprehension, she remembered Kate and checked to see if by some miracle the lass had stayed nearby. But nay, she was nowhere to be seen.

"This time I'll kill her; by God I will!" she vowed. She took off running, her stomach the size of a golf ball. All she needed now was to find out that Kate had already fallen overboard before the ship had even left the dock.

* * *

There were girls and boys running around everywhere; more than Kate had ever seen in one place in her whole life. But she didn't know how to join in. She couldn't do anything except curl up in a corner. Daddy wasn't coming with them, and when he'd held on to her, there'd been a look in his eyes—a scared look. She didn't know what to do about Daddy being scared. And there'd been so many new things.

The ride in the steam train was fun, sleeping all night in the special bed that came out of the wall. And Sydney was big and noisy; full of people and water. Cars and bicycles raced everywhere, and horses pulled carts full of food.

They had to jump on the tram really fast because lots of other people wanted to get on at the same time and everyone was in a big hurry here. When they got to the wharf and she saw the huge ship, she was too excited to talk.

But then she found out that Daddy wasn't coming with them. He was hugging her so tight and looking at her with that look. That scared look. When he let go, she just ran as fast as she could after Mummy.

* * *

Flo went screaming around a blind corner, risking life and limb, and searched for a familiar face in the crowd. That girl would be the death of her! One minute she fair could kill Kate, and the next she was terrified at the thought of losing her!

She noticed a group of children playing ring-a-ring o' roses on the other side of the deck, so she headed there in the slim hope that her nomadic daughter had been attracted by the game. At first she could see nought, and her heart began to sink. But then, thank goodness, she saw Kate curled up in a corner.

"Kate what are ye doing?" she demanded, doing a quick once-over to check for injuries—a common occurrence with this one.

The reply was little more than a whisper. "Daddy's sad, and I don't know how to make him better."

If Flo had felt like a sinner needing a reprimand before, she felt like a murderess deserving the death penalty now. "What nonsense are ye talking?" she snapped. "Daddy has tae stay and look after the farm. He'll be so busy time will fly, and we'll be back before he kens it." She lifted Kate to her feet, took her by the hand, and returned to the side of the ship, where people were waving goodbye. "Look, the ship is moving off now. Let's wave tae Daddy again. That will make him feel a lot better."

When they scanned the crowd on shore, Tom was nowhere to be seen. Flo's throat went dry. It would be awful to leave without a final goodbye.

"There's Daddy, beside the pole!" shouted Kate. "He's waving to us!" she called out, throwing her arms in the air.

Kate blew kisses, and Flo did the same, if only to make Kate feel better. Tom was waving back, and much to Flo's annoyance, she saw clearly the fear etched into his features. Even though she closed her eyes immediately, the image remained stamped. Kate was crying fit to vomit now. They would have to stay there until the ship sailed out of sight, or the child would be inconsolable.

Fifteen more minutes passed, and now the people on the wharf had become mere dots. "Let's search for our cabin, Kate," Flo said. "Ye could do wi' a sleep." She kept a tight hold of Kate's hand as they were being jostled left and right by hordes of people. The child leant up against her as they walked.

What an explosion of stimuli this was for a little girl going from a dairy farm to a big city and then an ocean liner. The two of them had a grand journey ahead, and the future was a mystery ready to unfold. And Kate was finally all hers.

21

One Month Later

Flo was perspiring, and her throat was as dry as the Sahara. Shipboard life was a world apart that pushed aside all thoughts of what was left behind or waiting before. For one month she'd flowed with the fantasy, free from any sense of guilt or responsibility. Now it was time to exercise a little caution.

James's eyes had taken on a look of hunger. Why had she accepted his invitation for a morning stroll around the deck? She'd found it amusing over these past weeks to experiment with her feminine charms and had certainly enjoyed the flood of attention that had followed. But there were men who didn't understand that it was all merely a game.

Too late she'd learnt that when an unmarried virgin flirted it was taken lightly but when a married woman did the same it was seen as an open invitation. Flo may have looked sophisticated, but she had not the stomach for adult games with men, and that she knew full well. She must summon up every skerrick of wisdom and woman's intuition she possessed to navigate this situation.

"Thank you for your company, James," she said with a smile that she hoped was warm without being an encouragement. "Thank God for the Punch and Judy show they put on each morn for the bairns. I think I'd be fair ready tae jump overboard by now without the occasional respite from Kate!"

"I'd be more than happy to mind her for you, Florence," he replied, a wee bit too eagerly. Till now it had been such a boon having keen babysitters that she hadn't given a moment's thought to the consequences.

"That's vera kind of ye, James," she replied. "It's not that I dinna want tae spend time wi' Kate. But I swear she must sit up at night planning how tae fit the most disasters into each day. I dinna ken how I've avoided a nervous collapse before today."

"It must be hard coping on your own" said James. "By the way, where is Mr. Millet? Passed away, has he?"

Here it was again. How easy it would be to merely say Tom had died, but she couldn't risk it with Kate around. "Nay; he stayed at haeme tae run our business matters. 'Twill be a good thing for us tae be separated for a time. I'll be reconnecting wi' kinfolk when I reach Scotland." *There, that sounded sufficiently vague. 'Twas friendly wi'out being a promise.*

"So you each have much to think about," said James with a new spark in his eyes.

"Aye, ye could say that," replied Flo, hoping her best protection was a hint of mystery. "Ye ken, James, I'm finding it a wee bit hot for walking after all. I think I'll be stopping at these chairs an' reading for a time. Ye have made the morning walk most pleasant." *Some erratic behaviour should addle him a wee bit.*

"At your service, lovely lady," he replied; then he kissed her hand and made his departure.

With a soft, low whistle of relief, she settled into a deck chair. All this grandeur and froth and bubble! Surely if a woman just used a wee bit of nous she could benefit from any help that was offered without stepping into abject immorality. Guilt gave her shoulder a wee tap, but she brushed it away. She didn't want anyone raining on her parade, including herself!

Friends back in dead old Singleton didn't even dream about a world like this. Mary Eastman was a good-hearted simpleton with the understanding of a gnat. And Irene belonged to that rare breed of women who truly loved their husbands. Flo hadn't wanted to burst her bubble by revealing what really went on in her own marriage.

Oh for heaven's sake, what was she doing thinking about Singleton? No fun to be had down that track! The entertainment director—aye, now he was what she called fun! When he'd discovered she sang and played the piano, he'd invited her to perform one evening after dinner. What a contrast to wretched church concerts!

Yanking at the drawstring on her bag, she rummaged around in the abyss looking for a novel that was in there somewhere. She finally found it, threw the bag onto the floor, and set about going through the motions of reading. After several minutes, she finally gave up trying to get past the first paragraph.

She realised it would be the black of night in New South Wales now. In a few hours, Tom would be getting up with the dawn. He'd start with the milking and watering and then ease off for the morning cuppa. The dams should hold up even if the rains didn't come this year. But whatever happened, he would get by somehow.

Och, fer God's sake! This is ridiculous! She let out a very unladylike curse, and the hapless book went flying from her hand across the deck. Was she going mad? There were witty, polished men at every turn vying for her attention. And had she felt even a glimmer of interest? Nay, she had not!

*   *   *

Nathaniel opened his eyes and realised that the outburst was over and he was shadow-boxing by himself on the deck. What a nightmare trip this had turned out to be! He was going to need a few more miracles between here and Scotland if he wanted to keep his five-star status.

To his relief, Flo got up mumbling under her breath, stomped over to retrieve the book, and then plopped back into the deckchair. If he and Imogen could just manage to keep her from serial adultery and Kate from landing in the drink until they hit land, they'd consider themselves two very blessed created beings. Of course this situation would be a lot more angel-friendly if they weren't working on a high-profile case.

Satan had shaken countless more of his screws loose with much ranting over the latest "souls that will make a difference" list released by his troubleshooters. Word was he'd been making life even worse than normal for his key henchmen while they tried to track the children down.

Now that Kate was one of the "suspects," Nathaniel and his team hadn't had a moment's peace. What's more, he'd been forced to do some more troop training, which had never been his forte. Thankfully Imogen had turned out to be a gem.

That angel had his work cut out for him keeping up with Kate. But he was very disciplined and obedient because of his stint in the Throne Room. And that, ladies and gentlemen, made the tricky area of job delegation a whole lot easier for the old CGM!

Imogen turned up out of nowhere then, and Nathaniel glowed red wondering if he'd said that last sentence out loud. But the moment passed when he noticed Imogen's appearance, which could only be described as dishevelled. He made a split-second decision to say nothing, knowing that the usually immaculate angel would be mortified to know that his angst was showing.

"Hello, comrade, how goes it?" he said, raising his arm in greeting.

Imogen checked to see that Kate had been left safely with Flo by a keen suitor before coming to sit on the deck railing. Nathaniel lit up with pleasure as they settled in for a chat.

"If you must know, I'm beyond exhaustion and into the twilight zone of chronic fatigue. Just remind me, Nathaniel—who am I, where am I from, and where am I going?"

"I've got too much on my plate already without having to remember your details as well, friend. How are you going with whatshername, by the way?"

"Up the creek without a paddle, mainly. There are so many opportunities to fail that I've gone into auto drive to avoid thinking about it. That girl has the energy of three men."

"That's tricky stuff, admittedly, Imogen, but great for character-building, all of it. Try looking after someone who's seriously angry and confused most of the time, and you'll really know about the twilight zone. I've started having conversations with myself just to confirm that I'm still here, and a new tic is developing under my left eye."

"So we're in the same boat, literally and symbolically."

"Yes, friend, you could say that. In fact, you did say it. We're in the same boat, heading for the same country, and we'll be in it together for as long as it takes!"

22

The docks of Aberdeen Harbour

The jug was so big that it took all of Kate's strength to pour some water into the basin without dropping everything. Standing on tiptoes, she splashed her face several times and patted it dry with a hand towel. She then climbed up onto the chair and stared closely into the mirror.

She didn't want anyone to know she'd been crying, because Mummy got very angry when Kate missed Daddy. It was wrong to miss Daddy when Mummy loved her so much.

But she so needed Daddy's hugs right now! Once again the tears started, and she began to splash water all over again, trying to be quick.

* * *

Oh, for heaven's sake! Flo thought. One minute Kate was in sight, and the next she'd disappeared! Flo was about to run in pursuit when she saw Kate coming out of their cabin looking like death warmed up.

"Ye frightened the vera life out of me, child!" she said. "Here we are, ready tae step foot on my haeme soil, and ye disappear on me. What on earth have ye been up to? Ye're saturated!"

"Sorry, Mummy."

"Well, hold my hand and stay close while we make our way down the gangplank. Are ye ready?"

"Yes."

"Come on, then."

Flo could feel her heart fair knocking against bones as she made her way down the gangplank, searching all the time for the familiar stern face. Aye, he would be sombre at first,

120

trying to hide his feelings, and it would take a while for him to open up. But she knew that he needed her and would want to have her all to himself.

He'd never had any time for bairns, but he would gradually come to care for his granddaughter. And besides, Kate would be out all the while, playing with cousins and neighbours. She heard a scrimmage of some kind o'er to the right and looked across.

Suddenly out of the crowd burst a man who called out her name and ran towards her with open arms and tear-filled eyes. 'Twas a stranger who looked all the world like her father! Before she could even partly grasp what was happening, he enveloped her in a bear-like embrace.

The episode lasted only seconds but had an impact like a head-on collision with a lorry. She just stood broomstick straight, staring at this person who was talking with the pace and volume of a cattle auctioneer. She thought of the novels she'd read that spoke of identical twins who changed places.

"Flo; I canna believe it's ye!" he said now, smiling and showing teeth that she'd never seen before. "And ye must be young Kate!" He swooped the girl up and spun around, much to her great delight. "What a stunning young lassie ye are! I'm yer Granda; did ye know that? Flo, I've brought the sulky along so we can fit all yer bags. Let me take ye both tae it so ye can relax whilst I fetch the luggage."

Within minutes Flo and Kate were seated up in the sulky while Alec hurried away looking like a man on a mission.

"Granda's nice, Mummy," said Kate, looking up at her from beneath fluttering eyelashes.

No doubt she was trying to figure out what was wrong with her mother. The truth was that Flo was paralysed with shock. It would be an understatement to say that nothing in that welcome scene had gone according to plan. He'd never said a warm, encouraging word in her life, yet already he'd held Kate and declared her to be a stunning young lassie.

*　　*　　*

Alec was almost too excited to think straight. The Lord was so merciful to give him this chance to make amends for the lost years with Flo. Life's tragedies had broken his heart, and he hadn't the energy for any pretence now. But in that nakedness he'd found a wondrous freedom and a chance to connect with his sons. 'Twas his hope that something similar might happen with Flo.

"Where are ye wantin' these, then?" said the porter as he separated off Flo's bags onto a trolley.

"O'er the way on that sulky, thankye," replied Alec, handing the young lad a coin. He found it satisfying to see his eyes light up.

As he returned to the vehicle, he made a vow before God to make every moment count.

* * *

The strangest thing was happening as Flo thawed out from her frozen state and watched her father stride along, chatting happily to the smiling porter. This change in his demeanour was so vast that it served as a contrast to highlight the way he'd been and the way things were when she was a bairn.

Pictures began to emerge from the mental coffin where she'd buried them when she'd left home. She saw the beatings, the relentless discipline, and that distant coldness that was always in his eyes. And all the while he'd harped on about his sickening religion and his wretched God.

How could she have forgotten even for a moment, let alone years? She had no idea what he was cooking up in his old age. Aye, but there was one thing for certain—she would never forgive him. Nay, never!

23

Aberdeen, three months later

The sounds of music and laughter coming from the sitting room seemed to be aimed directly at Flo as they swirled around her in a mocking chant. The Alec Forsythe she'd grown up with had died, and now here she was, living with a complete stranger. Not that she and her dad had ever been close. But whatever they'd been, they weren't that any more. She put her book down as she stood, and she tiptoed out of the library and across the hall to have a peek.

There was her father, playing the piano and smiling from ear to ear as he watched Kate dance around the room as if she were a prima ballerina. They didn't notice her, because they were both caught up in the joy of the moment.

A sharp pain pierced deep, and she felt as though her very soul was haemorrhaging. Holding back gasps of pain, she somehow managed the return to the library; she leant against the wall and slid down onto the floor.

With head on knees, she whimpered like a kitten. How had she forgotten the wretched truth of her childhood? Surely some form of amnesia had set in from the shock of finding herself married and living in Australia.

Too late her father was making a show of reaching out; aye, but she'd rebuffed every advance. The warmth and hugs which he showered upon Kate were as salt to her wounds. When had he ever played with her the way he was now playing with his granddaughter?

Finally she dragged herself up and walked across to slump back into the armchair. The pain of rejection remained and coloured her thinking as her mood became pensive. Over the past months here in Aberdeen, what had anyone actually done for her?

Back in Australia she'd dreamt of her kinfolk counting the days till her return. She'd imagined them spending happy times with her to make up for lost ground. But truth be told, for these past months they'd all been fitting her in around their busy schedules.

Heath and Charles had popped in a mere few times with their children, who were all years older than Kate. Each visit had been a struggle disrupted with awkward silences. She'd felt as relieved as they'd looked when it was over. Robbie had dropped his three around every day to play with Kate but hadn't stayed long himself. She and Robbie had nought in common.

Victoria was pleasant enough, and Nellie had visited. But she couldn't say they'd been knocking the doors down to embrace her. For sure both lasses looked very complacent; they'd done well for themselves, and that was a fact. To think that Victoria had caught the eye of Reverend Miller! He was fair attractive, minister or no, and had four bairns no less. Och, but she'd always been the maternal kind! Even simple Nellie had three, and she adored them all. She spoke about nought else.

They'd all been clever with their words. "Let's give Flo some time alone with Da," they'd said. Using that excuse, they'd fussed over Kate and oft taken her away for the day rather than stay.

Oh aye, everyone loved Kate, with all her energy and natural charm. She had her mother's thick chestnut hair but her father's olive complexion. There were none of the freckles that had haunted Flo all her life. And then there were those glowing emerald eyes. She'd rather die than tell Kate any of this. The lass was already enough of a handful without the complication of vanity!

And what a time of it she was having, playing all day with her cousins and neighbours. Every morn after porridge, she was out the door without a backward glance. Flo should have been glad to be free of her as well as Tom. This was her opportunity to revel in the beauty of her homeland and take pleasure in the company of her own folk.

But God help her, she missed the sing-song warble of magpies and the riotous laughter of kookaburras. She shuffled the armchair forward to be closer to the fire and sunk deeper into her woollen cardigan as she tried to stem the memories which now broke through and flowed free.

She hadn't realised it, but she'd grown accustomed to spending long summer evenings drinking cups of tea while sitting on the huge timber veranda after dinner. And in truth there was comfort to be had from the mooing and barking and crowing that went on around the place all the while.

Where it was grey here, back there 'twas all blue. 'Twould be spring soon, and the air in Singleton would be thick with the fragrance of blossom trees, sweet peas, and roses. Tom fully believed that there was no one in the world as wonderful as she, no matter what she did. Life was so strange. She'd never been short of attention from men, but she only ever felt safe with him.

* * *

Alec stopped playing and put down the lid of the piano in spite of Kate's protests.

"Granda, just one more song, just one more … pleeeeeease!" she whined.

"Nay, little one; there'll be no more for today," he said with a laugh. "Yer mother will be wonderin' what's become of ye, and besides it's yer bedtime and ye ken it!"

"Don't want to, don't want to, don't want to!" chanted Kate as she allowed him to hold her hand and lead her out of the sitting room.

"Ye must, ye must, ye must!" replied Alec, a grin splitting his face as they both entered the library.

And there was Flo, sitting in the armchair, looking as serious as all get out. His light mood vanished in a flash and was replaced with foreboding—a common experience with Flo over these last months. Kate leant up against him as if for comfort. His first thought was to get the lass to bed as soon as possible.

"Gie yer mother a kiss goodnight, young Kate" he said, "and if ye're in bed in ten minutes, I'll read ye a story."

"There's no need for that, Da," said Flo from the midst of her jumper. "I always read Kate her bedtime story, and tonight will nay be different. But I'll still be having that kiss, Katie."

The lassie didn't need to be told a second time. She kissed Flo with a mumbled "G'night, Mummy," then scampered off to the bedroom. There was silence between them both for a time. Flo was the first to speak.

"Well! What a cosy picture ye make between ye," she said without looking his way. Then, turning to face him, she added, "I canna recall e'er experiencing ought like it myself."

Nowadays Alec's emotions just refused to stay hidden. When his only daughter had left home with a stranger for a land at the end of the earth, he'd not shed a tear. Now his eyes were like brimming pools as he searched for the right words.

"Are ye not happy here, Flo?" he finally said.

"Nay, Flo isna happy here!" Her eyes challenged him. "Flo's vera unhappy wi' everything, including a father who's behaving like a complete stranger. Back in Australia people stay the same, and they actually care whether Flo lives or dies!"

She had always been his thorn in the side; too strong for a woman and too clever by far. Alec had tried to curb her spirit so she'd fit society's mould and find a good husband. But his efforts had only made it harder for her.

"I was thinkin' that ye didna care for us, Flo," he said finally. "Not that ye could be blamed for that."

Flo shot to her feet and faced him with her arms folded. "Why the hell would I come from the other side of the world tae see you if I dinna care?" she shouted. "It's ye who doesna care, Da!"

Alec's cheeks were rivers now as he stood his ground facing her. His mouth opened and closed several times, but nought came out. Finally, in little more than a whisper, he spoke.

"I care, Flo," he said. "I care. More than ye'll ever ken."

Flo's face began to crumple, and her shoulders shook. She looked like a lost little bairn, and Alec feared he would come completely undone. He reached out his arms, but she pulled away.

"Well ye've had a strange way o' showin' it!" she flung at him. "This place is a dungeon o' misery. I'll be goin' in tomorrow tae book tickets back haeme!" And with that she fled weeping from the room.

Alec stayed stock-still until he heard her slam the kitchen door. Then he put hands on hips and shook his head in wonderment. Was this a dream, or had he, Alec Forsythe, truly managed words straight from the heart to his daughter? And could it be that he'd said them without falling into a thousand pieces?

But beyond that, Flo had said that she cared! A flutter of hope like butterfly wings brushed past his spirit. Smiling through his tears, he felt a new boldness rise up within. A reckless plan began to form in his mind.

That hurricane of a granddaughter had caused a new fire to ignite in his belly. What a rollercoaster ride it was to keep up with her! But he never tired of hearing her chat away in her funny accent. And how he loved it when she called him "Granda" and held his hand.

He stepped over to the fireplace and stood gazing into the flames while he let himself dream. The lassie was hurting; a blind man could see it. And his Flo was aching beneath her pride. They needed him; he knew that as well as he knew his own name.

O'er these last years the Lord had enabled him to show his sons love with word and action. At the very least he'd made his peace with them and their bairns, and they would do fine without him. Victoria was the happiest he'd ever seen her. Aye, he could leave here with a clear conscience.

He needed to be wise in his approach. He would say that he wanted the chance to make amends with her before he died. She couldn't refuse him that! Then he would ask if he could come to Australia with them and spend some time helping on the farm. He was only sixty-seven years old and still fit. Aye, that was the way to go—one step at a time.

"Alec," he said, "there is still much tae be done, and ye're merely a lad!"

* * *

Flo was beside herself. She stumbled into the kitchen and set about clanking together a cup, teapot, spoon, milk, and sugar in a parody of tea-brewing. Breathing heavily, she reached for the piping-hot kettle which was bubbling away on the fuel stove. Her hand stopped in mid-air at the sound of footsteps coming from behind.

"Could ye put in enough for two, Flo?"

Her father's presence seemed to take up all the oxygen in the small room. It took her all her willpower to resist gulping for air. He'd just told her he cared, hadn't he? And surely she had seen tears in his eyes. She held her breath and turned to look into his sculpted face, clay now where it'd once been granite.

"What do ye want, Da?" she whispered.

"If ye could give me a few minutes, Flo," he replied, "I'd like tae put forward a proposition."

She searched his eyes for hidden dangers but found only clear pools. She thought mayhap he was senile. Who was to know? Only time would tell.

"Do ye want one sugar or two?" she said.

24

Flo wiped her face and neck with a damp flannel and made a final check of the kitchen. The flypapers dangling from the ceiling were black with dozens of the pests. There was nought for it but to put up fresh ones, or 'twould play on her mind. She set about detaching old strips while trying not to get her fingers stuck in the process.

After tossing them in the bin, she washed her hands before lifting the small tray off the bench. Then she fought her way through the plastic strips that hung across the doorway, nearly fell out onto the veranda, and finally plonked the tray onto the old timber table that Tom had made when they first moved here.

After plumping up the cushion in her favourite chair, she settled down with a grunt of relief for the first time since 5.00 a.m. Believe it or no, she caught herself humming while pouring out strong steaming tea from the old silver pot.

"By the look of it ye've learnt tae appreciate the wee pleasures out here in the Never-Never, Flo," she said while stirring in sugar and creamy milk taken from the previous night's milking.

Thank goodness Tom had made the extra effort to add a wraparound veranda when he'd built their home. It kept the house cool and provided for outdoor recreation when she was fed up with being in the kitchen but didn't feel like sweltering in the yard. Her eyes drank in the peaceful scene of open fields dotted with gum trees and cattle and paddocks already golden with wheat.

They'd been back on Australian soil for only two months, and already Scotland was a fuzzy memory. If she'd had any last doubts about returning, they'd withered at the sight of Tom striding up and down the wharf at Circular Quay, searching every face but wanting only one.

Kate raced into his arms, and he hugged her tight. Aye, he loved his daughter, but it was clear that Flo held the special place in his heart. His eyes had questioned hers as usual, and for the first time, she'd given the look of reassurance that he sought. That was the least she could do.

She took another sip of tea and shook her head with a sigh. Life has a way of knocking down your castles in the air and leaving you with some heavy bruising. She'd hoped for a knight in shining armour galloping on a white horse but married a farmer in work boots plodding along on old Violet! So she was not the princess she'd imagined herself to be. It is so sad when a dream dies. The hurt goes deep, and the grieving time is long. And all through the grieving, you must continue with daily chores, because life doesn't stop and wait until you feel strong again.

Tom had given Da a fair welcome on arrival. For sure, he was just glad to have his wife back any which way! Of course it helped that the man was as fit as a young bull and had soon shown himself helpful. Be that as it may, she was pleased to see them working well together.

Tom had thrown his energy into the farm when she left; he'd worked his heart out making sure it kept running. Of course his diet for twelve months had been scrambled eggs and strawberry jam sandwiches. He'd almost whimpered like old Spot when she'd first fired up the wood stove and started cooking.

But no more than a couple of days after his return, she started nagging him again. 'Twas the devil made her do it! And try as she may to be patient with Kate, the lass was already driving her mad. Since her time away, it was even harder than before to keep her inside with her mother where she belonged.

*   *   *

Alec chuckled as he watched the chickens fighting one another for the scraps he'd scattered. They squawked and flapped while the old rooster strutted around in his comical, disjointed way as if he owned the yard and was allowing this intruder to enter only because he'd brought food.

At the sound of the homestead door opening, he looked up and saw Flo step out carrying a tray. Once she'd had her moments of peace and quiet, she would summon them up for fresh-baked pikelets and tea. His mouth watered at the thought. Oh my, but he loved this climate! Outdoor living was a new thing for him, and how he relished it.

The Lord had once again turned his understanding upside down. He hadn't thought to be having a rebirth in the midst of his rescue mission. He was thriving in the Australian sunshine and becoming a picture of health; had even lost all trace of the rheumatism that had been his curse in the old country.

There was no end to the ways he could be of help here. Anyone with eyes could see that he was a fit, strong specimen of manhood and that Tom needed assistance. God willing, there just might be a place for him here for some time to come.

Kate had needs which her parents couldn't see; just as Alec had been blind to the needs of his own bairns. Oh, to have an old brain in a young body. There was no telling what a man might accomplish! Right now Alec's bones were telling him that the lass pined for company and her spirit yearned for feeding. Those months spent in Aberdeen had given her a taste for the company of lads and lasses. Aye, 'twas hard; and in no time at all she'd be starting her schooling. He strolled across to Kate, who sat stroking her beloved dog, Spotty.

"Ye're quiet, lassie; have ye time for a chat wi' yer old Granda?"

"I'm so sad, Granda. The hills don't have any heather or snow; just brown, brown, brown." She ground her foot into the dirt and stuck out her bottom lip in a perfect pout. "And there's no one to play with; only animals and grown-ups!"

"What an insult, young lassie!" Alec tried to look offended. "I'm neither an animal nor a grown-up; I'm a Granda. And that means that I'm more of a bairn than e'er I was!"

Kate tried to stop the grin that threatened to break open her pout. "You can't be a Granda and a child at the same time; that's silly!"

"Nay, for certain 'tis not," said Alec. "I'll have ye ken that I've hidden twenty eggs down in the chicken coop. It's my guess ye can't even count tae twenty, let alone find every one."

"I can too! I can count to one hundred! Lachlan taught me!" Now she was jumping up and down.

"Did he now?" said Alec, hands on hips. "Well, after we've had morning tea, let me see ye prove it!"

"I bet I'll find them before you count to one hundred!" she shouted. And with that she took off like the wind after Spotty, who'd cornered a screeching chicken separated from its nearly hysterical mother. With a laugh and a squeal she jumped onto the hapless dog and wrestled it to the ground.

Yes indeed, he'd be needing to keep his wits about him. His life's work on this earth was not yet finished.

*   *   *

Mummy was watching her from the veranda with that look. Kate went hot all over and rolled away from Spotty. She turned around to stop from crying, and there was Granda, smiling and giving her one of his secret winks.

"The good Lord loves ye, Kate, nay matter what ye do," he said. "And when ye have him wi' ye, there's need for nought else."

Her heart smiled back, and somehow she didn't feel so bad any more. She loved her Granda so much it made her tummy churn. Did that mean she didn't love Mummy and Daddy any more? *Maybe you can love lots of different people at the same time*, she thought. After morning tea she would stay inside and help Mummy.

Granda was sooo much fun, and the chores didn't feel as lonely when he helped her with them. They fed the poddy calves and hens together and collected the eggs. Granda rode on horses to round up the cattle, and he looked after the dogs. And he told her secrets that she must keep to herself—things Mummy and Daddy had never told her about.

There was a huge and strong God who made everything. God was good and kind and loved making beautiful things like roses and sunsets and special little girls like her. He loved her very much and listened to her when she prayed.

On Sundays Granda would play the piano and sing songs which he called hymns. The hymns seemed to go deep down inside her, and she carried them around in her heart like precious jewels.

*   *   *

Flo trained a possessive eye on her daughter over the top of the teacup. Kate now spent near every spare moment with Da, who was fair captivated by the lass's charm. A bout of jealousy punched her in the stomach, and hatred welled up uninvited. She cringed in shame and tried to control her wanton emotions. What kind of a woman hated her own daughter? She loved Kate! Three big gulps of tea went down in a flash.

Tom didn't seem concerned about the situation. She guessed he was grateful for all the help he was getting with the chores. To be sure, Da was showing himself useful in myriad ways, especially when it came to their social events. He'd been the very life of the previous week's party, with his "warm and friendly manner." *Will wonders ne'er cease?*

"Would the real Alec Forsythe please stand up?" she spoke out loud to the rose garden. He was trying his best to win her over, but woe betide him should he try to take Kate away from her!

Her somewhat bitter line of thought was cut short when Tom stepped into her line of vision on his way from the paddocks. He'd been up at four this morning helping one of the cows give birth, and she could see by the slow, deliberate walk that the man was fair exhausted. That husband of hers loved his animals, and that was a fact. He'd do anything for them, and they for him.

"Hello, Tom," she said. "Is Violet coming along well then?"

"She sure is, Flo, and we got us a beaut new little calf," he replied. "How long d'ya reckon it'll be before them pikelets are ready?"

"Och, ye must be starved, husband," said Flo. She drained the last of her tea and stood. "If ye wash yer hands, I'll be settin' out morning tea now."

Tom stood still, watching her with a smile. "Jeez, Flo," he said, "ever since you came back from Scotland, you've sure been talkin' with a strong accent!"

25

High on a throne of royal state … Satan exalted sat, by merit raised to that bad
eminence; And from despair thus high uplifted beyond hope.
John Milton, from *Paradise Lost*, 1667

The Kingdom of Heaven

Life didn't get any better than this for the old Nathaniel. The glory was so thick that he was
getting drunker by the second. *Oh hallelujah, bring it on!* He belted out the worship chorus,
arms akimbo, before abandoning himself to rip-roaring hysterical laughter.

"Oh yeah, it's my birthday! Oh yeah, it's my birthday!" he sang while stumbling around
doing some sort of version of the hula. No one had to show him how to party! In mid-dance
he turned towards the guardian section and tried to coordinate his eyes to check on Imogen.

"Oh yeah, it's my birthday … Oh yeah … it's my …" he mumbled while squinting to focus.
Wouldn't you know it; there was old sombre-wings sitting alone with head in hands. Nathaniel's
heart went out to the angel who felt things so deeply. He got down on hands and knees to better
control his direction and made his way across to offer some comfort and strength.

"There are no wordsh are there?" he slurred, placing a hand on Dashiel's shoulder. The head
had cleared slightly now with the result that he felt a little self-conscious about his condition;
but fortunately Imogen was very welcoming.

"Well, it's certainly hard to find the words, Nathaniel," he replied. "I'd forgotten how light
it is here. Yes, it's the light that has bowled me over the most. Don't get me wrong; I wouldn't
swap the experience of guarding Kate for anything. But I'll be totally honest with you; the last
decade has been tricky."

Nathaniel chose his words carefully, wanting very much to be encouraging. "It hash been a huge transhishion for you, Imogen, but the fact ish that you have kept her shafe, difficult though it hash been."

"Difficult for you two sluggards; easy for me!" came a deep voice from behind them. Nathaniel whipped around to face an enormous and fearsomely beautiful warrior whose face was split in half by a mammoth grin. He felt a millisecond of panic because he didn't know the angel from a bar of soap, but fortunately Imogen's eyes lit up with recognition and he greeted him warmly.

"Dashiel! What are you doing in the Guardian Section?" he cried. "It's been centuries! Did you know I was on guardian duty now? Oh, let me introduce Nathaniel, my Earth mentor. Nathaniel, this is Dashiel, a veteran warrior."

"Great to meet you!" said the warrior. He gave Nathaniel's hand a shake that threatened to short-circuit his life force. "I've actually learnt a lot about you recently. There's been talk around the traps about the great work you are doing to raise up excellent guardians."

Nathaniel was stone cold sober now. To his horror, a tell-tale flush of pride began to well up, starting in his chest. Without further thought, he dived down to brush off an imaginary speck from the hem of his robe while whispering "Pride comes before a fall, pride comes before a fall" in a desperate attempt to get the act back together.

He was still getting over the size and splendour of this guy who positively dwarfed everyone within cooee. *Cooee!? Oh boy, those years spent in Australia are beginning to rub off!* Vital seconds ticked while he composed himself somewhat and eventually stood up straight again.

"Thank you, Dashiel," he said with a smile which he hoped expressed authority along with sincerity. "Are you being prepared for an assignment at present?"

"That's very much the way it's looking, young guardian," replied Dashiel, smiling crookedly.

He felt momentarily miffed at being patronised. These warriors loved to be in control, so they turned everything into either a victory or a joke! But the miff didn't last long, because Dashiel's next words paralysed every line of thought.

"The good news is that I am apparently going to be working with a great team," he boomed. "The bad news for you guys is that you're it!"

Nathaniel did what he always did when he couldn't think straight. He chose the high road. There was nothing for it but to display a good attitude and get into the swing of things. "Well, if that's the worst news I get today, I'll be doing well!" he said with gusto. Unfortunately that proclamation sounded much louder than usual because of the sudden hush which had fallen over the room.

Yes, he was embarrassed beyond words. But as luck would have it, the experience was short-lived. The reason for this was the chill that had entered the place and was now creeping along his wings. He followed the direction of everyone's gaze and then fell into stunned silence.

The Accuser had actually dared to interrupt a worship session and was boldly approaching the throne. As he slunk across the floor, he turned and glowered at the heavenly throngs. His eyes showed pride and despair and the recklessness of one who had no hope. But there was no pity for him in this place. Here he was the enemy, driven as he was by hatred and terror to wage war continually for the souls of men.

"What is your purpose, Satan?" said the Lord, his voice like a thousand trumpets and his expression unreadable.

Satan turned to face the Lord and raised his fists in a gesture of defiance. "I bring a challenge for the soul of Kate Millet!" he cried in a hollow wail rather than a shout.

"What about Kate Millet? She is full of life and loves me with a simple and unshakeable trust!"

"She loves you because she has lived in a bubble! If life threw some tragedies at her, she would soon change her tune."

"She would continue to love, and she would stand!" said the Lord.

Satan was not to be denied. He was swaying back and forth, agitation and battle-lust showing in every movement. "Let me sift her!" he screamed. "She is proud and stubborn, and I know that she will rebel!"

All eyes now turned to the Lord as he pondered these last words. Nathaniel felt a sickening dread begin to form in the pit of his spirit. He was beginning to get a glimpse of the cross-generational work that the archangel had referred to, and it wasn't looking inviting.

The seconds ticked by. Only by supra-angelic restraint did he ward off the impulse to fly across the room towards the throne shouting "Nooooooooo!" at the top of his voice. Satan continued the challenge, sounding more and more like a belligerent child.

"Anyone in her situation would love you!" whined the one who had been given so much yet had still chosen to hate. "You said that she would make a difference, but if you let me sift her, she will come to nought!"

"Enough!" boomed the Lord. "You will say no more, Satan!"

Silence reigned, and Satan cowered now, the fleeting wave of confidence having left him high and dry.

Nathaniel watched mesmerized as his Master spent several moments more in thought. Surely he would send the intruder packing and they could continue on their happy, drunken way. Finally a reply came from the throne, spoken with quiet gravity.

"You will have no access to her until she has reached the age of twenty-one years," he said. His eyes surveyed the space above and beyond the assembled multitude as if measuring the future. "You can then sift her, but you may not cause physical harm. The harassment of the demon hordes will be a sufficient test. Now go!"

Satan flashed a look of triumph to his former colleagues before turning and scuttled across the room. Upon nearing the exit, he began to puff up with pride, ready for the return to his kingdom. A manic laugh faded into the distance as he catapulted back to Earth.

"Something tells me, friends," said Dashiel after a few moments' silence, "that I've just seen a glimpse of my upcoming Earth assignment."

Nathaniel reached out to Imogen, who was visibly shaken, and held him in a comforting embrace. Anything said now would sound trite; he thought it better to say nothing and appear wise. He could never in a million years argue with the Lord the way Satan did! It was not in him to rebel. So the path of obedience was his only option—a path that was looking decidedly rocky.

A period of respectful silence followed in the Throne Room, but inevitably a spirit of worship began to rise again. Wordlessly Nathaniel smiled to his two companions, and they smiled back. He could see in the set of their shoulders that they were resolute. The three of them joined in the singing, united by purpose, and Nathaniel once again, for the trillionth time, gave up his own will and surrendered in trust to the Lord.

Part Four

26

Tetrak squirmed and sweated over the test paper that his slug of a leader had put together "especially for him." What happened to good old-fashioned trust? That's what he wanted to know. He was already ear-deep in tough assignment issues without having to deal with this crap. He felt like killing someone. And as far as seriously bad ideas went, that was a winner. If he didn't get finished before Satan came back, he'd be in for a boiling-oil bath at best. There might be plenty of terminal losers hanging around the bottom rungs of Hell who worshipped the Great Leader, but he'd been through enough to know that the guy was a sadistic control freak. All of which still left him nowhere to go but back to the questions.

So what was number six about? It was asking whether he'd successfully seduced Eleanor. Was Satan a murderous megalomaniac? Of course he'd seduced Eleanor, years ago. She'd been a piece of cake. He ticked that one with a flourish.

Number seven read, "Do a report on all Eleanor's children and grandchildren. Include a projection analysis as to likely candidates for operating the gift of spiritual sensitivity." Well, there was an easy answer to that one. "All of her children are hopeless losers, and the grandchildren aren't much better." *How's that for a fricking projected analysis? Ten points for creativity?*

He enjoyed his private joke for a few seconds. Then the will to survive kicked in and he began to set out a businesslike report that he hoped displayed keen insight. His fingers ran across the keys faster than the speed of light until every dysfunctional member of the family was covered by a deep and perceptive account. *Brilliant!*

Finally he wrote the last sentence, a piece de resistance: "Beatrice's kids are too young to tell. But with the way she and lover boy are carrying on, they don't have a chance of growing up with any backbone."

Now to bike smoothly along to question eight: "Define your goals in regard to Beatrice O'Brien, who is a possible carrier of the gift. What systems have you set in place to break her spirit and gain control?"

Tetrak's tumultuous existence flashed before him as he freewheeled into a purple-level terror zone. Since when had he been told to set about breaking Beatrice's spirit? Wasn't she just a bit player in this whole sick soap opera?

He began to gag with horror and clambered across the room to vomit through an open window. Think—he had to think! After wasting precious minutes throwing up, he rushed back to the desk. Thoughts were flying around in his brain as if caught up in a twister as he tried to make up a plan.

Her marriage was as shaky as a jelly blubber on a tightrope; easy to kill and at least a start. But he needed more than that to break the likes of Beatrice. What about her parents? There was so much material there he didn't know where to start. Ideas began to surface, brilliant in their perversity. He started typing like there was no tomorrow to get them all locked in before he got beaten by the clock.

27

My heart is a lonely hunter that hunts on a lonely hill.
—Fiona MacLeod, from "The Lonely Hunter," 1896

North Sydney, Australia, 1917

Bea was seconds away from detonating. *Oh God, those eyes.* She would never be free of them. Grief and ecstasy rode side by side, and she chose ecstasy, abandoning herself to mindlessness. Whispered assurances streamed from another world and stamped their possession as she clung to a dream.

"You were born for this, darling; you and I forever and a day. Say that it's true, baby. Say that it's true."

"It's you, only you, Sean. Never another, now or forever."

For mere seconds they were one and there was nothing else but the sounds and tastes of their loving. The rapture carried Bea like a cork and then finally broke and crashed, leaving her grounded and struggling to collect her scattered thoughts and twisted emotions.

It took a minute for the follow-up wave of shame to hit home. She had given in to desire again when she'd needed to make a stand. Self-hatred turned her stomach to pure acid, and in disgust she turned to get off the bed. Sean's hand grabbed her by the arm.

"Where are you going?" he snapped.

"To the bathroom," she said, trying to yank free. "Let go of me!"

"Not until you tell me what's wrong. You wanted me as much as I wanted you, Bea; you know that."

She twirled in fury. "Yes, Sean, I know that! We both know that, don't we? Even when you've come home finally to us at two in the morning as drunk as a pig! You don't have to remind me of how pathetic I am."

"I said I was sorry."

"You always say you're sorry! I've been as weak as dishwater; I know that. But tonight was the last time. I mean it, Sean. You've humiliated me for the last time!"

Bea escaped to the kitchen and grabbed a basin to fill with warm water from the pot on the stove. Clean—she had to get clean! But she knew that he'd followed her; felt him standing just behind.

"You need more than water to rid yourself of me, woman," he said.

She slumped forward over the kitchen sink, basin in hand and naked. God help her, he was right. She put down the basin, stood to her full five feet two inches, and turned to face him. His mouth was set in a line, and his eyes were glazed from sex and beer. He was irresistible. When she spoke, her voice had a hollow sound to it.

"Yes, I need more than soap and water to clear up the mess that we make together."

"Are you saying I don't make you happy? That my love doesn't satisfy you? A few minutes ago you were looking very satisfied."

"Sean, I've never been so unhappy in my whole pathetic life. Your way of loving has twisted me in knots. Living with you has left me beaten and weary. The only choice I have is to live without you."

His laughter had an edge to it. "You're not making sense, Bea. I was your first. And I'll be your last!"

"Maybe so. And maybe there'll never be another for me. But I will live without you, Sean. I will."

Robert woke at that point and began to cry, followed closely by Michael, who called out to her in a half dream.

"Those damn kids; I can't stand it!" he shouted, ramming his fists into his ears. "Day and night we're never free of them!"

"Then go."

"What do you mean?"

"I mean what I said. You hate the children. You only come home to me when there's nowhere left to go, and you change jobs the way other men change shirts. Apart from passion, what else is there?"

"So you're serious."

"I've never been more serious."

There was a moment then which hung heavy between them. She scrambled for the right words but felt as helpless as a toddler looking into the lights of an oncoming train. Nothing clever came to mind.

"I want you to leave, Sean," she said in little more than a whisper.

He stood looking at her in silence as she headed into the bedroom to grab her dressing gown. Every other time, there'd been shouting and screaming, which only took them deeper into the pit. But this morning was different. The children's cries grew louder.

"Well don't expect me to help with them," he said, pointing to the other room.

"I can't remember the last time you did," she replied. "You'd better grab some clothes on your way out," she called over her shoulder as she plodded through the bedroom door and towards the nursery.

28

One month later

The children wouldn't be asleep for much longer. Bea reviewed her situation for the umpteenth time while battling against an encroaching terror. Thoughts sparred with one another as she tested dead-end solutions and roamed around the dingy room, stopping occasionally to gaze out of the one window as if maybe there would be an answer there.

That pointless action was of course born out of habit because her bedroom window back home had looked out onto a beautiful garden full of camellias and roses. Some part of her mind just couldn't accept the reality of a window which just looked out at other windows of other boarding houses.

It went without saying that the Smithtons had their hands full keeping this place running; particularly in the middle of a war. But that didn't help the fact that the food just seemed to get worse every week and the fleas and rats gave her nightmares. She'd count herself lucky if the children didn't catch the black plague.

The money that she'd managed to save was fast running out. Her life was a shambles after living with that man. What a fool she'd been with her heady dream about being married to a prince! The fantasy had done a nosedive the moment the Miguels had shut down the Flamenco Flames to work full-time in their market garden.

Their motive was admirable enough. The men were too old to enlist, so this was a way they could contribute to the war effort. Mind you, they were a big help to the Beatrice O'Brien effort as well. She and the children would have starved without the provision of fresh fruit and vegetables week after week. Even now they were generous to her without any strings attached.

But once they'd stopped dancing, her fool of a husband hadn't known what to do with himself. He'd been quick to try for work in a munitions factory to avoid pressure to enlist for overseas duty. What a weakling! She was humiliated enough being married to a coward, but what mortified her the most was his drinking. It was her worst nightmare to find herself with a husband who came home drunk. And not just drunk; sometimes nasty and looking for a fight.

He'd tried to hit her only once, thinking he'd have the upper hand because of her size. But he'd found out what she could do with her knees and fingernails, not to mention an empty whisky bottle! Just thinking about that night was enough to churn up all the anger that still fermented in her insides because there was nowhere for it to go. She was glad she'd sent him packing!

But she still ached for the man. And that was the horrible, degrading truth which she carried deep in her heart. Maybe it was because he was her first love and there was still a dream in her heart that was a long time dying. Or maybe she was just demented. And maybe if he came knocking again, she wouldn't be able to turn him away.

Once more she walked across to the little window and craned her neck to look beyond the next-door roof to the sky above. For a few moments she gazed with longing towards the patch of blue and tried to imagine a place where someone cared. But the luxury of hope was not an option for her. There was not a loving someone out there in the great somewhere who would bring a happy ending.

Her eyes wept silently. She was as alone as alone could be with two children under three to look after. Michael was incredibly beautiful with his black curls and those blue eyes which seemed to change according to the weather like the sea. And Robert was a sweet and gentle baby who in his first twelve months of life had been nothing but a comfort and joy. Those two precious little gems were the only good things that had come out of her whole wretched life.

Bea's heart welled up with love just thinking about them. Sean had been jealous of her maternal passion. The more she'd loved her sons, the more he'd rejected them. So she'd had to love them all the more to make up for it.

And what if the love ran dry along with the money? She didn't even have the energy to be angry any more. A wave of exhaustion left her legless, and she plopped down on an old timber chair to stare blankly ahead. He'd left the previous month in such a quiet rage. She hoped he wouldn't come back. What was the point? The only things he'd brought with him each time they'd given it another try were more anger and more heartache.

One thing she'd learnt well and truly over these last years was the value of money. Her father had been as cold as a fish and as lusty as an old bull, but at least he'd worked hard all his life and brought a solid wage home each week while his children were growing up. And now the old rogue was dead and buried.

Yesterday's funeral had been a circus of greed and torment. Just thinking about it set off another wave of grief—grief for the child that had been Beatrice Cutler. She must have been so unlovable for him to have neglected her the way he did.

Thank God the family hadn't rejected her when she turned up. There'd been no shows of emotion either, but that was all right with her. All she'd wanted to do was sit with them and get lost in her own thoughts. If the Smithtons hadn't offered to look after the boys, she wouldn't have had the energy to make the effort.

What a little band of hopefuls they'd been as they all gathered together around the solicitor for the reading of the will! Much to her secret shame, and beyond all logic, she'd been hoping there'd be a little bit of something in it for her that would help put food on the table. As it turned out, there was Buckley's chance of that happening because they were all in for the surprise of their lives.

Father had been keeping a secret—one that had no doubt caused him to die way before his time. For the last few months Harold Cutler had been broken and broke, swindled by his own accountant and unable to find a way back. So the news was, "Apologies all round, but sadly your father finished his life penniless and you have all, without exception, been left nothing." How ironic considering the only thing he'd ever given them was money!

Bea would take her mother in with her and have her mind the children while she went out to work. She could see no other way forward. It was clear to anyone with half a brain that that there were no offers of help coming from anywhere else for either of them. Stanley and William both had wives, careers, and children and had long since gone on with their own lives. Cilla had fallen on her feet financially but was already struggling to manage a huge household plus a baby and a rich husband.

At the mere thought of her sister, she smiled now in spite of herself. Cilla was a picture of prissy frustration. How that girl didn't die of boredom married to Neville only the gods knew. He'd be about as sexy as a post. What she needed was either a holiday in Italy where she could dance and sing in a city square or a trip to the country that included a really good roll in the hay.

A baby's cry interrupted those thoughts, and she wearily dragged herself upright. Discouragement hovered around like a cloud, but she fought against it, focusing her thoughts instead on the two little lives in the next room.

29

North Sydney, Australia, 1925

Blimey! The din was so bad Joe couldn't hear himself think, and the smell of sweaty bodies was nearly knocking him over. The thing was, if the pub wasn't packed on a Saturday, a bloke would be in a panic.

"The Gladstone closes in an hour, folks!" he shouted. He weaved his way through the drunken maze with a tray full of beer mugs. "Hey Pete!" he bellowed over the din, "open some windas, will ya! I'm ready t' pass out here! And where's Beatrice? She's s'posed t' be playin' the bleedin' piana!"

Before Pete could answer, Rosie let rip. "She's gone t' the bleedin' toilet, Joe! Is that still allowed, or are ya savin' money on toilet paper now!"

No one else would have got away with talking to Joe Gladstone like that. But when he looked across at Rosie, it was all he could do to stop from licking his lips. There she was, hands on hips and looking him straight in the eye, a picture of lust with her blonde curls, pouty lips, and breasts he'd sell his mother to get a hold of. He started blustering to save face.

"If I get any more lip from you, I might just start restrictin' everyone t' one visit a night!" he shouted.

"Go ahead. It'll be your mutiny, not mine," Rosie shot back.

Cheeky tart! While he tried to figure out what to say, Beatrice floated in all hoity-toity, cut across to the bar, and asked for a drink of water. She was an odd number for sure. Now, Rosie, he could figure out where she was coming from; but who could work this one out?

She was friendly enough but always a bit distant, as if she were a cut above. Not that anyone else noticed, but Joe always studied people really closely. He'd learnt to do that just to survive in this game. She made that piano come to life; there was no getting away from that. And the men all seemed to like her. She never took one home, though.

She wasn't his type—too skinny. But she was popular by the looks, and that was all he cared about for the moment. But he'd have to keep a close eye on her. He just couldn't trust a woman who never drank.

*   *   *

"Thanks for covering for me Rosie," said Bea as she seated herself at the piano. "I needed that break to keep from screaming in the middle of a number."

"No worries, luv. But be careful; he's watchin' you like a hawk."

"He's watching you too, girl, but for a different reason. And that's a situation that can turn really nasty."

"Yeah, he's hopin' t' get me in the sack. But fair dinkum I'd rather join a nunnery! Anyway, me boyfriend works at the Tivoli and 'e's got me a job in the chorus startin' in a fortnight. So even if I keep the old lecher at bay for another week, I'll be okay. It's different with you, luv; you've got those kids t' think of. So be careful."

"Thanks for the tip, Rosie. You've been a really good friend, and I'll miss you."

Rosie smiled and touched her on the arm before moving off, and Bea felt tears welling up inside her. She always came undone when someone was kind. Taking a deep breath, she began to play "Roll out the Barrel," turning on the charm and smiling at anyone who was looking her way.

But her stomach was in a knot because apparently Joe didn't trust non-drinkers and didn't seem to like her being so different to the other girls. He probably imagined that she was plotting to rob him blind. Piano jobs were as rare as hen's teeth, and she needed this job desperately. Maybe a change of tack would be a good idea.

As she continued to play, her mind approached the situation from every angle, and by the time she struck the last chords, she had made a decision. When Pete walked past, she called him over and asked him to bring her a whisky. He looked surprised, but Pete's philosophy on life was to never make waves, so he didn't say anything.

Seconds later she took the whisky that was offered and gulped down the first disgusting mouthful. That's when she noticed over the top of the glass that there was a man standing alone and watching her intently.

He was dark-haired and chiselled and sat alone, leaning back in a chair with one leg angled casually across the other. *Absolutely gorgeous. Probably married.* Bea downed the rest of the whisky and took a few seconds to catch her breath. Then she asked for a second one and went back to playing.

30

A semi in North Sydney

Michael checked the two oil lamps in the kitchen to make sure they were topped up and wouldn't go out. He hated the dark. Ebony padded in from the hallway and slid her teeth, head, and then body across his leg, leaving black fur on his trousers. Then she turned and slithered past in the opposite direction.

He picked her up and carried her over to the saucer of bread and milk that he'd set up in the corner of the kitchen and watched for a moment as she settled in to lap up the treat. He loved that cat; so black and shiny. It felt good when she snuggled on his lap or plopped onto the bed at night and pressed her paws one at a time into his back, purring loudly enough to wake everyone up. It would be really lonely without Ebony.

Robert was getting impatient. "Come on, Michael! You're taking ages!"

"Yes, I'm coming!" snapped Michael. He stepped back across to the kitchen table, where they were halfway through a game of draughts. They didn't really know how to play draughts, but there was no one to teach them, so he'd made up some rules. He picked up one of his draught pieces and jumped over about six of Robert's. That was the last straw for his kid brother.

"It's not fair! You always win 'cos you're ten years old! And anyway, this is a stupid game and I don't want to play any more!"

"Suit yourself, crybaby. I didn't want to play anyway!"

Just then a voice came from the sitting room. "Is that you, Uncle Henry? Uncle Henry, is that you? We're waiting for confirmation, Uncle Henry. Is that you?"

Robert jumped up and ran to the kitchen door. "No, Grandma; it's me, Robert!" he called out.

From the sitting room came loud guffaws of laughter, and Robert turned away with a puzzled look on his face and his bottom lip trembling. Michael hated it when Grandma was working. Mummy said she was doing things called seances, but all he knew was that it always felt strange and she always had people coming to the house whom they didn't know.

"Grandma's working, Bobby," he said. "Let's see if we can find something to eat."

The two of them rummaged around in the cupboard and found some stale bread, dripping, and a couple of slices of devon. Michael shared the findings with Robert and they sat down together to eat. For a few minutes they nibbled away in silence.

"I'm tired," said Robert, eventually rubbing his eyes.

"So am I. Let's go to bed. We can have a wash tomorrow when Mummy's home."

It was scary walking up the stairs at night. There were ghosts everywhere, and Mummy wouldn't be home for hours. They stayed close to one another as they climbed, checking behind them with each new step. Michael had to hide his fear so that Robert wouldn't panic, because if Robert panicked that'd be the end of it.

When they reached the top floor Michael thought he was going to die on the spot. There it was again, that cold something that always made him freeze up with fright. He stood, too terrified to move, as it wrapped around him and then began to push him towards the staircase. He was going to fall and couldn't even scream. For some reason he just didn't seem to have any strength at all, and everything in him felt like rolling over the bannister.

Then an amazing thing happened. Someone tapped him on the shoulder, and a voice came from behind saying, "Run, Michael, run!" He got such a shock that he jumped back from the stairs. The cloud lifted, and without thinking, he started to run.

He darted over to where he knew the matches were on the landing table, grabbed one, struck it on the flint, and lit the lamp. His hands were shaking like jelly, but he kept moving, lighting lamps in every bedroom until there was light everywhere. Then he set about checking all over until he was sure there was nothing there except Robert and himself.

That was when the shakes started over his whole body until he felt he was going to vomit. His mind went in circles trying to figure out what had just happened. He reckoned that this sort of thing didn't happen to other boys.

"Michael, I'm scared and I'm cold." Robert's voice, coming from behind, seemed miles away, but it got him moving again.

"It's all right, Robert" he replied. "You're just tired." He hurried across to the dresser and found his and Robert's nightshirts. There were voices downstairs, so he knew the door to the sitting room had opened and Grandma was taking the strangers to the front door.

The two of them stood still, listening while Grandma said her goodbyes. When the last one left, she walked back through the flat and out the back door to where the toilet was. Still keeping an ear open, Michael changed into his nightshirt and climbed into bed. Robert did the same, and they both lay still, waiting for sounds of her return.

A few minutes later, the back door opened and shut and they could hear her begin to potter around in the kitchen. Michael could tell by the noises that she was getting a warm drink of milk for herself before coming up to bed. His chest was all tight. *What if that thing on the landing comes into the bedroom before Grandma comes upstairs?*

Leaning over, he reached out and felt for the shoebox of treasures he kept under the bed. For one horrible moment he thought it wasn't there, but then his hand closed over it and he pulled it out into the open. Rummaging through the precious things, he finally found it—the little gold crucifix that the brothers at school had given him. They'd told Michael about his guardian angel and about God, who loved him and would keep him safe.

Now he sat gazing at the figure on the crucifix and tried to remember the long prayers that the brothers had taught him to say. *How do they go, now? "Hail Mary, mother of God," then something about a womb and someone called Jesus. Why did they make it so hard? And what is a womb?*

The only thing he was sure of was that the top boss was God, and God's name was Jesus, so he clung to the crucifix and whispered, "Help us, Jesus; please help us. I know you love children and keep them safe. We don't have a Daddy; we only have you, so please look after us." He continued to say the name of Jesus over and over until the pounding in his heart slowed down.

It wasn't long before Grandma's footsteps could be heard coming up the stairs. Michael loved his Grandma even though she was a bit strange, and he knew that she loved him. She came into their room and smiled at them.

"I take it you boys managed to find something to eat" she said. "I'm sorry the meeting went so long tonight. Sometimes that just happens and I can't do anything about it."

"That's all right, Grandma," said Michael, who was just relieved that she was with them upstairs. She shuffled into her room next door, and he started to relax. That was when he realised how tired he was. He snuggled down under the blankets with the crucifix still in his hand and began to drift off to sleep to the sound of Grandma opening and shutting drawers next door.

* * *

Eleanor finally found her nightie and placed it on the pillow feeling absolutely exhausted. In the next room, Michael was already breathing heavily. What a beautiful child he was! She'd never loved anyone in her life until him, and it had been just when things had seemed blackest that she'd found herself living here.

But she worried about him all the time. Life was so baffling, and she seemed to be confused more often than not. What would happen to him when she was gone? Beatrice had never managed to find herself another man, and the future was looking bleak, to say the least.

* * *

Bea leant on the door frame and signalled to the stranger called William to be quiet. Her eyes drank him in as he strolled into the sitting room and stood, hands in pockets, looking lazily around. *Absolutely gorgeous. And absolutely married.* She folded her arms and did a private grimace. Someone else owned him, and she just got to borrow him for the night.

What a difference a couple of whiskies made! She'd been living like a nun up till today, and in the blink of an eye tonight she threw off the black robes and got herself into a no-turning-back situation, still that lost teenager in the shocking red dress after several glasses of punch. She took a couple of very carefully thought out steps away from the door frame. *Oh God I'm tipsy!* This was dangerous territory for her.

"How long can you stay William?" she asked, trying to look him straight in the eye.

"I'm yours for two more hours, Madame," he replied, standing to attention and saluting.

"Well, before the power goes to my head, would you like a cup of tea?" she laughed back. *Keep it light, Beatrice.* "That's all we have other than water and milk. Not many wild parties in this part of town, I'm afraid!"

*   *   *

William smiled and took a couple of seconds to study the woman before him. Her attempts to focus on his face had made those enormous brown eyes slightly crossed, and her hair had fallen out of all of its pins, leaving a mass of black curls. She was obviously not used to being drunk and spoke like someone from the upper classes. Yet here she was, living in a tinpot semi and working in a pub. She came across as an odd mix of strength and despair. He just couldn't figure her out.

"Well in that case I choose warm milk," he said, stepping towards her. "And I think that you should sit for a minute while I get it." With one movement he picked her up and walked across to the lounge with her leaning against him, as light as a kitten. He placed her on the soft cushions, and she smiled into his eyes.

Oh brother! What had started off as a one-night stand was turning into something dangerous already. He'd always told himself that the fleeting liaisons he had through the years made it possible to stay with Winifred and the children. But the women he usually picked up in pubs were interesting only for one or two nights.

This one had the potential to be very interesting for a long time and could even threaten the fragile thread which still held together his marriage. Was he ready to cope with that scenario?

"Maybe we don't have time to heat up milk," she whispered dreamily, her eyes now luminescent pools.

William's mind turned to mush. "I think maybe you're right," he replied, sinking down onto his knees beside her.

*   *   *

Eleanor stood in the bedroom in a haze of confusion, trying to remember what she'd been in the middle of doing. She groaned quietly, willing her mind to clear, and finally recalled that she'd been getting ready for bed. No one understood how hard it was nowadays. Her guides were becoming more demanding and giving more and more directions. There'd been so many different instructions going through her head lately that there could be a brain haemorrhage round the corner.

Breathing heavily from the effort, she fumbled her way out of her clothes and struggled into her nightie. That was enough to tire her out completely but didn't guarantee a good night's sleep. Honestly, she'd sell her right leg if it meant not having to do the seances any more, but running them was the only way she could help with the finances and babysit at the same time.

She groaned quietly now as more messages began to come through. It used to be only Tetrak saying what to do, but now there seemed to be fifty different voices nagging continually. It was driving her mad. They had quietened for a short time there but now were back again, coming at her from every direction. The only way she got any peace at all was by obeying, but what were they saying now?

There were various orders, all of them conflicting, and Eleanor's confusion increased. She held both hands to her ears and rocked back and forth, begging the voices to stop. Her thoughts chaotic, she wandered out onto the landing, lunging around in the dark.

*　　*　　*

Michael sat upright, heart beating and tummy feeling bad. Someone had tapped him on the shoulder again, no doubt about it, but he couldn't see anyone in the moonlight which streamed through the window. Terrified, he scrambled under the blankets and curled up in a ball, but the tapping happened again. He leapt out of bed and ran to wake Grandma but took in a big gasp of air at the sight of her empty bed.

"Grandma!" he called as he ran out into the hall. "Grandma, where are you?" That's when the icy presence closed in again, and he was scared to the point of nearly blacking out. He stood stock-still with fright and then heard the sound of someone moving over to the side. When he turned and peered into the shadows at the side, there was Grandma, talking to herself and opening the top-floor window, which was directly over the street.

He stared in horror as she lifted a foot up onto the sill. *This must be a nightmare; one of those ones when you can't move!* He thought maybe he wouldn't be able to make any sound either. But a kid had to have a go! Michael put everything he had into screaming, but only a whisper squeezed out.

Perspiration was running down his face; this couldn't really be happening! He thought maybe praying would work again. "Please help us, Jesus," he squeaked. "Help me to help

Grandma." The paralysing fear started to lift then, so he opened his mouth, took a big breath, and screamed his heart out.

*   *   *

Bea leapt to her feet without thinking so that William rolled backwards and crashed down onto the floor. She stumbled towards the stairs, motivated by guilt as much as fear, trying to make her pickled brain function. If anything happened to one of those boys while she was carousing down below, she'd never be able to live with herself!

She took the stairs three at a time and first saw Michael, who stood like a statue on the landing, his eyes like saucepan lids. He was pointing to the window. Then she caught sight of her crazed mother, who was standing on the windowsill! She covered the few yards in a second, grabbed her mother by the nightie, and yanked her off onto the floor.

"What on earth are you doing, Beatrice?" demanded Eleanor as she rubbed her head and looked at her daughter indignantly.

"More to the point, Mum, what were you doing on the windowsill in the middle of the night?" shouted Bea. She was angry, frustrated, and relieved all at the same time and needed to let it all out somehow.

"They had a mission for me," wailed Eleanor. "They wouldn't let me go to sleep until I completed it!"

"Oh for God's sake, Mum! There is no 'they'!" Bea was roaring like a trapped lioness now. "There is just you—a silly old woman going balmy! Why can't you sleep at night like other people?"

"Because I'm not like other people, that's why! I'm special!" retorted Eleanor as she slowly climbed up onto her feet by grabbing the old dresser in the hall. "No one's ever appreciated me; not my husband, not my children. My own parents abandoned me." The mumbling continued as she gingerly felt her way back along the wall towards the bedroom.

"Well, tell 'them' that you're not doing any more bloody missions tonight!" yelled Bea to Eleanor's back.

"Mummy, why are you wearing your petticoat?" asked Michael.

His question jolted Bea out of her tirade. "I was changing into my nightie, honey," she said, hugging him tightly. "You're cold, sweetie. Get back into bed, and I'll come in soon."

"You promise, Mummy?" His voice was tiny, his eyes beginning to fill with tears.

Bea willed her mouth to turn up in a smile. "Yes, honey," she told him. "I promise to come soon." He looked at her with need in his eyes, but all she had left in her right now was a smile, so she stayed in position until he turned with head bowed and walked back to his bedroom.

Okay, now was crunch time. She wondered how much William had heard and what difference it had made. Bea held on to the bannister as if her life depended on it and began to tentatively walk down the stairs. With each step she regained her composure, and with effort she painted a smile back on her face.

Her mind searched for a witticism that would be appropriate for the admittedly insane episode that had just transpired. "Honestly, the break-ins around here are getting ridiculous!" *No.* "Would you believe my son and mother both had a nightmare at the same time?" *Worse.* Finally both feet touched down on floor level. Bea had such a mother of a nervous attack that it was hard work just to go back into the sitting room.

And there'd been no need to worry. The place was empty. "Well, what do you know?" she said to the couch. "Absolutely nobody here!" Then she stood, hands on hips, and looked heavenward. "Oh, would you look at that," she said, her voice as flat as the old rug on the floor. "Nobody up there either." Her words travelled as far as the ceiling, then crashed to the floor.

Suddenly nausea rose up in her stomach, causing her to bolt for the door and into the yard just before breakfast, lunch, and dinner came up in a foul wave. She stayed out there, holding on to the orange tree for comfort until the dry-retching stage was over. Feeling beyond vile, she returned to the kitchen to rinse out her mouth.

The idea had been to get drunk and loosen up so as to fit in better at the pub. Who'd have thought that you could be a failure as a lady, a tart, and a mother all in one night? This was not the result she'd been hoping for.

Worn out beyond belief, she gathered up her clothing, doused the lamp, and began the return journey to the top floor. A quick peek into the boys' room showed her they were now both asleep. *Thank the gods!*

"Oh well, back to living like a nun," she grumbled to herself before crossing the landing and aiming, fully clothed, for her bed.

*   *   *

Michael had called out to the Lord from the depth of his heart. Nimrad just couldn't stop grinning. He looked the generational demons in the eye and waited for the fallout to die down from the collective kick in the teeth they'd all just had. They hissed, stomped their feet, rolled on the ground, ran around in circles, and screamed. What a pathetic display. And it didn't change a thing.

A monkey could have figured out that Beatrice was racked with guilt when she decided to send the boy to a Catholic school this year. And Tetrak didn't give it a second thought, knowing that the head priest was steeped in religion and had no revelation of grace.

But Nimrad had pounced on his chance like a pro, even if he did say so himself. He'd managed to find one solitary brother who'd experienced the Father's love. Hallelujah, what cliff-edge stuff it was to go undercover into that den of judgement! There he was posing as a relative and asking the brother to spend special time with Michael while demons were circling him, trying to figure it out.

He'd only had a few minutes before his cover would be blown. Then he'd had to get out fast and just wait and trust that the brother's kind heart would win through. And tonight his efforts had borne fruit. For the first time in centuries, an angel of light had access here.

He was not afraid, having been anointed and prepared for such a time as this. He would always remember that day of destiny when the Lord had chosen him to guard Michael. The Birthing Room had been super busy at the time, but amidst the noise and excitement, the Master had looked him in the eye.

Oh, the wonder and glory of it! Even now he vibrated with ecstasy at the memory. The Lord had spoken volumes with his wonderful eyes, and Nimrad had understood that Michael carried within his character the seeds of victory. Fresh courage had pulsed into Nimrad's heart that day.

The road ahead for Michael looked fraught with difficulties now. Satan would be in a grandfather of a rage; of that there was no doubt. But for ten years Nimrad had been watching and waiting for a door to open. Now that the chance had come, he would not be found lacking!

*   *   *

Tetrak was shaking from head to foot, but there was so much generalised terror that no one was noticing. The atmosphere was crackling and swirling after that father of a malfunction. Death and Destruction were whimpering and screeching and already turning on each other. He tried to clear his head, knowing that Satan would be frothing at the mouth over this.

The gift had skipped a generation. How had they missed that? They'd got too sure of themselves; that was it.

He already had a migraine from being near the angel of light, and he felt about as threatening as a canary. The others were losing the plot big time, and there'd be full-scale panic soon.

"All right, you idiots!" he bellowed. "What is your problem?" He figured that if he yelled loud enough he might convince them and himself that he still had a hold on something here.

"But Tetrak … the angel of light … an open door … the Lord …" babbled Death and Destruction. "The Master will punish us! We'll be tortured! We'll be …"

"That's enough!" shouted Tetrak. "Shut up and get a fricking grip! Outside, all of you! Move!" They didn't have to be told twice and set off scurrying and falling over one another to beat Tetrak to the roof.

"Well, what were we supposed to do?" whined Murder. He was covered in scales and slime and stared at Tetrak through bulging blood-red eyes. "I thought we had authority here … Master," he hissed, pouring contempt on the word "Master."

Tetrak was stumped by that shot. For centuries the Cutler family had been controlled by Satan. At least that's what he'd been told. Or was he just a patsy that had been set up to fail? No, Satan couldn't risk playing around with something like this. And failure was not an option.

"Yes, we have authority here," he replied, staring back and injecting as much venom as possible through his eyes. Murder began to noticeably shrink. "But what we don't seem to have is demons who actually know what they're doing! Now all of you get out of my sight; I can't stand to look at you!"

Luckily His bluff worked. With much hissing, screaming, whining, and snarling, the demons searched every which way for dark corners to cringe in. Tetrak was left alone on the roof, holding on to his last shreds of composure while inwardly boiling.

The plan had been to kill Eleanor tonight so that Bea and her sons would be totally alone and unsupported. There was endless potential in that scenario for him to shine. He'd envisaged brilliant blows of discouragement which would break Beatrice and leave the sons unprotected.

So how had he finished up in the soup with an angel of light on the landing and Beatrice, Eleanor, and the kids all tucked up in bed asleep? Wouldn't his peers have a heyday with that one if word got out?

*   *   *

Nimrad waited until the last demon had left. When all was quiet, he entered the boys' bedroom to ensure their well-being. Michael was sleeping peacefully for the first time in an age, and even poor, tormented Eleanor would rest uninterrupted tonight. It took a child to see through all the rubbish and go straight for the truth.

*   *   *

Bea woke out of her stupor at 3.00 a.m. feeling sick fit to die. She leapt out of bed, made a dash for the window, and dry heaved for a couple of minutes, as there was nothing left in her stomach to bring up. She knew this was more than the alcohol. She hadn't had a period for weeks, ever since she let that no-good ex-husband break down her defences once again.

She just couldn't have another child, and that was all there was to it. Two was already too many! The sooner she dealt with it, the better; and tomorrow was her day off, so it was now or never. But somehow the line of reasoning didn't comfort her as well as it had in the past, and her throat tightened with emotion at the thought. *How can I go through with it again?*

*   *   *

Murder had already seen Bea heaving at the window and left his dark corner to slip into her bedroom. There she was, pathetic creature, arguing with herself and trying to "do the right thing." She would be easily swayed. He circled the bed several times, leaving a film of despair and discouragement all over her.

"It will be all over by morning," he whispered in her ear. "You'll have a short time of pain instead of months of discomfort, hours of agony, and a lifetime of misery."

Now she was crying. This was harder than the other times. She hadn't given it any thought before. He assumed she must be on some sort of temporary guilt trip, or else maybe he was losing his touch. Nothing would surprise him the way things had been going tonight. He stepped up the ante.

"You're such a hopeless mother already," he spat out. "How do you think you'd have a hope in hell of raising another one? And how long do you think you'd last at the Gladstone once they knew you were pregnant? You're nothing to write home about and easily replaced!"

*　　*　　*

Nimrad watched in agony. She had no idea how much she was loved, and the Lord had told him that the new soul in her womb was a girl who carried a blessing of friendship and comfort. He didn't have authority with her and could get himself into big trouble. But he had to do something.

"You're beautiful, Bea! And the Lord loves you more than you know!" he called from the doorway of the bedroom. "Stop and consider! Stop and consider!"

*　　*　　*

Murder was furious at the intrusion. He directed his blood-red lethal gaze at Nimrad and attacked, knowing full well that he had dominance with Beatrice. He sliced at the useless weakling with his claws and beat him to a pulp with his powerful feet. With a shout of frustration and contempt, he kicked the intruder out before turning his attention once again to Beatrice.

"You're a fool if you believe that!" he screamed. "No one has ever loved you, and once your children grow up, they will leave also! Get the knitting needle and pour the bath now while it's dark. Then you can rest on your day off. What alternatives does a woman like you have, anyway?"

*　　*　　*

Bea rose from the bed with a heavy heart. Why was a woman like her even giving this any thought? There was no choice for her. She was still alone, just as she'd always been. There was nothing for it but to go through the nightmare of aborting another baby.

She'd been a fool to let Sean back into her life after all these years, believing that he'd changed. Never again would she let him near her or the boys. Tears began to flow again as she squared her shoulders to prepare for what was ahead. Once more she would violate herself, and once more her bathtub would become a place of death.

Part Five

31

I cannot understand you Australians. In Poland, France and Belgium, once tanks got
through, soldiers took it for granted that they were beaten. But you are like demons.
Tanks break through and your infantry still keep fighting.
—A German prisoner of war during World War II

The Port of Tobruk, Egypt, 1941

Nimrad had an emotional moment at the sight of Michael in hard hat and khakis amidst sandy
rubble with his rifle propped at the ready. He was scribbling away in that ragged notebook with
a zeal that'd give Moses chiselling out the Ten Commandments a run for his money.

Other soldiers in the trench unwound by ribbing each other Aussie style and drawing
cigarette smoke into lungs already clogged with sand and dust. Their light banter even drew
a smile from Nimrad occasionally (when all was quiet at his post, that is). Aussies were good
together; gave each other truckloads of grace.

As usual they turned a blind eye to what they called "Mike's weirdo bouts." Well, "weirdo
bouts" was one way of saying it. "Obsessive angst-driven behaviour" was closer to the mark.
But in spite of the quirkiness, Michael was popular with his mates; he always pulled his weight
and had a quick wit that kept them laughing through black times.

He'd figured out his own version of normal. The circus he'd grown up in would send most
off into some twilight zone, but who could predict the human spirit? This one was a fighter.
No one knew he could see things others couldn't. He kept that fact to himself and accepted it
as just another piece in the jigsaw of his crazy life.

But what was that foul, nauseating smell that had started to drift up from behind? Nimrad
turned and saw Rejection, Murder, and Anxiety hovering and ready to pounce on Michael

at the first sign of weakness. He ignited with anger and sent a flash of righteous indignation hurtling towards them.

"Are you misguided or just sadly retarded demons? I vow you are doomed to disappointment if you are waiting for me to slacken my guard!"

"We are neither misguided nor retarded, angel; just joyfully expectant of victory in the knowledge that both Michael and his guardian are irrevocably flawed!"

What impudence! The ignorant clods didn't know who they were dealing with. The Lord had told him to guard Michael, and guard him he would! "How dare you insult a servant of the Most High!" he roared. He flew straight for them, a crackling, vibrating field of electricity flashing a sword that emitted shrieks of warning.

It took mere seconds for their bluster to evaporate. Anxiety was the first to crumble. "Crap! We're dealing with a maniac!" he screamed. "I'm gone!" Murder would have stayed on if Rejection hadn't turned inside out as he screeched to a halt, turned, and made for the hills yelling, "You are sooo right! And I am sooo out of here!"

One-to-one didn't suit Murder at all. With a shake of his fist and a hissed "This isn't over till it's over, angel," he scrambled to safety without as much as a backward glance.

"This isn't over till it's over?" What sort of a threat is that? Seriously, the pathetic rubbish I have to deal with! Nimrad was left to sizzle and fizz alone while he cooled back down. Once his anger had dissipated, he began to feel a little flat. He decided to try visualising some possible upshots that could be in the pipeline for him down the track as Michael's guardian.

Unhappily, thoughts of psychiatric hospitals, gaols, and emergency wards came immediately to mind, so he decided to steer away from that particular realm of thought. He knew that above all he must stay focused and vigilant.

Choosing to be positive, he breathed a heartfelt thank you for the assistance he'd had from battle-hardened warriors who still fought with courage after centuries of bloodshed. The splendid and enormous Zimron had recently arrived at Tobruk and often gave specialised attention to Michael so Nimrad had times of relief from the heavy load.

It wasn't rocket science to figure out that Michael was close to a nervous breakdown. His whole life had been a battle to survive, and now here he was, as nervous as a cat in a snake pit, trying to cope daily with the relentless push of the Germans. His courage was great, but he was still a time bomb set to go off. And Nimrad would be ready when it did.

*   *   *

How was a bloke supposed to get his mind together in this heat? Michael was jack of everything to do with the desert. You name it and he was sick of it. He determined that if he ever got out of this alive, he was going to live somewhere green and eat steak every night.

Everything he'd written was swimming before his eyes. Not positive. Even worse, his mates' voices were morphing into a foggy buzz. He probably needed to stop and take stock. But that was easier said than done, because the writing had helped to keep him going. Also, he wanted to record events as they happened, fresh from the oven.

If it was the last bloody thing he did, the book would get finished. One day there'd be a bestseller on the world's bookshelves giving minute-by-minute details of the horror story he and his mates were living through right now.

The title had come to him in a flash of brilliance: *An Aussie Battler at War*. Perfect! The contribution of the Aussies and the gut-wrenching loss of so many mates wouldn't go unheralded. He'd make sure it was filled with human interest pieces, funny quips, and examples of inspiring heroism.

The way he saw it, just the fact that he'd been able to keep going with it for the last two years while dealing with everything from smoker's cough to rampant diarrhoea was a miracle to write home about. Once again he tried to write, but his ideas were all over the shop.

Mum's face flashed into his mind followed by a familiar pain in his chest. She was like a lone exotic bird caught in a cage full of chickens and turkeys. It was a good thing she'd taken the time to teach him the piano. Not that he could ever hold a shine to her, but he wasn't bad.

The O'Brien School of Music; he could remember it like it was yesterday. They'd been good with the smoke and mirrors, the two of them keeping up the illusion of a large, flourishing music school. What he wouldn't give to hear her play now.

Then he thought of Robert and a knot caught in his gut, pulling at the silent panic he seemed to be feeling more often lately. That kid had always been too soft; made a bloke want to protect and somehow rescue him. But he couldn't make Robert be strong, couldn't make him fight. Caring wasn't enough.

In the back of his mind behind the memories grew the awareness of a droning sound that turned his blood to ice. Scared to look but knowing there was no choice, he turned in time to make out a surprise air raid that was closing in fast.

Mechanically he checked the position of the planes to see which way they were heading and could tell that a straddle of bombs was going to come mighty close to him. His stomach lurched, but survival clicked in and he took off.

This was definitely a "crucifix moment," so he plunged his hand into a pocket and closed it around the beloved trinket. Living with death had sure kept him sharp. He sent up a lightning-quick prayer and connected into the realm of light as he'd learnt to do decades ago. A gut instinct told him to run south when most were running west. Without taking time to think, he ran south.

The droning came closer and he ran on, fuelled by pure adrenalin and close to throwing up. Then, from out of the blue, what looked like one of the local Arabs appeared up ahead, waving to catch his attention. He waved back, and the bloke took off running. Michael squinted into the sand and sun and saw that the man was aiming for a large rock up ahead. He couldn't remember ever seeing it before, but he was low on choices so raced towards it with the fleet-footedness of the desperate.

The Arab disappeared behind the rock, and Michael followed. As he got closer he could see that it wasn't a mirage. Not only that, but there was a large hole which had been dug out underneath. Without a thought he hit the sand, rolled into the hole, and curled up into the foetal position, saying the name "Jesus" over and over.

A two-year-old would think this was bizarre behaviour, but it had worked when he was a kid; and anyway, when men were looking death in the face, there weren't many true atheists. Speaking of which, where was the man who should be with him in this hole, looking said death in the face?

The only thing he could see here was a terrified lizard. No time to think about that, because the straddle came closer, and as usual his heart pounded like a kettledrum. It was probably showing up on their bloody radar! Suddenly, without warning, he began to shake uncontrollably.

This was not positive; negative all the way. His vision became blurred and his thoughts began to tumble around, making him feel giddy. He wondered if he was dying, especially when pictures from his past life began flashing and twirling before his eyes. *Great work, Michael—playing the last post in a hole on the backside of the desert next to a lizard!*

There was his mother, laughing and saying, "You're indomitable, Michael. A brick wall wouldn't have a chance if it was in your way!" He remembered working at the local newspaper after school for extra money. At fourteen the world of journalism seemed like a pulsating, exciting fantasy land where all the people were rainbow coloured and larger than life. The deadlines and constant stress had made adrenalin pump through his veins like a drug.

Familiar faces and voices continued to fade in and out of consciousness. *Robert!* What would he do about Robert? Then there was the rotten depression and the newspaper closing down just when he was starting to do a couple of articles. After that he'd had to live on his wits in a thousand ways to survive.

Survive—he had to survive! The pictures began to grow dark, and as always his heart rose up against the forces which threatened to destroy everything he held dear. "I'm going to win!" he screamed at the fates. "I will win!" he roared as the mist closed around him and he was engulfed finally in total blackness.

32

Singleton, Australia, September 1942

Allen glanced up through his eyebrows to check Kate's progress. That letter needed to be done before lunch, and if it wasn't, he was damned if he knew what to do next. As he searched his brain to figure out possible damage control, the tapping finally stopped and he heard instead the heavenly sound of paper being wound from the typewriter.

He sent up a lightning eyes-closed thank you to whoever might be listening. He hoped she'd got it right this time, because what with the original and three copies plus three carbons, it seemed to take her forever to make any changes.

"Here's your letter, Allen," she said as she breezed into his office. "Would you mind checking now to see if it's right? I wanted to get down to the records office today in my lunch hour."

Obediently he began to read through the letter, mentally shaking his head in bewilderment. He was known throughout town as Allen Smithton of Wellesley, Smithton, and Cribbing Solicitors. But for some reason he didn't mind Kate Millet calling him Allen and telling him what to do.

Maybe it was because when she bounded in each morning with her red curls bouncing around and her face fresh and alive, she brought the sunshine with her. And maybe it was because he found himself chuckling all day at her various antics.

The idea of a girl who rounded up cattle and went to dance classes as well really played havoc with his mind. It was that combination of a farm-raised father and a city-bred mother that did it; rustic earthiness wrapped in catwalk glamour.

"Yes, that's perfect, Kate," he said presently. "Now why would you want to go to the records office, I wonder?"

"Oh a couple of projects in the pipeline, Allen. Nothing you need to worry about." Her head was tilted; one hand was on her hip. She was all instinct and no experience.

"Well, please report back when your mission is completed, Agent X. I'll be here keeping the home fires burning and straining under the tedium of it. Not everyone gets to spend their time living with danger!"

She threw her head back and laughed. "I'll keep that in mind, Commander," she replied with a salute.

*   *   *

After grabbing her bag, Kate ran outside and jumped onto her bike, mindless of stockings, high heels, and her new tweed dress. A minute later she was riding down the main street of Singleton and heading towards the outskirts of town, waving right and left to folks she'd known for a lifetime.

Shops gave way to houses and then open fields with their backdrop of gently sloping hills. She took a deep breath and let it out in a long sigh, content to be out in the wide open spaces. The railway bridge came into view now, which was good news because she was definitely beginning to work up a sweat.

Waving at a couple of soldiers driving the other way into town, she crossed the bridge. A smile broke out at the memory of Allen's comments. He knew very well that her father was working throughout the war in records and could look up the name of any soldier for private information.

She had no qualms about it. It was fine having an army base on the edge of town with soldiers coming through by the hundred, but they'd tell you anything! They were just passing through and living for the moment, and a couple of broken hearts here and there meant nothing to them.

Well, she might be just a country girl, but she was no pushover. No matter if a soldier was as handsome as sin, she'd make sure he wasn't married or towing a couple of kids before she got involved. She turned left after the bridge and headed towards the barracks.

Now what is it I still need to do today? There was that pile of paperwork to finish at work and the finishing touches for my dance costume. Then there was ... then there was ... Oh, dammit!

She'd forgotten to pick up Mum's dress. Guilt slithered around her intestines, igniting a flare-up of anger. Her mouth formed a straight, tight line where before there'd been an upward curve. Then it began to curve slowly but surely down.

Now she was going to have to rush like a frightened chook through the "to do" list at work in order to pick up the damn dress in time. Then she'd have to scream through the marathon ride home so there'd be time to milk the cows before setting Mum's hair ready for her precious garden party tomorrow.

Then, if she was lucky, she'd be sitting up half the night sewing her own outfit. Her mother had never wanted her to dance and didn't give a scrap about the solo tomorrow night. She was just in a snit because lately Kate had been paying her less attention than normal. The tantrum this morning had been ridiculous. Her mother was a child.

She'd tried to please her all through the years, but there was no amount of love that could make Mum happy. There was a whole world full of people who'd be happy to receive all the love that Kate had in her heart to give. She had decided that as soon as she was old enough, she'd get as far away as possible.

But then what would happen to Dad? He was so alone in the world. How would he be without her looking out for him? And what about Granda, who'd secretly given her money for lessons out of his allowance and taken over tasks that were too hard for her? He knew that she didn't have the build for heavy farm work!

Up ahead an old, fat blue heeler was running up to greet her, snarling and yelping with gusto as if he were a German shepherd cornering a rabbit. She skirted around him with the skill of someone who'd spent half her life on a bike and called out, "Go boy!" as she aimed for the army gates, which were now just ahead.

At the prospect of seeing Dad, she began to smile and the cloud lifted a little. She had a couple of very interesting prospects for him to check out. So many men and so little time! She waved and grinned at the sentry on duty, pedalled through the gates, and then made a right turn at the first hut. As a final dramatic gesture, she did a half turn outside the records office and skidded to a halt.

* * *

Tom heard a kerfuffle outside and looked up just as Kate came careering up to Records at a hundred miles an hour. She sent up a cloud of dust, leapt off her bike, and came bouncing in. His heart near burst with pride.

"Hello everyone; how are you all?" she said as she breezed through. "Hi, Dad! Had a good morning?"

Tom broke out smiling from ear to ear. His Kate was a bobby dazzler! She'd worked hard all her life; been a good help to him even though she was such a slight little wisp. Had always ridden into town on a bike to school and done her homework by oil lamp late at night after chores. Still managed to get A grades and turned into a beautiful ballerina, by jingo!

She was standing in front of him grinning, and then it dawned on him that she was waiting for an answer. For a few seconds he couldn't remember for the life of him what she'd asked. Then it came back to mind. "Can't complain, Kate. But I thought you was gonna run straight into the front winder just then! So what's on the books for you today?"

*   *   *

Kate was flushed and exhilarated after the ride and was free to be herself with Dad and his friends. With a laugh she stepped up onto a chair. "First, what do you think of my new dress?" she said, twirling around to show him the creation she'd finished making two nights ago.

Dad didn't have a clue about fashion, but she wanted to show it off anyway. "See Dad, this lilac tweed material is the latest craze, and the dress is cut on the bias, brilliantly tucked in at the waist with a belt, and finished at the neck with a Peter Pan collar!"

"Well, all I know is it looks great."

"Great observation!" she laughed as she jumped lightly onto the floor. Thoughts of Mum's outfit threatened to intrude, but she pushed them determinedly to the back of her mind. She stood to attention and clicked her heels together. "Now, Captain, down to business!"

"Okay, shoot," said her father, opening up the latest book. "What were the names of those codgers you wanted me to check on again?"

She threw her arms in the air. "Dad, you've got the memory of a sieve!"

"Rubbish! Come on, tell me again."

33

Singleton, Australia, October 1942

Well, Michael's life had never been boring; he supposed that was a positive. But then the list of negatives was getting longer every year. Growing up without a father had been pretty negative. Surviving the worst depression since the Stone Age and then three years of war against a madman had been right up there on the negative scale. But he reckoned that landing a six-month hospital stint in Sydney with his nerves shot to pieces had pretty much been the icing on the negative cake.

And what conclusion had all the whang-bang city doctors come to at the end of the six months? "Michael O'Brien has experienced a nervous breakdown and experiences an ongoing anxiety state." You didn't have to be a genius to figure that one out. He hadn't known his own name for a month. Even now he still had trouble stopping his hands from shaking.

These last five months at Singleton military camp had been easier to cope with. At least he'd been amongst other soldiers who understood things that couldn't be put into words. He strolled down the corridor of the rehab hut, willing himself to look relaxed when inside he was a bloody mess. They'd okayed him for transfer to the main barracks tomorrow, and he didn't want them changing their minds.

He was completely on his Pat Malone now; that was the bottom line. No point dreaming; it was up to him to cope and somehow get a life for himself. And the first step was to get out of this place before he went mad.

He stepped outside into the cool night air and lit up a cigarette—his twentieth today at least. No doubt about it; he was a nervous wreck. Fritz had done his job well with the old water torture method of regular bombing day after day, week after week. Alcohol was the only thing that seemed to help, and he'd given up trying to do without it. Whatever got him through another day was the go right now until things settled down further along the track.

Fifteen puffs later, he heard his mates long before he saw them. The hooting and laughing were loud enough to wake the dead, but they'd earned the right on the battlefields to make as much noise as they liked. Moments passed before the army jeep came careering around the corner and with a screech of brakes pulled up in front of the hospital hut.

"Welcome to the love chariot, Mike!" bellowed Richard, the loudest of the three, who was nicknamed "The Mouth" by his mates.

"Sorry, didn't catch that," replied Michael, putting his hand to his ear in mock confusion.

Richard stood on the seat arms, outstretched, and called out to the heavens. "I said, my young and very deaf friend, welcome to the love chariot! Tonight I will get lucky. I can feel it in my bones!"

Jack was driving. "You'll need to feel it somewhere else, Dicko," he said, straight-faced. "Dem bones, dem bones, dem dry bones won't do you much good on their own."

Michael smiled as he climbed in and sat next to his mate Buzz in the back seat. Jack stepped on the accelerator and roared through the gates of the army camp. They were all excited about the prospect of a good time at the Saturday night dance in town, so the jokes were coming thick and fast.

He joined in and kept the jokes coming, giving his rendition of a happy-go-lucky man-about-town. He'd learnt to do that over the years, but secretly he often felt as if he were on the outside looking in at other people doing their thing. Life was a bit of a film. Luckily they'd managed to get a hold of some whisky and beer.

The first sounds coming from the band playing in the local dance hall made his spirit rise. He always felt the closest to being alive when around music. The jeep sent dust flying as it swerved and pulled up outside the dance hall and they all leapt out and waved at mates who were thronging around outside.

"I'm not stopping out here with these losers, mates!" shouted Richard. "The action's inside, and it's ten guys to every girl!"

Michael wasn't arguing with that logic. He followed along with his mates and headed for the entrance. The moment he walked through the door, he saw her. *Oh man, a class act in a hay barn!* Against the backdrop of a country dance hall, she looked as out of place as a blood-red rose in a pumpkin patch.

She was shortish and willow-wisp slight; as delicate as his mum. A great set of legs, and extraordinary colouring. He slid away from his mates, who were frantically checking out unattached girls, and made his way along a back wall to a corner where he could see without being seen.

His sex-starved mates would be after breasts and hips in tight clothes, but he'd been taught to aim higher. He studied the way she carried herself and how she interacted with girlfriends as well as men. By some miracle she was dressed in the latest city fashion; elegant and understated. He couldn't take his eyes off her.

As she moved amongst the men, his experienced eyes recognised the teasing flirtations of an innocent who had no intention of following through on any of the delights which her eyes promised. Was he looking at a virgin with sophistication and spirit who lived in the middle of nowhere? Wonders would never cease!

He'd always done well with women, and this one was worth a go; worth coming out of hiding for. "You're irresistible, Michael" he told himself. "She'll be putty in your hands. Nothing ventured, nothing gained, et cetera, et cetera." With that he took a couple more swigs from the hip flask in his pocket, took a big breath, and began to cross the floor.

*   *   *

Kate decided that this newcomer was more than interesting. He was heading her way with the relaxed confidence of a man who believed that the room belonged to him. When he drew closer, she could see that his eyes were a liquid blue and that they were set like flint on her.

He looked much older than the others and had a gaunt worldly look so different to the open, fresh faces of the young men she was used to. Fear and attraction combined to flood her body with heat which she hoped wouldn't turn her face beetroot. With her heart fluttering, she nodded when asked to dance.

The dance floor was her domain where she was used to being watched and admired by male and female alike, so in spite of the firecrackers going off in her stomach, she sashayed forward, her outer confidence still intact.

Then the slow music for a jazz waltz began, and he led her wordlessly forward. Within seconds the realisation dawned on her that tonight the tables were turned and it was she who was speechless with admiration as this stranger took the reins and showed her what dancing could really be like.

Never before had she been led like this. The jazz waltz became a love song, and together they entered a timeless dimension where she was unaware of anybody or anything other than the perfect harmonising of their movements.

"Where did you learn to dance?" she whispered. "Someone must have taught you."

He didn't answer immediately, but after several seconds he replied, "My father was a dancer; didn't teach me anything but must have passed it along in the blood. But I'm more interested in you. You feel like a feather in my arms."

The words came as a surprise, because his voice was deep and smooth and he spoke with a city accent. She scrambled for something to say. "We did ballroom dancing at school," she finally breathed, "and I've been going to dance classes since I was ten."

He held her away from him for a moment, his face a picture of mock indignation. "And here I've travelled the world looking for the perfect partner, when she was in Singleton all along!" He looked up to the heavens. "That was a struggle I didn't need to have!"

"So were there some struggles that you needed to have?" she asked.

"Yes, the ones I couldn't avoid."

"You mean nuisance things like war and such?"

"Yes, war was one; and then there was the problem of an enemy who took the whole thing seriously!"

She threw her head back and laughed. He was fascinating. She couldn't wait to get down to records on Monday to make sure he wasn't married.

"I suppose you've got a name," he asked her now.

"My name's Kate. And yours?"

"Michael; Michael O'Brien. I kissed the Blarney Stone before the age of three and only got this far through the luck of the Irish."

34

One month later

Kate's ribs were sore from laughing all night. That man was a comedian, and the dancing—oh, the dancing was like something from a fairy tale. It had been a perfect night, and for the first time she was in love—truly in love—with a man other than Dad or Granda. Did that mean she loved them less? Mum had been sending thunderous looks her way all evening, but Kate was determined not to give way to fear. What a surprise she had in store for her if she believed that Kate still cared about her opinion!

She said her goodbyes to the last couple of guests just as Michael strolled over and placed a hand on the wall beside her. A thrill rippled through every nerve as he leant down and whispered in her ear.

"I'm beginning to develop a nervous tic trying to decode your facial expressions, young lady. So far we've had 'I love you,' 'I hate you,' 'I'm ecstatically happy,' 'I'm miserable,' and 'I'm angry.' And that's just in the last few minutes."

He was so delicious that she wanted to lose herself in him and forget everything else. "It's been a big night" was all she said, but her eyes said much more. He was streets ahead of any other man she'd met, and he'd know what to do.

"I say we take a walk in the moonlight to cool me down and hopefully warm you up," he said, placing his arm around her shoulder.

"Warm me up for what?"

"When it happens, I'll think of something. I never miss an opportunity."

She giggled and let him lead her outside and down the front steps. They wandered through the garden for a while in silence, listening to the crickets and drinking in the varied perfumes of spring. Once they were far enough away from the house, he stopped and turned to place a hand on each side of her head. For several seconds he just explored every inch of her face with those beautiful eyes, and then he gave her the sweetest of kisses.

It wasn't like the lusty breathless efforts she'd experienced with simple local boys or soldiers anxious to push things along. Like his dancing, it was a matter of hastening slowly. He didn't try to take it further but rather stopped and looked into her eyes again.

"You're not yourself tonight, sweetheart," he said as he stroked her hair. "Do you want to tell me what's wrong?"

How could she tell him what was wrong? It was so hard to put into words the different feelings that warred with one another when she thought of her family and the prospect of leaving home. While she struggled with these thoughts, he spoke again.

"You don't have to explain anything to me, Kate. You have your secrets, and I have mine. But there's one thing I want to make clear."

"And what's that?"

He spent a moment in thought before replying. "Meeting you has been like getting hit by a bus. It's wiped away any thoughts of women from the past and left me reeling from the impact, and right now there's only one thing I'm sure of."

"And that is?" she asked, her heart in her eyes.

"And that is that I've never known a woman like you. I am a crazy, mixed-up bastard, sweetheart, and that's a fact. But there's one pure and sane thing in my life right now, and that is the love I feel for you."

*   *   *

Flo stared into the blackness through the kitchen window, her cup of tea suspended between the saucer and her mouth. The night had gone well for sure. Aye, their parties were ever the place to be. But as always, the sight of the young lads in their uniforms had brought memories of Hamish to mind. He'd been so bonny and young and bursting with promise but hadn't had a chance against the bloody war.

Her father had delighted everyone earlier as always with his infectious hunger for life. A familiar mix of regret and resentment bubbled up at the thought of him. But in spite of that, she'd near burst with pride when he'd sung "Castles in the Air" in his thick Scottish brogue while dear Irene Drummond accompanied him on the piano. The words of the familiar old song began to play in her head as she remembered.

The bonny, bonny bairn sits pokin' in the ash

Glowerin' in the fire wi' his wee round face.

Laughin' at the fuffinlous,

What sees he there?

All the young dreamers buildin' castles in the air.

Nostalgia welled up, and tears pricked her eyes. "Castles in the air" was right! How she'd dreamed and dreamed as a young lass, and now her hopes centred around doing the most she could with what was.

And "what was" included her daughter, who was fair glowing like the moon tonight. Kate must have imagined that her mother was a naive fool; more fool her! Did she think that the new love interest hadn't been noticed even though he always came with a group? Or did she think they'd not been seen whispering sweet nothings just now before they disappeared off together into the night?

Well, she could think again, because from the first night that Michael had come to the house, Flo saw it all. Aye, he oozed charm and kept everyone in stitches, and it was as clear as the nose on her face that Kate was full smitten. There was a calculating quality to him, as if he'd spent his life thinking on his feet.

It hadn't taken long for a pattern to emerge. He hid it well, but the man was drinking three to everyone else's one. She'd caught his trick of taking a drink from a tray and then hiding it at the side of the room and taking one from another tray.

He was city born and bred, and Singleton wouldn't hold him. Aye, it was true that Tom knew from records that he was single, not divorced and had no bairns. To be sure, that may be enough for Kate, but it didn't satisfy her! Just what were his kinfolk like?

Flo had done her best to dissuade Kate from seeing the man, but she'd dug her heels in, damn her! The lass wore a new look of defiance and was keeping her distance. He was a clever one for sure, working to turn a lass against her own mother. Well, she knew his game. A power battle he wanted; aye, and a power battle he'd get!

35

Another month later

Flo's heart was fair pummelling her chest. With clenched teeth and strained neck she crashed and banged away in the kitchen in a bid to drown out the sobbing and screaming coming from the bedroom. God, what a tantrum! For weeks now her nerves had tottered on the edge of panic. But every instinct shouted that today was a crucial point in the battle, and she knew she mustn't weaken.

"God's gift tae women" would be waiting in town by now. Sure, and full livid he'd be! 'Twas true she'd pushed the limits by not allowing Kate to leave home. Aye, and the lass was to be twenty-one in two months. But desperate situations called for drastic measures!

Her mind was as clear as a bell. She'd remembered to hide the bike last night and organise for Kate's horse to be fully occupied today. She didn't want Kate galloping off down the road in a cloud of smoke. As it was, the lass came close to walking all the way!

A fresh wave of shrieks echoed off the walls of the bedroom, but she steeled herself against it. With any luck the man would have never been stood up before. She was betting on his pride keeping him away.

*   *   *

Michael lit up another cigarette. Calm—he must stay calm. Surely she wouldn't stand him up. She was crazy about him! No one had ever stood him up, and he prided himself on his judgement of women. There had to be another explanation.

Taking a deep drag of the cigarette, he kept one inch away from panic. This courtship had stretched his self-control to the limit. Blind Freddy could see that there was Buckley's chance of seducing Kate; marriage was the only way a man could have her. And Heaven help him, he was actually contemplating the big M for the first time!

This was crazy. He must be really going nuts to believe that a walking train wreck like himself could make a go of it with anyone, let alone a princess like Kate. But then again, his whole life had been crazy and the last few years had been total insanity. So why balk at the idea of marrying a girl who wore silk stockings and high heels and also milked cows? What was normal anyway?

The midday film had started an hour ago, and he was sure she'd been looking forward to it. He went back over the arrangements in his mind. They'd agreed that since he didn't have a vehicle she'd ride into town on her bike and he'd grab a lift with anyone who was heading in. What was he missing here? Her mother didn't like him; took pains to make that fact crystal clear. But surely she couldn't stop Kate from going on a date.

Or could she? In a moment of revelation, light began to dawn. He began to think back over the different times he'd caught Mrs. Millet looking across with an expression of something akin to hatred. But he hadn't worried, because the father and grandfather liked him, and Kate was old enough to make her own decisions.

She was so strong in every other aspect. Like the time he'd mentioned marriage. Usually when a bloke talked about that subject, a girl would give him her body as well as her heart. He wouldn't have to ever follow through with it. But she'd said they couldn't ever get married because he was a Catholic and she was a Protestant!

It had thrown him so much when she hadn't gone all gooey at the thought of being dressed in white that he'd started arguing that he never went to Mass. Just a Catholic school for a while, he'd argued, when his mother's guilt was getting the better of her. He'd even made a mental note to hide the crucifix he still carried around.

That was when he'd first realised he was in trouble. Why, he'd asked himself, was he trying so hard to talk a woman into being okay with the idea of marriage? And right now he was in big, big trouble, because the truth was he didn't give a damn about his pride.

What was terrifying him right at this moment was the possibility that either she was giving him the big heave-ho or the mother was a more potent enemy than he'd allowed for.

There was only one thing for it. He'd handle this the way he always handled a crisis: attack the situation front-on. He threw the cigarette stub on the ground, crushed it with his foot, and then began the long hike to the Millet farmhouse.

36

One hour later, Flo's heart stopped pummelling and began to sink. She knew she'd underestimated her opponent. Standing at the lounge room window, she watched tight-lipped as the distant speck began the long climb up the hill towards home.

As the speck drew closer, all hope that it wasn't Michael flew out the window. Damn, it was him all right! And she could guess by the angle of his head and resolute rhythm of his walk that he was full determined and in a red-hot rage.

So he wasn't playing games. He'd taken up the challenge and planned on a fight to the death. Panic gripped her at the thought of losing control. A ball of indigestion settled in her chest; probably an ulcer. She raced outside and did a frantic search for the men until, after minutes that felt like decades, she spotted them at the milking sheds.

She had to yell like a fishmonger to gain even a flicker of response from the two simpletons. They turned their heads in her direction, and she near toppled over with her frantic waving until they rose up from their milking and headed for the house. When they were within earshot, Tom was the first to speak.

"Is dinner early tonight then, Flo?" he said. *Wonderful.*

"Och, it smells delicious tonight, Flo" added her father. "We'll hurry through the last two cows and be straight back tae wash up."

"Forget dinner, ye idiots!" bellowed Flo. "Do I look happy to ye? Do I look happy?"

Alec stepped back two paces. "Well, come tae think of it … nay, not really."

"Exactly! And why? Because that slick city funny man is marching up the hill this vera moment tae steal our Kate out from under our noses!"

She roared and she stamped. But did it get them moving? Nay, it rendered them witless. They started fluffing about like headless chooks running in useless circles. *Lord Almighty*, she thought, *these men will send me daft!*

Aware of precious minutes slipping away, she tried to quieten herself and think. They were supposed to be the rational ones, fer God's sake! She got no further because the front door slammed open and into the midst of the chaos strode Michael without even ringing the bell.

"I want to see Kate!" he shouted, his face flushed and damp from the long walk.

"Well she doesna want tae see ye!" bellowed Flo. She summoned the effort to grasp onto the last vestige of reason.

"I would like to hear Kate tell me that herself, Mrs. Millett!" he replied. And with that he strode down the hallway.

Tom and Dad had looked surprised up to this point, but now they were fair open-mouthed in disbelief. Flo stamped her foot with impotent rage as she saw her world falling around her. Michael made his way through the house and into Kate's bedroom. Seconds later, without a word, he dragged the lass into the living room where now even Flo stood gawking like a stunned mullet.

*   *   *

Kate felt as if she were being sliced down the middle, and right at this moment she had the courage of a sick kitten. It seemed that all of her reactions were coming from either anger or fear. But right now the anger was so huge and so deep that it threatened to destroy her, and it was easier to go with the fear.

Michael seemed to be beside himself with emotion, and through the haze of her own pain, she could see that he was shaking. Suddenly, to her amazement, he shouted at the top of his voice.

"Now, Kate," he cried out, "do you love me?"

The three gaping heads of Granda, Dad, and Mum turned like sideshow clowns from Michael to Kate, and she heard herself mumble back, "Yes, I love you." The heads swivelled back to Michael.

"Right! And I love you!" Michael replied, looking like he wanted to kill someone. "Now I want you to answer me this. Do you or do you not want to marry me?"

Time stood still for Kate. Michael wanted to marry her. At last here was someone with the courage to stand up to her mother. Michael was stronger than her mother. Within the safety of that knowledge she chose anger, and the fear evaporated. Her words came out loud and clear.

"Yes, Michael!" she shouted into his face. "I want to marry you, and I will!"

37

Singleton, Australia, February 1943

"I've been to funerals that were happier than this wedding, Nathaniel." said Tristan as he scanned the church both inside and out. "Alec is the only one praying. But then again he always sends his best ones up when he's upset."

Nathaniel was about to commend Tristan for his valiant attempt at optimism when Imogen spoke up. "Tristan, the only ones who aren't upset are Michael and Kate. And that's only because they don't know what's ahead of them," he added in sombre "we're all going to be massacred" tones.

"Yes, amen," said Nimrad. The guy was so flat you could run over him and not know it. He'd been showing signs of spiralling downhill lately, and Imogen's words had the potential to send him over the edge. "And we don't have the luxury of ignorant bliss, do we, friends?" he continued. "We have a good idea of what's coming once Kate hits twenty-one: battles, battles, and ... oh yes ... more battles."

Nathaniel tried to ignore his own sense of impending doom and thrashed around for something positive to say. Then it came to him. "Remember what the Lord said, colleagues," he announced with gusto. "He told us that Kate would make a difference. Surely that is a positive in light of the big picture."

"Have you forgotten the other minor piece of info that the Lord mentioned, Nathaniel?" snapped Nimrad. "He referred to the 'demon hordes' that she'd be dealing with. Or, in layman's terms, those maniacs that I've been battling for decades with no end in sight."

Nathaniel's hackles stood on end. He would have more respect! "We're not the enemy, Nimrad," he continued, eyeballing the angel. "That is a very useful bit of info that you would do well to remember. In fact, to be more specific, you will need to develop and maintain a close liaison with us if you are to ever successfully complete your own assignment!"

The other guardians remained silent and watchful, and Nimrad looked from one to the other, fidgeting with his robe. Presently he turned his attention back to Nathaniel.

"I've spent so long working solo," he murmured, "that it's a little difficult to grasp the fact that I'm now part of a team."

"But grasp it you can, guardian, and I am determined that you will." He gave Nimrad a loving hug and then stepped aside as the others came across one by one to give comfort. Nimrad's eyes were glazed at first, then downright weepy, until finally he was crying like a baby. Decades of tension came pouring out, and walls of isolation crashed down—walls that he had needed for a time in order to survive.

Meanwhile, a spirit of encouragement broke through the clouds of uncertainty that had been casting their shadows over Nathaniel's mind. Hope blossomed, sending its perfume of joy wafting through his whole being. He'd just mastered what could only be described as a tricky episode. No doubt about it, he was growing some muscle!

Yes indeed, a new confidence was manifesting in his life. And confidence would give birth to an air of authority which by a process of natural progression would lead to success and ultimate victory. Oh, sing the hallelujahs and sound the trumpets! God was on the throne, and Nathaniel the Bold was doing his thing here on planet Earth! (In all humility, of course.)

*   *   *

The minister announced the dreaded words: "And now may I introduce to you Mr. and Mrs. Michael O'Brien!" Flo had fought in the only way she knew how, but to no avail. Kate had fallen for a soldier from another world and would soon leave her home and kinfolk. To be sure, life had many ironies

Numb with fury, she followed her daughter down the aisle and outside into the church gardens. There was the minx now, all smiles, not caring that her every move was like a knife being thrust into her mother's very soul. She pushed her way through the surrounding crowd until she was within inches of Kate's ear.

"Well, are ye satisfied, lass?" she whispered through gritted teeth. "Ye've broken yer mother's heart!"

* * *

Alec watched from a discreet distance as the bridal party stepped into the garden. His heart sat heavy in his chest. Aye, he liked Michael; but he knew that Flo's fears were not unfounded. The lad was fighting many demons and would be like the devil tae live with. Tom, always the peacemaker, hadn't spoken his mind, but he hadn't been his cheery self for weeks.

Through the church entrance came Flo, now with the look of murder on her face. He held his breath as she approached Kate and whispered words that caused the lass's whole countenance to change from joy to grief.

"Forgi'e them, Father; they dinna ken what they're doing!" he cried out from the depths of his spirit. "They dinna ken, Father! Grant us yer mercy and yer grace. We canna do ought wi'out yer grace tae gie us strength!"

He moved forward through the group of well-wishers and saw relief in Kate's eyes as she spied him coming towards her. Her eyes filled with tears, as did his, and she melted into his outstretched arms.

"I mustn't weep or my makeup will run," she said into his shoulder. "I love you more than I can say, Granda. And I love Michael enough to burst. But I'm happy and miserable. Mum is being horrid."

Alec knew that he must make every word count. "Forgi'e her Kate" he said. "She nay kens what she's doing; just lashing out in her own hurt. Remember the Lord. Promise me ye'll nay forget Him! He loves ye wi' an everlasting love. I've been young, and now I'm old, and He's ne'er let me down. Ye canna earn his love and will die trying. 'Tis a free gift."

"I'll try to believe that, Granda; I promise," she said. "I'll miss you a hundred times a day!"

* * *

As the old man and the girl embraced, the finger of the Lord touched them both. Light flooded the spot where they stood, and healing love tumbled in waves all around. Then, while

Nathaniel was observing the goings-on, something astonishing happened. The Lord turned to look straight into his eyes, igniting a roaring fire in his spirit so that he was alight and alive from top to toe. And wondrous rapture, the Lord smiled at him alone for at least ten seconds!

In those precious seconds, he understood that the Lord trusted him with things too precious to put into words. Kate was twenty-one now, and Satan's time had come. Blazing away like the original burning bush, he turned towards the waiting guardians, whose eyes were all targeting his face.

As he spoke, the words echoed in the heavy silence. "And now it begins," he said. "The enemy is mobilising. But the Lord has decreed that prophets and intercessors will come through this line, and it is our job to make sure it happens. Every generation must have those who will call out to the Lord for their fellow humans and also those who can see and hear when others can't. Up till this time we have all worked together. But from now on I must leave you for short periods, as there will be many different areas for me to cover and I must keep a handle on everything."

"What if Satan attacks during one of those short periods, Nathaniel?" asked Tristan, his eyes a study in blind panic. "The responsibility is so great!"

"In that case, Tristan I am convinced that you will all do famously," replied Nathaniel. "You will draw on everything you have learnt through the centuries, and you will not throw away your confidence. Those who are bold and run into battle gain the victory. Those who retreat find that they are alone and defeated."

As the wedding bells rang out in the small churchyard, the drumbeat of battle resounded in Nathaniel's spirit. A war cry rose up from amongst the guardians, who were all faithful to their Lord—of that he was sure.

His eyes drank in their radiant faces, and he silently pledged to apply to his own life the advice he'd just given them. Wherever the mission took him and whatever happened, good or bad, he determined to always fight and not retreat.

38

Specialised Administration Demons (SAD), Hell

Tetrak felt that maybe he should fake being deaf or brain-dead, or maybe just get the blazes out of here and never look back. He curled up in the foetal position and tried to disappear into himself as the signal came through more and more clearly. Now he could hear the voices of the messengers travelling through the airwaves and calling his name.

There was no way around it. He was being summoned to Cavern Central and would have to face the music. He unfurled and lay back with eyes closed, trying to lighten up. *Nah, meditation never worked in Hell; better to stay wired.*

There had to be a way out of this quagmire he'd stumbled into; it was just a matter of figuring out a fabrication that could hold water. He began sifting through the facts around what Satan ominously referred to as "The O'Brien Family Stuff-up."

Fact number one: he'd failed in his first task a couple of decades ago. He hadn't managed to push daft old Eleanor off the windowsill. So Beatrice hadn't had to do two jobs, and her sons hadn't been left totally abandoned and therefore open to Tetrak's notorious powers of seduction.

Fact number two: somewhere in the middle of the fiasco that had followed the windowsill screw-up, a wretched angel of light called Nimrad had mysteriously turned up on the landing. Tetrak knew that there was no point trying again to unravel that one, because after every previous attempt he'd ended up in a catatonic state of confusion—unhelpful to say the least.

Fact number three: when he'd finally managed to drive Eleanor crazy so that she actually walked off the roof, it turned out that his timing had been up the creek. To quote the Master, it had been "a Gross Miscalculation on Tetrak's part." Lo and behold, Satan hadn't wanted her walking off any roofs once there was an angel of light on the scene. Who would've known?

The old Eleanor had left a bunch of disembodied spirits wandering around, and Mr. Conscientious had gone ballistic, flashing sword, bombs, fists, elbows, and knees in a blur of light. Demons went screeching in every direction and didn't stop until they'd got enough galaxies between them and the swirling dervish.

Fact number four: according to info received from his gloating competitors, he'd failed to achieve what was ostensibly a key goal in this whole lousy assignment. Apparently "The CGM Extraordinaire" aka "Tetrak the Great" was supposed to ensure that the family line of psychics continued uninterrupted, and he hadn't figured out that Michael was the perfect candidate to be next in line. So he'd let the golden boy slip through his fingers.

Where was the upside here? He'd just spent critical minutes on a total waste of time! The message was booming through again. "Tetrak, come immediately to Cavern Central!" If ever there was a crunch time for him, this was it. How do you talk your way out of four consecutive malfunctions?

He glanced around the office which had been his home for decades. His eyes caressed the instruments of torment that were all set up in display cases, much to the envy of countless rivals. On the left was the door to his own personal torture chamber, which had taken years to set up and was perfect for anger projection. Who knew where he'd be after this? Feeling like a condemned man going to the gallows, he stepped out into the corridor.

The screaming and wailing of the damned irritated him even more than usual. Right now he was definitely not in a good mood, and the sound of souls in torment was to him like a red rag to a bull. He stopped several times to mercilessly whip the noisier ones, gaining some relief from their cries of anguish. Then, just before he began the main descent into the bowels of Hell, someone shouted his name and he looked around. It was Eleanor.

"Oh God, Tetrak, help me!" she shrieked. "I'm burning in oil! It's agony beyond anything I could have imagined, and I'm so alone. Help me, dear friend and guide!"

This was just what Tetrak needed to prime him for the meeting with Satan. He grabbed a cauldron of oil and threw it onto the stupid crone so that it ignited immediately. Spurred on by the sounds of her screams, he began whipping her, continuing until his fury was spent. He shouted obscenities and curses at her until she was finally silent, then turned the temperature up higher and went on his way, ready to fight for his life.

Thanks to that stroke of luck, his brain was now working at top speed. The Master hated weakness, so he knew he must not show fear or remorse. He must convince Satan that all goals were still well and truly on course and that a succession plan was in place. *What is the plan; what is the plan?*

When the dreaded CC loomed larger than life up ahead, he still hadn't figured out what to say. He pondered how he could make four failures seem like temporary hiccups on the pathway to roaring success. He stood finally before the entrance, still mentally debating various arguments which could postpone his possible demise.

"Well, what are you waiting for, worm?" came the voice of doom from inside. Tetrak stepped through the doorway.

The Master was pacing back and forth, surrounded in swirling shadow and an aura of incomparable evil. When he turned to face the door, his eyes were deep crevasses of iniquity and hatred, and they rendered Tetrak completely awestruck. But he had not gained his high position by being vulnerable, so he fought to keep a clear head. As much as he admired this great leader whom he'd followed from Heaven to Hell, it was essential to come in on the attack.

"You've interrupted me at a crucial stage, Master!" This was stated with as much authority as he could muster. "My plans are at a vital point, and I must remain vigilant!"

"What crucial stage? What plans, Tetrak?" replied Satan in subdued tones. Then, in a shout that could be heard for millennia, he came in for the kill. "As far as I can see," he screeched, "you have no plans, crucial or otherwise!"

Tetrak's body was numb with terror, but as luck would have it, his brain was still working. "My plans to isolate Beatrice and her sons and bring them into a state of complete bitterness so that they will all turn to me just as Eleanor did!" he shot back, holding his ground. *Holy cow, Tetrak; where did you drag that from? You're brilliant!*

"You seem to be forgetting the lone but nevertheless highly significant fact that Michael has managed to snare Alec Forsythe's granddaughter, you retarded idiot!!" screamed Satan.

"Robert's close to breaking, Master!" The brain was in overdrive now; anything could come out of his mouth. "We've achieved access there through Rejection. As for Michael, we can call in Anxiety, Rejection, Anger, Addiction, and Paranoia, to name a few; and the time is ripe for us to set in motion the sifting of Kate allowed by the Lord." This was planet-shaking stuff. He even believed his own story.

Satan stood as still as a corpse now and began to channel power through the chasms that passed for eyes. A tangible current of dread emanated from them and encircled Tetrak until the chances of him fainting on the spot were ninety-nine out of one hundred. "You have already failed me before, Tetrak," he breathed. "It cannot happen again. Do you understand?"

Tetrak understood perfectly but was incapable of speech, the temporary rush of adrenalin having drained out through his toes. Instead he turned and shuffled away, numb from the brain down. As he blindly manoeuvred back through the maze of corridors, he heard a scream to the right.

"Help me, Tetrak!" came the shrieked cry of a pathetic lost soul. "Please have mercy! Help me!"

Grenades of hatred exploded in his belly, and he galvanised into action. "Shut up!" he shouted as he reached for an iron bar.

Part Six

39

God and devil are fighting there, and the battlefield is the heart of man.
Fyodor Dostoevsky, from *The Brothers Karamazov*, 1879

Sydney, Australia

Beatrice winced as the kid missed the key chord yet again. What was she going to do with the poor child? While Richard bowed his head and mumbled an apology, she formed her mouth into a caricature of a smile and determined to come up with something encouraging.

His mother was a battle-axe with pie-in-the-sky expectations, and Bea's heart went out to him. On the other hand, it was 4.30, said battle-axe was due any minute, and Bea needed to put food on her own table. She could tell the woman that there was more chance for her pet cat to learn to fly than there was for Richard to be a pianist, or she could say nothing, continue booking up private lessons, and live another day.

Within seconds she made yet another decision that went against her heart but catered to the fight for survival.

"Don't worry about that chord, sweetie," she purred, sliding onto the piano stool beside him. "It's very difficult, and you played the rest of the piece beautifully! You've been working so hard today; it's time for you to stop and rest. Mother will be here any minute."

The child broke into an expression of adoring gratitude, and just at that moment the matriarch herself appeared at the door. The pudding face lit up with approval, and Bea imagined how she and Richard would look right now from Vera Bollingsworth's perspective. She'd see a cosy scene of pupil and teacher sitting together at the piano, her son smiling adoringly up at his tutor. *Bingo.* One thing had gone her way this week.

"Madam Beatrice said I played my piece beautifully, Mother!" said Richard as he stood and edged towards Vera, his eyes pleading for reassurance. What it would do for him to get a hug, perhaps, or a smile, or even a "hello, how are you?"

Vera swallowed up all the air as she swept into the room and grabbed his hand. "Splendid, splendid! Here's your two shillings, Beatrice. God knows these lessons are costing a fortune, but it's worth it to know Richard is progressing as he should. Sorry I can't stop to chat. Come, Richard. Thank you, Madame Beatrice!"

"Goodbye, Vera," said Bea as she put the two shillings into her purse. "Keep practising, Richard!"

And with that they were gone. What a flashback to her own childhood! The only difference was that she had actually had talent. Mind you that had got her squat in the love department, but at least it had warded off the humiliation of failure, which would inevitably come for Richard.

She couldn't afford the luxury of feeling compassion for the boy—of feeling anything at all, in fact. It weakened her resolve to keep on fighting from one day to the next. A fringe-dweller, that's what she was; carrying around her bags of broken dreams and looking through windows at people living their lives. She pushed to the back of her mind the mental picture of those young eyes so hungry for love and went into the kitchenette.

Gathering up into a bowl the bread scraps that had been saved over a couple of days, she selected a bottle of milk from the icebox and poured the contents into a bowl. This was her favourite time of day—the peace and quiet of dusk. She strolled out onto the spacious veranda and placed the bowl onto the black and white tiles. It was only a matter of seconds before the cat brigade started to turn up, coming from all directions.

How beautiful they were; black and slinky, ginger and cheeky, grey, mottled, and striped. Each one was a study in perfect coordinated grace. She leant up against the doorway and watched her precious feline friends congregate at the spot which had been the scene of many a past feeding frenzy. Soon there were six of them hungrily slurping at the milky mixture, and as usual each one studiously observed personal space decorum.

Her heart went out to these stray animals who were alone and unwanted. They were no less regal because of life's abandonment and were worthy of respect; so quietly independent, carrying themselves with dignity and bowing to no one. She lifted her arms in a full stretch, breathed in deeply, and then slowly lowered her arms again as she exhaled and looked around her.

The old Victorian edifice she now called home was similar in many ways to the mansion of her childhood. This one was not so grand now, of course; it was all run-down and divided up into four separate flats. But at least she'd got to live in the plum flat with the bay window and chandeliers thanks to regular revenue from piano lessons.

And she'd been able to grab the flat at the back of the house for Michael. He felt at home here in the inner-city ambience of Glebe, and the rent was low enough for him to afford, which meant that he was better off than a lot of returned soldiers. But young Kate was looking far from impressed.

What madness had led Michael to think that the girl would switch easily from a safe little dairy farm to his life here in the back blocks? Just thinking about it made Bea cringe for a second with shame. There was no doubt in Bea's mind that he loved the girl. But he was out of his league and behaving like an idiot. Well, it wasn't her place to interfere. She would just be there as a friend and try to be part of the answer, not part of the problem.

Feeling suddenly very weary, she picked up the bowl—which was now licked clean—and turned to go back inside before the late-afternoon temperature began to drop. She hadn't seen Robert for years now. What on earth was he getting up to? His pattern was to make contact only when he was desperate, so she supposed that no news was good news. But that man was a constant worry, always hiding behind something or someone. He was brilliant on the piano, but she'd never been able to find a way to help him do anything with it. All he'd ever had to do was burst into tears and Michael would jump in as the big protector. Well, her baby must have fallen on his feet in some way, or she would have seen him before this.

40

Sydney, Australia

He was literally burning up with envy. Michael looked away as the journos began rushing through the doors, pumped with adrenalin and frantic to get their stories ready before the 6.00 p.m. conference. He felt like telling them where they could stick their stories and where they could go while they were at it.

Michael's life stank. When he'd first started with the *Herald* he'd been a skinny teenager and was just getting a go on when Wall Street fell. They'd taken him back after things got moving again, and he was settling in okay when—what do you know—the bloody war broke out. Which all went to prove what he'd always known: Michael O'Brien was born under an unlucky star.

It wasn't the newspaper's fault, and they'd given him the chance to start at the bottom for the third time, but right now he wanted to shoot the whole place to kingdom come. He was occupied with getting his personal monster back in the cage when Jim Mason catapulted across the room—in a total mess as usual, and looking for help.

"Would you help me with this jumble please, Michael?" he gasped in between huge intakes of air while handing over a third of the pile of notes he'd carried in. "I think I'm onto a winner today; got a great angle!"

Michael skimmed over the page of illegible scribble. "Anything else you want? Like maybe a miracle healing, or a parting of the Red Sea?"

Jim laughed good-naturedly. "Just a bit more cooperation and a bit less cheek!" he shouted over his shoulder as he settled in front of his own typewriter and picked up the phone to make some last-minute calls.

Michael began to collate Jim's info, and the green-eyed monster stirred again in his gut. He glanced at the clock to see how much longer it'd be before he could hit the pub and get as much grog as possible into him before closing time. "Oh, great line of thought, genius," he whispered. "Guaranteed to make you a champion!" He knew there was greatness in him if life would just give him a chance. He wound paper and carbon into the typewriter and began to hit the keys with a vengeance.

As the minutes rolled by, he got caught up in the task of beating the time limit, and in spite of himself, he began to enjoy Jim's story. That guy had a gift for nailing issues that would hit their mark with the public.

Lately he'd been delving into the workings of the ACTU, which hadn't been around long but was already a force to be reckoned with. According to Jim there were whispers around that they were pushing for the basic wage to be lifted. They were talking about it even hitting the seven-pound mark. *Ha! And maybe one day pigs would fly!*

He'd also looked at surveys on the subject of men returning to the workforce after active service. They were taking over jobs that women had held throughout the war and had expected to be welcomed like heroes. But surprise, surprise, the women were up in arms about it. The girls had enjoyed going out to work and having their own money, especially when they'd had the use of all the childcare facilities which had been set up because of the special circumstances and would now be shut down. They'd got used to being paid 90 per cent of the male wage during wartime and were jacking up now about being back to 54 per cent. And the politicians were shocked.

That proved once and for all that politicians were nuts. How much better would his life have been if his mother had earned decent money and had the use of childcare? Anyway, they could make all the fuss they liked, but it'd be a cold day in Hell before female wage rates came back up or childcare facilities became the norm.

He was finishing the last sentences as Jim hurried over, reams of paper under each arm. "Thanks a million, mate," he said brightly as Michael added his typing to the clutter. "Lucky you, here it is five o'clock and you've finished for the day while I've still got to face the gladiator ring and sell my story. And between you and me, behind all the bravado I'm scared rigid that it's maybe just a load of old codswallop."

What a great opportunity to hit a guy while he was down! Michael paused just long enough to shut out the voice of temptation and push down the spiteful retort that had got as far as his neck. "No, mate," he said finally, "the story's good. I'm betting that it'll go over well."

Jim stopped still for a moment. He'd seen many answers to prayer over the years, and in a split second he sent one up for this likeable bloke who seemed to have so much against him. "Give him a break, Lord," he said in his spirit. "He just needs a break!" Then he said out loud to Michael, "Thanks, mate, I reckon you will too. Your time will come." He gave Michael a thumbs-up sign before running towards the conference room.

*　　*　　*

Jim's prayer sent a wave of glory washing over Michael as he gathered his things and prepared to leave the office. Envy shot through him as if the hounds were after him, and Nimrad stepped into the middle of the wave and then turned to look directly into the face of his old adversary Tetrak, who was shaking from head to foot. He kept his gaze steady even as the demon gradually stopped shaking and began to puff himself up to twice his size, spitting out curses and spreading tattered wings.

"Damn you, Nimrad!" he screeched. "I've been in this family for centuries! Do you imagine you can dislodge me?"

Nimrad remained unmoved. Tetrak was the first to break eye contact, and he began to pace back and forth in an agitated manner.

"Where are you, Envy?" he growled, eyes darting around the room. "The longer you hide, the angrier I'll get, coward!" With that he disappeared through the wall.

"Oh, brother," said Nimrad to himself, "if I were Envy, I'd stay hidden. It would surely beat the alternative!" He looked around just as Michael was hurrying through the main door with his hat already on and cocked at a Frank Sinatra angle. Following close at his heels were Drunkenness, Shame, Frustration, Self-hatred, and others Nimrad didn't recognise.

There was also an expression on Michael's face that was a bit troubling; it was a sort of "angry young man with big chip on shoulder meets frightened little boy" type of scenario. He took a moment to send out a request for assistance.

"Got a bit of a situation here," he signalled. "Backup would be helpful." Having done that, he summoned courage and sped after his charge. It was good to be part of a team.

*   *   *

Michael travelled at a rate of knots partly to get amongst it at the pub and partly to burn off some emotion. Jim's kindness had nearly been his undoing back there. "'Your time will come,' 'Your time will come'" he muttered to himself while negotiating a flight of stairs leading down to the main doors of the Herald building. With his luck that time would probably come just before he got hit by a train! What was a bloke supposed to do?

Once outside, he stopped to light a cigarette and checked his watch. Ten past five already. There were only fifty minutes left to get drunk enough to calm the panic gripping his chest. He took a deep drag on the cigarette and then took off again, trying to look relaxed while making a beeline for the pub. "Stay calm, Michael; look normal, Michael," was the secret mantra going over and over in his head. He had to resist the urge to break into a full gallop for only another few yards, and then he was home free.

When he finally pushed through the doors of the pub, the din inside was unbelievable and he could hardly move through the crush. But even in his present restless state, Michael took two seconds to admire the beauty of the old bar with its intricate woodwork reminiscent of a bygone era.

Once was a time when there would have been pool tables, comfortable couches, and beautiful furniture in here. Now, of course, there was the six o'clock swill, with the usual maniacal throng standing ten deep and close to mass hysteria. To his relief he spied three of his drinking mates—Dick, Robbo, and Bert—who waved him over.

"G'day Mike," said Robbo. "Thank God you're here. Now we can activate plan A."

Robbo was good-looking in a clean-cut blonde way. He'd fallen on his feet when the opportunity came up to do management training at the David Jones store in Elizabeth Street, but he hadn't forgotten his old war buddies. Every afternoon he still ran all the way down to Hunter Street to join them in the old Grand Hotel.

"Glad to be of service, mates! I hereby declare my absolute commitment, even unto death, to do all in my power to beat the system. And that means any system!"

"Jeez, you are so full of crap, O'Brien," said Bert. "All I want to do is get some grog into me before six o'clock!"

Robbo took charge. "Okay, mates, let's just do it. Everyone ready … forward … ho!" With that the four ex-diggers joined the fray in front of the bar and with absolute dedication began to push through with every ounce of energy they had. "It won't be easy, men, but haven't we dealt with worse than this in our time?" he yelled, holding up his fingers in a victory sign.

Michael deliberately/accidentally trod on the toe of the man next to him. "Hey, watchit ya mug!" shouted the guy, hopping around in a circle. This created just enough diversion to allow for substantial progress in the relentless push forward.

"Over here, Marj; for Chrissake, over here!" came a cry of desperation from his right.

"No Marj, here! Three beers over here!" shouted another, this time from the left. Finally Michael hit the front and caught the attention of said Marj, who was one of eight barmaids and barmen allocated to the "panic hour."

"Four beers; thanks, luv!" he roared over the din. "They're for me and my mates over here!" he added pointing at the others.

"You mean you an' your fellow hooligans doncha?" replied Marj, a good-natured girl in her mid-twenties.

"That's one way of looking at it, sweetheart. I personally like to think of us as philosophers."

"Well at least you got mates that achuly exist, so that's a bonus. There's plenty round here who sit talkin' to the air all afternoon. Here y' go, luv. Enjoy."

Michael paid her the money and began the precarious trip back holding the beers above head height. He regained "corner central" without losing a drop just as the other three arrived as well, each carrying four drinks. They turned to face the wall and formed a semi-circle, then placed twelve drinks on the floor at their feet and began to down the other four as quickly as possible. With any luck they could get that lot down and manage another sixteen before closing time.

* * *

Nimrad was losing strength fast here while the darkness was rapidly gaining ground. So much for the "yay team" thoughts he'd had a while ago. He checked the place for any possible assistance, but all the other guardians that he could see had their hands full with their own assignments.

A couple of nasty pieces of work were beginning to take an interest in him because they'd noticed that he was unsupported. One of them was only medium height but had a long periscope for an eye and was frequently swivelling it in his direction, while his mate was covered in giant porcupine spikes and was looking him up and down with an expression that could only be described as expectant.

This was the ultimate conflict situation for a guardian. His charge was busy drinking himself into oblivion and needed close supervision, but if Nimrad didn't get out of here quick smart, his action days might be over. For a few moments he was riveted to the spot with indecision, which was all they needed.

They began to close in, both salivating at the thought of a possible massacre, and Nimrad involuntarily stepped back, only to bump into someone. Cold terror flushed through his spirit, but then the flight-or-fight instinct took over and he turned to face his tormentor.

Astonishingly, there was Nathaniel himself, as large as life and smiling like a Cheshire cat! Emotion welled up in Nimrad like a river and choked off any words he might have thought to say had he been able to think.

In a microsecond Nathaniel enveloped him with light and heat and yelled, "Let's get the cowards, Nimrad!" Together they charged towards the would-be attackers, who both screamed and made a mad dash for the other side of the room and disappeared through the wall.

Nimrad took a moment to gather himself together. When he finally spoke, it was in a voice that was not much more than a whisper. "For a moment there I thought I was done for, Nathaniel. I truly didn't know what to do.

"The trial has been long and relentless, friend; no one is more aware of that than myself," said Nathaniel after some minutes.

"You've been gone for months, Nathaniel; much longer than anticipated." Nimrad had regained his voice and was in no mood to beat around the bush. "It's been difficult, to say the least."

"I know it has," replied Nathaniel, "and in some ways it will get harder from here. But at least I can report that everything has been set in place ready. I've been training a new guardian to look after Florence. His name is Klandis, and even though he's a rookie, I feel confident that she is in good hands for the time being. What that means is that I can stay with you and Imogen until things ease off."

"Imogen will be relieved, I can tell you," said Nimrad. "Kate's his first case, and there have been a few too many shocks for him lately. I can't wait to see his face when you walk in!"

Nathaniel was pensive for a few moments before responding. "No doubt that would be worth seeing, Nimrad, but my gut feeling is that it would be best if I go ahead to support Imogen. You have been refreshed now and are all right for the time being. Your main task at the moment is to concentrate on getting Michael home in one piece!"

"Well, I can't say I'm happy about that," replied Nimrad. "This place is not a barrel of laughs and is as lonely as all get out. But I'm a guardian, which means that I guard, right?"

"Right!" said Nathaniel with a grin. He blessed Michael and then headed off, giving Nimrad a wave as he went.

41

Glebe, Sydney, Australia

Michael swayed from side to side in front of the gate which led to home and certain trouble. He was way beyond seeing double; quadruple at least. "So this is home sweet home," he muttered. "What a joke! A bloke'd be more at home in the loony bin!" He held himself as straight as possible, trying to locate the latch of the gate, then said defiantly, "Only came here 'cos there's no one left to drink with anyway!"

His mind was going in circles. This whole marriage thing was too hard; too damn hard. Kate wanted his heart and soul and nothing less, "Just a bit of breathing space, Kate," he mumbled, "that's all I ask. A bit of breathing space!"

Everything'd been hunky dory when they'd been in her world on "Purity Planet." But it all hit the fan back in his world, which apparently was "disgusting" and "abnormal." What was "normal" anyway? *Musn't weaken; must stay strong. I've been through a war, dammit; I can handle one woman!*

Gingerly he reached out and grasped around for the latch, thrust open the gate, and lurched forward, still mumbling quietly. He stopped to relieve himself behind the hydrangea bush, then aimed his body towards the front door, which opened just as he reached it.

*   *   *

Kate looked at the drunken apparition standing in the doorway and felt like shooting him on the spot. What had she done to deserve this degradation? Her girlhood dreams were shattered and lying in a heap, and she felt as if she were rummaging around in the wreckage trying to find two pieces to fit together.

"Hail to the bewful Kate! Step aside, woman, an' let me come in!"

Kate watched quietly as Michael stumbled past her into the tiny kitchenette and opened the oven to retrieve his dried-up dinner. "Do you remember what you promised me before we were married?" she said, quietly standing with feet apart and arms crossed.

He turned around, dinner in one hand, holding on to a chair with the other. "I remember the 'till death do us part' bit. Nearly ran out the door screaming, I did. But knew that if I did, it'd make your bloody mother happy, so stayed m' ground."

Kate saw the challenge in his eyes but kept her composure. She wouldn't be pulled down to his level.

"You promised me that after we were married you would never have another drink!"

"Well, here's the latest news flash, princess. I lied! Oh yes, as shocking as it might sound to your greener-than-green ears … I lied. Guess what, Kate; out in the real world, not everyone grew up playing with cows and horses, and not everyone tells the truth all the time!"

Kate suddenly sprang into action as Michael stepped from the stove to the table. She grabbed the plate out of his hand and tipped the food into the bin.

"Well, that was brilliant! And your point, exactly?"

"My point is that no man has ever treated me like this and I'll be damned if I feed you one more time! Just go to bed."

Michael executed a very shaky exaggerated bow. "Don't mind if I do, your majesty. Can't wait to get out of here!" With that he wove his way towards the bedroom looking pleased with himself, as if he'd said something intelligent.

*   *   *

Nathaniel shrugged and rolled his eyes at Imogen and Nimrad. Michael had just hit Kate with the feeblest exit line of the decade, and now here he was talking all the while in a stage whisper while Shame and Rebellion whispered encouragement into his fuzzy brain.

"Who does she think she is? She's so self-righteous; always looking down on everyone else!"

"That's right! You don't have to put up with that. Give her an inch and she'll walk all over you!"

"Who does she think she is?" echoed Michael. "So stuck up; if I give her an inch, she'll take a mile!"

Nimrad couldn't stay silent any longer. "You love her, Michael!" he called out.

Michael stopped his mutterings and stood still for a few moments. "Love's a bitch!" he said finally; then he made a beeline for his bed.

Nathaniel turned his attention back to Kate, who had slid down into a chair and dissolved into tears. Imogen was holding a wing over her for protection and at the same time was swishing his sword back and forth to fend off Self-Pity, who had sneaked in from the right.

"Satan's net is drawing tighter, Imogen" he said.

"Yes, I know! What should I do? How can I help her?"

Nathaniel's heart went out to Kate and Imogen. He was about to reach across to them when suddenly the enemy executed a surprise attack and a grenade of hatred came hurtling into the kitchen. Nathaniel let out a roar and deflected it, giving Imogen such a fright that he threw his arms in the air and screamed like an emergency siren. Instantly he realised what had happened and felt totally embarrassed.

"Sorry about that, guys," he mumbled, burning with humiliation. "Feeling a bit edgy lately."

Nathaniel struggled to keep a straight face. "I'd say that's an understatement, wouldn't you, Nimrad?" he said with a wink.

Nimrad crossed his arms and assumed a serious expression. "You appear to be more than a bit edgy at the moment, my friend. Not surprising considering Michael's award-winning performance just now. Wouldn't you agree, Nathaniel?"

"Absolutely! Michael outdid himself tonight in the way of idiotic behaviour. He delivered one of the most breathtaking self-destructs I've ever seen."

Imogen just stood with his mouth open, looking from one to the other. After some seconds, Nimrad's grave face cracked open into a broad grin and Nathaniel began to break out into short bursts of giggles. Imogen joined them in spite of his worries, and gradually the giggling developed into unstoppable, tear-inducing, gut-shaking laughter which lasted for several minutes.

Finally the refreshing wave of joy passed. Nathaniel closed his eyes and sighed with pleasure, then looked up to see incredulity on the faces of various shady-looking characters who were watching from the garden. At the sight of them transfixed with mouths agog and eyes bulging open, he started chuckling again.

What a powerful weapon joy is. The fact that heavenly angels could laugh in the face of such darkness was something their enemies could not comprehend. It threw demons into absolute confusion and undermined their confidence every time. His thoughts were interrupted at that point by Kate. The girl was now talking to herself as well as sobbing.

"What am I going to do?" she cried. "It's too hard; too hard! How can I raise a baby in this hellhole? It's hopeless!" She wrung her hands in despair. "I won't even tell him yet. Why should he have the joy of knowing when he doesn't even deserve to be a father!"

Nathaniel winced as Kate's words went out into the heavens. News of her pregnancy would travel like wildfire through enemy ranks. Already her negative confessions were drawing the darkness to her like a magnet and a heavy fog was closing in accompanied by creatures of darkness. This was no time for bravado; he decided to summon aid.

He'd expected to be given some backup foot soldiers, but within seconds, who should descend through the ceiling of the kitchen but the magnificent Dashiel! Once more he was struck by the beauty of this towering warrior who shimmered with electrical energy and emitted a heady fragrance of roses and jasmine. For goodness' sake, why would a magnificent specimen like this be called upon to help in what was surely still a domestic situation?

Nathaniel was relieved, overwhelmed, and embarrassed all at once. Consequently he leapt forward and hugged the guy in greeting before remembering that warriors were not really into the sensitive bonding thing. For a moment he panicked because Dashiel froze, unable to respond to such a display of emotion. He dealt with the situation by saying the first thing which came to mind.

"I heard you were in the Middle East, Dashiel. Not enough to keep you busy there?" He surreptitiously took a step back.

Dashiel's shoulders relaxed, and his face softened. "Didn't want to miss the chance to check up on you, my friend," he replied with some bluster, his eyes focused somewhere above Nathaniel's head. "Heaven knows you need monitoring from time to time." He redirected his gaze towards Nathaniel and smiled. "No, actually I was called in here to get an update and acquaint myself with the present situation. Never a dull moment around your territory, Nathaniel; and a tricky section of the territory it is!"

Nathaniel was still trying to fully process this new development of receiving help from someone as high-profile as Dashiel. Amongst other things, he felt concerned for the warrior, who he knew had spent aeons negotiating crucial warfare in the skies over Jerusalem. He'd won many victories; no doubt about that. But Nathaniel thought he surely must be in danger of burnout!

"I'm glad you're here, Dash" he said. "You and Zimron are the ones who are always called in at critical points. I've continually tried to do my best, but I must say it has always been a relief when you've turned up in the heat of battle."

"You've underestimated yourself for centuries, Nathaniel" replied Dashiel, giving him an affectionate push. "It's no small thing that the Master wanted you for this assignment. He is breaking chains which have existed for generations and needed someone with your loyalty and tenacious courage'

"Um, I think I'll go and check on Michael." Nimrad's voice was a quiet squeak from behind them.

Nathaniel turned to find Nimrad and Imogen both standing riveted to the floor and looking totally stunned by the celebrity visitation.

"Oh yes, excellent," he said to Nimrad. "Lord knows what could be going on there by now. Imogen, looks like the fog's lifted in here and things are under control again."

"Yes, I believe everything's going extremely well, Nathaniel," replied Imogen.

"Everything's great, really great!" said Nimrad at the same time. He flashed a facial contortion that passed for a smile, then took off at a rate of knots for the bedroom.

"Well, just wanted to let you know that I'm on call for you at the moment," said Dashiel. "And don't worry about me, Nathaniel," he added with an affectionate smile, "I'll make sure that I don't burn out!"

Nathaniel mentally kicked himself. *Rats!* He realised he must have slipped back into his habit of thinking out loud. How awkward.

"Are you up for a quick meeting outside before I go?" said Dashiel over his shoulder before ascending and disappearing back through the kitchen ceiling, leaving only the smell of roses and jasmine.

"Uh, yes, that would be great!" shouted Nathaniel. "Be back soon, Imogen," he told his charge before hurrying after his newfound friend in a flurry of feathers.

*   *   *

Kate quickly escalated from weeping to bone-shaking sobs. When they finally ran their course, she did a mammoth nose blow and eye blot. There'd been so many reasons to fall in love with that man, and now there were just as many reasons to leave. So why was she still here?

Admittedly he was the only man who'd ever touched her, and still the only one who could. All the more reason for him to treat her like a princess, just as the men in her life always had. Yes, he was battling to find his place in the chaos after the war, and when he was sober she still saw in him the potential for greatness. But what about her?

The bottom line was that she had nowhere to go. She could never return to her mother in Singleton; nor could she stand the humiliation of contacting old friends. As for Michael's friends, they didn't even bear thinking about. They were tacky, cheap drunks, the lot of them. And that included the women. What a disgusting thing Kate found it to see women getting drunk, and it put her teeth on edge to hear their working-class accents!

She pounded the kitchen table with her fist and sat upright, anger rescuing her from the dead end of despair. If he imagined that she would one day make friends with those people, he had another think coming! *And there'll be no more dinners left in the oven when he comes home late!*

She decided the precious life growing inside her would remain a secret for a while longer. She would send a letter to Granda tomorrow telling him, and that was that. She would walk with head held high and carry herself above the immorality of Sydney.

* * *

Imogen looked around with some apprehension. Pride sauntered forward out of the shadows, clearly confident in the authority Kate had just given him.

"Do you dare stop me, Imogen?" he challenged. He was one of the smallest of the demons, and heart-stoppingly ugly; he reminded Imogen of a monkey with slimy skin instead of fur. But his voice and manner were arrogant and patronising, as if he imagined himself to be enormous and breathtakingly beautiful.

"The time is not right for that, Pride," snapped Imogen, infuriated and frustrated at the same time. "But I look forward to the day when I will squash you like an annoying ant!"

Pride broke into crackling laughter before resuming his haughty expression. "You really do tend to run ahead of yourself, Imogen," he croaked. "You're still very new to the whole guardian thing and, to be totally honest, haven't made much of an impression so far. Maybe we can have this conversation again in a hundred years. That is, if you're still around by then!"

Imogen flinched and then sagged as the dagger of discouragement slashed into his spirit. He looked on helplessly as Pride placed a heavy black cloak around Kate, who sank deeply into it and sighed as if with relief.

* * *

Nimrad found Michael lying in a drunken stupor, surrounded by enemies who were putting nightmares into his head. They were generational demons who had access at this point, but Nimrad had authority to preserve Michael's life, so he positioned himself on guard to make sure that the lifeline was kept in place. The scene resembled a torture chamber. Sheets and blankets had been thrown back, and pillows thrown to the corners of the room. Michael was in a lather of sweat, tossing and turning and tormented to the breaking point by Death and Anxiety.

"You cannot have him, Death," he said. Although Nimrad spoke in little more than a whisper, Death stopped as if struck and swirled around to confront him.

"As usual you've got it all wrong, Nimrad, you incompetent fool," he hissed. "I have full permission from Michael himself to do what I want." He was blanketed completely by a cloak of a black cloud which sent waves of icy cold air floating around wherever he went. The stench which emanated from the cloud was almost unbearable, but through the centuries Nimrad had trained himself to ignore it.

Nimrad raised his voice in righteous anger. "Do you think I suffer from dementia, Death? I was there when Michael called out to the Lord!"

"He desires me!" shouted Death. "I am the ticket out of this mess that passes for his life!"

Nimrad had had enough. He roared out his challenge. "You lie, Death! He is a fighter and an overcomer! Even as a child he rejected you!"

Death screamed and lunged at Nimrad in a rage. Nimrad tried to reach for his sword and call for help, but the cold was paralysing in its intensity. Then he began to gag as the stench of the repulsive creature became overpowering. Icy tentacles of hopelessness reached deep into his spirit, and despite the best of efforts, he began to sink. Through the mist of despair he called out to Michael's spirit.

"Fight, Michael!" he cried. "Fight! … Fight!"

Nimrad felt close to expiring and was struggling futilely against the bloodlust euphoria which was empowering his enemy. What a victory it would be for Death if he could eliminate the sole angel of light who had been muddying Satan's plans for so long! He couldn't believe that after all his hard work it would finish like this.

*   *   *

Michael was running for his life through the desert, terrified beyond description. The more he tried to run, the slower he seemed to get, and always there was that sense of impending doom which was inescapable. He searched desperately for a safe place, but as far as the eye could see there was only sand.

Closer—the threat was getting closer. And now he was hardly moving. Where was his crucifix? The priests had told him about the love of God and the power of that cross! It had helped before. It was his only hope! The terror loomed huge, and with every last ounce of energy he tried to scream.

*   *   *

It seemed to be coming from miles away—a muffled noise that sounded like faint static. However, it was not static but a voice. In fact it was Michael's voice, which was getting louder by the second. But what was he was saying? As he strained to listen, Nimrad noticed that his strength had stopped waning and in fact was coming back in waves. And now, as the seconds ticked by, he found that he could make out the words.

"The cross!" Michael was shouting. "The cross! God, help me! I call on the power of the cross of Jesus!"

Death groaned in anguish and shrank to a tenth of his former size. Anxiety rushed from the room, emitting blood-curdling screams of terror; Death followed, growing smaller by the second. Nimrad stood swaying in the middle of the room, trying to gather his scattered wits and get his bearings. Then he remembered that his charge needed protecting and turned to check the bed.

There was Michael, lying motionless now with mouth open and snoring loudly. Nimrad smiled and shook his head. "Well I'll be a monkey's uncle" he whispered, remembering that it was good for angels to use the colloquialisms of whatever era they were working in. It helped them to empathise. "You're a ball of surprises, Michael!" He walked across, blessed the exhausted human, and sat on the bed beside him.

*   *   *

Nathaniel returned to the kitchen after a short but satisfying in-depth vision exchange with Dashiel. Who would have thought that the two of them could get to that point? He intended to share some new insights with Imogen, but one look told him that the guy was really struggling, to say the least, and needed to be uplifted. He lunged around in his mind for something positive to say, then gave him a big, warm smile.

"Be encouraged, Imogen! There have been many good reports about your work going back to Office Central. The talk is that the rookie guardian is coming through stage one with flying colours."

"Oh, good to hear, Nathaniel. And what did the reports say under the heading of 'Attitude'? There were myriad times when I wanted to hand in my resignation, I can tell you!"

"Well, my friend, unfortunately for you the Lord has seen that you've metamorphosed into a brilliant guardian, and he has no plans to send you back to worship duty."

Imogen sighed dramatically with hand on heart. "Oh, the price of success!"

At that point their banter ceased abruptly because a damp fear was starting to infiltrate the little kitchen. Kate became agitated and began to pace around the room, talking to herself and slicing her fists through the air. Nathaniel and Imogen gagged into their robes as a smell like that of dog manure wafted into the air. Into the midst of this scenario stepped Tetrak, with none other than Satan by his side.

Nathaniel sent a red alert to Nimrad, who joined them immediately; and the three angels stood together facing their ancient enemy, having been well taught to always show a fearless and united front. Godly authority welled up like a fountain within Nathaniel's spirit and spurred him to move past panic.

"You never learn, Satan! How dare you defy the armies of the Most High God?" His voice vibrated with authority, startling the demons that'd been coming in from all directions to watch this interesting turn of events. They all looked absolutely astonished at his boldness and murmured amongst themselves.

"Shut up, all of you!" bellowed Satan, who then proceeded to stand absolutely still, breathing heavily with eyes closed for a full minute.

The tension in the room increased so much that Nathaniel almost expected the windows to shatter and the doors to fly open. Nimrad and Imogen both unconsciously crept up closer to him on either side, but he decided this was not the time to make an issue of it. Finally Satan addressed him directly.

"You know very well, manager, that I was given permission to test Kate once she turned twenty-one, and that is exactly what we have already begun to do. Now the time has come when I myself will move in closer, while you must retreat." There was no smugness or even excitement in his expression; just the look of a person obsessed with his mission.

"She is from a line of righteousness, Satan!" Nathaniel cried out. He was way past pretending to be cool. "You will pay for your arrogance!"

"But her mother has rejected the Lord, and now Kate will be mine and Michael's pathetic attempts at faith will go down with her!" said Satan, breaking into an attempt at a laugh, which caused him to look totally demented. "And that will be the end of your 'righteous line,' Dashiel!" With that he lifted the end of his black cape, twirled around, and disappeared. His demonic entourage followed, expressions smug and shoulders back, having been buoyed by Satan's comments.

After several minutes of astonished silence, Imogen spoke out. "I don't think I can bear this, Nathaniel. To have to give way to that scum!"

"We will teach you how to work from a distance, Imogen," replied Nathaniel. "It was easy to trust the Lord in the Throne Room, but now you will have to learn how to believe on the coalface."

42

Singleton, Australia

Either Flo was getting harder to handle or Alec had finally gotten old and weary. *Lord, this is madness*, he thought. Here he was, hiding in his room like a scared wee lad while Tom took the main brunt of the tongue-lashing. What was he, a man or a mouse? "Choose to be a man, Alec; choose to be a man," he whispered, resting his forehead against the bedroom wall as Flo's voice reverberated along the hallway.

"Believe it or not, husband, it is not my idea of heaven to spend all day picking up after two absent-headed men who can't find their way from one end of the house to the other!"

The shouts were loud enough to wake the dead. There was nothing for it. Tom needed him. He sighed deeply, prayed for strength, and resolutely stepped out into the hallway just as another barrage opened up.

"I swear you two have got hay for brains! You're messy and absent headed and as useless as a tick on a dog! What have you got to say for yourself, Tom?"

A few seconds of silence followed, and Alec stayed rooted to the spot, waiting for what was sure to be a sorry comeback from Tom. Then it came.

"Jeez, Flo. I didn't think we was that messy!"

Alec winced as Flo cranked her yelling up to an ear-piercing level.

"*Were* messy, Tom! You didn't think you *were* messy, not *was!* When are you going to learn to talk properly?"

"Well ... I guess never, seeing as how I haven't learnt by now."

"Heaven help us," Alec breathed.

"Oh for God's sake! What in the name of Heaven am I doing here with the two of you?"

Alec risked a quick peep into the lounge room and saw that by a stroke of luck both Flo and Tom were facing the other way. It took a mere split second to decide that he should head for the back door and out into the open air. Without another thought he took off at top speed, which at his age was one notch above a fast crawl. Several minutes later he made it to the first hiding spot, which was the backyard dunny.

A short break to check if he'd been seen, then on to the chook shed and safety. He was exhausted and sweating like a pig. He leant against the back of the shed, gasping for breath and drinking in the comforting sounds of clucking and cheeping. As usual, memories of Kate flooded in now that he was alone with the fields and animals. The chooks had been the source of so many games …

"I can hear the chickens, Granda … down by the wheat paddock!"

"Aye, lass; Spottie's chased them all the way. And if yer mother finds out, we're in big trouble."

"Come on, Granda; we've still got time to get them back before dinner. Can't you run faster than that?"

"No I canna, lass … what d'ye think I am, a green lad?"

"Well you do act like one sometimes. Oh look, there they are! Spottie's rounded them all up in the corner of the spare paddock!"

"They're terrified, the poor wee things. We'll have tae round them back into the chook yard."

"You naughty boy! Oh look, Granda; he's so proud of himself!" …

Tears filled Alec's eyes. No matter how hard he tried, it was nay possible to get past the grief of her leaving. He understood why she didn't visit, but life was so empty without her. "Heavenly Father," he whispered, "I thank Thee for the gift of Kate; for a second chance in life. I thank Thee for her joy and light and her heart full of love for me. Wherever she may be, please help and comfort her and show Thyself real. Gie Michael the shove that he needs to make it, and please have mercy on Tom." Now the tears flowed unrestrained. "Help them, dear Lord; they all need Thee so much. And please gie me strength to make it to the end!"

Suddenly a pain the likes of which he'd never known gripped his chest, and he found it almost impossible to breathe. He clutched the windowsill of the shed and waited for the pain to pass, but it only increased and moved up the side of his neck and down his left arm. For several minutes the agony continued, and then his vision began to cloud. For the first time

Alec began to think that he might be dying. His next thought was of Kate and the news she'd written about in her last letter.

"The bairn, Lord! Please take care of the bairn. Keep it from the devil and catch it in angel arms when Kate gies birth." Nausea began to come like a tidal wave so that it was overwhelming, and he began to lose consciousness. As darkness increased, he thought of something else he wanted to say. "Lord God, please forgive my human weakness. Receive me into Thy kingdom."

Then something incredible happened. A creature—nay, two creatures—appeared shining amidst the darkness, glorious beyond anything he'd ever imagined. And one of them was talking to him.

"It's your time, Alec," said the taller of the two, who was the height of two men and radiant white from head to foot with golden wings. His face was luminous and beautiful, and he was smiling straight at Alec.

"You're my guardian angel!" gasped Alec.

"No, Alec," replied the creature. "Tristan here is your guardian, but I know you very well and was summoned to be here at this awesome moment. My name is Nathaniel."

Alec was about to reply when another crushing pain hit his heart, causing him to fall to the ground. Suddenly there was nothing but a glorious feeling of lightness and peace, and then the impossible happened and he was floating upwards with these magnificent angels. When he looked down, there was the chook shed, and beside it the body of an old man.

"Are they going to be all right, Nathaniel?" he asked.

"You've done all you can now, Alec," replied the luminous one. "Your time is up, and you must leave them to come with us. But the Lord is well pleased with you, as you will discover. Welcome to your reward!"

Alec glanced back just once as Singleton became a dot, but already he was caught up in the glory of the peace and love, which were increasing by the second. Faster than the speed of light they travelled up through the earth's atmosphere and then out into space until every last feeling of heaviness disappeared.

Oh, the glorious lightness! The wonder of feeling so free! Into the midst of his reverie came the sound of music so glorious that it caused his spirit to ignite, and he gazed around in rapture to find the source. In the distance was a golden city more radiant than the sun which beckoned and pulled like a magnet. He was coming home!

43

Glebe, Sydney, Australia

Kate turned on the tap and cupped her hands to capture some water. She filled them once to slurp hungrily, then again to rinse her face. The laundry was already like an oven; a girl could collapse trying to get the washing done. She began to transfer clothes from the old copper to the rinsing tub with her laundry stick and fought against the desire to sit down as the water bubbled and steam filled the room.

The air was as thick as pea soup, and overwhelmed her so that she dropped the clothes and stopped to grip the side of the tub. She took several gulps of air and reached for a damp cloth, then stopped with the cloth in mid-air at the sound of her name being shouted by someone standing outside. She managed to get herself to the door of the laundry and was greeted by a young boy who was smiling and holding up a piece of paper.

"Are you Mrs. O'Brien?"

"Yes, I am."

"Telegram for you, ma'am."

The boy handed it to her and hurried away. Kate was glad he didn't hang around, as she was in no state for a conversation. She leant against the door frame while she opened the telegram and began to read.

GRANDA DIED SUDDENLY YESTERDAY AFTERNOON OF A HEART ATTACK STOP FUNERAL ON WEDNESDAY STOP HE WOULD WANT YOU TO COME STOP

Kate stood stock-still, closed her eyes, and groaned. *Not Granda! Anyone but Granda!* He had been larger than life, her best friend, her confidant. She drew comfort from just knowing that he was there. His letters kept her sane in this hellhole; how could she go on without them? Anxiety tightened its grip, and she fought for some sort of control over her thoughts.

The first thing that came to mind was that she mustn't cry. She absolutely mustn't start crying, because then she wouldn't be able to stop and it'd be all over. "Breathe, Kate," she whispered, "breathe and think what you need to do."

But after several deep breaths she was still just going into more and more of a downward spiral. Something had to be doen. She looked around, frantically trying to remember what she'd been doing. *Oh the washing, that's right.* And now she had to get the clothes out on the line. Yes, that was what she had to do—get the washing out on the line.

Kate strode over to the sink and started to manically feed dripping clothes into the wringer while turning the handle like a glassy eyed robot. She watched with fascination as the water was squeezed out of a jumper and the garment passed out the other side of the wringer as flat as a pancake. She fished more clothes out of the boiling water and turned the handle of the wringer faster and faster. The most important thing in the world to her right now was to get that washing out.

Finally the last garment landed with the others, and then Kate picked up the laundry basket and headed out the door. The combination of bright sunlight and unshed tears had a blinding effect, but after a few seconds of blinking and swaying she crossed to the line and began to hang clothes out as if her life depended upon it. This was perfect timing. The clothes would catch the hottest part of the day and be ready to be brought in mid-afternoon.

Like a woman possessed she mindlessly jabbed pegs onto clothes. All feelings of lethargy left so that within minutes she hung out a full load of washing and stood back to watch it waving in the breeze. Now that disgusting outside toilet needed cleaning, as well as the communal bathroom. No one else in the house ever thought to clean them except Bea and her.

You have no one now. The thought struck her mind as clearly as if somcone were standing right there at the line. It stopped her in her tracks as surely as if she'd hit a brick wall.

"My father loves me!" she said out loud.

Your father is no match for your mother. You are alone and unprotected.

"I have Beatrice!" That tiny woman had been a friend; no judgments, never intrusive.

Beatrice is Michael's mother, came the reply. *You've done nothing for her. She will always put him first. Where is your safe place?*

"No!" cried Kate with her hands over her ears. "Don't leave me, Granda!" she shouted. "I need you more than ever! Please come back!"

She began to walk aimlessly around the yard, trying to keep from toppling over the edge into despair. She thought she must be going mad, talking to herself like this. What was the point of washing or cleaning—or anything, for that matter?

You might as well just run under a bus, said the voice. *No one cares anyway. What is the point? What is the point of anything?*

"Yes, what is the point? What is the point of anything?" That fighting spirit she'd had as a girl must have died somewhere along the way. For months now she'd been just willing herself to get up each day and go through the motions of living. What sort of existence was this for herself or the child she was carrying? Desolation began to encircle her soul and then tighten, leaving her feeling terrifyingly, absolutely alone. She wept in anguish, groaning and gasping and searching in her mind for something that would provide hope.

But there was no way out of this nightmare that she'd stepped into like a naive child, and no end in sight. Gradually the tears subsided and there was nothing to do but stand staring into space. With grim resolve she turned around to head for the backyard gate and the busy road beyond.

That was when, amazed and embarrassed, she realised that someone else was in the yard. An elderly woman dressed in lilac and pink stood holding the gate open. Had there been someone there this whole time? She had a lovely, kind face and was smiling at Kate. Just the sight of her gave Kate comfort.

"Oh, I'm so sorry if I scared you, dear," said the woman in a gentle, warm voice. "I must have come into the wrong yard. Does a Susan Miller live here?"

"No, I'm afraid not," replied Kate. That voice was a soothing balm to Kate's spirit, and she just stood staring at the woman.

"Are you all right, dear?" continued the stranger. "If you don't mind my saying, I couldn't help noticing that you're pregnant, and it's so hot today. But aren't you good; you already have your washing out. I always say that having a baby is one of the most significant things a human being can ever do."

How did she know about the pregnancy? "My Granda just died," said Kate. She was still riveted to the spot, completely caught up in the woman's aura, and for some reason wanted her to know about Granda.

"Yes, I know, dear," replied the woman, "but his prayers remain with you. And your father needs you. What you need to do is stop and rest for a moment. Make yourself a nice cup of tea and then start to pack your bags."

Kate finally found the ability to move. She swivelled around to look at her washing, which was drying so beautifully in the heat and breeze, and thought about the woman's suggestion. That toilet really, really needed a clean. Perhaps she would deal with that first, before it got too hot, then stop for a cuppa.

"Thank you for your kind words," she said, turning back to the woman. "I think I'll just clean the—" *For heaven's sake!* The woman had left without saying a word. Kate hurried over to the gate and looked first one way, then the next, but there was no sign of her anywhere. *That old woman can sure get up some speed!*

Well, it was too hot to be running after her, and Kate didn't have much time. Singleton was going to be a nightmare, but it would be the last straw if she missed Granda's funeral. There was a lot to do, what with packing and organising a train ticket, and Dad needed her more than ever. Of course he'd never admit it, because he wouldn't want to put her to any trouble.

She stopped to consider Michael. He had always been fond of Granda and would probably consider coming along. Her lips pursed as resentment flared hot and fast. No, she would not tell him. Let him see how it felt to have no idea where she was or when she would return. *Let him simmer and worry for once!* He had pushed her to the side. He was not allowed to be part of this sacred time in her life.

*   *   *

"Well done, Imogen! You demonstrated creativity there and achieved a great result from a distance. I thought the pink and lilac colour combination was a nice touch." Nathaniel pretended not to notice the fact that right now Imogen was visibly shaking and groaning with his arms tightly crossed. No doubt about it; this guardian tended towards a melancholic disposition. The best way to handle him was to keep things as light as possible.

"I thought I was going to lose her, Nathaniel," Imogen said in a voice barely above a whisper.

"But you didn't lose her, Imogen, and that's the bottom line," replied Nathaniel, trying to play the whole incident down. Things were moving too fast at this point to allow for the luxury of self-examination or panic. "I'll call in extra backup for you for the funeral."

"You're leaving?" Imogen looked up for the first time in minutes, his eyes like saucers. "What about Kate?"

"Kate's busy cleaning a toilet rather than running under a bus thanks to you," said Nathaniel in what he hoped was a voice of authority softened by kindness. "The reinforcements will be here soon. I'll wait with you until they come."

44

Singleton, Australia

She'd kept it vaguely together so far, but now was like a dead woman breathing, unable to register any sort of emotion. There was no sadness, anger, hunger, you name it. Crying was out of the question, even though it would maybe have done her good to cry.

The sight of Granda's coffin floating along in slow motion up front was just simply impossible for her to handle. Even the sound of Mum and Dad arguing in the back seat didn't move her. Her eyes remained riveted on the hearse directly in front as their voices drifted around in the background.

"Stop fussing, Tom," Mum was saying in between copious sobs and much blowing of her nose, "you're annoying the daylights out of me!"

But Dad just couldn't stop fussing. "I can't help it, Flo. All of us are gonna miss the old bloke ettingg' huge; etting' surer. But you're etting' yourself in such a state."

"I am not in a state! I'm just letting out my emotions in a normal, healthy way, unlike some people around here who shall remain nameless!"

"That's not fair, Flo. We all show our grief different. Our Kate's just as upset as the rest of us."

"Well you could have fooled me. I haven't seen any sign of her caring about anyone much for years."

Kate waited to see if Mum's words would hurt or make her angry, but there was no reaction at all. At least something was going her way today. To think that the previous night she'd started to nurture hopes of staying here for a while to get a break from the sardine can she'd been living in. Boy, had that been a dream. So this was what it felt like to be between a rock and a hard place.

The hearse turned into the old cemetery and wound through gardens which were a masterpiece of red and white roses. Those blooms were meant to give comfort, but all they did was cheapen Granda's passing by daring to open to the sun and celebrate life. He had loved flowers. "God's handiwork," he'd called them.

"Y' see this rose, young Kate? Look how it starts out scarlet in the centre then fades tae pink. And the fragrance! Och, what an artist is our Lord!"

Kate noticed that they were slowing down, so steeled herself for the burial ahead. She summoned the courage to peep out the window, and at the first sight of the grave knew that the only way to get through this agony would be by somehow finding a place of solitude and safety. Gradually the hearse came to a stop, and she quickly slipped out, made her way to the gravesite, and checked out the surrounding area.

Over to the right was a cluster of grevillea bushes where it would be possible to watch the proceedings alone. A crowd was beginning to gather, and each person was too preoccupied to notice her at that point, so she kept walking steadily, avoiding eye contact and hoping against hope that no one would call out her name. Finally she made it to the bushes, let out a huge sigh of relief, and positioned herself in the midst of the flimsy hiding spot.

The sounds of crying, noses being blown, and awkward conversations faded into the background, and the sombre faces of lifelong friends became a blur. Her focus was riveted on the coffin, which carried the precious person who had filled her days with sunshine and hope.

Minutes dragged by, and the minister from the Singleton Presbyterian church began to recite the twenty-third psalm, which had been one of Granda's favourites. Reverend Sutton was sincere, no doubt about it, but somehow that psalm wasn't coming alive today the way it had whenever Granda had read it out to her. He used to say it like a love song, and she used to hang on every word.

When he got to the last verse, there'd be tears in his brown eyes. "Surely goodness and mercy shall follow me all the days of my life," he'd say; then, after a pause, he'd close his eyes and say the last line: "and I shall dwell in the house of the Lord forever."

Now came the part she'd been dreading—the lowering of the coffin. "Ashes to ashes, dust to dust," recited the reverend as Granda disappeared into the ground. Kate held on to a branch with both hands to stop from throwing herself in with him. Mum dropped something into the hole, weeping loudly and Dad tossed in some soil he had scooped up with his hands. Then a couple of workers started to shovel soil into the grave.

Kate withdrew in horror and clung to a nearby fence. She couldn't take her eyes off the gravesite as the soil methodically covered the coffin. A huge part of her was being buried with him, no doubt about it, and she would never be whole again.

How was a person supposed to deal with this? Her responses were all over the place anyway now with the pregnancy, and there was her wonderful, lovable Granda, disappearing for good under a pile of dirt. From the time she'd first met him, her life had stepped out into the sunshine as if he'd been given as a gift especially to her. And now he'd been taken away at a time when she needed him most.

Finally the bubble of her emotions burst. As if escaping from demons, Kate ran like the wind to the hearse and ripped open the door. She jumped into the front seat, slammed the door, and cried her heart out until there were no tears left.

45

Singleton, Australia

Any more hours spent just sitting here in this old armchair and Kate might end up stuck forever in her childhood bedroom. She was everywhere and nowhere at the moment. Her mind was completely awake, batting ideas back and forth, her body was refusing to budge, and her emotions were red raw. What was a person supposed to do with all that?

There was nothing for her here; no safe place. Mum was impossible now, and Dad was a mess. Back home at the ranch Michael would be furious. She sank deeper into the chair at the thought of facing the man again. It had felt so good to just take off on Tuesday without warning and without even telling him about Granda. But now, in the light of day, it was not looking like such a good idea.

He always said that he was just trying to get on top of his shattered nerves and build a life for them both. According to him, the alcohol helped him cope. He could never figure out why she didn't just keep the home fires burning while he tried to sort everything out. They might as well have been on different planets.

She groaned and closed her eyes, trying to make her mind slow down. Dusk had begun to settle in, and there was some comfort to be had from the sounds of birds all around. Magpies warbled, kookaburras laughed, and cockies screeched as they sought out others of their kind to settle down with before dusk began to close in.

If she'd married one of the countless country boys who'd come knocking, maybe this is what it would have been like every day, settling down at dusk with her husband after a hard day's work in the fields. But none of them had thrilled her like Michael.

He could charm a bear out of its winter sleep and make even a corpse laugh with his wit. There were so many sides to him that were hard to understand. He was a man of the world, and she felt like a child compared to him. She was going to have to do a lot of growing up very quickly if there was going to be a chance to make their love work. One day, when she had the energy.

At least Beatrice would be there for her in Sydney. That woman had definitely been round the block several times. Not that she was a tart; far from it. But always kind. No pressure or expectations; just quiet acceptance.

She decided to have a go at praying. What harm could it do? Speaking in a whisper she began. "God, if you are there, could you please look after Bea and help her? She's been so kind to me; I've grown to love her very much and I'd like the chance to show how much I appreciate her. Amen."

From now on the baby was her top priority. The very thought brought on waves of panic as well as guilt. Hadn't she contemplated jumping under a bus until that lovely lady had commented on the pregnancy? What sort of a mother was she going to be? Into the midst of these troubled thoughts came her father's voice from the doorway.

"How's it goin' Kate?" he said, his face a picture of weariness on every level.

"I'll be okay, Dad," she replied in monotones, "but I have to return to Sydney. Mum and I are not good for each other right now." Wow, what an understatement! Dad didn't argue. Judging by the resigned look on his face he knew she was right.

"Well, look after yourself and the little nipper," he said after a few moments.

Something about his voice made her stop and study him for a moment. He really was a dear and undoubtedly adored her. When had he tiptoed off the main stage of her life and settled himself in the wings to watch from a distance? Had she been so self-absorbed that she hadn't even noticed?

"Yes I will, Dad; I promise," she replied with as much reassurance as possible. "Could you book a train for me for tomorrow morning? I'll try to sleep tonight and be off first thing."

He gazed into her eyes for a moment, his own brimming with tears. "She doesn't mean what she says, Katie; she's just real mixed up sometimes."

Kate didn't answer straight away, as neither of them was in a hurry anyway. But no longer was it in her to bite back her words.

"That's not true, Dad, and you know it," she finally replied. "Mum does mean everything she says, and she's not mixed up. Her words are used as a weapon to cause you and me pain because of her own unhappiness."

He bent forward and held on to the doorjamb, visibly shaking and then sobbing. Kate held her breath as he reached for a handkerchief. That was the first time she'd ever voiced what they both knew to be true, and she wasn't backing down now. Finally he blew his nose and, leaning back on the doorjamb, spoke in not much more than a whisper.

"But it's me that's made her unhappy, Kate. I didn't satisfy her, not at all. She just stayed with me out of pity."

That was just the detonator that Kate needed to send her up out of that chair and onto her feet. "Don't talk like that, Dad!" she cried, tears welling unbidden. "You didn't make her unhappy! She was already unhappy when you found her. But what you did was let her wallow in her self-pity without ever challenging her to grow up!"

He let the words sink in for a minute. "You're right, Katie," he said at last. "It doesn't do any of us any good when I never stand up to her. I haven't had much to do with love except for you. You always loved with your whole heart, no questions asked."

"Dad, just because I loved Granda too didn't mean that I loved you less. You knew that didn't you?"

"Katie, I've never been so happy as the day when you came back on that ship. I was nearly out of my mind thinkin' I'd never see you again. And if the price of having you back was sharin' you with Alex, then I was glad to pay it."

"I love you so much, Dad; it hurts all over."

It was wonderful to hug her father again the way she used to before life got so confusing. When they'd both finished hugging and crying, he placed his hands on her shoulders and looked her straight in the eyes.

"I'll try to be stronger, nipper, but make sure you learn from my mistakes. That man of yours has got boatloads of unhappiness stored up from before you found him. Don't take it on board like I did, don't let him wallow in it, and don't let him take it out on your kids."

46

The cigarette smoke was so thick in here that Bea nearly collapsed face down on the keyboard from asphyxiation. She was beginning to get a really bad feeling about this place and had already started to toss up how necessary the money really was. The scared "I want to curl up in a ball" Bea was looking for the exits, but unfortunately the terrified "How will I survive?" Bea was mentally processing the week's bills. Terror won out over mere fear this time round.

The Cross had always been one of her favourite haunts, and the bohemian scene was where she'd felt the closest to belonging anywhere. It was comforting when artists, musicians, writers, and actors could gather together and let their eccentricities hang out in safety. When Pearl Brennan had said there was a job going at the Sundown Hangout, she'd trusted her old friend and taken it sight unseen. But then again, she hadn't seen Pearl for four years, and obviously a lot of water had gone under the bridge since then.

By the looks of it, the old Pearl had got more desperate and less discriminating and was not just working behind the bar for her spare cash now. The American GI she was plastered all over was half her age and already sloshed. Not that Bea could blame the woman. She and Pearl had both given up hoping for a fairy godmother decades ago.

But this place was a living hell. She'd pictured an arty cafe ambience but had landed in a sleazy club full of Americans, prostitutes, and underground-looking characters, mixed in with strippers and even a sprinkling of camp couples.

She finally got to the last chord of "Wish me Luck as you Wave me Goodbye" and forced a smile for the dozen or so who clapped. A glance in the direction of the wall clock told her there was one hour left on her shift and also alerted her to the approaching presence of the manager, Cliff Bell.

"Is everything okay, Cliff?" she asked nervously. At maybe six foot three, dressed totally in black, and smoking a huge cigar, he was one scary character.

"Yeah, it's fine, Bea. But I think it's time for some slow, sexy stuff. Can you do 'Wonder When my Baby's Coming Home'?"

"Sure can," said Bea, holding her face in the smiling pattern. "I get the idea."

"When the Yanks get sentimental, they spend more money; you know how it is," said Cliff, giving her a pat and an intimate wink before ducking away as quickly as he'd come.

If there was one thing she knew, it was "how it is." Tossing that thought aside, she plunged into the first notes of the requested song. After the first couple of verses, she looked up from the keyboard and for a second froze mid-chorus. A camp couple had just entered the club laughing and cuddling, which wasn't what had grabbed her attention. The attention-grabber was the fact that one of them was her son Robert.

By instinct she looked away immediately and focused on her piano in an attempt to get herself together. Questions crashed into one another as they plunged around in her mind. Why hadn't he told her? Did he think she didn't care? Did he hate everything about her life and want to reject her and all she stood for? Had he left her for good? How could she have missed something as huge as her baby looking for love with a man?

Somehow she got to the end of the song. With her heart pounding like a war drum and sweat breaking out everywhere, she finally got the courage to look up from the keyboard. Her eyes flitted back and forth, taking in the whole club, but he was nowhere to be found. *He couldn't have left! Surely he wouldn't just leave!*

She jumped up from the piano stool and began running throughout the club, searching every face and ignoring the strange looks being slanted her way. This was possibly borderline hysteria, but Bea couldn't stop the tears that were flowing now or the panic that escalated as she ran out onto the street and frantically looked from right to left.

It was devastating to see him after all this time without being able to make contact and express her love. Oh how she loved him! She began to sob with the anguish of a mother grieving for a lost child. She assumed he must have seen her playing and been so disgusted that he couldn't get away quickly enough. *He must really hate me. My baby hates me.*

* * *

Robert ran as if the hounds of Hell were snapping at his heels. He couldn't feel the pavement anymore; just the blind panic that drove him forward as he knocked people out of the way and tried to ignore Matthew's shouts.

"For Christ's sake, Robert, stop!" yelled Matthew. "You don't even know where you're going, you twat!"

The guy was right. He started to slow down, then finally stopped in the middle of the pavement and just stared into space. The only cohesive thought happening in his head was that it was a matter of life and death to be away from that place and the accusing eyes of his mother.

There was no mistaking the matter. She'd looked his way, stopped dead for a couple of seconds, and then gone back to playing as if she were performing at a concert recital instead of banging away at the Sundown Hangout. Probably horrified. Maybe a potential heart case. *What is she doing in a dive like that anyway, for God's sake? Talk about a square peg in a round hole!* At that point his thoughts were interrupted by the sounds of Matthew gulping for air beside him.

"Anything you want to tell me about, sweetie?" he said between gasps. "You know, like the odd troublesome mental illness or such. The sort of thing a person can forget to mention."

"My mother was in there," replied Robert without turning to look at Matthew.

"Oh shit!" said Mathew. He was silent for a few moments. "What was she doing in a place like that? Does she work for the Salvation Army or something?"

"Not funny, Matthew!" shouted Robert. "How do I know why she's there? All I know is that my whole life I was never good enough, and just when I was starting to feel okay about myself, bingo—there she is again!"

"Maybe she didn't see you, sweetie" said Matthew. "Where was she, anyway?"

"Playing the bloody piano, that's where!" yelled Robert. "She saw me the moment we walked through the door and nearly fell off her stool!"

That was when he noticed that Matthew was shooting furtive looks to the side and turned around to find that they'd gathered quite a crowd. He cringed with embarrassment and once again had to face the fact that the two of them presented a strange picture to most people. The shame that he saw in Matthew's beautiful face cut to the bone. When would the pain ever end? Would there ever come a time when they could just be themselves without being treated like criminals?

Without another thought he grabbed his lover by the hand and ran across the street, trying to block out the mental picture of those faces looking at them with either contempt or mockery. Matthew had gone really quiet, and his lips were pursed, both definite signs of being more than a little upset. Robert was going to have to make amends somehow. They reached the opposite pavement, and he stopped for a few seconds, trying to figure out what to say.

"Matthew, honey, I am sooo sorry," he said finally. "You haven't done anything wrong, and I was taking my anger out on you."

"And just why are you angry?" replied Matthew in a tiny voice. "She was just playing the piano."

Robert tried to keep his irritation in check. "My mother had great dreams for me," he said in measured tones. "She wanted me to become a world-changing pianist, amongst other things, none of which I did. The last thing she expected …" he hesitated for a split moment to find the right words.

"Was to see you walk into a dive with a poofter," snapped Matthew. "That's what you were going to say, wasn't it?"

"Of course I wasn't you idiot!" he bellowed, arms akimbo.

"Well don't worry, Robert; you don't have to be ashamed of me anymore!" spat Matthew as he flounced off, his eyes brimming with tears.

Robert sighed and watched him go. He did love Matthew, but the sulks and tantrums could get pretty exhausting. He needed to be alone for a while to get his head together. Mother had looked like an angel sitting at that piano, so petite and delicate, her beautiful black hair thick and shiny.

There was a big, huge pool of grief at the bottom of his soul and a little boy inside who wanted to run into that club, embrace his mother, and pour out oceans of love. He adored her. But it was unbearable for him to even think of the disappointment he'd always seen in her eyes whenever she'd looked at him.

He could never be Michael. It was crazy dreaming of things that could never be when he'd finally found love and a community of people who accepted him with no strings attached. There was no going back for him, and that was all there was to it.

47

Glebe, Sydney, Australia

Damn! How is a bloke supposed to find his way when there are four of everything? Michael held on tight to the front fences of the street leading home and pulled himself along as if climbing Mount Everest. He knew the house ahead was his because it was the last one on a corner. If it was in the middle of a row of terraces, he'd be up the creek without a paddle right now.

"No reason t' come home anyway," he mumbled to himself. "The wife's left, there's no future; I'm just a drunk without a cause." He slowly manoeuvred his way through the gate and continued the litany. "Yes, Michael, a drunk without a cause; without a cause, that's you." At that point he noticed through the alcohol haze that Mum's light was on. "Well, well, well!" he said, going cross-eyed in an attempt to focus. "Mother's been partying! Naughty, naughty."

He waggled his finger back and forth and began to lumber towards the door of Bea's flat. There were two steps to negotiate, which according to Michael were two steps too many at the moment. He got down on his hands and knees and crawled to the front door, then pulled himself up on the doorpost and was about to knock when the door opened.

"Oh my God, Michael," gasped his mother. "How long have you been drinking?"

"An' a very good evening to you too, mother!" replied Michael. "Been drinking for 'proximately thirty years, give or take a decade."

"*Tres amusement,* Michael," said Bea. "For heaven's sake, come inside and do your collapsing on the lounge instead of the veranda."

"Need help with that," said Michael, grasping the side of the doorway like a drowning man hanging on to a life raft. "Big step in the way." He let Bea transfer his left arm from the door frame to her tiny shoulder and lead him from the veranda to the lounge. With a sigh of relief he collapsed onto his back and remained as still as possible, waiting for his head to stop spinning.

"Where's Kate?" asked Bea. "She'll be worrying about you."

"She's left me." There, he'd said it out loud; the thing he'd been thinking for days but hadn't wanted to face. Kate had left him. "No note, no phone call, no nothing, mother, just … kaput!" he said with a wave of his hand.

"She's left!" exclaimed Bea. "And you haven't said anything? What if she's hurt, kidnapped, or lost? Don't you care about anything, Michael?"

"Rang Singleton." He didn't want to talk about this but knew his mother wouldn't let it drop. "Tom's a hopeless liar. She's there, Mother; blind Freddie could see that. Or rather deaf Freddie could hear that."

"Why don't you chase after her? We both know she's had plenty of reason to leave!" She was pacing back and forth, and Michael was getting giddy watching so he closed his eyes. "At least look at me when I'm talking to you, Michael!" she shouted, making him feel even worse.

"Whose side are you on, anyway!" He sat up for emphasis, which turned out to be a bad idea. "I'm your son, remember? You taught me everything I know!" He collapsed back onto the lounge. "She left me, Mum. Not chasing after her," he added in a little voice.

"I can't understand why you're just going to let a girl like Kate slip through your fingers, Michael," said Bea.

"That's jus' one of a million things you don't understand, Mum," whispered Michael. He was on the brink of a migraine here, and his mother just wouldn't let up.

"What do you mean by that?" she replied. "I understand a lot of things."

"Well you don't understand me! "Me—Michael; that's what you don't understand! And what's more, you never did!" And with that he pulled himself upright, held on desperately to the end of the lounge, and turned towards the door.

"I'm off to bed, Mother … good night!" he snapped with as much dignity as possible in the circumstances. Then he felt his way along the back of the lounge, lunged towards the door, and opened it. He was feeling moderately better after dumping a load of misery onto his mother but knew it wouldn't be long before the guilt set in. To his relief, she didn't follow, so he proceeded to slide along the wall and make the long and foggy journey to his own flat at the back of the building.

48

Glebe, Sydney, Australia

Nimrad looked hopelessly at the comatose figure on the old double bed. Michael's snoring was loud enough to bring down the walls of Jericho, but his brain was out of action. Rejection and Self-Pity had created a blackout which rendered him impotent. So now Beatrice had no one at her darkest hour.

He transferred to Beatrice's flat hoping to find some way to intervene and found himself face-to-face with Tetrak, who was pacing restlessly and vibrating with bloodlust. Nimrad's heart sank at the sight of Beatrice, who sat at her piano playing classical music, her face streaked with tears.

Grief had stretched his cape to cover her, so the spiritual atmosphere was icy cold and putrid. Rejection was circling and emitting a chant which was stirring up waves of evil all around.

"You've failed, Bea. Failed in every area," he repeated again and again. "The world would be better without you. Better without you."

"No!" cried Nimrad. "It's a lie, Beatrice; a lie!" Already he could feel himself weakening and could see that she wasn't hearing him. "You are loved, Beatrice. People need you," he added in what was now only a whisper.

Tetrak broke out into hysterics. "Nice try, Nimrad," he finally said through gasps of laughter, "but there are no prayers registered for Beatrice, and there are curses aplenty. I can't even believe you have the hide to come here."

"She is loved," whispered Nimrad. "I love her." But already Grief's tentacles were immobilising him. The level of excitement in the room now rose to fever pitch, and Nimrad turned to see who had entered the atmosphere.

Satan glided onto the scene, making all the others look clumsy in comparison. He had coloured himself red and gold tonight; Beatrice's favourite colours. Bea stood now and wandered across to look at photos of Robert, Michael, and Kate which she'd placed on the sideboard. Her eyes filled with tears again at the sight of the beloved faces. "I've made a mess of everything," she whimpered, "and I wanted to at least be a good mother."

"Of course you did," replied Satan, "but you just don't have it in you, do you?" He watched with satisfaction as she broke down into uncontrollable sobs. She blew her nose and sighed deeply. "I broke my parents' hearts, shattered my sister, married a loser, and now my children despise me. I'm a zero; my life has been for nothing." Again she began to weep. "It's all been a big, fat zero."

Nimrad's spirit was wrenched at the sight of Bea's despair. Tears of compassion flowed as they had for so many others, and he searched frantically within the prayer waves in the hope that someone somewhere had thought of her.

And there it was; a childlike but heartfelt appeal on Bea's behalf. It was the first ever from Kate, but the depth of her love had injected it with power. He could see that the simple request had reached the throne, and the answer had already been activated. Relieved and invigorated he resolved to stand his ground by her side until help arrived.

49

King's Cross, Sydney, Australia

"Shut the hell up Matthew! I can't stand your nagging one more second. Do you understand?"

There was not one aspect of Matthew's expression or stance that said he intended to shut the hell up. Robert had managed to lose himself in an alcohol stupor, and when he'd dragged his eyes open, there he was, ready to start up where they'd left off.

"Oh, for crying out loud! You drive me up the wall. I think I'll shoot myself just to get some peace."

Matthew brushed away a lock of hair that had fallen over his forehead. The nervous action, along with his resolute expression, was impossibly endearing.

"Robert, I'm not going to let you bully me." His shaking fingers fiddled with the buttons on his favourite velvet dressing gown. "For Christ's sake; she's your mother, and you love her to pieces. It's not as if she beat you or threw you out on the street or anything. You're absolutely devastated, and I haven't had a wink's sleep worrying about it! Anyway, for all you know she might be beside herself as well. You know where she lives, so why not just go around for a visit? You don't have to take me along; she'll need to build up to that slowly. We don't want to give the poor dear a heart attack."

Robert felt like a monster in the face of Matthew's generosity of heart. His Dutch courage went galloping out the door and left him standing naked and with no arguments left. "You know that I'll hate you for this in the morning," he said.

"It's already morning, sweetie. By the time you get up and dressed and catch a tram, you can be there at first light. You can talk things through over a nice cuppa or whatever people with mothers do."

"And are you prepared to clean up the mess if it all goes to pot?"

"You know that I am."

50

Glebe, Sydney, Australia

Robert stepped out of the tram and stood on the street trying to gather together any crumbs of courage he could find in the corners of his heart and mind. Soon people began to give him strange looks. What were they all doing up at this unholy hour on a Saturday morning anyway?

Well, he'd come all this way, and Matthew would give him hell if he backed out now. He closed his eyes and exhaled slowly before setting out on the final leg of the journey. Matthew was right; this situation had to be made clear once and for all, and there was just the slightest possibility that the conclusions he'd jumped to were all wrong.

He turned the corner resolved to see the whole thing through, and marched through the gate with the look of someone about to face a firing squad. After a moment's hesitation he stepped up onto the veranda, and entered through the open front door. There on the lounge, crying her eyes out, was his mother.

51

Glebe, Sydney, Australia

As Glebe got closer, Kate's nerves got tighter. The tram pulled up close to the back gate, and her heart started playing the bongos. *What do you say at a time like this? "Sorry to disappear on you like that, Michael; Granda died!"*

"There y'go luv" said the conductor. "Home safe and sound."

She rummaged in the bottomless pit called a bag and finally found her key before clambering down onto the pavement. "Thank you very much," she said in princess tones. Her address might be Glebe, but it didn't mean she'd had a Glebe upbringing!

That spurt of pride carried her to the back gate, which she pushed open with a flourish. But then it all evaporated, leaving her frozen in mid-step, suitcase in hand, and seriously wondering about the upshot of her wacky behaviour.

Michael was usually home on Saturday morning. When she turned up he might be sad or he might be furious. He'd been very fond of Granda and might be upset about missing the funeral. Or he might be plotting her demise. Maybe he couldn't care less.

Dammit! When did I become such a sap? She'd never been like this before Michael. It was time to throw all sappy behaviour out the window—or over the fence in this case. After a passionate "Come on Kate, you can do this!" and several mammoth inhalations and exhalations, she strode down the path, through the open kitchen door, and into the middle of somebody's nightmare.

The place was stuffy, smelly, basically unloved. It looked like there'd been a dozen chooks living there at some time in the distant past. Generally speaking, it was disgusting by anyone's standards. And there in the middle of it was Michael, out cold.

She dropped her bag onto the kitchen table and stood with hands on hips, looking around the revolting pigsty. Should she be angry because he was such a pig, or relieved because he was obviously beside himself? How did life manage to get this complicated?

After some thought, she decided that a heart to heart chat with her kind mother-in-law was the way to go. Bea would be able to tell her how Michael was. A half smile found its way to her face at the thought of that woman, who'd been such a comfort; no judgements and no expectations.

With that in mind, she exited the kitchen door, crossed the backyard, and rounded the corner of the house to follow the pathway which led to the flat at the front. She hurried up the steps and into the lounge room. There on the lounge was Bea, fast asleep, and beside her on an armchair was a small version of Michael.

*   *   *

Robert continued to observe the exotic creature who'd just landed in the room. Her brilliant green eyes were taking in everything, and it wasn't long before she noticed him curled up in the chair. She took just a moment to study him.

"You're Robert, aren't you?" she said without averting her gaze. "You look so much like Michael, except a little smaller."

"I see you are a kind person," he replied. "I am half Michael's size."

"The eyes are a dead giveaway."

"Yes."

"Why are you here?"

"I saw Mum last night at a club and came round this morning to attempt reconciliation. When I arrived she was at the point of despair. Apparently she'd had a bad session with Michael right after the shock of seeing me with my boyfriend. No telling what would have happened if I hadn't turned up. Someone somewhere must be looking after her; I sure haven't!"

To Robert's amazement, her eyes filled with tears. "Robert," she said, "it's good to meet you. My name's Kate, and I'm Michael's wife."

And with that she left.

*　*　*

Michael tried to drag himself out of bed. He cringed when he remembered what he'd said the night before. Mum was the only person who'd ever really known him. Michael closed his eyes and tried to take in that terrifying fact. He probably looked like a crazy person sitting there in the middle of his mess, but he didn't give a damn.

He sure as hell didn't have the energy to figure out what was going on between Kate and him. She must have had her reasons for going AWOL, but he wasn't up to hearing about what a hopeless husband he'd been. It was hard enough feeling like an abusive monster of a son.

"I can't believe that I dumped my garbage on you last night, Mum," he said to a framed photo which smiled back at him. "What a champion! And the joke's on old Michael, because no one else cares whether I'm alive or dead." He groaned and bent over forward, raking his hands through uncombed hair. How was he ever going to get over this guilt? "I'm sorry, Mum," he said, his voice clear and echoing in the eerie stillness. "You deserved more, much more."

Memories rose up of his little wisp of a mother protecting Robert and him from the bullying waste of space that passed for his father. Michael used to curl up in bed in a scared little ball and listen to the commotion when she refused to let Dad back into their flat. She always stood her ground, no matter how drunk or abusive he was, and finally he would always give up and leave.

She'd stood her ground last night too when her own son had turned up at the door blind drunk. His animal instinct had been working even though most of his brain had shut down, and he remembered that she'd shown no fear. She'd challenged him to want more, go higher; and her words had hit their mark even though he'd thrown them back in her face.

Kate had never fought back. That was the trouble. She'd never looked scared, just disgusted. Bit by bit she'd just drawn back more and then finally shut the door. How do you get through to someone who won't fight back? He wished she could see that he was just trying to tie together enough frayed loose ends to make some sort of life for them both.

He'd never worked out how to get rid of the anger that raged in his gut or the fear that one day she would see through to the scared little kid inside. He could scrape by in life with the gift of the gab, but inside there was always that bubbling cauldron going on. Somehow it had helped to know that Mum knew and understood.

The nightmares were still haunting his sleep, courtesy of the bloody war. Last night it had come again, the one where he was trying to run through sand that kept slipping away from under his feet. Every time he looked down, he saw bodies of mates lying face up with eyes wide open, staring at him. Just thinking about it brought on new waves of crippling grief. It had helped to write about his nightmares in his letters home to Mum.

Music had always echoed through their homes down through the decades. She was just as brilliant playing classical as she was beating out the latest hit dance songs. And then there were the children's tunes she used to teach to the young girls from that posh private school nearby. Michael could never understand why those lessons were so important to her. She had one favourite that she used to sing over and over until he knew every bloody word. How did it go again? Oh yes, that was it:

I'm a little doll who was dropped and broken, falling off my Mummy's knee.

I'm a little doll who has just been mended, so won't you tell me please?

Are my ears on straight, is my nose in place,

do I have a cute expression on my face?

Are my blue eyes bright, do I look all right

to be taken home Christmas Day?

Michael let the rest of the song play over and over in his head. She used to really bounce along the keys, singing it out loud and finishing with a flourish of chords. It brought a smile to her face, but not a happy smile; more of a wistful one.

"I never figured out why that song meant so much to you, Mum" he said, voice breaking and eyes streaming. "You always seemed so tough. I thought I could throw anything at you and you wouldn't break." Michael held the photo up and studied it for a moment. Her black curls cascaded nearly to her waist, and those brilliant black eyes seemed to leap from the frame. He shook his head and whispered, "You might have fallen, but you didn't break."

*   *   *

Kate finished dry retching next to the hydrangea. If there'd been even a crumb in her stomach, it would have come up. At this rate she was going to be so skinny that she'd end up looking like a snake that had swallowed a cat for lunch.

God had answered her pathetic prayer only hours ago. Granda was right; it was time for her to grow up and think of the big picture. She hadn't had to build up fighting muscles with Granda and Dad loving her no matter what she did. But all the rules had changed now, and bad things don't go away if you ignore them. The more she ignored Michael, the worse he got.

She'd never felt guilty before; there'd always been someone else to blame. But no doubt about it, guilt is the worst thing that can happen to a person. It knocks the very life out of you. Michael was crazy with guilt about his mother and brother, and she was just crazy with guilt about everything. She couldn't have picked a worse time to walk out. And she hadn't got back to visit Granda when she knew how lonely he was without her.

Footsteps came up behind her. It was Robert, the midget version of Michael. She smoothed back her hair, stood up straight, and turned to meet him.

"Hi Kate," he said in a croaky voice. "If you don't want any visitors, I'll understand. I just feel like jumping off the fricking gap right now. Not that it's your problem, for crap's sake."

"No, please don't go, Robert. Michael's wallowing in the depths of our flat, and I'm not in a hurry to go there. Are you drowning in guilt like me?"

"Going down for the third time and not sure whether I want to come back up."

"At least you did come back home to reconcile. There must be some comfort there."

"I ran away from her like a mongrel dog. Where's the comfort in that?"

"But you changed your mind and returned wanting to make amends. And you came at a crucial time."

"All of which doesn't change the fact that Michael and I have a lot to answer for."

Kate wanted to sleep for a month. "Have you had the chance to talk with her properly yet, Robert?" she said.

"Are you kidding? I don't know where to start. She was just ecstatic that I came back and fell asleep exhausted on the lounge."

"No, I'm not kidding. Go back there and just sit quietly for a while and make peace with her."

She could see that her words had hit home. He stopped and pondered them for a while. "I'll see you later," he finally said.

"Yes, see you later," she replied.

Once he was gone, she went back to trying to think. *What on earth can a person do with this much regret? What drawer can you put it in?* She considered that if she'd made a habit of going back home for visits instead of sulking behind her pride, maybe life would have been a little better for Granda and he'd have lived long enough to see his great-grandchild. If she hadn't walked out on Michael, maybe he wouldn't have dumped all his junk on Bea's doorstep and she wouldn't have been driven to the point of despair.

She couldn't get over it, under it, around it. No matter where she went in her mind, it followed her. *This is impossible! Unbearable!* She began to rock back and forth with her arms wrapped around her middle. *What was it that Granda told me about guilt? It hadn't meant much at the time.* She racked her brain to remember. *That's right; he'd been feeding a poddy calf at the time.*

"I've made more mistakes in life than ye ever will lassie," he'd said. "We start off light and free like this calf, but then our sins build up till we can scarce live wi' ourselves. The wonder of it is that when we confess our trespasses, our Heavenly Father forgi'es us. But the great miracle, Katie, is when he takes our load of sin and guilt away and washes us clean and gi'es us the strength tae live again."

Could that possibly be true? Should she dare to try it? She felt she surely couldn't lose anything by trying. And anyway, nothing could be worse than what she was going through at the moment. She started to pace, arguing back and forth around the point.

*　　*　　*

According to Nathaniel's calculations, she hadn't washed her hair for a week. Her clothes, which were usually smart and immaculate, were wrinkled and thrown together. All of her life the girl had been thin, but after weeks of barely eating she was literally skin and bone.

The darkness was closing in, but he could see that she had some fight rising up. Spiritually speaking, the noise and stench were intensifying by the second as demons of all shapes and sizes grunted, snorted, screeched, and even laughed hysterically. This was their moment, and their time was short, but they were absolutely sure that Kate was on the brink of breaking.

Tetrak was doing a war dance in the centre, his face a picture of bloodlust and ecstasy. The heavenly angels stood at the ready, and all eyes were on Kate.

"She's so alone down there," said Imogen. "I can't bear it!"

Nathaniel heard Imogen's words like a faint background noise. He was careful to remain completely still, because deep in his spirit there was expectation. Something was happening. He just knew it, even though there was no visible evidence.

The atmosphere was shifting. Kate had stopped rocking in despair and instead was pacing around, muttering to herself.

"Look closer, my friend," he whispered. Imogen turned a puzzled countenance towards him before swivelling back to the battle scene.

"Can you see the significant thing that is happening right now?"

"No, Nathaniel; but I'm sure you're going to tell me."

"Kate has had a thought."

"Hallelujah."

"I don't know what the thought was, but it's having an effect. It's something new that she's decided to chew on."

"Okay."

"And something is beginning to rise up on the inside."

"Not feeling the love yet, Nathaniel."

"Well, you're not Robinson Crusoe there, friend. Neither is anyone else."

Suddenly Kate stopped her pacing, stood stock-still for several seconds, and then, to the amazement of the gathered throng, dropped to her knees.

"Oh God, please help me!" she cried out. "The agony's too great. Please forgive me and take it away. I'm sorry! I am so sorry! Forgive me for my pride and selfishness and stupidity! Please give me the strength to do things your way."

Oh glory! You could have knocked every created being over with a feather. Immediately the darkness dispersed, and within milliseconds angels of grace swept in and sent every bewildered demon packing. A lightning flash of courage flared and went deep into Kate's spirit, zapping away all passivity and replacing it with boldness. Nathaniel had been dreaming of this moment for decades. He made a beeline for Tetrak and sliced him from top to bottom with his sword.

"You dare to defy the Most High God?" he roared. "From this moment on, your authority has been dealt a death blow!"

"I don't think so, Nathaniel!" replied Tetrak. "As if a weasel like you could touch me!" Swearing and cursing, he grabbed his sword and tried to draw it, only to find that it would not budge. Frantically he tried to lift the weapon, which he'd always mastered brilliantly, and uttered another curse against heaven. But Nathaniel raised his sword again and, as if in slow motion, sliced it through Tetrak's spirit from right to left.

"Your days are numbered, Tetrak!" commanded Nathaniel. "Do you wish to continue?"

For the first time, Tetrak looked around and discovered that he was the only demon left. He began to retreat, hissing and squeaking and oozing slime. With a shout of "You haven't seen the last of me yet!" he turned and scuttled off like a terrified crab.

Then the Lord stepped into the scene.

All of the angels fell to their faces in ecstasy and worship, and Nathaniel was caught up for a time in his adoration, trying to find words which would adequately express how it felt to be in the presence of such glory. But all he could say over and over again was "Lord, you are so beautiful! You are so beautiful!" When finally he was able to sit up and check out his surroundings, the room was empty

* * *

Kate charged across the yard to the back of the house, kicking an old wine bottle out of her way. She couldn't believe her own stupidity. How could a girl spend a lifetime with someone like Granda and never give God a go? She'd just been zapped with peace and love that were beyond her wildest dreams. Not only that, but she felt able to kill giants! Any God who could do that sort of a miracle was worthy of her time and energy. She would love him just as much as she'd loved Granda!

"Things are going to be different around here, Kate," she muttered while aiming for the door of their flat. "You've been a turkey long enough!" Without hesitating, she flung open the door.

Michael was slumped in a lounge chair. He had a fortnight's growth, tousled hair, and bloodshot eyes and was staring at her as if she'd just landed from the moon. This was not the time to mince words.

"I know you're distraught," she announced. Her voice was so clear that it took her by surprise. "But you really do need to stop whipping yourself and begin to find a way to keep on living."

Michael just kept staring, and for a few uncomfortable seconds she remembered her unkempt appearance. But he didn't seem to be noticing that; he looked more like he'd seen a ghost. She decided to push forward regardless.

"As for me, I just told God how sorry I was and asked him to forgive me for making so many gigantic mistakes. I can't tell you how much better I feel after that." Michael's lips were moving, but nothing was coming out, so she continued. "Michael, perhaps you could ask God to help you with the log-sized chip you carry around on your shoulder," she said in the same voice a person would use to offer someone a cup of tea.

"The reason I left was that Granda died and I was too angry with you to tell you." Now her eyes were getting wet and her voice was going croaky. "He was one of our greatest supporters. But we do still have one another. All of our arguing has just sent us around in a thousand circles, and no one is ever going to win. As a matter of fact, if you want my honest opinion, I think we've both lost."

Michael looked as if he wouldn't be able to comprehend anyone's opinion, honest or otherwise. She sensed a movement at the window and saw that Robert had come round to join them. He came to stand at the door, eyes glued to her.

"We chatted and hugged and cried, and she's fast asleep again, so I thought I'd come to see Michael," he said. Michael was looking like a rabbit caught in headlights.

"The three of us really are a sorry lot" she said, eyes welling. "We can't undo what's done though, can we? Maybe with heaven's forgiveness we can dream about starting again and building something new."

It was time to pull out her ace card. "There's something I haven't told you, Michael." She paused to steel herself. "The truth is you're going to be a father." She took a quick peek and saw that he was still looking moronic but seemed to be listening.

"Yes, Michael, we're going to be parents. So there is every reason to have hope for the future and work together to do as good a job of it as possible. I've decided to forgive my mother and pray for her instead of trying to pretend she doesn't exist."

There was still no sound coming from Michael, so Kate decided "in for a penny, in for a pound" and plunged on. "Eventually you really do need to get that book of yours written. For the time being you must keep your job at the newspaper. I realise that. But once we've finished having our babies, I can help with the finances."

"Something else you don't know is that I did actually manage to get my dance teacher's certificate at the age of eighteen. Miss Susan said that I was not only a talented dancer but also a gifted teacher. So I will be able to start running dance classes, and you will be able to get on with your writing. And by the way, we're going to start going to church. Robert, I'm so glad you came back. You must come and visit often."

This seemed as good a time as any to finish up, so she willed herself to turn and exit the place. She figured it'd be best to leave the brothers together while she paid Bea a visit. Once around the corner and out of sight, she spent some time leaning against the side of the house, shaking her head. *Did I really just say all those things? Yes, I certainly did.* Well, there was no gain in retreat.

*   *   *

Michael was still unable to move. Kate had finished her oratory, which might as well have been in French for the little he understood of it. But as she marched away, the magnificent creature who had stood beside her remained and smiled at him.

"My name is Imogen, Michael," he said in the sweetest tones Michael had ever heard. "I know you can hear me. You have been given the ability to connect with the spiritual realm, just as Eleanor was. But Eleanor sought to enlarge herself and so opened up to the darkness. Your heart is different. You desired to connect with someone and something bigger than yourself, and you yearned for the sunshine above the clouds that covered your life. Even as a child you called out to the Lord of Light and so since that time your guardian, Nimrad, has had access to protect you."

Another glorious being stepped into his line of vision. *For Pete's sake! These are guardian angels and they are talking to me!* His body was totally immobilized, but his spirit had never felt so alive. The one called Imogen was the tallest and was breathtakingly beautiful, with huge, translucent blue eyes and wings which were made up of radiant silver and gold feathers.

The newcomer, Nimrad, was shorter but strong and was decorated with the colour beige, which most people wouldn't see as very macho but which he carried off well. He had silver eyes which seemed to be looking into Michael's soul and a face which was borderline scary except for the softness around his mouth. As Michael studied him, he began to speak.

"You feel responsible for your mother and baby brother." His voice was deep and vibrant and strong. "But their choices are their own, not yours, Michael. It's time to take stock of your own actions now. Stop worrying about Robert; he has a special friend who supports him.

I know it's been a hard road back from your breakdown, and it's true that your life has been tough. But that doesn't excuse your recent obnoxious behaviour. The only way you're heading with such an attitude is down. You have a wife who needs you, young man, and a baby on the way!"

Then they both disappeared. Michael felt his body coming back to life and gradually started to move his arms and legs. Robert had come across to check that he was okay, and he looked concerned. He smiled, and Robert smiled back.

Slowly Michael stood and took in his surroundings. The room which had been giving him such nostalgic comfort up till a few minutes ago now seemed lifeless and meaningless. He had wanted to stay there forever, but now all he wanted was to get out quick. *What was it Kate said? I need to write my book, and she is going dancing. And we are going to be parents!*

"Do you think she'll insist on taking me to church too, Michael?" It was Robert's voice. "Matthew wouldn't like that. He'd sulk for a week."

*   *   *

Kate embraced Bea, her heart bursting with joy. "Sorry to wake you, Bea but I had to tell you all the news! I'm pregnant, and the future is looking promising for us. We appreciate you more than we can say. I, for one, will always be grateful for your unconditional support."

Bea smiled through bleary eyes. "My dear, it is I who am grateful to you for loving that larrikin son of mine and sticking in with him. If I can still be part of your life as you move on, I'll be a very happy woman."

"How wonderful that you have your son back!"

"Oh, I can't tell you how close I came to giving in to despair. Then suddenly, out of the blue, after a whole night of no sleep, there he was. I thought it was a hallucination!"

"But it's a real flesh-and-blood son, and he loves his mum very much," said Kate.

52

Singleton, Australia, one week later

What was it about chooks that was soothing? Flo didn't have the faintest idea but was desperate for anything that gave even a few seconds' comfort, so she continued standing there long after she'd thrown the scraps on the ground and collected the eggs. She closed her eyes and let the sound of their cluck-cluck-clucking rise up around her like a soft blanket until she first heard and then saw Tom walking towards her from the milking sheds. The setting sun behind threw him into silhouette, and as he came closer he made an impressive figure, still upright and sinewy from a lifetime of hard physical work.

All her life she'd worked hard to build as many friendships as possible in her desperation to feel loved and important. For as far back as she could remember, she'd been trying to get her father's attention and had always longed to see him look at her with pride. She'd placed a lot of hope in Kate too. The only person she'd totally taken for granted was Tom. How ironic that now, in her last years, he was all she had.

"I reckon those chickens are good and fed, Flo," he said to her now from outside the chook yard. "You comin' up to the house or settlin' down here for the night?"

Flo smiled in spite of herself. "I'm coming now, Tom. Dinner's ready on the stove, and there's custard for dessert."

The two of them began to stroll towards the house side by side, both silently taking in the grand show that the sun was putting on as it settled itself down for the night.

"He stole her from me Tom," Flo said presently.

"Who stole what?" replied Tom, looking totally bewildered.

"Why Da did, of course!" *Honestly, the man is as thick as three bricks!*

"Alec?" said Tom, now looking decidedly anxious. "Alec stole what?"

252

"He stole Kate from me," said Flo in measured tones. "I went all the way to the other side of the world tae see him, and all he e'er saw was her from the moment her feet set down on Scottish soil."

"That's not fair, Flo." Tom had stopped walking now and was standing with a hand on each of her shoulders. "She was just a little nipper, and she had enough love for all of us. But you wanted her all to yourself."

What had got into the man? He'd never spoken to her like this! "I just wanted my father tae love me!" she cried. "But he had eyes for nought but Kate!"

"No, I saw in his eyes how much he loved you. Maybe he didn't know how to say it in words, but he always loved you. Always."

Tom's words, spoken with such gentle strength, proved to be Flo's undoing. She broke down into chest-shaking sobs, and Tom took her in his arms. "He couldna talk tae me," she said between loud sniffs, "and I couldna talk tae him. And now he's gone. And she's gone!"

As he held her close, she surrendered to a delicious wave of self-pity for just a wee while. Finally it passed and she stood up straight again. Tom produced a hanky which she immediately put to good use. Then he began to speak.

"Somethin' happened to me a couple of days back out in the south paddock, Flo," he said in his slow, ponderous voice. "I was ridin' along on old Violet and thinkin' about Alec—what a great bloke he was and how he did okay in life in spite of some of the tough things he went through." He was quiet for a few seconds then. Ideas didn't flow quickly with Tom. Then he started again. "I got to thinkin' about the God of Alec and the God of the Salvos and how that God seemed to look after them. And I thought about you, Flo, and how miserable you've been. And you know what I did?" He waited for her to answer.

"No I don't, Tom. What did ye do?" *If only he'd just get on with it!*

"I decided to have a word with God. I said, 'God, I know you've got a lot on your plate and all, but I know Alec'd be up there with you now, and we're both missin' him somethin' fierce. My Flo is about as miserable as a lost child right now, and I was wonderin' if you could see us through this hard time. I've messed up somethin' terrible, and I'm more sorry than I can say.'"

"That was nice, Tom." Flo was curious now to hear the outcome of the story. "And what happened?"

"Well, Flo, I felt a peace come over me sort of like warm oil that went right down deep inside; sort of down into the part where my heart is. And I felt as if someone gave me a big hug right there while I was sittin' on the back of old Violet. And I just knew, deep down inside like, that God loved you and He was goin' to look after you."

Flo looked into her husband's eyes. Eyes that held no guile. She had tested him to the limit and rejected him in as many ways as possible. But now, finally, she knew beyond a shadow of a doubt that he would never reject her. And maybe, just maybe, God wouldn't either.

"There's something I didna tell ye earlier, Tom." She spoke with as serious a tone as she could muster.

"Yeah? What was it, Flo?" Unconsciously he dropped his hands and stood up straight with his legs slightly apart as if preparing for enemy attack.

She looked him straight in the eye. "Well now, it's crucial that ye should know an important detail regarding dessert. There's nay just custard, ye know; there's apple pie as well. I was going to save it for when the Ramsays came over tomorrow for afternoon tea, but I think we should have it tonight. I'll throw together some cookies in the morning."

"Great decision, Flo!" He put his arm over her shoulder and turned towards the house. "Great decision!" he said again, grinning at her like a Cheshire cat.

53

Singleton, Australia, June 1946

Michael slaughtered cigarette number twenty-two, grinding it to a slow, agonising death in the choc-a-bloc ashtray. If this lunacy took much longer, he was going to lose it in a big way and welcome his first child into the world blind drunk. He was acting exactly like the guys in the movies, pacing up and down in a white room that looked like a prison cell without bars and looking continually across to the only door in the place in the mad hope that some sort of human life would finally come through it.

What sort of antiquated system would stop a man being with his wife at the birth of their baby? It had taken every ounce of his limited self-control to avoid throttling the antiseptic nursing sister earlier. You'd think that he didn't have a right to be here. Kate had been in there behind that door for hours now, and if anyone should be with her, it was him. Suddenly, as if in answer to his thoughts, the door opened and the sister from hell appeared. She was not a happy camper.

"We have a situation which is extremely irregular, Mr. O'Brien," she announced, sounding and looking as if she'd just sucked a lemon. "Your wife is having problems and needs ether. She absolutely insists on seeing you and is making such an appalling fuss that the doctor has given permission—"

"Where is she? Get out of my way, woman!" roared Michael as he pushed her aside and rushed into the labour ward, his heart nearly exploding in his chest. No need to ask directions. Kate was yelling loud enough to bring the fire brigade.

He thrust open another door, and there she was, looking like the wild woman from Borneo. Red hair was everywhere, and her eyes were glazed from hours of agony. For one horrifying moment Michael thought he was going to faint, but he was snapped out of it by Kate's words, which she was bellowing like a barmaid.

"They're going to put me under, Michael, and they wouldn't let me see you first! I had to fight like a mad thing just to see my own husband!" Then another pain hit and she began to scream.

The horror of the situation pushed Michael past woozyness into an adrenalin rush. "What do you want me to do?" he found himself yelling.

The pain subsided and Kate continued. "I want you to stay in this room until the baby's born. And the moment it comes into the world, you have to commit it to the Lord. Do you understand, Michael? I asked God to get us out of our mess and promised to dedicate our baby to him. I couldn't care less if everyone thinks we're demented; please promise me that you'll do that!"

"I promise! Now take the ether, for God's sake, Kate!" Michael knew he was shrieking like a lunatic, and yes, everyone did think they were beyond demented. *Oh, who gives a shit?.* Kate was all he had left in the world, and he was not going to stuff up this time. The doctor was telling her to count to ten with the cloth over her mouth and she looked as if she weren't going to last past five. Finally there was blessed silence as she sank into a deep sleep, and then the doctor's calm voice resonated from behind his mask.

"Just step over to the side, please, Mr. O'Brien. We have to do a forceps delivery here."

Michael was only too happy to move to the side and let the experts take over. A possible blackout was still only a jug full of blood and guts away. He closed his eyes and tried to calm himself. "Oh Jesus, take care of her. Please keep her alive," he prayed. "Please give me the strength to do what she asked."

When he opened his eyes, there was Imogen, smack in the middle of the circle of medicos. He was going like the clappers, anointing everyone's hands with heavenly oil. He stopped periodically to ward off what Michael could only guess were enemy attacks and also to work with the doctor. His hands were actually inside Kate's body, helping to guide the baby out into the light.

Oh brother! This was definitely not the sort of stuff that you drop into conversation at parties!. And it was absolutely, definitely, not something that Kate should ever hear about. You just don't discuss angelic visitations with a girl who's grown up with cows.

Now the doctor was inserting the hideous forceps, and in spite of himself Michael watched transfixed until he saw the head being pulled out. *What did people do before ether?* The body slid out next, along with copious amounts of blood, and he could feel himself beginning to fade.

"You're on, Michael!" It was Imogen's voice. "No need to do anything fancy; just short and sweet."

A cry hit the air. "You have a healthy baby boy, Mr. O'Brien," said the doctor, who now stood offering the baby for him to hold. Michael was beginning to develop an unhealthy affection for the man but was careful to keep that a secret. He gathered his shattered wits and stepped up to the plate.

"We agreed on the name David for a boy," he announced to the masked faces in the room as he tentatively balanced the tiny bundle in his arms. "On behalf of my wife and myself, I dedicate David O'Brien to God. I pray that he will walk with the Lord all the days of his life. Amen."

Once more everyone galvanised into action to take care of Kate. One of the nurses took David and whisked him away somewhere, and Michael gratefully accepted the arm of another nurse who led him towards the door. Just before exiting he looked back and found himself face-to-face with Imogen, who smiled and gave him a thumbs up, then disappeared.

Part Seven

54

I thought he was a young man of promise, but it appears he is a young man of promises.
Arthur James Balfour, as quoted in *My Early Life* by Winston Churchill, 1930

Avoca Beach, New South Wales, 1968

This place was heaven on earth. Kate anchored her brain for two seconds by thrusting her attention onto the view. It was totally divine. But she was no angel, and she sure as eggs wasn't floating on a cloud. Dusk was beginning to turn the water fluorescent, and a gliding pelican was surfing wind currents above the ocean. And she was uptight. Well, "two notches short of panic" would be a better description.

What bad luck for Suzanne that she'd been the last pupil to leave again today. Not the girl's fault, of course. But Kate had still snapped her head off. A huge hands-on-hips sigh was followed by a quick "Sorry about that, Lord!" prayer, and then she set about opening the windows of the dance studio to get rid of the smell of sweaty bodies.

She began her stretches and checked out the reflection that looked back from the wall mirror. The leotards still looked okay because her figure had stayed intact. She thanked the Lord for that; it'd be a bit hard to give private select ballet lessons looking like a blimp!

She absolutely refused to dress her age, especially when it came to hair. And she absolutely refused to be bored or boring. Thanks to Dad's genes her olive skin was standing her in reasonable stead.

"Brave little face," she said to the mirror. "Carry Mama through the change and she'll be grateful forever."

After a few more minutes of deep breathing and stretches, she was still as edgy as an athlete fronting up for an Olympic final. She paced back to the open windows in the hope that the ocean panorama would work its old magic once again. Somehow there'd always been a dollop of eternity here at home central that revealed itself through the unhurried rhythm and endless waves, and often she'd been able to capture little snapshots of heaven when she looked out.

It had even worked during those happy-crazy days of juggling two teenagers and a dance studio. She might have been chronically tired and brain-fuddled and going down for the third time, but just a moment spent gazing at the waves could give that glimpse of paradise that would get her through. Her eyes searched now, hoping for another miracle.

Walkers were beginning to come out from fibro burrows for late-afternoon exercise. Figures were silhouetted against the water, making their way in line formation up and down the beach. Dozens of multi-coloured lorikeets were descending in pairs onto the pine trees and chirruping loudly to one another as they jockeyed for their sleeping posts on the branches. It was undeniably wonderful.

But it wasn't working for Kate today. *Oh well; still neurotic.* Time to execute plan B. She headed for the kitchen. Before climbing the stairs, she thought it a good idea to see how Michael was going in the study. She knocked on the door and at the sound of a grunt opened it a couple of feet. He was totally absorbed, scribbling with pencil on one of the hundreds of sheets of paper that were strewn around him.

"Finished the first draft sweetheart?" She attempted to keep her voice calm.

"Yes, but it's total crap!" So things were business as usual here by the looks.

"Would you like a coffee?" she ventured. It was going to be a job getting him ready to leave in an hour; she thought it best to start moving him gradually.

"Yes, thanks," was the reply. "When do we have to leave?"

"In forty-five minutes," she lied. But it was just a white lie for a good cause. "I'll have the coffee ready for you in the kitchen," she added, and then made her way upstairs.

A few minutes later the coffee was brewing on the stove and the glorious aroma wafted up her nostrils. Back on the farm a pot of tea had been the answer to everything, but now coffee was where it was at. She poured some into her favourite red mug and added plenty of full-cream milk—fattening, of course. You can take a girl out of the dairy farm, but you'll never take the dairy farm out of the girl.

After the first yummy sip, she stepped out onto the huge veranda. It had taken a tooth-and-nail fight to have this area included. Granted, it was a fight that had stretched the budget and marriage to within an inch of disintegrating; but it was a fight worth having nevertheless. Countless hours had been spent here with family and friends. There'd been Deep & Meaningfuls (her favourite), counselling sessions (exhausting but strangely satisfying), plus noise and laughter aplenty.

Their beloved ten-year-old Labrador plodded across to her side. "You love it here, don't you Lightning?" she said as he gave her hand a wet kiss. "But you'll have to wait a while for a w-a-l-k. I'm not in the mood." The crucial word was spelt so as not to give him false hope at the sound of it. She patted him affectionately and then crouched down to give him a hug. Lightning rolled over onto his back, and Kate stood and began to give him a tummy rub with her foot. Her troubled mind began to ease a little. When did a mother stop being a mother? David might be twenty-two years old and over six feet tall, but she just knew he was going through something huge right now. And there was absolutely nothing to do but pray.

"He's going to be fine, sweetheart," Michael's beautiful mellow voice broke through her thoughts. She turned, and there he was, all craggy and rumpled and looking into her soul with those impossibly blue eyes.

"I know that in my head, Michael, but my heart's a whole other story." Her eyes feasted on the sight of him. She put down her mug and reached out.

Michael wrapped his arms around her and held her close. "Well, unlike you I can't have my head and heart in two different places at the same time. The bad thing about that is that I get bored easily. The good thing is that I don't get confused." He stopped to look down at her, his eyes sparkling, and she laughed in spite of herself.

"And your point, Einstein?"

"My point, oh confused one, is that I am totally clear about the fact that he's going to be okay," said Michael. "So where's my coffee?"

* * *

As she bounced off to the kitchen, Michael took a minute to calm down. The ugly demon that he'd seen harassing her moments ago had finally fled. It had looked like a wild boar and was charging towards her over and over. When he'd spoken out the name "Jesus" to the repulsive creature, it had trembled with terror. But it had still stood its ground and looked him directly in the eye as a challenge for some time before disappearing. The less Kate knew about that right now, the better.

Kate emerged back onto the deck with a coffee, and his gut tightened with desire at the sight of her just as it had for more than twenty years. She placed the mug on the timber railing, and he took her into his arms. She snuggled in close, and Michael relished the feel of her petite body, so vibrantly alive.

"Everything's going to be okay, Sweetheart," he whispered.

"He's carrying so much responsibility, Michael," she replied in little more than a whisper.

Michael stroked her hair and kissed her cheek and forehead. "Yes, I know, honey; but the Lord answered all your prayers for me, and I was a borderline maniac. David's a saint by comparison."

She looked up into his face with her mesmerising green eyes and gave him one of those smiles that made his stomach turn to mush. "Well, you're not a saint, darling; that's for sure. But you're a delicious sinner, and my brain's beginning to feel like cotton wool. I vote we get ready to go before I forget what day it is."

"You're probably right, damnit. Am I OK to go like this?" *Best to keep things natural and moving forward.*

"Yes, as long as you brush your hair and tuck in your shirt. I've already got my outfit sorted, so I'll have a quick shower and be dressed in no time."

Michael called out as she skipped downstairs. "You'd better be! I'm already picturing you in the shower!"

The echo of her laugh in the stairwell was music to his ears. He listened for the sound of the shower running and then began to pace the floor. "Please protect him and honour him, Lord," he prayed, "because he honours you. I know that you want to grant him his deepest wish, because he's always loved and served you. Lord, what he wants more than anything in the world is for you and your angels to turn up in a tangible miracle-working way whenever he preaches. He longs to see people healed and transformed. Grant him that wish, please, Lord—tonight and always!"

He continued to pray for several minutes until the concern he'd been feeling lifted and peace began to settle in his heart. Then he remembered that he was supposed to be straightening himself up to leave so began to wander around looking for a comb.

Rifling through the stuff on the sideboard, he noticed one of the numerous copies of the newspaper article that Kate had cut out of the *Sydney Morning Herald* a year ago. Good old

Jim Mason. He'd always been a great friend even when Michael had been a nervous basket case back at the *Herald*. He smiled with pleasure as he read the words:

There were many who predicted that Michael O'Brien would be a one-hit wonder after the enormous success of his first effort, *Aussie Battlers at War*. The general consensus was that he had no more material to draw on. But the reasoning of this columnist at the time was that a guy who can write virtually a whole novel while in the desert in the middle of a war is not to be taken lightly.

Congratulations, Michael. You've proven me right and the critics wrong three times over, and your latest thriller, *Would You Like Cream with That, Sir?*, set in wartime London, kept me on the edge of my seat. I didn't eat for two days. What's next in the pipeline?

Good question, Jim. Once again he was going through the mind-numbing angst of thinking that everything he'd written over several months was garbage. And of course there was that constant nagging fear that maybe he was a four-book wonder. If he hadn't discovered Kate in that old Singleton dance hall, he would have just given up years ago and drifted into a permanent haze of alcohol.

And without Kate, he and Robert would have lucked out at first base in their second run for brotherhood. He finally located a comb and began to tidy his hair. Kate had pushed for Robert to chauffeur David tonight as part of her ongoing mission to raise his self-esteem.

Fair enough, the guy had gone through a lot of changes lately, but Michael still had some monster doubts about where he was at in his head. Then again, he'd been wrong a thousand times before. One could write a book on that subject alone.

Just then the door burst open and Lucy exploded into the room flushed and glowing with life and the beauty of youth. Unlike her mother, she was turning out to be very voluptuous, which was always a worry for a father, and she looked scarily like Grandma Flo. His chickens had sure come home to roost!

"Hi, Dad," she said. "This is Steve!"

A twenty-one-year-old kid with legs up to his armpits followed her in, hands in pockets and shoulders hunched forward. He looked everywhere but Michael's face and said hi to the lounge room wall. Michael hated him instantly. He was also struck by the fact that Lucy was close to the age Kate had been when he had snatched her away from a cosy, secure home to live with an old, life-weary, battle-scarred war veteran, aka himself.

Why hadn't Tom at least tried to run over him with a tractor or hit him with a hosepipe? The old codger must have been secretly horrified but had never said a bad word to him. Well at least both Flo and Tom had lived long enough to see their daughter happily ensconced in her dream home and married to a "successful writer." And Bea, bless her heart, was over the moon to see her sons reconciled and her oldest baby making something of his life.

"I was worried we'd be too late to catch you," said Lucy. "Can we come with you guys? My car is playing up."

Instantly the words "And where's Wonder Boy's car?" sprang to mind, but what came out of Michael's mouth was "Yes, that's fine. Your mother will be ready soon."

As if on cue, Kate came bounding up the stairs then, and her face broke into an excited grin. "Oh, hi darling!" she exclaimed. "Hello, Steve, how are you? This is great! We can all go together!"

"Very well, thank you, Mrs. O'Brien!" said pathetic WB, who had miraculously come to life and gone all talkative once Kate had entered the room. That boy was going to get his hands on Lucy over her father's dead body!

Kate poked her head out the front door. "Uh oh, it's as dark as Hades out here," she called out. "Get a load of the black clouds, guys! We're in for a grade-ten storm."

Michael had never heard of a "grade-ten storm" but was used to Kate making up her own version of the English language. "Yes, we'd better get going; those grade-tens are a menace," he said, glancing out through the window. "It'll be six o'clock soon, and we've got a drive ahead of us to get to the Entrance."

"I'd better put Lightning inside," said Kate. "If it starts thundering, he'll be terrified and we'll find him catatonic in a corner somewhere."

"Good thinking," replied Michael. "I'll start the car and turn it round while you do that."

He grabbed a couple of umbrellas and hurried everyone out to the Holden station wagon. As they clambered in, a massive streak of lightning flashed above them, followed by a thunderclap so loud Michael could have sworn the sky had split open. He turned the car round, and a few seconds later Kate came running out and jumped into the front seat just as the first big drops of rain began to hit the windscreen.

55

Main road to the Entrance, New South Wales

Robert decided there was a first for everything. Trying to drive through a hurricane was one example. He held on to the steering wheel for dear life and prayed that his VW wouldn't get blown off the road and out into the blackness, which he knew was just bush, rocks, and then a drop.

The lightning flashes were scaring him spitless, and the thunderclaps were just about breaking his eardrums. The message coming from his knotted stomach said that God was expressing majestic disapproval because it was Robert driving and not someone else.

He was beginning to break out in a nervous sweat. Fair enough, considering he was trapped in a car in a cyclone with his nephew, who just happened to be a holy man of God who talked to angels; and who'd wanted to be at the hall by 6.30, which was now.

Not to mention David's minder in the back seat, who had the personality of a brick wall but apparently could "see" things in the spirit. Between the two of them, they would've seen right through him by now and figured out what a fake he was. This was nightmare material right up there with leeches and quicksand.

When Kate had asked him to help out in David's church as a deacon, she'd made him feel so good about himself that saying yes had been a no-brainer. But then, after the spell had worn off, he'd made a point of reading in the Bible the bit about "the requisites of a good elder."

How the hell was a bloke supposed to live up to all that? For starters, the closest thing to a wife that he'd ever had was Matthew, who was noticeably male and noticeably camp. And as for the bit about being in control of your household, forget it. He'd never come anywhere near being able to control Matthew.

Third, and by no means least, apparently he and Matthew were not supposed to be attracted to one another. *Man, it's going to take a boat load of miracles for that to happen! Easy for you, Davey boy; difficult for us!* There was David, already up with God and the angels at the grand old age of twenty-two. Robert had been selling porn up at the Cross when he was twenty-two!

Just as he was starting to feel a panic attack coming on, the traffic moved forward and they began to make some headway. They rounded a bend and the cause of the hold-up came into view. There was a mother of a collision up ahead, and lights flashed from police cars, ambulances, and breakdown vans. Just beyond all that insanity, it looked like things were flowing more smoothly. Robert found he could breathe again.

"I'm really sorry about this delay, David," he said.

"You're not responsible for the storm, Robert," the kid replied. "If we're late, we're late." Then he placed his hand on Robert's shoulder and said, "Peace, Lord; give my uncle your peace. And we call down your mercy on these accident victims Lord. In Jesus's name we assign angels to minister peace and comfort and we bind the spirit of death."

When David touched him, Robert felt something like electricity go through his whole nervous system. Within seconds he felt loved and somehow knew that everything was okay. In fact, he knew that *he* was okay, which was an even bigger miracle.

"No sign of this storm easing off, Ken," said the kid to his offsider as if nothing much had just gone down.

"Doesn't look promising," replied Mr. Personality.

"Yeah, but it's not far to go now," added Robert, trying to sound normal while attempting to figure out what had just happened to him.

David studied him for several less-than-comfortable moments. "You have a kind heart, Uncle Robert," he finally said. "You'll make a great deacon."

Robert glowed from head to toe. It had been a long time since he'd been a great anything. "Thank you, David," he replied. "I'll be praying for you tonight."

*   *   *

David said a whispered hallelujah as they pulled into the community hall car park. The rain was still bucketing down, and the welcoming committee consisted of three men who looked over seventy and were standing in line carrying giant umbrellas. What did they think he was, an octogenarian?

He went through the motions of greeting the men, introducing Ken, and thanking Robert, but all he wanted was some time alone. The most talkative welcomer was called Pastor Bill, who was scarily zealous. On and on the guy babbled without stopping for breath while the three of them fell over each other trying to get David inside and get the umbrellas down at the same time.

"We're privileged to have a young man of your spiritual calibre at Prayer for Revival Ministries, Pastor David. We've heard all about the miracles that follow your teaching wherever you go and the angelic visitations that you have experienced. We want you to know that we have prepared ourselves spiritually and mentally for this conference and are ready for anything that the Lord would care to bring to us. I say that in all humility, of course. Would you like some warm soup and toast?"

David counted to three and breathed deeply. What he thought was, *First you leave me to organise my own car and driver—hence the beat-up VW driven by Uncle Robert, who's been a Christian for five minutes. Then you offer me food when I need to be praying!*

What he said was "That's not necessary, thank you, Pastor. But I won't lie to you; I'd sell my grandmother to have time alone somewhere."

Their eyes nearly rolled back in their heads, and he could see their mental jaws drop. They'd probably expected him to talk like a character from the King James Bible. "Um yes, I'm sure we can find somewhere," said Bill finally as he led David and Ken inside and started searching. "It's certainly a great day we're living in when God is sending us saints like you to manifest His wonders. Let's try this door."

Behind the door was a smallish square room with timber floorboards and plain wooden chairs around the perimeter. "Not Buckingham Palace, but it'll do the job," said David. "If someone could come and get me in an hour and a half, I'll be set."

"So ... you won't be there at the beginning of the service."

What David thought was *Brilliant maths work, Bill!*

What he said was "No, but don't worry, Pastor. I'll be there, and it'll be good. If my uncle could pick me up in an hour and a half, I'd be one very happy little vegemite."

"Right. So we'll send Robert around to pick you up here in an hour and a half."

"That would be great; thank you."

The smile that David had kept fixed in place had made his face ache. He walked Bill through the door and stepped aside to let in Ken, who immediately made for a corner of the room and settled into one of the wooden chairs. He closed the door and leant back against it with his eyes closed for several seconds.

"In the name of all that's holy, what a pig's dinner of a mess this is!" he broadcasted to the empty chairs.

"I dunno about that," replied Ken. "These guys might not look too polished, but I'm picking up good stuff here, mate."

"What I'm picking up right now is the band rehearsal going on next door, and I'm here to tell you that the piano's out of tune and the bass is off the beat."

Ken looked up with eyebrows raised and an expression that said "How long am I going to have to put up with this?" It took him a few seconds to reply.

"Well, for us plebs who aren't musically minded, there are other variables to consider." He spoke in quiet, rational tones that left David feeling like he'd been doused with iced water.

"Such as?" He wasn't through with being cheesed off yet.

"I'm seeing that there's been buckets of tears shed here, mate; buckets. And I'm seeing hours and weeks of prayers that have been ramming through the barricades of Hell and pounding on Heaven's doors."

"Just what I needed, Ken; my prayer partner going all poetic on me" laughed David. Ken looked at him with as much humour as someone on death row.

"They mean business, Dave, and they've paid the price. They've fasted, prayed, and worked together to save up the money to have you here for three days. They've printed fliers and gone out into the community to invite people along."

"Right. Point taken."

Ken had been his travelling companion and prayer partner for yonks. He was a cool guy and great intercessor, but they were as different as water and fire. Ken was as steady as a rock and had never been known to lose his temper or outwardly rebel against anything.

But David refused to give in to condemnation. At least he possessed the boldness to go where others feared to tread. Friends could give support, but the buck stopped with him, and it was he who stepped out in front of the firing line night after night. He was the one who had to look the devil in the face and step forward no matter what.

He missed Tammy way too much and couldn't wait to finally get married. Then they'd be able to travel together and (more importantly to him) have some of the amazing sex he'd been fantasizing about. He was relieved that at least his parents and Lucy were going to be here tonight. They knew he was just flesh and blood like everyone else. Meanwhile, he had to somehow start getting his act together.

Ken was already sitting with head in hands, praying privately, unfazed by the fact that they were in the middle of nowhere in a cyclone with a small band of well-intentioned believers who were busy crucifying the musical genre. Wouldn't it be just like God to display his power and bring a tidal wave of miracles to a place like this!

He began to pace around the room, calling out to the Spirit of God. *Oh man is this tough!* David wanted to be anywhere but here. No sane person would ever want to be a chosen one with a calling. He'd fought against it and spent years floundering around trying to find the exits, but every attempt at rebellion had left him drowning in misery.

He stopped pacing for a second and thought about that. *What sort of retarded thinking had led him to imagine that it was possible to stand against God?* As that thought began to have an impact, his anger morphed into healthy fear and he began to talk for his life.

"I'm sorry, Lord," he breathed, eyes closed and hands on forehead. "I must be out of my mind to be struggling like this. I let it all go now and surrender to you. Have your way, God. Have your way." It was time to align his mind with the word of God. He began to speak out powerful promises from the Bible.

"The Lord will never leave me or forsake me!" he repeated over and over. "No weapon formed against me will prosper! If God is for me, then who can be against me? Those things that are impossible with man are possible with God!" Now the anointing began to come, and he said with absolute resolve, "I will not throw away my confidence, because in it there is great reward!" and then, "God didn't give me a spirit of fear. He gave me a spirit of power, of love, and of a sound mind!"

A little later there was a temporary glitch when the congregation began to throw their whole hearts into singing out of tune and off the beat next door. He flinched a couple of times, whispered, "Oh you're joking!" then resumed, going from one end of the room to the other, praying and bringing every thought into focus.

Finally he gave the Lord full sway and stood absolutely motionless with arms lifted and heart open. He stayed like that for several minutes, and then the spirit of the Lord began to pour out wave after wave of his love for the hundreds who had gathered in the hall. This proved to be David's undoing.

He wept as if his heart would break as dozens of faces appeared before him. They were the faces of hearts desperate for hope and comfort, hungry for God's love, exhausted from struggling to please him. Without a doubt they were ready to pay the price of revival, to do whatever it took to open the way for God's peace and miracle-working power to be unleashed.

What they needed right now was to rest like children in the arms of a kind and merciful divine Father. They understood holiness and faithfulness and sacrifice but had not experienced God's unconditional love or the full power of his spirit. Bit by bit the weeping subsided, but now David had seen the Lord's heart for these people. Now wild horses couldn't keep him from the battle.

"In the name of Jesus I bind every demon of Hell from holding anyone captive in this hall tonight!" he shouted.

A huge streak of lightning split the room in two and was quickly followed by a crash of thunder which nearly knocked him over. Then his eyes were opened to see demons scurrying away in all directions. However, one remained still.

Tetrak, the one who had challenged and harassed him since childhood, stood his ground. His eyes were red pools of hatred, and they searched David's face for a sign of weakness. The anointing burst into flame in David's spirit and he gladly responded to the challenge, never letting his eyes falter.

"There is no place for you anywhere, Tetrak!"

"I have infiltrated for four hundred years, you puny child! My strength is returning, and my target is you. Do you imagine you are a match for me?"

David was on fire now and spoke with an authority which was not his own. "Be silent, demon! You don't have the authority of an ant!" he declared. "The scriptures tell me that you have no hope and no future. They also say that no weapon of yours can harm me because I belong to the Lord. Leave now without looking back!"

Tetrak let out a blood-curdling scream and disappeared in a split second. Rain pummelled the roof and wind rattled every window, but the room began to fill with light and warmth. David dropped to his knees in worship as the Spirit of God saturated every corner of his soul.

Once again he'd found the eye of the storm—that place of perfect peace and rest. Time stood still. Nothing mattered to him but the need to express love and adoration over and over. He did not have the luxury of wandering off and doing his own thing. This was what he was made for, and this was where he must stay.

After what could have been seconds or hours, somewhere miles away there came the sound of knocking, and the door was opened by Robert. But he was only able to get out "David, it's time" before crumpling in a heap because of the pea-soup presence of God which was now in the room. They left him there for a short time, and then Ken lifted him to his feet. Robert stared mutely into Ken's eyes, blinking and trying to get his bearings.

"Can you remember where the hall is, Robert?" asked David. Robert attempted to speak but gave that up as a bad joke and instead pointed across to a door.

"Good work, uncle!" David was all smiles now. "Thank you for the prayer cover, Ken!"

"My privilege, pastor," replied Ken, straight-faced except for the slightest of smiles. "Couldn't do it without you, my faithful friend. Now let's go preach up a storm to match the one outside!"

*   *   *

Robert gazed drunkenly at David's retreating back. He couldn't talk or coordinate his movements, but he felt amazing! "This is better than drugs or sex," he mumbled, "which is something I never expected to hear myself say." Gingerly he swayed over to the side of the room and plonked onto a chair, legs akimbo.

Visions of Matthew popped into his mind out of the blue. Then, even more out of the blue, tears began to well up at the thought of his precious partner who'd been a true and faithful friend for so many years. Why the hell Matthew had put up with his shit for so long was one of the world's greatest mysteries.

So much had happened in the six months since they'd visited that church to hear David preach. They'd gone only as a favour to Kate. But who could say no to that angel of a woman?

And then, of course, once David had started his golden oratory, it was all over, bar the shouting. The two of them had fallen over one other running to the altar to give their hearts to the Lord.

He leant his head back against the wall. What did the future hold for them now? No one had warned them that it was agony when the Holy Spirit came into your heart and opened your eyes to the truth. They'd spent months just crying out for forgiveness and trying to keep up with all the changes that were taking place in their souls. Where would they both be in another six months? Suddenly it seemed crucial that he speak to Matthew come hell or high water. He fumbled around in his pocket and found a couple of twenty-cent pieces.

After making a couple of attempts to stand up, he finally admitted that it was a no go and instead opted for slumping down onto his hands and knees. He scrambled out into the hallway and spied David, who was having a conversation with a blank space, which was a bit unsettling. But then again, Robert didn't have a leg to stand on, literally, because he was crawling like a dog towards the spot where he'd noticed a public phone on the way in. He hoped that by the time he got there he'd be able to put together some decent sentences.

He spotted the phone up ahead and nearly wept with joy when he saw that there was a chair next to it. "Focus, Robert," he whispered as he pulled himself up and sat with a thump. Now came the hard part, where he had to put the coins into the slot. This took longer than the sitting-on-the-chair scenario, but finally the coins were in and the number was dialled. After several rings he heard Matthew's beloved voice.

"Hello, Matthew here," he said in his best modulated phone manner.

"Matthew, it's me. I'm sorry if I'm a bit incomp … incompre … um … hard to understand at the moment."

He could hear Matthew's intake of breath. "Robert, you're drunk! You're supposed to be driving David to that meeting thingy!"

"No, it's okay." *Isn't it just like Matthew to be concerned about everyone's safety?* "Believe it or not, I'm cold stone shober. Can't explain now."

"I bet you can't."

Suddenly Robert felt an uncontrollable urge to cry. He began to sob like a baby, and the more he cried, the more sober he became. Then the blubbering gradually settled down and he moved into everyday weeping, sniffling, and hiccupping like an idiot.

"To say that I'm worried right now would be an understatement, sweetie," said Matthew finally. "What's going on?"

"I love you, Matthew; you're the best friend I ever had," said Robert, relieved to find that he was articulate again. "You've put up with my crap for all these years, and you only ever wanted the best for me. The future for us is a fricking mystery. Maybe we haven't got a future. All I know is that when I think of the past, I feel like a worm. I don't deserve your love or your forgiveness; I've been a bastard."

Matthew was silent for a short time. Just when it seemed he wasn't going to say anything, he started to speak quietly and clearly. "Robert, listen to me" he said. "You used to mouth off sometimes with big-sounding words, but you wouldn't hurt a fly. I knew you wouldn't ever hit me and you wouldn't ever leave, and those were both firsts for me."

"Oh Matthew, you deserve so much more," sobbed Robert. "Please forgive me for the way I spoke to you over the years and for all the times I didn't show how much I loved and appreciated your beautiful heart."

Now it was Matthew's turn to cry; not clumsily like a malley bull, but softly and with dignity like a cat. Then there was the delicate sound of a nose being blown. "How can you doubt it, Robert?" he said at last. "Of course I forgive you. You didn't know what you were doing."

* * *

Nathaniel checked one last time to make sure that each guardian in the room was attentive and that every strategic entry point was covered. He knew he must stay calm, in spite of what the Lord had told him. The enemy must not be alerted by even the tiniest spark of excitement.

The demons knew that David was a force to be reckoned with, but even David didn't realise how much the Lord planned to do tonight in this old wooden church hall in the middle of nowhere. The place was spiritually like a bomb ready to explode, and he was beginning to feel decidedly unsettled, if not apprehensive.

Just then he felt a tingle of excitement and sensed a familiar presence. David was approaching. Nathaniel's face broke into a smile just thinking about that colourful young man who'd communed with the Lord even in the womb. He'd been given to the Lord at the point of birth and possessed a natural righteousness salted with earthy mischief.

But that didn't negate the fact that Nathaniel's job here was a lot trickier than normal, what with David's high-priority classification. Wouldn't Satan like to get his hands on the human who was the product of Michael's turbulent heritage and the rocky country stream that had spawned Kate?

Eager to check on proceedings, he maintained an expression which he hoped spoke of mild boredom while he passed through into the area behind the main hall. David's guardian Lancello was walking ahead to ensure a safe passage. Nathaniel stretched his neck to the side to see who David was talking to, and there was Zimron in all his splendour.

Well, so much for playing it cool. Nathaniel had kept a lid on things so far, but once Zimron walked into the place, even the total dullards were going to guess that something big was going down. He thought it best to forget about the mildly bored expression and go for something more along the lines of fiercely determined.

Michael's brother looked like he was finding it a bit hard going being a rookie deacon. He was down on all fours in the corridor, and his eyes were nearly popping out of his head at the sight of David talking to nobody. After tonight he wasn't going to be surprised by anything. The group drew nearer, and Nathaniel shimmered all over with delight and expectation when David saw him.

"Hi, Nathaniel, looks like things are hotting up around here."

"Hello, young David. Yes they are. It's wonderful to see you again, Zimron." The warrior nodded and smiled but was too keyed up for light chat.

"Let's get into it, then," said David as he pulled aside a ceiling-to-floor curtain to enter the main hall.

At the sight of Zimron entering with David, every angel and demon became electrically charged and instantly galvanised into action. Nathaniel took off, fiercely-determined expression in place and sword at the ready. Suddenly the hall filled with warriors from Zimron's top elite troops. And glory hallelujah; they were led by the magnificent and perfumed Dashiel!

All-out chaos erupted. The electrical system went haywire so that sound equipment went silent and lights flashed on and off, sending deacons scurrying to find the main circuit box. Humans were reacting to the charged atmosphere, some panicking and grabbing onto friends, and others screaming and looking for the exits. Pastor Bill, who'd been desperately filling in with amusing chit-chat while waiting for Pastor David to arrive, was now staring in horror at the bedlam that had broken out in the room.

To Nathaniel's relief, the warriors moved like lightning; within seconds all demonic activity was brought under control. The sound system started working again, and the lights flashed back on. Humans settled enough to go from panic to nervous bewilderment.

Pastor Bill mopped his brow with a handkerchief and was opening his mouth to speak again when he noticed that David had stepped into the hall and was being led to his seat by a deacon. With a louder and higher voice than usual, he launched into an introduction.

"Now comes the time we've all been waiting for" he bellowed. "We have the privilege of welcoming to our conference a remarkable young man. Pastor David O'Brien is being used mightily by the Lord in our time to bring the tangible presence of God into churches everywhere. Many thousands have had their lives revolutionised by the signs and wonders which follow him wherever he goes, and untold numbers have come to know the Lord through his ministry.

"We at Prayer for Revival Ministries may be small in number, but we have a huge dream to see revival spread right across this beautiful country of Australia. Ladies and gentlemen, Pastor David is contributing mightily to that very end. Please give him a warm welcome this evening!"

As David stepped up onto the stage to a standing ovation, Zimron approached Nathaniel. "We need to position warriors behind every person present, Nathaniel," he said. "These people have been through extensive sifting and cleansing and have gained the favour of God."

Nathaniel knew that the Lord intended to move mightily in signs and wonders tonight and that people would come to the Lord in unexpectedly high numbers, but he was beginning to suspect that there was more in the pipeline than that.

"What exactly are you saying, Zimron?" he asked, almost hoping that Zimron wouldn't answer.

"I'm saying that this is the fulfilment of your mission which began one hundred years ago, my friend" replied Zimron with just the glimmer of a smile. "David and those at Prayer Revival Ministries believe they are here for one weekend, and you believe that it will be a glorious and significant weekend. But you are all wrong."

Nathaniel blurted out, "Are you serious?" but he then immediately eliminated that notion as bordering on the ridiculous. *When is Zimron ever not serious?* "My apologies," he whispered to Zimron's blank face. "Please continue telling me how wrong we all are." He kept back the last part of that sentence, which was "except you, of course." Warriors didn't understand sarcasm anyway.

"Let me inform you, Nathaniel," continued Zimron, "that the Lord intends to establish a revival head office here with miracles and wonders as everyday occurrences. Consequently, floods of humans will head this way and the meetings will continue every weekend for years."

"Oh a thousand hallelujahs!" shouted Nathaniel, his imagination crunching into overdrive. "Jails and hospitals and psychiatric institutions will empty because of the healings and deliverances taking place!"

Zimron continued without missing a beat. "The members of this congregation will cope with the practicalities because they are hard-working, faithful, and patient. David is young and energetic and has Tammy by his side. She is the perfect complement for him, and together they are admirably equipped for this work. Nevertheless, they need much backup from us if they are to withstand the challenges which will surely come from Satan."

Nathaniel's head was swimming. He'd gone from colourful outburst to speechless in the swish of a wing. "So ... w-w-what you're s-saying," he began, then he gave up trying.

"Is that we'd better get moving!" stated Zimron, and then he took off at the run.

Nathaniel accelerated into fourth gear from a standing start while still trying to process what he'd just heard. One sure thing was that if tonight was the culmination of his mission, then this was no time to mess up. He hurried to alert all the guardians to be extra vigilant with their charges and worked with Zimron to position a warrior behind every person present.

Once he was sure that all was in place, he got busy finding the right spot in the hall. He settled at the side to drink in the sight and sound of David, whose golden words carried humans into the realm of faith and enriched everyone who heard.

It was indeed true to say that the Lord chose the most unlikely vessels to fulfil eternal purposes. Wasn't the old Nathaniel a perfect example of that one? He concentrated on the words David was saying now and got so caught up with listening to what was being said that it took a moment to notice the fragrance of roses and jasmine that had begun to waft around him.

"These are great days, Nathaniel." It was Dashiel striding past in all his beauty, luminous with vibrancy and controlled excitement.

"Yes indeed." No point taking up a warrior's time explaining that he was pretty much in the dark here, so he focused back to the pulpit.

But more interesting than the pulpit right now was Zimron, who at this moment held a huge torch which he was about to set alight with a burning red heavenly ember. As the ember came in contact with the oil-soaked torch, it caused six-hundred-foot-high flames to leap into life. Nathaniel was mesmerised.

"Well what are you waiting for?" asked Zimron out of the blue.

"I'm not waiting for anything," replied Nathaniel, his feathers prickling. "I'm just trying to keep up with what's happening from one moment to the next!"

"Is that right?" laughed Zimron, his stormy eyes flashing. That was a first—Zimron laughing. "And what would you say, my friend, if I said that you have been chosen to set the revival torch to the anointing oil?"

"Are you serious?" Nathaniel shouted. Yes, it was ridiculous to ask a warrior if he was serious; but just a second ago he'd been laughing!

"Frankly, Nathaniel, I can't guarantee what I will do if you ask me that question again! As sure as I'm floating here, I've never been more serious! Here, take it for Heaven's sake!"

Nathaniel was thunderstruck. He was flashing beams of light for miles, but who cared? The Lord had chosen him to ignite a revival fire, so he must have gained divine favour! Grasping the torch with both hands, he held it high and waited for the outpouring of oil.

David had been preaching his heart out, but at that moment he looked across the room directly at Nathaniel and lapsed into complete silence. People began to cough, rustle and cross and uncross legs. Finally he turned back to them and in hushed tones began to speak.

"Friends, the Holy Spirit is about to enter this hall in great power. It is the time for all of us to stand together, raise our hands into the air, and call on the Lord."

The little congregation stood and began to pray earnestly for God to pour out His presence. Nathaniel could see that they wanted this more than anything on the face of the earth. They had prepared themselves in as many ways as possible and were ready. As their soul-deep cries rose up and their hunger pulled on the Lord's heartstrings, the oil began to fall from heaven.

Nathaniel was heady with a mix of anticipation, awe, and compassion for everyone present. The first wave of anointing entered the hall, and with his spirit vibrating he touched the red-hot oil with the flaming torch. Immediately revival fire exploded into the hall and pandemonium broke out.

Humans began to laugh, cry, fall over, and shake as their mortal bodies were impacted by divine power. "Oh glory, glory, glory," muttered Nathaniel as he drifted across the room checking for any areas that needed extra help. He scanned the place from north to south, and his eyes came to rest on Kate and Michael.

Kate was lying curled up on the floor, her face a picture of serenity. The Lord was dousing her with much-needed peace. "Rest, dear Kate," he whispered. "The Lord has placed many in your path, and you have given yourself to loving them all."

"But I failed with my mother," her spirit replied. "I didn't care enough!"

Nathaniel considered his response. "No, Kate; the problem was that you cared too much and your heart could find no middle ground." His words hit their mark and she began to weep, pouring out a lifetime of grief.

"I couldn't help her. It was impossible; impossible."

"I know. But that was not your job; it was Tom's. Let it go now and thank God for the ones that you were able to help."

She let out a sigh and fell silent. Next to her Michael was standing with arms spread wide, thanking God repeatedly for all of his blessings.

"Life's much better without a monkey on your back," said Nathaniel.

"That's stating the obvious in a decidedly obvious manner," replied Michael's spirit.

"You're honest and bold, Michael. With a combo like that, obvious is the best way to go."

"Ouch, that's my Achilles' heel you're so flippantly discussing."

"Maybe. But it's also been your salvation. Because of that honesty, you knew that your own strength and goodness would never be enough; and because of that boldness, you had the courage to ask for help and forgiveness from someone greater."

"I've offended many."

"And challenged many. It is the truth that sets humans free."

"I wounded Kate."

"And you've already confessed a thousand times."

"I hurt the person I love the most in the world."

"Yes, you did. But it's over, Michael. Kate forgave, and God has forgiven and forgotten. Let it go."

Michael's arms slowly lowered, and the furrows of his brow disappeared. Beside him was Bea, who remained on her chair, sitting at ease with eyes closed and a smile on her face. He grinned as the Lord's love for her wrapped around him.

"The Lord is good. He's kept you fruitful in old age."

"Yes. He forgave so many things and showed himself merciful to me."

"Because he loves you so much, Bea."

"Yes, yes, I know." And with that she lifted her arms in a gesture of worship and surrender.

Meanwhile, a guardian reunion was in full flow nearby. Imogen, Nimrad, Tristan, and Caleb were chatting happily, and they flashed with pleasure as Nathaniel drew close. He embraced each one and entered wholeheartedly into the joyful tête-à-tête. Tristan was the first to congratulate him.

"I didn't know a century ago that I was working alongside a future celebrity. Congratulations, friend!"

"Come, now," Nathaniel replied, "I think the word 'celebrity' is a bit of a stretch." *But only a bit.* He was thankful that last thought had stayed in his head. "And I've been hearing things on the grapevine about you, Tristan. You were awarded a merit after your good work with Alec.

"Yes, yes, the rumours are true. But you and I both know that I was a mere speck of down fluff away from complete failure when you came into the picture and offered assistance. Alec came up with so many unpredictable variables."

"From what I hear, he's doing the same in heaven," added Caleb. "But you can never accuse him of being boring."

"How's Tom going?" asked Nathaniel. "I haven't seen him for a while."

"He's going gleamingly, although it took him a while to adjust when he was promoted so far above Flo. But he and Alec work wonderfully well together."

"Excellent."

The angels stopped their chatter when they realised that Imogen and Nimrad had been seen. Michael was gazing at them both and grinning.

"Would you look at that," he said. "Our faithful guardians are still guarding faithfully!"

"You've done well, Michael" said Nimrad. "Now follow your wife's example and rest in the love of the Lord." With that Michael fell in a heap next to Kate.

"It's wonderful to see you all," said Nathaniel.

"Sincere congratulations, Nathaniel," they replied in unison.

"Favour well-earned," added Imogen. "By the way, it looks like Lucy is coming along nicely. The new boyfriend has a minus reading in the confidence stakes, but Kate has already got him in her sights."

"Brilliant!" said Nathaniel. "We must fellowship soon. But meanwhile there's work to be done here. I love you all and would be bursting with pride if it was permissible."

Off he went, flying back and forth to check out the entire goings-on. He didn't want to miss a thing. Everywhere humans were laughing, weeping, and rejoicing as David moved amongst the crowd, ministering to all who were hungry for truth. Oh, the wondrous chaos and sounds of revival! He was thrilled to his toe tips. Then he heard something more wonderful by far. The voice of the Lord was resonating above the din, and he was calling Nathaniel by name.

"Yes, Lord?" he cried out over the din. "Speak, for your servant heareth!" Admittedly that last bit was a trifle over the top, but right now he felt more than a trifle over the top.

"David is our weapon of truth and love, Nathaniel, fashioned over many lifetimes."

"He is a beautiful human, Lord."

"Much will be expected of him, but also much will be given. He will marry soon, and I will surround him with men and women of integrity."

"It comforts me to know that, Lord."

"A great century's work, manager. You are highly favoured."

"Thank you, Lord! I live to please you!"

"And Nathaniel …"

"Yes, Lord?"

"Your first assignment as a cross-generational manager is finished. And one more thing Nathaniel."

Uh Oh, what now? "Yes Lord?"

Well done, CGM! Well done, good and faithful servant!"

Printed in the United States
By Bookmasters